RISE OF THE ELDER

D.K. HOLMBERG

ASH PUBLISHING

CHAPTER 1

Rsiran Lareth crouched on the rooftop, staring down at the darkened street below. Lights flashed throughout the city, ones that would only be visible to him, and his connection to the lorcith. One of his knives hovered over the ground, sweeping through the streets as some sort of lantern that he used to pierce the darkness between the other bright lights that he saw.

With his cloak around him, he was nearly invisible. Not quite as invisible as Haern would be with the strange shirt of Venass that he possessed, but still dark enough that none but the strongest Sighted would be able to notice him.

As he sat on the rooftop, he focused on the sense of lorcith, listening for it. To this, he added his connection to heartstone, searching for both. When it came to Venass, he didn't know which they preferred to use.

The streets around him weren't as familiar as those of Elaeavn, but then Elaeavn was no longer the city he knew. The council had made certain he didn't feel the same welcome within the city, and ensured he was considered a threat. It was a position he knew all too well.

"I don't see anything." Jessa crouched next to him, completely silent. Were it not for the heartstone charm she wore, he wouldn't have any way of knowing she was there. She barely moved—barely breathed—her training as a sneak making her practically invisible. Rsiran didn't need to see her to know the lines of her face, the way her brown hair swept down to her shoulders; he could see those without opening his eyes. Neither did he need to see her to know she was worried. Each night spent here left her more anxious.

"You don't need to see anything. They're down there."

"I know you think this is how we're going to get access to Venass, but it's dangerous."

Rsiran turned toward her. "Everything's dangerous these days. Living in the trees is dangerous. Training the others to fight is dangerous. Everything."

"I thought you liked that we were back in the trees."

Rsiran thought of the simple structures that had been built in the Aisl Forest. There had been a time when he wondered what it would be like for his ancestors, back at a time when their people still lived within the branches, close to the Elder Trees, but now that he'd had the chance to experience it, the thought of his smithy and the warmth of the forge or even the regular heavy weight of the hammer as it struck metal appealed to him. He missed those comforts.

First, they had to stop Venass.

A flicker of lorcith, barely more than a fluttering, pulled on him.

Rsiran tapped Jessa's hand—their signal for her to remain where she was—and he Slid after it. When he emerged, he was near the center of the city. A wide-open courtyard surrounded him, one that he'd been to several times before. A dark shape moved along the edge of the courtyard, and from that person, he sensed the lorcith.

He *pushed* one of his knives so that it floated toward the other man, giving him enough light to see by. The man seemed to notice the knife and spun around, a crossbow aimed at him.

Damn!

Almost too late, he Slid, emerging near the man. Rsiran *pushed* on the lorcith that he detected, sending the man slipping along the cobbles and away from him.

"Lareth," the man said in a soft whisper.

Rsiran couldn't tell if he knew this man. He wore a long, black cloak with a hood that covered his face. A band of metal pierced him. That lorcith would be what gave him abilities much like what Rsiran possessed.

"You were foolish to come to Cort," he said.

"I have my reasons."

The man chuckled. "Reasons? Did you come to die? Because that's all that can happen here."

All he wanted to do was to capture one of the Venass fighters. He needed information.

Rsiran ignored him, *pushing* on a pair of knives and sending them streaking toward the man. Neither struck. He vanished in a Slide so fast that Rsiran struggled to follow it.

When he emerged, he did so behind Rsiran.

"You don't think I can handle one of you with the ability to Slide?" Rsiran asked.

"One?" The man flickered as he Slid forward, no more than a step.

Rsiran readied a pair of knives, but had a growing uncertainty rise within him as well. Had he underestimated Venass? There were plenty of their agents moving through Cort, enough that it gave Rsiran an easy reason to justify the amount of time he spent here, but those he'd found had been easy to subdue.

"If there were more than one—"

A chill worked up his spine and he Slid, emerging on the edge of the plaza. Another Slide took him to the far side, and then one more took him back to the opposite side. Each time he emerged, he felt the uncomfortable sense that others able to Slide appeared, but Rsiran couldn't see them.

Pulling on five of his knives, he sent them away from him, bringing them back as soon as they reached the pits of darkness pooling around the courtyard. Something flickered, and Rsiran hesitated, *pushing* one of the knives in that direction.

There he saw three others, all with crossbows.

Bolts loosed at him.

Rsiran Slid, emerging on top of one of the nearby buildings. His heart raced. If there were that many Venass near him, he needed to be more careful.

As he emerged, he realized that they had followed him.

Damn.

Another Slide, and this time, he emerged near the heart of

Cort, with dozens of towering buildings on either side of the street. Lorcith lingered along the street in places where he'd left it, giving him more light than he'd otherwise have in the darkness.

The sense that others trailed him remained.

Rsiran spun, looking for signs that they had, but found nothing. That did nothing to settle his racing heart. He should have expected Venass to begin hunting him; after all, he'd been the one hunting them for the last few months, searching for those with heartstone and lorcith buried within them so that he could trace it back to his grandfather. So far, none knew how to find him.

And worse, they didn't know how or where to find the crystal.

More than anything else, that was what he wanted to find. The other crystals were still safe, protected by the way that he'd used the energy of the Elder Trees to seal them off, but he needed to find the missing crystal to secure the seal. Not only secure it, but to find some way for him to stop Venass. That was all that mattered now.

The others of Venass might be out there now, but that didn't mean that he could do nothing. Stepping into a Slide, he paused in the space between.

As always, the smells of lorcith and heartstone swirled around him, almost as if this place fed on the energies of those metals. The air had a muted quality, one that made it seem both lessened and strangely more real than when he was on the other side. From here, he could access the power of the Elder Trees, and could use that power.

There was another benefit to standing in this space between, one that only he could reach. The power of the Elder Trees refreshed him, filling him with their energy, building his strength. As he bathed in that, he didn't worry about injury or pain or fatigue from Sliding. All of that went away. It was in this place that he'd seen Della healed, where he'd helped Haern, and where he never feared those more powerful than him. It was not a place he could live—he didn't even know if he would be allowed to remain for much longer than his brief visits—but it was a place where he felt connected to the Great Watcher.

Rsiran drew on his renewed energy and then Traveled.

Traveling as he did, separating himself into two, allowed him to leave his physical body behind while his mind could then Travel anywhere in the outside world, invisible and undetectable by most. Traveling while in-between was the only way he was able to use the power of the Elder Trees. This time, he emerged in the courtyard where he'd found those with the crossbows.

Two Venass soldiers lingered in the shadows, hiding near the long walls surrounding the courtyard. Using the power of the Elder Trees, he *pushed* against them, securing them to the ground so they couldn't move. They wouldn't cause him any more trouble. There were others who would take it from here.

Rsiran needed to find the others.

Connected as he was to the Elder Trees, he sensed the pull of heartstone and lorcith like a sharp tugging at him, drawing him through the city. Traveling to the next place where he detected the metal, he found two more Venass soldiers. He incapacitated these men the same as he had the others.

How many remained?

He still hadn't found the lead Venass. That was who he *wanted* to find, and once he did, he hoped that he could take Rsiran to Danis. Once he stopped his grandfather, he could end the war, bring the guilds back into Elaeavn, and perhaps finally have peace.

He noted a surge of heartstone, and it was near another, one that he was close to.

Even in this insubstantial form, his heart raced.

He Traveled toward it.

There, Jessa stood with eyes wide, her body stiff as the Venass fighter held a knife to her back. When Rsiran appeared —Traveling, not Sliding—the man smiled broadly.

"I know you're here, Lareth."

"If Rsiran is here, then you're in trouble," Jessa said.

Rsiran admired the steel in her voice, and the ready way that she stood, prepared to dart forward, and away from the knife. How could he have left her alone like this? Of course Venass would come after her. They knew how important she was to him, and they knew the lengths to which he would go to get her back safely.

"Mr. Lareth seems to think that he is safe wherever he Travels. He will find we have learned, and that we will not be so easy to dispatch."

Rsiran drew upon the connected energy and *pushed*. Power surged from him and slammed into the man from Venass. It washed over him, dissipating as if there was nothing to it.

The knife pressed forward. "As I said, you will find that we have learned, Lareth. Too bad that you have not."

The man's knife started forward, and would stab into Jessa. Traveling would give Rsiran no way to help her. He needed his physical body.

In a heartbeat, he returned to the in-between and Slid back to Jessa, emerging behind the Venass fighter.

Rsiran *pushed* on the knives he carried, *pulling* on the heartstone piercing the Venass fighter at the same time. His knives met resistance. This man was strong—stronger than most of the Venass he faced—but Rsiran had learned tricks while facing Venass that he could use.

Holding onto the sense of lorcith within Ilphaesn, a sense he could detect even here, he *pushed*. The knives sliced forward, slipping through the resistance, slowly moving toward the other man.

The Venass fighter's face tightened in a mask of concentration as he resisted.

Rsiran *pulled* on the heartstone piercing the Venass fighter, and *pulled* on the lorcith he had, as well, dragging him away from Jessa. She jerked free and stumbled away.

The Venass man fought a moment longer before releasing the resistance in a soft snap of power. As he did, he flickered, and faded from view, Sliding away from them.

"That… was a little too close," Jessa said.

"They were expecting me."

"You knew it would happen. How many Venass have we taken out since we came to Cort?"

Rsiran closed his eyes, trying to remove the image of the knife in Jessa's back. How much longer would he have to worry about her, and worry about the next attack, or the next? He'd lost her once, and vowed not to let that happen again, but what if he couldn't prevent it? What if he wasn't strong enough to stop Venass? They continued to progress, to find newer and newer ways to use powers they siphoned off the connection to the metals, and he didn't progress nearly as quickly. They had more experience and more time working with the metals than he had, and he didn't doubt that they would eventually find some way to hurt him—either directly or through Jessa. His battle against them had changed him. He'd now killed, over and over.

Was that what he was to become? Was that what it would take to defeat Venass?

"Rsiran?" She rested her hand on his, and he opened his eyes, meeting her deep green eyes. "I've seen that look from you before. I know what you're thinking."

She probably did. Jessa didn't need to be a Reader with him. With her Sight, she managed to catch the worried lines on his face or the pull of the muscles in his cheeks, or countless other ways that she had of knowing him that he didn't understand.

He took a deep breath, his gaze flicking to her sharp jawline that softened as her hair framed her face, falling to her shoulders, so much longer than when they had first met. In that time, she had changed, getting both softer and harder than she had been. Rsiran had changed, as well, no longer the fearful boy afraid of disappointing his father. Now he had others he was responsible for, more than just Jessa and his friends, but all the guilds.

"I'm thinking that we need to get back to Aisl." That was the name the guilds had given to the camp they had made within the Elder Trees. They had named it after the forest and the trees, a name that felt both fitting and simplistic. Rsiran hadn't objected, though they had asked his opinion. He had the sense he could have overridden it, made a suggestion to the rest of the guilds that would have been listened to and acted upon.

"That's not what you're thinking. You have that look, the one you get when you think you need to keep me safe. I know that look, Rsiran."

"I... need to find a way to draw them out. If they're still here, it means they still search for the crystal, and if I can have them chase me, that takes away from their ability to search."

"Isn't that what we're doing? Isn't that the reason that we came here so that you can get connected with whatever other groups are needed so we can find the crystal?"

"That's why we came, but that's not what we're doing. I've been using this time to hunt Venass."

"And the guilds are thrilled you have."

Rsiran nodded. The guilds had suffered under Venass. Many had died, fighting a war many within the city didn't even know existed. Now those who remained trained, learning skills to better fight, ignoring their guild abilities for now. "As much as I want to find the crystal—and I think we have to find it—there's a part of me that's angry about everything Venass has done and wants only revenge."

"If this is all about revenge—"

"I know. It can't be. I understand, but that doesn't change the fact that is what is driving me. And now... now it seems Venass has discovered a way to resist the power of the Elder Trees. That was the only advantage we had. What happens if they figure out a way to keep me from Traveling? What if they keep me from reaching that power in the first place?"

They had so few advantages when it came to Venass that they needed every one they *did* have, which was why Rsiran and his abilities were so useful. Or had been.

"What are you saying?"

"I don't know. There's just so much to accomplish. I need to find the crystal quickly. That can't be out there unprotected. We need to take back the city. And then we need to destroy the rest of Venass."

"I know this."

Rsiran nodded. "You do. The others... they grow comfortable in the forest. To them, there's safety there, and they've separated themselves from the rest of the world, letting the power of the Elder Trees keep them protected. But they can't be safe there indefinitely. Venass has already destroyed one of the Elder Trees. If they manage to destroy another, if they find a way to overcome even that protection—or worse, reach the crystals —we'll lose."

"I know," she said again.

"You know, but the others let themselves forget."

"What do you want to do?"

Would she go for what he wanted? There *was* safety within the trees. It was the only place they had that really was safe right now, but it was a safety that might not last for much longer. They needed to take advantage of it for as long as possible, so Rsiran had time to find the crystal. "I'll need your help with the others."

She eyed him sharply, a question lingering in her deep green eyes.

"They trust you."

"They trust you, too. You're the smith guildlord. More than that, you're the one who helped them find safety in the first place."

"They trust me, too, yes. But there's something else I need to do, and I can't worry about whether Aisl will prepare. That's what I need you for. You can gather everyone together, get them ready for what we must do next."

"And what is that?"

Rsiran knew that even though she hadn't said anything about the fact that he intended to leave her behind, that didn't mean she wasn't angry. She planted her fists on her hips and waited for him to answer. If his answer didn't satisfy her, she mightn't let him leave her behind, and he wasn't willing to risk angering her by sneaking off without her.

"Once I find the crystal, we're going to attack the city."

CHAPTER 2

T he Aisl Forest let little light through the upper branches, leaving much of the forest bathed in darkness. This part of the forest had a weighty sense to it, one that came from the stillness to the air mixed with the heavy earthy notes, but the weight came from more than that. There was power within the forest, a power that kept the guilds and those with them safe.

The space between the trees had changed in the last few months. Buildings built from wood harvested in other parts of the forest wove together, forming simple homes. Upper branches were bound together with vines and ropes, turning the thick branches into pathways that hovered above the forest floor. A few children played, though not as many as in the city itself. Everyone else worked with a hushed intensity.

In some ways, Rsiran suspected the forest looked as it once had, in the time before their people had left the trees and formed the city by the sea. Della might know—her ability granted her a way of looking back, a way that let her see into the past, so that she could understand what once had existed—but she never revealed anything about what she knew, keeping those ancients secrets to herself.

Jessa released Rsiran's hand as they reached the forest. She glanced over at him, a worried frown still creasing her brow. She might agree with him—at least, he *thought* she agreed with him—so far, she hadn't said that she didn't. But that didn't mean she liked what he intended.

"When do you plan to leave?" she asked.

"I won't stay gone. I can always return."

"Return from where?" came a voice from behind him.

Rsiran spun to see Haern approaching. He walked with something of a limp, and the scar along his face twitched, a sign that something bothered him. A coin flipped between his fingers, dancing across them before returning to his palm to start again.

"Cort. Trying to find information about the crystal. If your friend wouldn't have taken off..."

"He can't help you with what you need to do, or how you're going to find what you need to know."

"And what is that?"

Haern fixed him with a hard gaze. "You don't return."

"Haern!" Jessa said.

Haern shook his head. "If that's where you two have been running off to," he started, ignoring the heated stare from Jessa, "then you need to stay buried. Let the others say what they want about you."

"And what do they say?" Jessa asked.

Haern smirked. "You *are* gone for hours at a time. That sort of thing gets tongues wagging, if you know what I mean."

Jessa punched his shoulder.

"We have other things we're worried about besides... well, besides *that*," Rsiran said.

Jessa turned her glare to him. "Really?"

Rsiran flushed. "It's not *all* about that," he said quickly. He couldn't deny he and Jessa had snuck away to have time together. Camping in Aisl felt too close, even though they slept in the open. There were just too many people around, and it made him uncomfortable. He'd rather be within the Ilphaesn mine, or better yet, in the smithy he'd been forced to abandon when they left the city.

"What do you mean we need to stay buried?" Jessa asked.

"In Cort. I can only imagine you're doing it to draw out information about the crystal."

"That's what we intended." Jessa glanced at him, and Rsiran tried to hide the rising flush within him. "So far, Rsiran prefers to hunt down Venass."

"They're moving openly outside the city," Rsiran explained.

"They move openly in the city now, too," Haern said. "Is that the best use of your ability?"

"How many will die if it's not me?"

Haern flipped a knife quickly and then sheathed it again. It happened so fast that Rsiran took a step back. It was easy to forget how skilled Haern was—or had been—but seeing his dexterity, and the skill he'd honed once more, always impressed Rsiran.

"You're not the only one in this, Rsiran. There are others

who can fight. Who *have* fought. They need to keeping fighting. And you need to use your ability for more than killing."

It struck at the heart of what had bothered him while in Cort. With every Venass fighter he killed, he felt a part of himself slipping away. He needed to refocus on the crystal. That was what was important.

"I know," he said.

"You think you can prevent more from dying?" He turned toward a small group standing near one of the massive sjihn trees.

Miners Rsiran knew, working on creating a tunnel beneath the forest. They had the opening framed and secured, but others worked alongside them. The guildlord had come to him asking his opinion about whether they could and should dig toward Ilphaesn. The guild wanted to ensure control of Ilphaesn, fearing what would happen if the Elvraeth council— and those who remained in the city—managed to secure the lorcith. They were now aware that Venass had infiltrated the city and the palace. Having access to Ilphaesn would grant Venass even more potential than they already had.

"I think I can try," Rsiran said.

"Try. You're one man, Rsiran. You're powerful, and you've grown more competent in the time I've known you, but you're one man. This is war, the kind these lands haven't seen in many years. We do what we can. We fight as we can, for what we know to be right. Some are going to die. The Great Watcher knows we'd like to save as many as possible, but that isn't the way war works."

Rsiran remembered the last attack on the city, the way so

many died, leaving the guilds reduced. Even that served the council, he now suspected. Could they have been after that all along? Did they really think to weaken the guilds by allowing Venass to destroy them? Once they did, Venass would control the city, not the Elvraeth, regardless of how powerful the council thought themselves.

"I've got to find the crystal first," he said.

"That's what you can do," Haern agreed. "But you can't do it as Rsiran. You can't be running through a city Sliding around and taking out the Hjan." He flashed a wolfish grin. "Most outside of Elaeavn don't fear our kind. Some don't care for us. They might respect us, but that's where it ends. You've already seen how there are others with abilities you don't possess."

"I've faced the Hjan, Haern."

"The Hjan. Those within Venass. They're one kind of awful. There are others as well. The Hjan fear them less than they fear you, but that doesn't mean they aren't out there."

"Like your friend Carth."

"She'd be one, but there are others like her, only they don't make their way to these lands very often anymore."

"And they once did?"

Haern shrugged. "I suspect they did, but like I said, it's been a while since they've been seen in these lands."

Rsiran wondered if he could Travel to those other places. Sliding put him at risk, especially if he didn't know where he intended to go, but with Traveling, he could float above the land, a projection of himself. He suspected he could use Traveling to help him find a safe way to Slide.

"What does all of this have to do with me getting the information that I need?"

Haern looked around the clearing, eyeing those standing too close to them before leaning toward Rsiran. "You have responsibility now, Rsiran. You can't go running around putting yourself out there in the way you're going to need to in order to make this work."

"What way will I need to?" He hadn't given much thought to what he'd be required to do, only that he agreed he needed to find some way to discover what might have happened with the crystal. When it first disappeared, he'd thought it might have been Venass, but they didn't have the crystal. The guilds needed to find it before Venass.

"You'll need to be harder. Darker. That's the only way you'll find information, and that's what we really need right now. After you get that, you can take on Venass all you want."

"You want him to take on another name?"

"Another identity. Wear it like a disguise. Use that to get information he would not be able to obtain as Rsiran. Like I said, there are those who respect people from Elaeavn even if they don't like them. Make himself useful, make himself dangerous, and he'll be able to learn much more than he would otherwise. That's what I want from Rsiran."

Haern met Rsiran's eyes. "You've got the necessary talent for this. I've worked with you enough to know you have the skill, but what you're going to have to work on is the attitude. You have to be willing to go darker than you've ever gone if you're going to convince others you're truly an assassin. Then you go after the jobs. Then you can learn what happened to the crystal."

"And then we can get on with pushing Venass out of the city."

Haern nodded. "There's that. Like I told you before, I can get you started, but you're going to have to do the rest yourself. You're going to have to actually do the work."

"What kind of work?" Jessa asked.

Haern flipped a knife between his fingers. "My kind."

Jessa laughed. "He can't kill for money."

"Why not? There are plenty of people out there who deserve to die."

"Deserve?" Rsiran asked.

"Think of Danis. You don't think he deserves to die? Think of how you had to kill Evaelyn. What would it have been like had you been willing to kill Josun?" Haern shook his head. "Not all men are good and noble, Rsiran. Not all will give you the same respect you give them. You're going to have to do things, get your hands dirty, if you want to protect those you care about."

"If he does this," Jessa asked, glancing over to him, "what do you suggest?"

"First, he's not Rsiran. Pick a name. Something that sounds... intimidating. Easy to say. Something with meaning. Then you have to start getting yourself known. Cort is as good a place to do it as any. Make sure others know you're there. Let them know what you can do. And you'll probably have to hide your ability with lorcith. That's a sure way for Venass to know it's you. You should Slide. Don't want to hide what will make you the deadliest, but the rest… that's only going to get you discovered and draw the attention of Venass when you don't want it.

"We can talk more about what you'll need as you get established, but you're going to have to get in there, and you're going to have to prove that you belong. Just being of Elaeavn, and just having skill with knives, doesn't mean you're worth more to them than another assassin. Hell, there's another Elaeavn assassin working in Eban, and he's got a terrifying reputation." Haern smiled slightly. "Whatever you do, be careful."

Rsiran could only nod. What else was there to say?

When Haern left, Jessa turned to him. "Now I'm even more convinced that you shouldn't do this. You'll be risking too much, Rsiran."

"And I was thinking the opposite—that I have to do this. If that's what it takes to get information from that world, then I have to get into it so we can learn where the crystal might be."

"We don't even know if you'll find anything!"

Rsiran shook his head. "Venass doesn't have the crystal, and we know it's gone missing, and that someone has it. Rumor is all that we have to go on at this point. If this doesn't work out, we'll keep looking."

"Or you'll be dead." Jessa shot him a hard look. "You heard Haern. There are others with abilities, Rsiran. *I've* seen men not afraid of those from Elaeavn! You go out there, and something happens to you…"

Rsiran pulled her close, resting her head on his shoulder as he comforted her. "Nothing is going to happen to me. We've faced worse."

"You don't know that." Her voice was muffled against his shoulder, but he could tell she fought back the urge to cry.

"I know whatever we might find is nothing compared to the threat of Venass. But first things first. I'll find the crystal."

"When do you intend to start?" she asked.

"Soon." He didn't know when, but Cort no longer made him nervous. There might be those from Venass, but if he didn't go looking for them, he wouldn't need to worry as much about them. Knowing they were out there gave him the advantage, and he would follow Haern's advice, and assume another identity.

"What are you going to call yourself?"

"I haven't decided. Haern said it should be something memorable."

"And frightening. You want people to hear it and know that you're not someone to take lightly."

"You don't think Rsiran does that?"

She smiled and patted him on the chest as she took a step back. "Rsiran does well enough, but I know you. We'll have to come up with something that works."

"Maybe Brusus will have a suggestion," he said.

"If you can separate him from your sister long enough to get a word in with him."

Rsiran smiled, thinking that for some, the changes that had taken place over the last year had actually been good. Not only for him—being able to use his ability to Slide openly and without fear that he might get caught put him in a much better place than he'd been before—but for those like Brusus, a man who'd been lonely before, searching for answers about his family the same way that Rsiran had searched for answers on his.

"I'm sure he'll take time for me. If not, I'll just go to Alyse and ask her for permission."

They stood together, hugging lightly, and laughing. Even as they did, Rsiran couldn't shake the sense they were in something of a calm before the storm. All he waited for was thunder and lightning to announce what was coming.

CHAPTER 3

T he tavern stunk, nothing like the Wretched Barth, even
in the time between Lianna's ownership and when Rsiran's sister started cooking there. The air smelled of sweat and
mold and old ale, making him disinterested in the food on the
table in front of him—a stack of dried beef and carrots nearly as
dry. His mug of ale sat untouched as well.

Rsiran wore a heavy dark cloak he left draped around his
shoulders. He scanned the tavern, looking for the man Haern
had put him in contact with, but saw nothing to give him the
sense the man was there. The place was crowded, with people
pressing up against him all around, the waitresses trying to
squeeze into open spaces, and too many tables for the size of
the tavern. Nothing like the spacing found within the Barth
where he could actually have a quiet word with Jessa and the
others. This place—a tavern called Silver Cat—was all noise and
commotion.

A man staggered toward him and slumped onto the stool

opposite Rsiran. He looked at him through reddened eyes he rubbed vigorously, as if trying to shake sleep from them, and belched loudly. The sound was lost in the din around them.

He leaned forward and breathed out with a fetid breath. "You him?"

Rsiran tensed. Wasn't this the reason that he'd come? He needed to make connections, and he had to start low. That was what Haern had suggested. He wouldn't be given the plum assignments until he'd proven himself. Haern hadn't been able to tell him how long it might take, only that he might need to deal with it for weeks. Time they didn't have. Somehow, Rsiran would have to make a name for himself more quickly.

"Who are you looking for?" Rsiran asked.

"They tell me you take jobs," the man said. He eyed him slowly, starting at Rsiran's hands and working up to his face. When he reached his green eyes, he leaned back with a start. "Maybe you the wrong man."

He started to stand, and Rsiran grabbed at his hand, holding him down. "I take certain jobs," he said carefully. He still hadn't settled on a name. All the suggestions that Brusus had were either ridiculous or too complicated. To think Brusus had the gall to suggest that he call himself Sira the Slayer.

The man jerked his hand free and rubbed where Rsiran touched. "Don't think you're quite the one for this," he mumbled. He turned and staggered away, leaving Rsiran debating whether to run after him. That was his one lead. Haern had promised to get him started, but now even failed at that.

Rsiran pushed away his plate and stood. He fought through

the crowd and made his way outside where he breathed in the cool night air, letting it fill his lungs and wipe away the stench from inside the tavern. He was tempted to Slide back to the Aisl, but he wouldn't yet.

Wandering through the streets, he let his mind wander, reaching for the sense of lorcith and heartstone. He detected it all around him, in some of the shops to the distant presence of Ilphaesn. It pulled at him all the time, a constant comfort, and one he was thankful Venass had not separated him from. In some ways, he needed that connection even more than he needed the ability to Slide. Without his ties to lorcith, and to heartstone, he couldn't be the smith he wanted to be. He wouldn't be as skilled as he was left with only Sliding and Traveling.

Stepping around a corner and into an alley, he started when a dark shape dropped from a rooftop to land in front of him.

Rsiran readied a pair of knives, already *pushing* them away.

The figure darted over him, spinning as he did, somehow seeming to pull the shadows around him. Rsiran had seen something similar only once before. But it wasn't a man.

"Carth."

She crossed her arms and stepped deeper into the alley. "You recognize me."

"I recognize what you do."

She stepped forward, smelling of a strange mix of spice and heat. "Not many have such an ability. I have known another, but he is... unique." From the light coming off his knives, her deeply tanned face glowed, though her dark hair remained obscured in the shadows.

"What do you want with me? Do you intend to come for Haern again?"

Her eyes narrowed at the mention of his name. "Not Haern. He'll pay for what he did, but perhaps you were right in leaving him for now."

"He's under my protection."

Saying it sounded ridiculous, but Rsiran didn't want Carth thinking she could return to Elaeavn—or Aisl, if they remained in the forest for much longer—and come after those he cared about. Haern had done things in his past, but he had changed as well. And Rsiran needed him for the upcoming battle with Venass. Of all those allied with him, Haern might be best equipped to handle the attacks.

"Is that a promise?" Carth asked.

There seemed something more to the question, a weighting that he didn't fully understand, but perhaps that didn't matter. What mattered was that Carth left Haern alone. If Rsiran had to work to protect him, it would take time away from other things he needed to be doing, things like finding the crystal.

"Just... just leave Haern alone."

"As long as Venass remains a threat, I'll leave Haern in your custody. Beyond that, I make no promises, Rsiran Lareth."

"Why do you care so much about Haern?" he asked. Haern hadn't been willing to share what happened, only telling them that Carth resented something that had happened when he had still been with the Hjan.

"You know what he is."

"Was. He's not with them anymore."

"That does not change what he did, Rsiran Lareth."

"He's not the same man you knew."

"Perhaps."

Rsiran *pulled* his knives back to him, tucking them into his pockets. "Why did you find me, Carth?"

She leaned forward, a smile on her face. "You intrigue me, Rsiran Lareth. You spend weeks in Cort chasing Venass and then return to hide in the Silver Cat?"

"I need to find something."

"You search for the crystal."

He tensed. Carth possessed enough ability that he actually worried about her intentions with the crystal, even if she claimed she had no real interest in it. If she attempted to reach it before him, he would have no choice but to beat her to it—or stop her.

"What do you know of it?" Rsiran asked.

"I know that it is not in Venass. If they possessed one of the great crystals, they wouldn't be searching the countryside as they are now. That they are as active as they are…"

Rsiran had thought the same thing. Venass would have moved differently had they already possessed the crystal. The fact they remained in Cort as well as other places suggested they didn't have the crystal. It was a fact Rsiran counted on.

"You believe that you can gain insight by hiding in taverns?" Carth asked.

"Not in taverns. I…" He hesitated, not certain that he should admit to Carth what he intended.

She smiled, almost Reading him. "You think to ingratiate yourself into the darker side of things in Cort? You cannot do so as Rsiran Lareth," she said.

"That's what Haern said as well."

"In that, we agree. You will need to prove yourself worthy if you intend to reach the thief-masters. That's where the real knowledge lies."

"I'm trying."

She smiled again. "You need help."

"And you're offering? I thought you didn't want to do anything that might help Haern?"

"This would not be helping Haern. This would be helping Rsiran Lareth."

Rsiran glanced down the alley, his mind racing. "Why would you be willing to help me?"

Carth started toward him, shadows sweeping around her as she did. Rsiran considered it a trick of his imagination, but as he watched Carth and looked for any evidence that might be the case, he saw none. "You shut down the forge, did you not?"

Rsiran blinked. "How did you know about that?"

"It's my business to know about things, Rsiran Lareth, especially when they involve Venass."

"What do you care about Venass?"

She breathed out and shook her head. "They have caused enough trouble, I think. It is time they lose the power they have stolen."

"There's more to it than that."

"There is, but that is of little importance to you."

"I think I should decide what is important to me."

Her smile faded, and Rsiran wondered if he might have pushed too hard. "Venass and the Hjan violated a peace accords. Many have suffered."

"That's your only reason?"

"That is reason enough."

Rsiran could tell there was more to it, something Carth didn't want to share with him, and he wondered what it might be. Had the Hjan attacked someone she cared about as well? "What do you intend to do that can help?"

Carth flowed past him. There was really no other way to describe it. "You need credibility, Rsiran Lareth, but you cannot obtain it easily, nor quickly. I believe you feel some pressure of time?"

Rsiran nodded. That had been his fear—wasting too much time trying to establish himself risked the crystal disappearing for good. More than that, it risked Venass gaining more strength. "That's why I went to the Silver Cat."

"A reasonable place to start, but it will take you at least a year to get the name and access that you desire."

His heart sunk. A year. He had no reason to doubt that Carth told him the truth.

"I see from your expression that is longer than you intended," Carth said.

"You knew that would be longer than I intended. Did you come to taunt me?"

"On the contrary, Rsiran Lareth, there is something that I can offer you."

"What is that?"

Her smile shifted, fading from one that made her seem slightly amused to a darker, almost predatory grin. "A name."

CHAPTER 4

R siran remained motionless on the rooftop, watching for signs of movement around him. A dozen lorcith knives were stationed along the roof, giving light only he could see. A dark hood covered his head, and the slick fabric of the strange shirt Carth had given him made him uncomfortable. He couldn't deny the benefit to the fabric though. It was much like the one Haern possessed, one that seemed infused with shadowsteel, with the intention of drawing the eye along the surface. It would mask him from anyone Sighted. For anyone without any abilities, it would practically make him invisible against the night.

A name. That was what Carth had offered, and one that Rsiran had heard whispered before: Lorst. By taking the offered name, he became indebted to Carth, but what other choice did he have? They couldn't wait for months for him to legitimately earn a name, not when Carth and her network already had one ready—almost as if she had planned it.

Rsiran still didn't know what the price for the name would be. He had little doubt she would extract something from him.

The city beneath him was different from Cort. Roofs had angular lines with heavy slope to them. People moved below him, some soldiers of a city guard and all armed with swords. In the time that he'd observed, he realized they weren't the ones to fear. It was the men hiding in the shadows, moving quietly from alley to alley that he needed to watch. They were men who worked for the thief-master.

That was whose attention Rsiran—Lorst, really—needed to get.

He came to Eban with the reputation earned in Cort, one Rsiran hadn't earned, but *someone* had. There wouldn't be a way to earn such fear without actually doing something. Stories of Lorst spread throughout Cort, and some of them were brutal, leaving Rsiran wondering if he really should have assumed the name. It was too late to back out now, especially now that he finally had a lead on the crystal, and wasn't that the reason he'd come here in the first place?

Carth crouched next to him. He hadn't expected her to accompany him, but wasn't surprised when she'd asked him to carry her with him. She barely made a sound, even her breathing nothing more than the whisper of wind.

Rsiran wondered how she managed such quiet, but almost didn't want to ask. The longer he spent around her, the less confident he felt that he would be able to defeat her if it came to a real fight. She seemed completely unfazed by his abilities, not concerned at all about the fact that he could *push* on metal. And there was the strange way the shadows shifted around her that left him uneasy. The more he saw it, the more convinced he was it was real.

"You see him?" she said softly. Her voice carried to him, but he doubted that it carried any farther.

"I see him."

"That is your target."

"What did he do?"

Carth swiveled her head toward him, her eyes catching some of the moonlight. "Does it matter?"

"Yes."

She sniffed softly. "You are more like him than I would have believed possible."

"Like who?"

She shook her head. "A friend."

"What do I need to do?"

"You remove the target, Lorst. Doing this will get you notice. In Eban, that matters more than other places."

"What did he do?" he asked again.

Carth slipped down the roofline, still as silent as she had been the entire time she'd been next to him. She peered toward the street, as if seeing something he could not. Rsiran wondered again if she were Sighted or if her ability to pierce the darkness came from her strange connection to the shadows.

"Like many in this city, he's a thief and a murderer."

Rsiran laughed bitterly. "I thought you said Lorst was hired by a thief and a murderer."

She nodded. "Many jockey for power here. To them, it is nothing but a game."

"And that's how I will find the crystal?"

She shook her head. "There was no word of the crystal in Cort. Nor in Asador. I have checked Jhandur and Loash and neither has what you seek."

"It could be in Thyr."

This time, she did look back. "It could be. But if it were, do you not think Venass would have learned? That city is theirs as much as Elaeavn is your kind."

"Why here, then?"

Her lips curled slightly, the barest beginning of a smile. "Here... here there is word that another has come."

"What kind of other?"

"Your kind."

Rsiran breathed out. That was more than she'd shared before, keeping it from him as if she feared that he might not Slide her to Eban. "My kind. There are Forgotten in many places, Carth."

She raised a finger to her lips. "Careful with my name here, Lorst."

Rsiran frowned. He hadn't expected her to be concerned about him using her name. What was it in Eban that worried her?

"It is more than another of your kind in Eban. It is whose attention they have attracted."

"And whose is that?"

"A man I have learned not to underestimate. And neither should you. That is why this must appear as realistic as it can, otherwise Orly will know. He's as dangerous an unpowered man as I have ever encountered."

Unpowered. She said it almost with an offhanded air, but

the way she spoke of Orly had something of... not fear, but *respect*. Rsiran suspected that it was difficult to earn Carth's respect.

"And this Orly might help us find the crystal?" he asked skeptically.

Rsiran didn't know many from outside of Elaeavn, but those he'd met so far had wanted nothing more than to harm his kind. He thought of the men who had tried to abduct Jessa, the same kind of men who had attempted to use her before she had come to Elaeavn, men who wanted nothing more than to sell her into slavery. That kind of man would not be interested in helping them. That kind of man would want only to hurt them more. If this Orly was like that, Rsiran would need to be prepared for someone nearly as bad as Venass.

"I do not think he'll help, not unless it is in his interest to do so. That's why you need to make it so that he's interested in you, Lorst."

Rsiran could swear that he felt a surge of power as she said the name, almost as if she were trying to Compel him into believing that it was actually his.

"You should not wait, Lorst. Your opportunity with this man will soon disappear."

Rsiran stared down at the street, watching the man moving into the alley. As they had been promised—at least, as *Carth* had been promised—the man they sought wore a dark red sash around his waist, tied so that the ends dangled down.

"Does that signify anything?" he asked Carth.

"Not anymore," she said softly. "He long ago abandoned what it meant."

Rsiran waited, hoping that she would say more, but she didn't.

With a sigh, he Slid from the rooftop, emerging deep in the darkness of the street below. As he did, he readied a pair of knives, preparing to *push* them.

Heat surged through the street.

Rsiran tensed.

A shape appeared from the shadows, and Rsiran noted that it was the man with the sash. "She sent you?" he said.

Rsiran hesitated. The man unsheathed a curved sword he hadn't seen before and stood with it in a relaxed grip. His posture made it look as though he was experienced with his sword, reminding Rsiran of the Neelish sellswords. Fortunately, he didn't need skill with his sword to face the man effectively.

"Who sent me?" Rsiran asked. He readied a Slide, as well, in case he needed it. Carth wanted him to kill this man, but he couldn't do it without knowing *why*. There had to be some reason for others to want him dead, and he agreed that not all men deserved to live. Some needed to be removed from the world.

The man stalked toward him. "She should not be here. She is the one to violate the accords. A dangerous game she plays, but it is one she cannot win. Not with *him* involved."

"Who do you think I am?" Rsiran asked.

The man took a step forward. "A fool. You come here, thinking you have power, but there is no power other than those who serve the Hjan."

"The Hjan want only power."

"As they should. They have proven they can use it. Few can say the same. It's time the A'ras side with them."

It was a term he didn't recognize, one he would need to ask Carth about. If there were others like him... they could be useful. "They have proven they will do anything to obtain it, and will harm any who try to stop them."

Why was he bothering to debate with this man?

Yet he knew the answer. He couldn't do what Carth wanted of him until he knew whether he *wanted* to do it. Killing in self-defense was different from a cold-blooded murder. Was he that man? Could he ever be that man?

Only, wasn't this war? Hadn't he been drawn into a deeper and more dangerous conflict than he had ever known? He would have to do his part if they were to survive. That meant he had to kill, even those who weren't trying to harm him at the time. Just because he wasn't threatened by the man now didn't mean he wouldn't try to harm Rsiran in the future.

"Only because others are not strong enough to possess the power they have been given. Some must have it taken from them."

With that, he swung his sword.

Rsiran wasn't ready for what happened next. There came a surge of energy, like a flash of heat, that sent Rsiran flying back toward the wall. Had he not readied a Slide, he would have slammed into it.

Instead, he flipped through his Slide, emerging on the other side of the man.

The sword swung toward Rsiran again, and again power surged from the man, only this time, Rsiran was ready. He Slid forward, catching the man's sword with a pair of knives, *pushing* on them to knock the man back.

The man gritted his teeth and slipped back a step, then swung his sword toward him again. This time, more power than before surged from him, and erupted around them.

Rsiran lost control of the knives he *pushed* as he went flying.

He *pulled* the knives toward him as he Slid, emerging briefly on the street before Sliding back down the alley toward the man.

He had underestimated him.

Rsiran hadn't expected that kind of power in Eban. He didn't know what the power was, or how the man managed to assault him, but it wasn't the same kind of power that Rsiran used, and it didn't appear to be like Venass.

With a quick Slide, he emerged back in the alley.

The man was gone.

Rsiran didn't think he Slid. The power he used was nothing like power of the Great Watcher, and he didn't seem to have used the metals the same way that Venass did—Rsiran would have detected either heartstone or lorcith.

A surge of heat came.

Rsiran Slid, emerging at the back of the alley.

Where he'd been standing, a blast of fire now erupted, and the man stood with his sword.

Rsiran couldn't help but marvel at the man's ability. He possessed something so different from the abilities Rsiran had, and something that would be useful in facing Venass, if only they would have a way of getting the man to side with them.

Another thought—one that was more troubling—came to

him. What if there were others like this man? What had he called himself... A'ras? Rsiran needed to keep that term in mind, but he had to complete this first. If he couldn't find a way to defeat the man, then it wouldn't matter.

Pushing on the lorcith knives, he Slid forward, emerging long enough to *pull* on them as well. He Slid again, this time jerking on the knives, *pulling* them toward the side. With each Slide, he changed the direction of the knives.

The man took a step toward him. Rsiran *pulled* on the knives, Sliding as he did, so that when he emerged, the knives were already moving, and went soaring toward him, catching him in the chest.

The man fell in a heap.

Rsiran approached carefully. He toed the sword, intending to kick it away.

Carth landed next to him. She glanced at the man before shaking her head. "Don't."

"Why not?"

"The blade is poisoned. A dangerous kind of poison if you were to touch it."

Rsiran glanced at the sword thankful that he hadn't been hit by it during the confrontation. "What do we do with him?"

"You leave him like this. Others will find him."

"How will Lorst get credit for this?"

She kicked a toe at his knives. "These will remain. They are your calling card."

"Mine or Lorst's?"

She arched a brow.

How would Lorst have lorcith knives as his calling card?

"You've been planning this, haven't you?"

"I always plan."

"But for this? You knew I'd need your help. You prepared for Lorst."

She smiled tightly. "You needed my help, much as I need yours. Come. Now we wait."

"For what?"

"For your summons."

CHAPTER 5

When it came, Rsiran wasn't fully prepared. Carth helped him get ready, but he collected the knives that he needed, wishing he had access to his forge so he could create more. He supposed he could find a smithy outside of Elaeavn, but searching would take more time than he had. The dozen or so knives that he had would have to be enough.

"Where do I need to meet him?" he asked as they crouched on another rooftop, this time with a silver sliver of moon shining overhead. The streets were busy at night, filled with soldiers and thieves and other people, all making their way along the streets. Noise and commotion followed, something that was much louder than he'd ever experienced in Elaeavn. There, the sea often covered most of the noises of the city, a soothing sort of sound that was a constant presence.

"He has called you to his home," Carth answered. "Such a summons is more dangerous than meeting on the street. It is a sign he has taken Lorst seriously. You should know there are others with skill he has hired for some job."

"Is it common to hire more than one?"

"For particular jobs, he has been known to do so."

"And this job?"

"I suspect there is something else at play here. You must discover what it is, and be ready."

"The crystal?"

Carth frowned thoughtfully. "Perhaps. I don't know if he has discovered the crystal or if there is something else at work here."

"And you think that I should go?"

"Can't you free yourself if you are in danger?"

"There are ways to trap those who can Slide."

She smiled slightly. "I have heard you don't have the same limitations as others with your particular ability."

"I can get free of most traps, if that's what you're asking."

"Most?"

It was his turn not to answer. He wouldn't share everything with Carth, not when she had made it clear that she wanted to know more than he was comfortable sharing. "Where do I go?"

She pointed to a place where two men stood guarding a door. Both held crossbows and wore swords sheathed at their sides. "That will be your entrance. Behind there, you will find more men armed with weapons. You must not touch any of them. Let them claim your knives. I can see you will find a way to recover them if needed."

"And then?"

"Then you will hear what Orly has to say."

Rsiran held his breath and Slid. If this was what he had to do in order to find information about the crystals, then he was going to do it. He emerged in the alley near the men and walked carefully toward them. They watched him approach, both men with hands going to the hilts of their swords.

"Orly is expecting me," Rsiran said, trying to sound harder than he felt.

The men exchanged glances. "You're Lorst?"

Rsiran didn't know what Orly expected Lorst to look like. It was possible Carth had made him appear different, or less threatening—or even more threatening.

"What were you expecting?"

The man nearest snorted, eyeing Rsiran from his head to his feet. "Looks like Galen in some ways."

"Don't tell Galen that," the other said. "He'd likely kill you for suggesting he looks like someone else."

"Who is Galen?" Rsiran asked.

"Thought your kind all knew each other," the first man said.

"My kind?"

"Yeah. Green-eyed kind. Tall bastards, ain't you?"

The other glanced at his friend. "You should be careful—"

Rsiran flipped a knife so that it sank into the wood frame next to the door. He gave it the slightest *push,* not wanting to actually hit the man but wanting to show that he was more dangerous than they suspected. It was the kind of thing that Lorst would have done.

"Orly. He called me, I believe."

The nearest man smiled in spite of the knife that had nearly connected with his skull. "Ah, maybe you *are* him. None

seen him—you—before, so don't really know. Thought we'
test it."

Rsiran reached past him and pulled the knife from the wall
and slipped it back into his pocket. Had he *pulled* it, he would
have revealed his ability, and he had no interest in doing that. It
opened him to more questions and ones that Lorst might not
have the answers for.

"Am I to remain standing here or will you take me in to
see Orly?"

"You'll need to leave the knives behind. And any other
weapons you might carry with you, like swords or darts."

"Darts?" Rsiran asked.

They nodded.

Rsiran took the knives in his pockets and handed them to
the men. "I'll be returning for those."

"Only if Orly decides you should."

Rsiran actually smiled. "I'd like to see him stop me."

He worried for a moment he might have gone too far.
Would they think him overly arrogant, or would they believe
that to be the way Lorst would act? Rsiran hadn't learned how
deeply Carth had seated the rumor of Lorst, and whether he
would be the kind of person to act arrogant, or whether he
would be more the silent but deadly type.

"Think Orly might like this one," one of the men said.

They led him into a narrow hallway where they placed his
knives. Rsiran maintained his connection to the knives, ready
to *pull* on them if needed, but worried the distance might actually create problems. If he *were* to need the knives, he could be
too far away and might not be able to call to them.

They guided him to another pair of men. Both were enormous, incredibly muscular, and moved with a sure grace that suggested to him they were more deadly than the outer guards had been. Neither appeared to carry swords, though Rsiran knew from experience carrying a sword didn't mean you knew how to use it.

They stopped at the top of a long stairway. "Down," one said.

Rsiran expected them to lead him down, but they didn't.

At the bottom of the stairs, he paused in front of a door. What would he find on the other side? A man dangerous enough that he warranted Carth's respect. Possibly dangerous enough he could harm Rsiran, but Rsiran took some comfort knowing he could Slide away if needed. But this man might have insight about the crystal. That was what he needed more than anything else.

He didn't even have to knock, and the door swung open. A darkened room on the other side greeted him. Shelves lined the walls. He noted bottles of wine and dark liquids, as well as the expected books and papers. A thick, plush chair of red velvet— the color reminding him in some way of the man he'd killed in order to obtain the summons to come here—sat angled in front of the hearth. A thick carpet underfoot screamed wealth.

A smallish man stepped forward. He had a plain face and short gray hair, but his eyes warned Rsiran toward caution. They were hard and flat and nearly the color of his hair. "Lorst, I presume."

Rsiran tipped his head. "I am Lorst." It felt easier each time he said it, though it still didn't feel natural to him. Less awkward than the first time he'd used the name, but he needed to accept it or he risked discovery.

"You come with quite a reputation. I had not expected to find you in Eban."

Rsiran shrugged. "Cort has grown less interesting."

Orly arched his brow. "Indeed? From what I hear, Cort has a different problem these days. Perhaps that is the reason you have ventured away?"

He knew about Venass. Did that mean that he knew the truth about him as well?

Rsiran trusted Carth had provided him with the identity that he needed, but if she hadn't... he would already have lost his opportunity to discover what Orly might know about the crystal.

Before coming here, he would have thought it unlikely that a man without abilities would have access to the crystals, but seeing Orly, and noting the flat way he watched him, one that was a mixture of disinterest and strength, made him realize that Orly might know much more than Rsiran would have expected.

"Borders don't matter so much to me," Rsiran answered. He had already decided he would reveal his ability to Slide, so Orly needed to know he could.

"There are others without such concern as well. They have a different interest, though."

"I don't really care about such things," he said. "I'm more concerned about jobs. That *is* why I'm here, isn't it?"

Orly turned to one of the shelves and pulled down a flagon of amber liquid and poured two glasses. He offered one to

Rsiran, which he took and sniffed, but didn't sip. "Direct. I think we will get along well then, Lorst."

"Do we need to get along?"

"It would help, I think. There is another of your kind who challenges me in the same way. I would prefer if we got off on a better footing."

Rsiran wondered who Orly might mean. There was someone Carth had referenced, as well, though she hadn't explained more, and then there was the person the guards had referenced as well.

What was his name?

"Galen and I are nothing alike," Rsiran said. If he was wrong in throwing out the name, he risked offending Orly, but if he was right... there was the potential he would find it easier to get into his good graces.

Orly's flat eyes narrowed slightly. Enough that Rsiran knew he had gambled well.

"Yes, well he is part of the problem now. I had found him to be a useful resource, but he can be... troublesome. I would rather not have the need to eliminate him, but when his quirks begin to impact my job, then it is time I remove him. Are you willing to do that, Lorst?" He took a swig of his honey-colored liqueur and left the cup at his lips, waiting for Rsiran.

Rsiran set the glass down. He wouldn't drink from Orly's cup, not without knowing what he might have placed in the cup. "That is the job?"

Orly nodded. "Twenty gold tils if you remove Galen of Elaeavn. Is that a problem for you?"

Rsiran bit back the first response that came to mind. Killing in general was a problem, and this was killing for money. At least now he knew a name, but he still didn't know if this Galen would lead him to the crystal. He needed to check with Haern to learn whether this man would have had access to the crystals. Could he have been someone of the guilds with access?

"Lorst? Is it a problem?"

Rsiran shook his head. "I doubt Galen will pose much of a problem for me."

Orly turned back to his shelves and pulled another bottle from it, swirling it around. "You might find he is more trouble than you expect. He certainly is for me. But if you remove him as a threat, I think twenty gold will be well earned. Him and a woman he's with."

From his tone, Rsiran could tell he was unconvinced Lorst would succeed.

What kind of man was this Galen?

Had he made a mistake in coming here and offering himself for this task?

Not if it ended with him finding the crystal. That was worth it, even if he had to kill.

A nagging sense in his stomach made him wonder if it really was, or if he was doing something as terrible as what he accused Venass of doing.

"Which is more important to you—Galen or the woman?"

Orly tipped his head and frowned. "Does it matter?"

A troubling thought came to him. If it meant finding the crystal, it didn't.

CHAPTER 6

The heart of the Aisl Forest was difficult to reach, especially now that the guild maintained it as a home. In the few days that Rsiran had been gone, he found several things had changed. Not the least being the sheer *number* of people in the forest.

When he emerged from his Slide—one of the few who could actually reach the heart of the Aisl by Sliding—he looked around trying to take stock of all the people. Had the guild brought more here, or had some come without having someone to guide them?

Rsiran reached for a sense of heartstone, listening for the telltale sign of Jessa's necklace, and found it above the smith guild tree. Rsiran Slid to the tree and emerged on a long, flat section of the branch. A cluster of three women stood near the trunk on a wide platform, and Rsiran recognized Alyse with Jessa, but not the third woman.

"Rsiran!" Jessa said. She hurried to him, not concerned

about the narrow branch she used to reach him. As she embraced him, she whispered in his ear. "Did you do it? Is it done?" Her tone was much more worried than it had seemed when she first greeted him.

"Not done. I have the assignment, but don't know whether it is the person who might have the crystal."

Alyse approached and Jessa stepped away from him. "Where have you been?" With her fists planted on her hips and her jaw jutted out, Alyse came across angrier than she should be. Brusus's presence had softened her before now.

"There are things that I need to do, Alyse. I have certain responsibilities—"

She smiled and the firmness faded. "I know your responsibilities, Rsiran. I'm only teasing you. Brusus tells me you've been looking for the missing crystal."

Rsiran wondered how many knew about the crystal. For so long, few within Elaeavn other than the Elvraeth even knew the crystals existed, and now everyone in Aisl knew about them. Then again, that fit with Rsiran's plan for the crystals if they were ever able to reclaim the missing one. All gifted with abilities should be given the opportunity to hold them, not only the Elvraeth.

"I've been trying. I'm closer than I was before." He glanced toward the forest floor far below and the dozens of people there that hadn't been here when last he had been in Aisl. "How did so many find us?"

"Not find," the third woman answered. As she turned, he recognized her, but not because of the guilds. He had known her growing up, when his father had sent him on errands for the shop. Malina was a weaver, and had apprenticed nearly the same time as he had. Her raven black hair cascaded down her shoulders, and eyes of a moderate green watched him with curiosity.

Rsiran glanced to Jessa. "How many of the other guilds did they bring in?"

"It was Alyse's idea to bring the other guilds to Aisl," she said. "Not all came, but those who have... they have skills the rest of the camp lacks. We're building a new home here, Rsiran."

Rsiran surveyed the camp. This was never meant to be their home again, only a place where they could regroup and prepare for the coming war. The longer they stayed and became established, the less likely it was the others would want to risk war in order to return to their city. And he didn't blame them. He didn't want a war, either, but he wanted to return to his smithy. He was smith born and carried with him the blood of the smiths. And he was sure the other smiths would want to have access to their smithies.

"Home? This isn't our home. Not like the Barth and the smithy and the shores."

She smiled at him and hugged him tightly. "This doesn't have to be *our* home."

"There are some who might choose to remain," Alyse said. "You know our people came from the trees before we went to the shores. Some want to remain here now that we have come back."

"Would you?" Rsiran asked.

Alyse's nose crinkled. "Not here. This... this isn't for me. I would rather return to Elaeavn, and to the tavern and the kitchen and Brusus." Her voice trailed off as she spoke, and Rsiran smiled. To think that Alyse would ever have come to a point where she would want to return to a tavern amused him. In some ways, she had changed as much as he had. And seemed happier for it.

"Brusus wouldn't stay?"

"You know him well enough."

Rsiran did. The idea of the Brusus that he had known staying in the forest actually amused him, too. Brusus wasn't meant for this life. He might not even be meant for the life he now lived, abandoning his work as a thief that had defined him for so long.

"Where is he?" Rsiran asked. "Or Haern. Either could help."

Jessa frowned. "What is it?"

"The price for finding the crystal. I need to know if it's one that I am willing to pay."

"You need to," Jessa said. "If Venass gets the crystal…"

"I know what we fear happening if Venass gets the crystal, but I don't want to do something that will change who we are." There was a part of him that feared going farther than he already had. If he did that, would he be any better than those he tried to stop? "I'm not willing to go as far as Venass."

Alyse watched him, the familiar concern crinkling her eyes. "Brusus returned to the city. He wanted to check on the Barth. It's locked up, but he wanted to make sure it's not looted while we're gone."

"Is that safe?" Rsiran had returned to Elaeavn a few times since they'd left, but each time, he'd been concerned about what would happen and whether he would get caught. The council wanted to find him, and he didn't know if there was anything they could do to hold him, but now that they worked with Venass—presumably to keep the city safe—the guilds were *not* safe.

"He took Haern. They will be as safe as they can be."

"How did they return?" Walking was dangerous. Better to Slide, but without Rsiran to help, they wouldn't be able to Slide.

"Valn."

That made him feel a little better. Valn was capable, and skilled at Sliding. In the time that Rsiran had known him, he had gained more strength, honing his ability so he could carry two with him when Sliding a reasonable distance, something Rsiran didn't think he would have been capable of before the fight with Venass.

"Then I'll find them."

Jessa reached for him, but he stepped away, not willing to take her with him into the city. *Pulling* himself into a Slide, he emerged in his smithy.

Light filtered through dirty windows. A bin of lorcith glowed softly. The forge was cold, the coals sitting untouched for weeks and actually dusty. The long table where he'd stored his forgings now had only a few items of iron and steel, nothing of real value. He glanced to the door, and saw the bars of heart-stone he'd placed there were still secured. As far as he knew, there wasn't anyone else with the ability to Slide past heart-stone. Danis might be, but then his grandfather had used Venass knowledge to recreate many of Rsiran's abilities. He held out hope that being born to his abilities gave Rsiran an advantage, but didn't know if that was actually true. Venass might have discovered another way to use their skills, especially with so many of them studying and trying to learn how to stop him.

Would he ever be able to return here?

There was a time when he had feared being discovered, but that was in the past, much like his fear of discovery from Sliding. The smithy was *his*, and he hated that he had to stay away from it. Maybe it was safer than he realized. If no one else could Slide to it, then it was possible that he could return, if only to use the forge.

As he wandered through the shop, he found footprints in the dust that weren't his.

His gaze shot toward the door. Had he been mistaken? Was it *not* locked?

But no, the lock was in place. Bars of solid heartstone infused in place, set along the walls so that only someone like him would be able to even Slide in, and no sneak should be able to get past the lock on the door.

But it was unmistakable that someone had been here.

Not as safe as he had hoped then. Once Venass was taken care of, it would be safe to return. It had to be. The thought gave him extra incentive to finish what needed to be done.

A rustling sound behind him startled him, and he Slid toward the wall.

Rsiran *pushed* a pair of knives away from him, but saw nothing. Had he imagined the sound? He didn't think so, but there wasn't anything here that would explain what he'd heard.

He studied the inside of the smithy, trying to settle his

nerves. He shouldn't stay here. Even if it was safe, there were other things he needed to do.

Pulling the knives back to him, he Slid to the Barth.

The inside of the tavern carried with it the memory of scents from when he'd been here last. There was the scent of bread, an old yeasty odor of ale, and that of cool ash of the hearth. It seemed strange to see the Barth empty like this. Though it wasn't the first time the Barth had closed since he'd started coming to it, this time had a greater sense of finality to it.

Rsiran sent knives sweeping around the tavern as he looked for signs that Brusus or Haern might be here. There were none. The tavern had none of the dusty footprints his smithy now had, almost as if Brusus had come through and swept and wiped down the tables, keeping his tavern ready for the next guests. Knowing Brusus, it was possible he had, in spite of the danger.

The kitchen was equally empty. Lines of pots and pans hung on hooks, and stacks of plates were arranged neatly on a counter, waiting for the next meal preparations. A loaf of old bread rested on the counter, the crust slightly moldy.

"Thought you were busy establishing yourself." Haern stepped out of the shadows, a heavy cloak covering his shoulders and hanging low to the ground. A gleam of steel reflected from beneath the cloak from knives or possibly a sword, but not lorcith or heartstone made. Now that the guilds were gone, there were no constables to limit access to weapons.

"Where's Brusus?"

A door opened from the back of the tavern, and Brusus

stepped inside. He noted Rsiran immediately, and the flash of cold along the bracelets Rsiran wore let him know Brusus attempted a Reading.

"Damn, Rsiran! You don't need to scare us like this."

"Alyse told me you'd come back to the Barth."

"Yeah, well I can't leave it to rot. Have to make it appear that someone is coming through here or someone else might think it's theirs to come and squat. Be harder to get back once this is all over."

Rsiran appreciated the fact that Brusus was planning for a time after the war, especially after seeing those in the Aisl and their plans to remain.

"Besides, I got to check on your smithy, as well, so you can thank me for that."

Maybe Brusus had been the one to enter the smithy. He *was* a skilled sneak once upon a time, though maybe not as skilled as Jessa and certainly out of practice. There hadn't been a need for Brusus to sneak into places—or Jessa, for that matter—since meeting Rsiran.

"I've been working with Carth," Rsiran admitted.

Haern's jaw clenched. "That's a dangerous plan."

"She promised to leave you alone."

Haern glanced to Brusus before turning his attention back to Rsiran. "What do you mean that she promised? She use those words?"

He nodded. "Until Venass is taken care of. I'm not sure what she intends after that, so we've got time."

"You've got time," Haern said. His hand slipped beneath his cloak, and he pulled out one of his knives and started flipping it. "Damn woman wants me dead, and can't say I don't deserve it for what happened."

"We'll figure it out," Rsiran said.

Haern grunted. His knife spun in his hands before he slammed it back into a sheath beneath the cloak. "Not something here you can figure out, I don't think, not with Carth. This isn't something you'll be able to Slide me away from, Rsiran. She's got her network, and then she's got her informants. The damned woman is patient, so I don't doubt she'll find me."

Rsiran had seen that skill firsthand, and didn't know whether he would be able to protect Haern if it came to it, but he didn't intend to let Carth take him. "I told her I needed you for the fight with Venass. She wants to see them removed as well."

"Sure she does. They been attacking those she's aligned with for years. Had some kind of agreement once upon a time that protected both sides, but it was violated. Were it not for that peace, I wonder if Venass would have ever gotten as strong as they have."

"The accords." Carth had mentioned the accords, too. Saying that Venass and the Hjan had violated them. Rsiran also remembered hearing of them when they'd tracked down the man Isander. He, too, said the treaty between the Hjan and C'than had been broken by the Hjan.

"What she doing for you?" Haern asked.

"Gave me a name," Rsiran said, wondering what Haern might know about the accords.

"A name?"

Rsiran nodded. "As an assassin. Carth gave me an already-established identity to use."

"Ah, hell," Haern muttered.

"What is it?" Brusus asked.

"She planned this. No reason for her to have an identity for him unless she was planning it. Something like that takes time to establish. That was what I was trying to help Rsiran do on his own, but it'd take time to get established. A month or so to make the right connections, another month to use those connections to get the better jobs, and then he'd have access to the real power."

"We don't have that kind of time," Brusus said. He leaned on the counter near the bread. Rsiran wondered why the loaf remained here when everything else had been cleaned out, but with Brusus, it was probably something sentimental.

"And Carth knew it." He turned to Rsiran. "She's using you for something."

"I know."

Haern blinked. "You know?"

"She had to have planned it for me to be able to take on this identity. I don't know when she would have started establishing it, but Lorst was a known assassin when I took it."

"Lorst?" Haern frowned, rubbing at the long scar running along the side of his face. "Damn her, but she even picked a good name for you, too. Hints at another man, one who struck and disappeared. Even the Hjan feared him."

"Who was he?" Brusus asked.

Haern sighed. "Doesn't matter. Not now, at least. Now all that matters is that Rsiran owes Carth for this name." He looked over to Rsiran. "Did it help? If you're going to have something like that, it's got to be useful."

"That's why I wanted to find you. Lorst was offered a job."

"What kind of job?" Brusus asked. He leaned in, and his eyes practically sparkled.

Rsiran realized a part of Brusus missed the subterfuge he'd once been a part of, but in the time he'd known Alyse, that part of him had disappeared. No, it was more than that. It was since taking over the tavern. He'd done it claiming he wanted to honor Lianna's memory, but there had been more to it for Brusus. Having the tavern gave him a real sense of permanence in the city, something he struggled to have as a child of one of the Forgotten. But gaining that respectability came at a price, one Rsiran was glad Brusus had been willing to pay.

"Lorst is an assassin," Rsiran said. "There's only one kind of job."

"Who?" Haern asked.

"That's why I came here. I wanted to know if you'd ever heard of the target."

"Not the target. Who hired you? Where did she have you go?" Haern's knife flashed through his hands again, spinning rapidly. Without *pushing* on one of his lorcith knives, Rsiran wouldn't have the same control. Haern remained deadly dangerous.

"Eban. A man name Orly."

"Damn," Haern whispered. "Who's the target?"

"There were two, but both were from Elaeavn. Some woman, but that seemed almost an afterthought, and a man. Galen. I think Orly feared him."

Haern sighed. "You can't kill Galen, Rsiran."

"You know him?"

"Know of him. Met him once. Not many actually know him. What I've heard makes it clear that he doesn't deserve to die."

"He's an assassin," Brusus said.

Haern shot him a hard look. "So was I. Think I deserve to die?"

"Well, not *now*. I didn't know you back then." Brusus smiled widely, but it faded when Haern didn't follow suit.

"How long have you known Della?" Haern asked Brusus.

"What kind of question is that?"

Haern stared at him intently. "Answer it. How long have you known her?"

"Nearly all my life."

"How long have you been close to her?"

Brusus frowned, his bright green eyes flaring. Rsiran wondered if he attempted to Read Haern, but Rsiran had made bracelets for everyone, wanting to protect those he cared about —and might work with—from the risk of Venass Reading them.

"Five years. Maybe a bit longer. Before that, I visited often enough."

"Ever see someone else working with her?" Haern asked.

Brusus smiled again. "Della doesn't have anyone working with her. You know that well enough, Haern. Not anyone else with her particular gifts."

Rsiran's heart fluttered, and a nauseated sense rose in his stomach. "Della once had a student. I remembered her saying something about it," he said softly.

Haern nodded slowly. "She had a student. An apprentice. A

young man named Galen exiled from the city long ago. Rumors of him began about ten years ago, not long after he left Della." Brusus's face had paled. Haern shook his head, sighing. "So you see, Rsiran, you can't kill Galen, even if that's what it would take to recover the crystal."

CHAPTER 7

The night hung heavy and still, blackness covering everything. Rsiran remained motionless in the shadows, staring at the roofline, watching as he did. Lorcith knives stationed along the street gave all the light that he needed, more than enough for him to see the man crouched on the other rooftop.

"That's him?" he asked Carth.

She stood near him, nearly motionless. Rsiran couldn't even detect her breathing. "That would be Galen. He's an interesting man."

Rsiran had returned to Aisl searching for Della. He'd wanted to ask her about Galen, but she'd been busy with Luthan, the two of them speaking softly. She had waved him away when he'd appeared in her home, something that Della had never done before. What would he have said anyway? Would he have told her that he'd been hired to kill her former student? Rsiran had learned enough about him from Haern to know that Galen was regarded as a skilled assassin, and now Rsiran was somehow supposed to kill him—and *not* kill him.

How would he learn what he needed to find the crystal if he did this?

No answers had come, not that he had expected them. There weren't any answers about this. It was the first step as he began to determine what he needed to do to stop Venass.

"What's he doing?"

"Probably the same as you."

"I doubt that."

Carth turned slightly, enough that he could detect the heat rising from her. "Galen has a certain moral compass. He chooses jobs based on whether they should be completed, not so much for the money involved."

"You respect him." That didn't seem quite right. Orly respected Galen. But the way that Carth spoke of him was something more.

"He is unique of your kind."

"He's one of the Forgotten." That had been a surprise to learn. Haern didn't think Galen was Elvraeth born, which made it less likely he was aligned with the rest of the Forgotten, but he hadn't known what Galen had done to deserve the punishment. Probably nothing more than insulting one of the Elvraeth. Had Rsiran more time, he would have asked more questions. Della would know, but Rsiran could also have asked Luthan. The abilities for the former member of the council had served them well since he had joined them. But that would have to wait.

"Perhaps by his people, but not by all." Carth peered into the night. "What do you plan, Lorst?"

Rsiran swallowed. Each time she said his name, it felt like she forced it on him, giving him an uneasy sense. "I shouldn't kill him."

"I don't know if you could."

"Why? Because he's of Elaeavn? You've said he can't Slide, and I've faced others with lesser talents and come away."

"None like him."

Rsiran wondered if he should fear and respect Galen, or if he should be jealous. "There's the other job Orly hired me for."

"That would be the real job."

"I thought the real job was Galen."

"That is what Orly wants you to believe. Galen would have been hired the same as you."

That meant the woman, then. "What could be so important about a woman that he'd hire multiple assassins?" Rsiran asked.

"That is the question you must answer."

She stepped into the shadows and left him alone.

Rsiran watched the rooftop until Galen disappeared. He moved fluidly and jumped from the roof, disappearing into the tavern across the street.

Long minutes passed. Rsiran preferred to wait, hoping Galen and the woman he appeared to be guarding—not attempting to kill if Carth was right that he'd also been hired—would come back out of the tavern. It would make it easier for him to go after them. He could grab them, Slide them away from the city, and determine why Orly wanted them dead. He might even be able to arrange to make it look like they were both dead.

But if he had to go into the tavern, then there would be a greater challenge.

Shadows moved across the street, drawing his attention.

Rsiran counted six moving toward the tavern.

With the light from his knives scattered along the street, he could see they were all armed. As he watched, he noted another figure moving. No, not moving. *Sliding.*

Was there another assassin with the ability to Slide?

Lorcith pulsed.

Not an assassin then. One of the Hjan.

Damn. If they were after Galen or this woman, then Rsiran needed to get there first.

He Slid to the street, emerging near the tavern. One of the men approaching stopped, and quickly unsheathed his sword. Rsiran hated that he would be forced to attack, but he couldn't risk getting stabbed in the back while trying to reach Galen.

He *pushed* on a knife, sending it toward the man's leg, catching him in the thigh. When the man dropped, Rsiran *pulled* the knife back to him.

Two other men approached the tavern. Both wore two swords and one carried a crossbow. Rsiran sent a pair of knives at them, dropping them both.

That left three men, but he no longer saw them. And the Hjan. Where had he gone?

Rsiran slipped into the tavern. Music washed over him, loud and bawdy, and the crowd in the tavern all attempted to press around tables. Buxom serving girls with painted faces made their way from table to table, pausing long enough to touch men's hands or thighs before moving on to the next table.

Where was Galen? For that matter, where was the Hjan?

There was a door at the back of the tavern, and he started toward it when one of the serving girls approached and stopped him with a smile. She had reddish hair and pale skin, and her eyes were a light blue. Her hand reached for his shoulder, and she smiled widely.

"You need a little affection, big guy?" She ran her hand along his arm, and Rsiran took a step back, startled. She gasped playfully and touched a finger to her lips. "Maybe you prefer it slower. That's fine, too. Price is the same."

Rsiran flushed as he realized what she implied. He quickly scanned the tavern and realized *all* the women working their way through the tavern did the same thing. Was this what it was like outside of Elaeavn?

"I'm fine," he muttered, trying to push past her.

Her smile widened. "I don't doubt that you *are.* Why don't you let me see what those arms of yours look like. Big enough to be a blacksmith, you are!"

"I am a blacksmith," he said.

Her eyes widened. "Well then, how about you show me your hammer?"

Rsiran tried squeezing past her but couldn't. It was as if the woman intended to delay him. Could she be working with them?

As he watched, he realized other women worked on two men he assumed were assassins. They wore dark cloaks, and the bulge beneath one of their cloaks made it clear that he carried a sword. Rsiran didn't know how many carried swords openly in Eban—probably more than in Elaeavn—but the man worked to push past the short woman running her hand along his arm.

Damn.

Rsiran *pulled* a knife free. "Step aside."

The woman's eyes widened. "No need for that. We can play rough if you want."

"That's not what I want. Now move."

He made a slight movement as if to stab at her, and the woman jerked back. Rsiran used that opportunity to Slide past her, and emerged closer to the door. As he did, he heard a scream.

Damn!

He Slid toward the door. Emerging on the other side, he found a line of bodies. A figure flickered along the hallway, and Rsiran *pushed* three knives toward him as he Slid.

He emerged as one of the knives caught the Hjan in the back. Rsiran *pushed* on it, sending others that missed, and tried *pulling* on the lorcith implant. Something obstructed him.

"You won't get them first, Lareth," the man said.

They knew he was here.

He needed to keep his identity secret. If Galen or the woman discovered him here, and learned he wasn't the person that he appeared to be, he wouldn't have the chance to learn whether they had the crystal.

"Not Lareth. I'm Lorst."

The Hjan's eyes narrowed at the mention of the name, and

Rsiran realized that he'd made a mistake. Using all the knives he carried, he *pushed*.

One of them caught the Hjan and he started to fall. As he did, he Slid, disappearing.

Rsiran pulled the other knives to him. A flicker of light appeared, and the door opened. Without thinking, Rsiran *pushed* his knives at the door.

A man appeared in the doorway. "Galen," Rsiran said, trying to sound intimidating, flicking his gaze to the dark-haired woman behind him. She was beautiful and had deep green eyes. His wrists went slightly cool as one of them tried to Read him. Rsiran worried that someone might be listening, so added for Orly or the woman's benefit, "There's enough coin in this for us to split."

Galen's eyes widened slightly. "I need supplies."

His hand moved.

Rsiran had heard the rumor of darts being used, and knew to be careful. He Slid, appearing inside the room.

Something streaked through the room, but missed him.

For a moment, he detected another surge of lorcith somewhere nearby, likely from within the tavern, and realized the Hjan hadn't completely disappeared.

Rsiran Slid again, this time appearing in the far corner of the room.

Something came toward him, and he started to slide, but felt a piercing pain.

He resisted the urge to scream. Pain seared through him like nothing he'd ever experienced, in some ways worse even than when Venass had used the shadowsteel explosive on him, but this was different. His body didn't work, muscles that should answer refused, and he fell.

Galen was every bit as dangerous as he'd been warned.

He tried to stand, but couldn't.

That left only one option.

Rsiran focused on Della, and *pulled* himself in a Slide, praying that she could heal him in time.

CHAPTER 8

W hen he emerged, he heard the noise around him but couldn't speak. His head started to feel heavy, and Rsiran realized that he was having difficulty breathing. He smelled the heady odor of the mint tea Della favored, and was thankful he'd had the strength to Slide here. He could have tried going to the space between Slides, but he didn't know if that would heal him.

Hands reached him and rolled him. Rsiran wanted to scream, to say something, but couldn't.

Then a thick substance was pressed into his mouth. As it worked its way down his throat, the sensation eased. First his breathing returned, then his strength followed.

"What happened to you?" Della asked. She tottered around so that he could see her, and she held a slender rod in her fingers. That wasn't right. It was a dart. Galen's weapon of choice. "Where did you find this?"

Rsiran worked his tongue over dry lips and sat up. He

rubbed his arm where it still throbbed from the dart. "I tried to come to you, but you were busy with Luthan."

"Busy planning for the return, but not too busy to talk you out of doing something foolish. Where did you get this?"

"Eban."

The green in her eyes surged a moment. "Why would he be in Eban?"

"You know, don't you?"

She turned her attention back to him and frowned. As usual, Della wore her hair in a tight bun, but a few strands managed to get free, and stuck out wildly from her head. "Know? Of course I know. I've been keeping track of that boy since the fool council sent him away."

"What did he do?"

She waved a hand. "Nothing but try to protect me. Same as you would, I suspect, but you both would do it in your own way. How did you end up on the receiving end of this?"

She rolled the dart between her fingers and then flipped it toward the hearth. When it hit the fire, blue light exploded briefly from it. What did Galen use on his darts? Something fast-acting and painful. Had he not had the ability to Slide as he did, Rsiran would have died.

"I'm trying to find the crystal."

"Galen doesn't have it. He's been gone from the city far too long for that."

"I don't know whether he does, but there was an awful lot of power sent after him. Either Galen, or the woman with him, knows something."

"Woman?"

He nodded.

"Did you see her?" He nodded again. "What does she look like?"

"Dark hair. Green eyes. If she had been inside the city, I would have said she looked like one of the Elvraeth."

Della breathed out. "Stay here."

"Della?"

She didn't answer, just disappeared from the small hut. Rsiran leaned back, staring up at the branches bent overhead, covered with massive sjihn leaves, with only a smoke hole open. The hut was an impressive creation, more so because Della had already managed to make it her home.

Luthan appeared, Della with him. She tapped Rsiran on the shoulder. "Tell him what you told me."

The old councilor studied Rsiran with a frown. He had thick eyebrows and thinning hair, and wore a thin robe in spite of the cool of the forest. "What did you see, Lareth?"

"I told Della. Her old student."

"Not Galen. What of the girl?"

"A dark-haired woman. I said she had deep green eyes, and I would have thought her Elvraeth had she been in Elaeavn." Rsiran sat up quickly. "Is she one of the Forgotten? Do you think she could be working with Venass? Could Galen?"

Della waved a hand. "Galen does things for reasons of his own, but I doubt he would be doing anything that would attack Elaeavn."

"He's an assassin, Della."

"Perhaps by title, but he fights a different battle than most."

"Then what?"

"Could it be her?" Della asked.

Luthan rubbed his chin. "I don't see how it would be possible. She attended the Saenr. She wouldn't have been able to reach Eban."

"Who are you talking about?" Rsiran asked.

Luthan shook his head. "There was a Saenr before we lost the crystal. Naelm's daughter Cael was able to access the crystals. Afterward, he never spoke of how it went, but she disappeared. I heard rumors that he searched the city for her. Later, there were rumors he searched outside the city for her."

"The timing is a challenge," Della said.

"Not only the timing, but she would not have managed to take one of the crystals during her Saenr. Few even manage to hold them, but to take it from the chamber?"

"By the time she had her Saenr, the tree that crystal is tied to would have been damaged. The damage might have allowed her to take the crystal," Rsiran said. If it was true, that Cael was the woman he'd seen in Eban, and that she stole the crystal… He stood and started pacing. Was it possible he'd been close to the crystal in Eban, only to nearly lose it to Galen? If so, he needed to go back. His strength began to return, but he still felt slightly weakened. "Without the power of the Elder Trees to hold the crystal, there would have been nothing preventing her from taking it."

"That is not the way of the Saenr," Luthan said. "These are the youngest of the Elvraeth, and they are given the opportunity to witness the Great Watcher. Most only see the crystals. The few who manage to hold one… they are given something that—"

"I know what they are given," Rsiran said. "Just as I know it shouldn't be only the Elvraeth given that opportunity."

"We can debate the philosophy of the crystals, but—"

"Yes. Let's debate the fact the Elvraeth withhold them from the rest of the people of Elaeavn. The crystals—at least those who would be able to reach them"—and Rsiran wasn't sure how many would even be able to, but thought more should be given the opportunity—"belong to all the people."

"Lareth—"

Della stepped between them. "You must return to find her," she said to Rsiran. "If she does have the crystal, or at least knows what happened to it, we can finally begin to get closer to discovering a way to return it."

"I intend to do more than return the crystal," he said.

Della's eyes narrowed. "I do not think you are powerful enough to heal the Elder Tree, Rsiran. As much as you might want to do so, I think that power has been lost."

"We won't know until we obtain the crystal."

She nodded. "Return this Cael to the Aisl, and do it without harming Galen if you can."

"If I can." He thought about how quickly Galen moved, and the way that he tossed his darts. Rsiran didn't know if he'd be able to avoid another dart catching him, and if he did get hit again, if he'd survive. Galen might actually be of help to them with the coming fight with Venass, if only they could convince him to join them.

That would be of secondary importance. First, he had to find Cael and see if she knew anything about what happened to the crystal. If she did, either she would lead him to it, or she would tell him where to look.

Before leaving, he debated finding Jessa and telling her what happened, but it would only worry her. "Don't tell her I was here."

Della smiled. "I'll keep your injury from her one more time."

Luthan frowned, but Rsiran didn't remain to explain.

He Slid back to Eban, and emerged in the street.

A massive fire burned behind him, in the direction of the tavern. What had happened?

As he stood focusing around him, he detected lorcith flashing. Not only lorcith, but there were occasional flashes of heartstone.

The Hjan were here.

He needed to find Galen.

How long would he have been gone? Possibly ten minutes. Maybe a little longer. If Galen had been in the tavern, he would only have had time to make it a short distance along the street.

Rsiran Slid toward the tavern, emerging nearby. The heat from the fire pressed on him, nearly overwhelming him. He searched the streets and noted the throng of people pushing in from the south, carrying buckets from the nearby river.

Galen would have gone the opposite direction.

Rsiran Slid, emerging a street away. There were fewer people, but still more than there had been. He paused, focusing on lorcith and heartstone, but detecting neither before Sliding again. This time when he emerged, he saw a couple hurrying along the street. They would look like any other couple out at night if not for the fact that they stood nearly a fist taller than anyone else in Eban.

Before he could move, there came a flicker of lorcith.

One of the Hjan appeared in front of Galen. Rsiran hesitated. If Galen was as good as he'd heard—and seen firsthand, he should have no difficulty with the Hjan.

The man moved out of the shadows, his face becoming clear.

Rsiran gaped in shock.

The Hjan resembled him, and near enough they could be mistaken for each other.

Rsiran heard their voices. Galen seemed to believe the man in front of him *was* Lorst. The false Lorst spoke, taunting Galen, then he attacked, Sliding away from Galen as he did. A knife shot toward Galen. It sank into his stomach and he fell.

Rsiran Slid, but he was too slow.

The Hjan grabbed the woman and Slid.

Galen managed to sit up and grab the Hjan by his boot. All three disappeared.

When Rsiran emerged from his Slide, the street was empty.

His heart hammered in his chest. He'd lost them.

With one of the Hjan Sliding them out of the city, they could go anywhere. Galen had been injured, and there would be no way to stop the Hjan. Rsiran didn't expect a young Elvraeth woman to manage to fend off one of the Hjan. Which meant that Venass had the crystal.

He closed his eyes. Could he lock onto the sense of lorcith that he'd detected?

Normally, it wouldn't be a problem, but there was too much

lorcith around him, most of it he'd brought, forged himself, leaving him more attuned to it. Without a connection, he couldn't reach the sense of lorcith that he'd noted when Hjan had been here.

They were gone. And with them, the possibility of finding the crystal.

CHAPTER 9

The Aisl should have welcomed him back. He should have found the crystal—or at least Cael—and returned with a plan for restoring the crystal, even restoring the Elder Tree. Instead, he returned a failure. Venass had Cael, and likely had the crystal. He had nothing other than more questions.

Rsiran realized his mistake; he shouldn't have mentioned to the Hjan the name he used. They had taken advantage of that, and now... now the Hjan used that name to attack Galen.

His bracelets went cold, and he looked around the clearing. There weren't many Readers willing to attempt Reading him, knowing he wore the heartstone bracelets, but Della still attempted from time to time. A part of him wondered if she even managed to get past the barrier created by the bracelets, but she would never admit it if she could.

He found her near the base of the alchemist tree. Della stood with Luthan and Ephram, all of them staring at the tree.

Massive branches still carried leaves, but to Rsiran, the sense of the Elder Tree was darkened.

Sliding to them, he emerged to see them standing as if waiting for him.

"What did you find?" Della asked.

"Another reached them before me," he said.

"What do you mean by another?" Luthan asked.

Rsiran turned to the Elvraeth councilor. "There was another who reached them first. A Hjan who," he hesitated before going on, "looked something like me."

"Why would the Hjan care if they had someone who looked like you?" Ephram asked.

Della studied him intently. "They know, don't they?"

He nodded. "When I first found Galen, I came across one of the Hjan and made the mistake of revealing myself."

Worse, he hadn't been fast enough when facing the Hjan, and that had been with only *one* of the Hjan. What would happen when there were many more? They were getting increasingly skilled, making it so that he struggled to stop even one without letting him escape. How would he manage to stop all of them, especially Danis?

"And they have Galen and the girl," Della went on.

"Della," he started, "Galen... he was injured. The Hjan—"

Della closed her eyes, and Rsiran thought that she might be mourning the loss of her former student, but when she opened her eyes, she turned to the north and stared at the line of trees. "Galen lives. And I don't think he's alone."

"I saw—"

"I don't know what you saw," Della said. "But I have told you about the gift I received when I held one of the crystals. That allowed me to heal, but more than that, it connected me to those I care about." Her eyes dropped to his bracelets. "Most of them. Trust me when I tell you that Galen lives."

"Do you know if the Hjan have him?"

She shook her head. "It's not like that. I can... find his mind... That is the only way to describe it. Nothing more than that. It is not directional."

"If the Hjan attacked this man, they would have killed him," Ephram said.

"Then they escaped?" Rsiran asked.

"He is more resourceful than most give him credit for," Della said. "It is the reason I sent him to Isander to train."

"Isander?" Rsiran asked.

Della nodded almost absently. "He is someone with a different set of skills."

Rsiran frowned. It couldn't have been a coincidence, could it? The man who had trained Haern also trained Galen? And Rsiran had met Isander, even if Isander had been unwilling to help.

He started away, gaze sweeping through the clearing as he searched for Haern. There were different questions that he had now, and he didn't think that Della would be able to answer them, not if she didn't have any way of tracking Galen. Knowing that he lived was enough for now. If he could find him, and if he could get to Cael...

"Rsiran?" Luthan said, hurrying to catch up to him.

Rsiran glanced over to the elderly councilor. "What is it?"

"A... thought. We need to remove the risk of Venass from

Elaeavn, but we will need the council's support." When Rsiran arched a brow, Luthan pressed on. "I know how you feel about the council, especially after the way it appears they sided with Venass."

"Appears? I think we can fairly confidently say that they *did* side with Venass. You were abducted, Luthan."

"And rescued. But if you find Cael, we will have a different kind of leverage, at least with Naelm. If we can get her, and get to the council... It might be a way of getting the city back without heavy fighting."

Rsiran started to shake his head, but Luthan was right. If they could do anything to end it without a battle, he had to try, didn't he?

"I'll find her. And the crystal."

A relieved expression swept over his face. "Good. I trust that you'll do what is right."

"I'll do what I can."

He started away from Luthan, frustration beginning to bubble up within him. If the council hadn't sided with Venass, none of this would have been an issue. The guilds shouldn't be solely responsible for protecting the city, not if the Elvraeth truly believed they were meant to rule. The Elvraeth should take an active role as well. If Luthan believed the council would help, Rsiran needed to know what help they'd find in the palace. More than that, he needed answers.

An idea came to him, and he Slid before he thought too much about it.

He emerged in the Floating Palace, bypassing the heartstone that prevented others from Sliding into it. Lights glowed in sconces around him, and the halls were empty. His heart hammered as he hurried through the halls.

What was he thinking? Returning to the city was dangerous, and now he was going to the one place that would be the *most* dangerous if caught?

Rsiran checked his knives, ensuring he had enough if it came to it. Even better, there were dozens of knives within the palace now, some of them forged by his own hand, giving him an even greater connection to the metal. Others were forged by ancient smiths, and he'd often longed to have a chance to study the craftsmanship, but had never had the time. Now he wondered if he ever would.

He paused at the massive doors leading into the council hall before Sliding past.

The hall was dark, and as he *pushed* a pair of knives around the room for light, he saw it was empty. The enormous table that took up most of the middle of the room was darkened in shadows. A jagged rent at one end of the table told him that *something* had happened here.

Rsiran Slid, this time emerging in one of the upper floors of the palace. He focused on lorcith, letting the call of the metal draw him from place to place, having no other focus about where he'd go to search for Naelm.

The first room was nothing more than a storage room. In it, he found a couple of lorcith knives—some of the earliest that he'd created. Brusus had used them to trade for information. He *pulled* them, and noted the lesser skill that he'd used when hammering them. These had been formed when he first began working with the forge, a time when he had still been some-what hesitant, even if he hadn't known it at the time.

Rsiran pocketed them. They were his, regardless of how the Elvraeth had come to possess them.

The next room was someone's quarters. The room was empty, and the knife he'd sensed hung over the fire, crossed with one made of steel. He *pulled* on this one, as well, returning it to his pocket.

The third room where he detected lorcith, he found no knife.

Rsiran focused on the awareness of the lorcith that he detected. As he did, he realized that it wasn't a knife at all, only shaped similarly.

Next, he stopped outside a closed door further along the hall. Another sense of lorcith came from the other side.

After Sliding inside, a crossbow bolt flew at him, striking him in the leg.

Rsiran bit back a scream as pain surged through him.

A dark-haired man—the same one who had looked so much like him when he had attacked Galen—stood holding a crossbow.

He felt the poison coursing through him.

"You are a fool, Lareth. First you come to Eban, and now to the palace? Do you really think you're so powerful that you can stop—"

He didn't let the man finish.

Rsiran *pulled* himself in a Slide, and grabbed the man before pausing at the place in between Slides, where he used the power of the Elder Trees, letting it fill him, healing the injury from the crossbow attack.

The Hjan tried to jerk away, but Rsiran wrapped him in bands of power from the Elder Trees.

"Where is Galen?" Rsiran asked, pulling the crossbow bolt from his leg and tossing it on the ground next to him.

"That's what you're after? You really care that much about the man?"

"Not the man."

"The coin? Perhaps we have misjudged you, Lareth." He smiled darkly. "Or should I say Lorst?"

Rsiran used the energy he alone could manipulate here and twisted it more tightly around the Hjan. "I think either will work. Where is he?"

The man's face started to turn purple, and Rsiran eased back on the power. "Escaped. Why else would I be in the palace?"

The comment made no sense to Rsiran. "Where is he?"

The dark smile returned. "He returns to Elaeavn with the girl. There's nothing that you can do about it, Lareth, unless you intend to actually kill him yourself, and I think you found he is unique in how he can escape."

Rsiran was getting tired of all the praise heaped on Galen. "Where is Danis?"

The Hjan's mouth tightened.

Rsiran pulled on the power, squeezing him again. "Danis. Where is he?"

"You won't find him as easily as that. You can torment me all you like, but I don't know how to find him." He smiled at Rsiran. "You'll have to kill me, if you have the stomach for it."

"I have something else in mind."

Rsiran struck the Hjan on the back of the head, knocking him out. Holding onto the man tightly, Rsiran Slid him to the inside of Della's hut in the Aisl. Once there, he waited.

It didn't take long for Della to come running into the hut. "What did you do?"

Rsiran nodded to the Hjan. "His plate. Can we remove it?"

Della sucked it a sharp breath as she stared at the man he'd brought back to the camp. There was no denying the resemblance. "Rsiran—where did you find him?"

"Doesn't matter now. Can we remove the plate?"

Della placed a log in the hearth, getting the flames rolling even more. She made a slow circle around the man, pausing at his head. "Haern was able to successfully remove his plate, but he hadn't been as connected. I don't know how they fuse it to the person."

"I can do that, but can you heal him."

Della looked up. "Is that really what you want to do? It might be better were we to let him die."

"No. We need answers, and we won't get them with a pile of dead Hjan."

Della nodded slowly. "If we do this, you will need to remain here as I do."

She gathered a few sharp implements and crouched in front of the Hjan's face. Della pressed her fingers against his skin, running them along the scar before taking a deep breath. She looked up at Rsiran, and her eyes blazed a green so deep that they were almost black. "You will have to act quickly. Once the plate is removed, I will need to heal him. I suspect he will fight."

"He's unconscious."

"There are other ways to fight, Rsiran."

She placed a sharp knife to the scar and made a quick incision.

Rsiran expected blood to pour out, but it didn't. He saw a flash of metal beneath, and Della peeled the skin back, revealing the size of the plate. Only at the edge of the flesh did it bleed.

"Now, Rsiran."

He focused on the plate, and *pulled*.

Always before when detecting the metal buried in the Hjan, there had been something that limited him. Now that the flesh was peeled back, he realized the limitation came from the skin overtop.

The plate resisted him.

Rsiran *pulled* again, this time with more strength.

Della pressed down on the Hjan. Muscles in her arm quivered, and her jaw set in a tight line. "Quickly now."

Rsiran *pulled* again.

The door to her hut opened and Luthan entered. He scanned the hut and hurriedly joined Della, crouching next to her without saying a word. He pressed his hands on the Hjan's shoulders, as well, giving her support as they held him to the ground.

The plate began to move, but still it clung to him.

Rsiran had to try a different approach. Pulling it off the Hjan wouldn't work, but could he change the metal, perhaps change the shape? Lorcith couldn't take on another shape once forged, but he'd never tried using his connection to it to try before.

This time, he *pushed* and *pulled* at the same time. He didn't want to remove the plate, only to deform it and change the focus of energy from it.

The lorcith buckled slightly.

He pressed harder.

The lorcith resisted, but Rsiran focused on the sound of lorcith, on the song he heard from unshaped lorcith deep in the mines of Ilphaesn, and sent that as he *pushed* and *pulled*.

The lorcith softened.

The Hjan screamed.

Rsiran quickly wrapped the lorcith into a tight roll, and *pulled*.

It came away quickly, separating from the Hjan, and he dragged it free. Once free of the Hjan, he sent it to the fire and let the lorcith not only grow hot, but burned off the remnants of the Hjan in a flash of horrid green. He started to pull the lorcith out of the fire, but sensed from the metal that it wanted to remain, so he left it.

Turning his attention back to Della, he saw her and Luthan whispering softly to each other as they worked on the Hjan.

"The defect will require much healing," Luthan said.

"I can see that."

"You cannot risk such strength. We will have need of your strength."

"There is no other way, Luthan."

Rsiran crouched next to her. "There might be."

Rsiran reached for her hand, then grabbed onto the Hjan and *pulled* them to the place between Slides. As he emerged, power flowed around him, even more potent now that he was at the heart of the Aisl Forest with the Elder Trees physically near him.

"Rsiran—"

"We need to do this, Della. We need to know what they intend, and we can't continue to kill them. When this is over, will we exterminate all of Venass?"

"You have compassion, and that is a valuable trait, but when it comes to Venass, that compassion might not be well placed. Those you speak about have done unthinkable things, many that we cannot begin to understand."

"Someone once said the same about Haern."

Della's eyes softened. "Haern… he is unique in that he chose to leave Venass before he managed to sink too deeply. These men, this is something you're taking from them. They might not *want* to remain this way."

"Then we give them a choice. Later. For now, we need information."

He *pulled* on the power of the Aisl Forest and funneled it into her. Rsiran had done something similar once before, using the same technique when Della had nearly died while trying to heal the Elder Tree. Had it not been for her, the smith tree would have died as well. Would they have lost another crystal then? Losing even the one was too much. At least he could help Della, much like this place restored him when injured or weakened.

Della focused on the Hjan, letting her hands trace over the man. As she did, the skin slowly knitted back together. Rsiran could see what she did, could watch the way that she used the power and let it flow through her.

The Hjan shook.

Then he woke.

He glanced at Della and then turned to Rsiran. He tried something—likely trying to Slide—and his eyes widened. "What did you do?"

"The same as I'll do to the rest of the Hjan. I removed the ability you stole. And now you'll answer questions."

With that, Rsiran Slid them back to Della's hut.

CHAPTER 10

"I don't see anything," Jessa said.

They stood on a wide plain far outside of Eban searching for Galen and Cael. Should it surprise Rsiran that she was Naelm's daughter? In a twisted way, it made some of his decisions make sense, possibly even the decision to allow Venass access to Elaeavn.

In the distance, a forest lined a wide river, and farther still, the vague outline of the city rose. This was the direction Amin had told them to go, and even if Rsiran didn't fully trust the Hjan, it only took a few moments to check.

"Maybe they turned a different direction," Jessa went on.

"He said they returned to Elaeavn," Rsiran said. "There are only a few options if they intend to go by road."

"We could wait for them to appear. Then we could grab them."

Rsiran let out a long sigh. "Della doesn't think that we *should* grab them. Just keep them safe and take the crystal from them."

"You don't need to take them, then."

He didn't, but Della thought he needed to pull Galen in for some reason. "The crystal needs to return. If that takes Cael bringing it back..."

"If it reaches the city, the council will gain control of the crystal. That's not what we want."

"The council won't. I intend to see to that."

"How?"

Rsiran surveyed the landscape again. They weren't here. Della would have detected had something happened to Galen, and she said he was still out here somewhere, if only Rsiran could find them. It would be easier if the damned man had lorcith on him.

With another long sigh, he Slid her back to the Aisl.

"I need to return to Elaeavn for the next part," he told her.

"You can't take on the council on your own."

Rsiran didn't argue, but he thought he *could* take on the council if it came to that. It was the presence of Venass he couldn't, but now they had another way. He might not trust Amin to do anything other than betray them, but he could use him and what he knew.

"I don't need to take on the council, only convince them we'll return the crystal. Luthan claims—"

"I know Luthan claims the council only cares about the crystal, but do you really believe it will be easy to expel Venass from the city? Do you think to convince the council they supported the wrong side and simply ask Venass to leave?"

"Not easy, but necessary."

"Rsiran..."

"What choice do we have?" he asked. "This *has* to be the first step. If we can reclaim the city and push back Venass, then we have only to take the fight out of the city. When I find Danis—"

"When you find Danis, what do you really intend to do? You intend to destroy him?" She turned to him and took his hands, and stared into his eyes. "This is your grandfather, Rsiran. I've seen how much you struggle with the idea of harming family."

"He's not family."

She squeezed his hands. Rsiran breathed out, trying to let the anger he felt toward Danis ease away from him, but not certain if he could. Too much emotion was tied up in what Danis had done, the way that he'd destroyed his family.

Jessa pulled him through the forest, leading him toward the row of huts that had been built at the edge of the clearing, between the massive sjihn trees. As she did, he realized where she took him. A steady hammering came from somewhere behind the row of buildings.

"I don't need to see him."

"Don't you? Since you returned with him, you haven't taken any time to sit and speak with him. You're the guildlord, Rsiran."

"The guildlord of what, exactly? Until we return to the city, we don't have anything we're guilds of. Everything I have come to know is gone until we take back the city. That involves attacking Venass that might be there."

"I'm not saying that you can't do that, only that you can't be so focused on it that you forget what you've committed to. Our people had guilds before we ever moved to the city. You were the one to tell me that."

"They weren't the guilds," he said.

"Fine. Clans. The idea is the same. Now come on. You need to meet with your guild. And your father."

When they reached the row of huts, she guided him between them. Rsiran was surprised to see that a massive fire buried deep in the earth burned, the coals hot enough to melt steel... which was exactly what the smiths used it for. Someone had fashioned an anvil out of a thick stump of sjihn wood, and three men stood around it, taking turns hammering.

As Rsiran approached, Seval stepped off to the side and smiled, wiping his hand across his forehead. "Guildlord," he said with a smile. "You finally have come to inspect our forge? The masters have approved it, but I suppose we should formalize it and have you grant it final approval."

Rsiran hadn't known he was expected to approve a smithy. Did that mean he could formalize his own when they returned? The guild had pressed him to return to his family smithy, but he'd preferred to remain in the one he'd acquired from Brusus. There was familiarity to it.

"You have my approval," he said. "I should have returned to check on the guild sooner. I'm sorry, Seval."

Seval nodded. "You're the guildlord," he said, as if that answered everything. "Have you finished with what you plan?"

Rsiran suspected Seval only wanted to return to the city. Since he felt the same way, he understood. "Not yet. Now we have a new plan, one I hope will lead us back into the city."

Seval looked to the pit and then to the stump, a troubled expression on his face. "That would be good." He leaned toward Rsiran. "We're going to be short on weapons, Lareth. Only a few of the masters are comfortable making swords. They're learning, but to truly make a fine blade... well, you have to listen to the lorcith if you intend to use that, or you have to fold the steel more than most believe if you go that route. We could really use your guidance."

Rsiran glanced to Jessa. Was this why she'd brought him here? Had she known he was needed?

Delaying a little so that he could help the guild wouldn't cause too much trouble, and it *would* be good to swing a hammer again, even if it wasn't his own.

"I don't think you need me, Seval. You've learned to listen to lorcith as well as most, and Luca..."

Seval nodded. "Luca can hear it, but he still doesn't have the technique. Most of us don't, not even Neran, and it turns out he can hear the lorcith damn near as well as Luca. Seems Venass did us a favor by forcing him to listen." He smiled and pointed toward the makeshift anvil. "Come and work with us a bit, Lareth. The others would do well to see the guildlord in action."

"I..." He took a look around the small clearing, noting the pile of metal to one side, iron and lorcith and a few pieces of grindl. A small table was set with tools. Younger men worked to bring logs toward the pit, keeping the coals burning hot. In many respects, this *was* a smithy. "I think I can do that for a while," he said.

Seval clapped him on the shoulder and looked over to Jessa. "Are you okay if we borrow your man for a bit?"

She clasped her hand around the charm she wore, bare of flower as it had been in the days since they had come to the

Aisl. "I think I can get along without him for a bit. See if you can beat some sense into him."

"What kind of sense?"

"The kind that shows him he needs to remember his other responsibilities."

Jessa shot Rsiran a victorious look and turned away.

She *had* planned this, though he still didn't know *what* she had planned. Just getting him to the smiths wouldn't have been all that she wanted; there must have been another reason.

"What can I do?" he asked Seval.

The master smith grinned at him. "What can you do? You're the guildlord, Lareth!"

"You wanted me to help with sword making?"

"That would be a start." They stopped at the anvil, and Rsiran realized that his father was one of the men working there alongside Master Eldon, the man he'd rescued from Asador when the Forgotten had grabbed him.

His father eyed him strangely as he approached, and his eyes narrowed even more when Seval handed him a hammer before turning to the coals and pulling out a lump of lorcith. Since he'd rescued his father, Rsiran hadn't worked near him. It had been… a long time since he'd worked at a forge with his father, and seeing the expression on his face, Rsiran wasn't sure his father wanted to work with him.

"Give the guildlord some space," Seval said.

"We were crafting a few blades," Eldon said.

Seval grabbed the blade that rested on the anvil and held it up. "Looks finished. Now, let's see what a real blade master can make."

Eldon nodded, and his father's eyes narrowed even more.

Rsiran flashed back to when his father had caught him making a sword out of lorcith. That had been the trigger that had sent him to Ilphaesn, the trigger that had started all of this for him. And now... now he had come full circle, asked to demonstrate blade making, not only to the apprentices around them, but also to the masters. It felt surreal, as if more a dream than anything. Stranger still, he actually *knew* he was the right person to demonstrate this. Rsiran had spent countless hours making knives and swords, much more time than any of the master smiths.

"Are you certain about this piece?" he asked Seval.

"Luca chooses them," Seval answered.

"Thank you for continuing to work with him."

"Ah, Lareth, he is a pleasure. In time, he will be quite skilled."

Rsiran swung the hammer a few times, focusing on the lorcith. He'd never forged out in the open, never before with the sun high overhead, or trees all around. In this place, he felt a different sort of peace than he did even in his smithy. It was *right* that he use the hammer here.

As he listened to the lorcith, he knew Luca had chosen well. The piece sang, a strange sort of song, one that called to him, letting him know it would be willing to take on any shape asked of it, but that it would easily form a sword.

Rsiran hammered.

The first strike jarred through him, strange after all the time away from the forge.

The next came more easily, as did the one after that. With each blow, he fell into an easy sort of work, a pattern of hammering steadily, pausing long enough for someone—Seval, he realized, now acting as *his* apprentice—to flip the metal. Rsiran was drawn into the creation, hammering easily, muscles he hadn't used in weeks thrilled to be back at work.

The blade took on a pattern, slowly curving rather than straight as so many were that he made. As he forged, he realized it called for something else, and it took a moment to realize what it was.

"I need heartstone," he said.

Seval shook his head. "We have none, Lareth. The camp…"

"Heat it while I'm gone," Rsiran said.

He Slid to his smithy in Elaeavn and grabbed a section of heartstone from the bars on the wall, pausing long enough to look for additional footprints in the dust, but found none. Then he emerged, holding only a small piece of heartstone in his hand.

Seval was setting the blade back on the anvil.

Rsiran realized that dozens of people watched him. Most were master smiths or their apprentices, but a few others joined, as well, standing back along the line of huts. Miners and alchemists, and even Sarah standing with Valn. Why had they come?

The song shifted, and Rsiran's attention returned to the sword.

He handed the heartstone to Seval. "Moderate heat. I need a soft glow but nothing more."

Seval nodded, not minding the fact that Rsiran directed him.

Rsiran took up the hammer, working at the lorcith portion of the blade. He turned it over as he hammered, now working with smaller strokes. The metal folded neatly, a dimpled and almost wet appearance to it, and soon, the hammer wasn't enough.

He began *pushing* on the metal. Using that technique, he managed a finer control, and created a small depression in the middle of the blade. With each breath, he felt as if he got stronger, almost as if the work he did here energized him, bringing him closer to the smith rather than the man he had been of late.

Seval handed him the heated heartstone.

Pushing on the heartstone, he layered it into the depression, creating a pattern on the blade. He repeated the same on the other side, smoothing it out, and using a combination of *pushing* and *pulling* on both lorcith and heartstone, he sealed the two metals together.

The sword was almost complete, but needed an additional flourish. The song in the metal practically begged for one.

Rsiran held an image in his mind, and *pushed*.

The pattern took hold.

Lifting it carefully, he took the sword to a quenching bucket and cooled the blade.

As he held the sword, he noted the way colors swirled off the blade. There was a sense of power emanating from it, and it reminded him of the way power radiated from the Elder Trees.

"It's beautiful," Seval said.

Rsiran looked up. Only then did he realize that everyone stared at him. "I... I'm sorry, Seval. I got caught up in the work. I didn't demonstrate anything."

Seval grinned at him, sweeping his hand around him in a

wide arc. "I think you demonstrated far more than you realize, Lareth. Everyone here had the chance to see a true blade master work. May I?" he asked.

Rsiran handed him the blade, giving it up reluctantly.

"The detail on this is outstanding. The lines... the way you used heartstone and lorcith together..." He turned the sword over, letting the sun catch the other side before handing it back to Rsiran. "Place a hilt on this and you have yourself a blade deserving of a name."

"I can work with the smiths more at another time," he said.

"They would appreciate that. Perhaps you don't need to demonstrate *this* much detail," he finished with a smile.

Rsiran started away, and his father caught his arm. There was a pained look on his face, but the words that came out of his mouth were not what he expected. "I was wrong, Rsiran."

"Wrong? About what?"

His father swept his gaze around the small clearing behind the huts. "About so many things, it seems, but mostly about you. That," he said, nodding toward the sword, "is a work of such skill, I cannot imagine how you created it. Seeing some of what you have forged makes me feel like an apprentice again struggling to figure out how the masters managed their work." He let go of Rsiran's arm and sighed. "The masters were right choosing you as guildlord."

He held Rsiran's gaze a moment before pulling away and making his way back toward the other masters, leaving Rsiran standing alone. Across the clearing, Jessa watched him, and he sighed as he nodded to her.

CHAPTER 11

T he city of Eban had a certain darkness to it, one that the
dozens of lanterns and candles burning in the windows
did not erase. Rsiran stood on a rooftop, looking down toward
Orly's hiding place, watching for movement. He carried his new
sword, the hilt he'd placed on it simple, contrasting with the
finery of the blade. There was something about the sword he
hadn't determined yet, almost like he was somehow connected
to the Aisl, having forged it there.

"Do you intend to attack?"

Rsiran spun, and Carth smiled at him with a flash of teeth.
How had she managed to sneak up on him so easily? She wore
dark leathers the seemed to draw the darkness of the night
around her, and her black hair seemed one with the shadows.
Only her bright eyes—eyes that practically glowed—penetrated
the darkness.

"Not attack. I want answers. I need to find Galen." The more
he thought about it, the more he realized he needed to find him

before Galen reached Elaeavn. He couldn't risk the crystal reaching Venass first.

"He escaped you."

Rsiran sniffed. "Not me. Another attacked who claimed to be Lorst."

Carth smiled. "A clever trick, don't you think?"

"You knew?" Rsiran shouldn't have been surprised, but if she had known of the plan, why hadn't she shared it with him? Didn't she *want* to help Galen?

But clearly, she didn't. All she wanted was a way to reach Haern.

"It is my business to know, Rsiran Lareth."

"Rsiran? Not Lorst?"

She studied him, standing casually as she did. "I do not think the assassin suited you all that well. You might be many things, but assassin isn't one of them."

Rsiran didn't know if that was a compliment or if she insulted him. He decided it didn't matter. What mattered was getting the help he needed so he could find Galen, and then Cael. Once he found them, he could find the crystal. That was his focus right now.

He hoped that with the crystal, he could restore the Elder Tree, and use that to defeat Danis and the rest of Venass, but what if he couldn't restore the Elder Tree? Rsiran didn't know if he needed to do so in order to stop Venass, but he suspected it would help.

"You knew there was one of the Hjan pretending to be me?" he asked.

"Not you. That was Lorst."

"That was the real Lorst?"

Carth stepped closer to him. As she did, the darkness of the night seemed to close around him, almost as if she quenched the light from candles below, even muting the light he saw from the lorcith and heartstone he carried. "There was no Lorst. He was a creature of my creation. But it does not surprise me the Hjan would discover the deceit and use it to their advantage. They have done the same many times before."

"What are you after, Carth?" Rsiran asked.

"The same as you."

"I want the crystal returned."

"You want the Hjan destroyed."

He didn't turn away from her gaze. "Not only the Hjan. Venass as well."

Carth nodded. "They are similar but not the same. Venass seeks power, while the Hjan use the knowledge gained by Venass to enforce their agenda."

"My grandfather leads Venass."

The statement managed to get the biggest reaction he'd seen out of Carth. "Danis Elvraeth is your grandfather?"

"Apparently."

Carth tipped her head to the side, studying him for a long moment. "You didn't know."

"Not before all this started. I never knew him. None of my family, really."

"What will you do when you find him, Rsiran Lareth?"

"I intend to stop him and keep him from harming anyone else. I failed the last chance I had. I won't make the same mistake again."

"Neither will he."

"What does that mean?"

"It means that Danis Elvraeth learns quickly. Each set back is a lesson for him, each an opportunity for him to grow stronger."

"You sound like you know him."

Carth stared at the street below them, a tight expression on her face. "I have chased him for many years, Rsiran Lareth, only to have him escape."

"Why do you chase him?"

She turned and met his eyes. "The same reason as you. To end him."

A chill raced up Rsiran's back. He'd seen the easy way Carth managed to overcome whatever Rsiran could do, almost as if she anticipated his every move. If Danis could easily get past her, what chance did Rsiran have against him?

"You'll do that?"

"I'll do anything to achieve his capture. Even die."

"And if I get to him first?" Rsiran asked.

"It doesn't matter who brings down the boar, only that everyone shares in the feast."

"We could work together," he suggested. If Carth fought with him, they might be able to end the fight more quickly. Wasn't that what they would both want?

"Unfortunately, Rsiran Lareth, I have other responsibilities."

He wondered what those might be. Carth found him easily when in Eban, and unless she could Slide, she would have to move from here slowly. "More important than stopping Venass?"

"Do you think you're the only one who wants that? That you're the only one who tries?" She laughed softly, and her voice drifted into the night before disappearing. "The Hjan and Venass have survived countless threats in their pursuit of power. This is not the first time they have played this game, but Danis might have miscalculated this time. I intend to take advantage of that." She crouched, readying to jump. "Leave Orly. He's not a threat."

"I didn't intend anything with Orly other than trying to understand what he might know about Galen."

"Galen will return to Elaeavn. That is your play, Rsiran Lareth."

That was the same thing that Amin had told him, but he hadn't wanted to trust him. "Venass rules in Elaeavn."

"Venass has shown force to Elaeavn, but they do not rule. Ruling has never been their ambition."

"I don't know how you can say that after seeing what they've done."

"I've seen it far more than you can imagine. They work in the darkness, gaining power and strength. Perhaps the endgame is ruling, but for now, they wish to remain in shadows. That is also their mistake."

"What is?"

"The shadows belong to me."

With that, she leapt from the roof, soaring higher than she should have been able. As she landed, she disappeared.

Rsiran stared, unable to take his eyes off the spot where she landed. Who *was* Carth?

A soft noise below drew his attention. On the street, he saw movement and realized Orly emerged from his home surrounded by nearly a dozen men. Rsiran noted two of the men appeared to be Neelish sellswords. He might be able to bring them down, but there would be a cost.

Orly hurried along the street before turning a corner.

Rsiran considered following, but what would he gain if he did? Carth was right—he needed to find Galen, and he wouldn't do that tracking a thief-master in Eban. He might not even find him by returning to Elaeavn, and if he did, it still might not matter, especially not if Cael didn't have the crystal.

What he needed was to leverage what he knew and use it. What he really needed was to reclaim Elaeavn from Venass, and force the council to assist.

Maybe there would be a way without real violence, but it would risk himself. That didn't worry him, but it would anger Jessa.

Rsiran Slid, and emerged in the Aisl.

He focused on heartstone and found the piece that he wanted, Sliding to it.

High in the trees, he found Haern.

"You should be careful when you Slide. You could fall from here," Haern said, barely looking up.

"I could Slide if I fell."

"If you hit your head before you could Slide?"

Rsiran shrugged. "I know my abilities, Haern."

"You have grown more skilled, but that can make a man careless. That's all I'm trying to tell you. Don't get careless. We need you to face Venass."

Rsiran settled onto the branch next to Haern. Few of the

massive sjihn leaves obstructed the line of sight here, giving him the ability to see all of the forest floor spread below. "You didn't tell me that Carth wants to bring down Venass as much as we do."

Haern closed his eyes. "Only Carth knows what she wants."

"Who is she?" he asked.

"You mean *what*, don't you?"

That was the question that had plagued Rsiran, but he didn't know if Haern even knew the answer. "What. Who. They're the same, aren't they?"

"Maybe with her. She's unique. Perhaps the last of her kind."

"What kind is that?"

"Carth comes from a land far to the north, a place from across the sea. She would have remained there if not for the Hjan. That was one of their first mistakes, and possibly the worst. Had they not drawn her attention…" Haern smiled. "But they did. I did. And now she is here."

"You don't know what she is either, do you?"

Haern shook his head. "I know that she's skilled in ways that we are not."

"Gifted by the Great Watcher?"

"Not the same way that you and I are, but she has gifts of a sort. I don't know that anyone really understands the extent of her gifts other than Carth herself."

"I asked her to join us in the fight against Venass."

Haern smiled. "Imagine she threw her support right in."

Rsiran laughed. "She said she had other things that she had to do."

"Don't mistake that for not helping. Carth fights Venass, so she'll do whatever she needs in order to accomplish what she seeks."

"Then why has she helped me so far?"

"Because it suited her. Like everything that Carth does, it matters if it suits her goals. If not, then she won't assist. Somehow, you fit in with what she has planned."

"If she'd share what she has planned, we could be a part of it."

Haern shrugged. "Perhaps. That would be the easiest for us, but Carth has one of the sharpest minds I've ever encountered. If she's planning something, there are layers to it that you and I cannot imagine."

"Sounds like the way Brusus used to describe Josun."

Haern laughed softly. "I suppose it does." He shook his head. "He's one we haven't seen again."

"Not seen, but he's still out there, and now he's sided with Venass." It would make him more dangerous, more powerful even, and Rsiran dreaded facing him again, but he would have to. More than even knowing what he must do to stop Danis, Rsiran's fight would not ever really be over until he dealt with Josun. "I need to return to Elaeavn. I'm going to face the council."

"As guildlord?"

Rsiran shook his head. He'd considered going as guildlord, but that didn't have the weight that he needed. "As myself. Naelm needs to know what I'm willing to do if he continues to side with Venass."

"And what is that?"

Rsiran sighed. "Something stupid. That's why I need your help."

"When are we going?"

"Soon. I have to find Valn to set something up first, but then we'll go."

"Where?"

"Back to Elaeavn."

CHAPTER 12

E laeavn was quiet.

The city often had a stillness to it, especially at night, a time when few people moved along the streets and there were only the sounds of the gulls circling or the steady washing of the waves along the shore. Tonight, there was something more to it, though Rsiran couldn't place his finger on what he sensed.

He walked the streets of Upper Town, keeping to the shadows, taking in the destruction leveled by Venass, wondering if the city could ever really recover. How could the council have allowed Venass into the city? Didn't they see what Venass intended?

Maybe they did, and didn't care as long as they retained their rule.

That had to change, like so much else had to change.

Even when he'd lived here, he hadn't taken the time to walk through the city and appreciate it this way. Most of the time, he had Slid, using his ability to avoid the streets. Jessa had always tried to get him to walk, to learn the alleys and other parts of the city that you couldn't learn without taking the time, but he'd never felt the need.

"You're quiet," Haern said.

"What's there to say?" He stopped, continuing to hug the shadow of the buildings. "The city is different." Both men wore shirts of a fabric that seemed to make them one with the darkness around them, keeping them hidden from view, a fabric Jessa claimed was designed so that even those Sighted could not discern its presence.

"It's not changed quite as much as you think," Haern said. He held a darkened blade of heartstone and lorcith, one he carried only at Rsiran's insistence. Its soft blue glow that only Rsiran could see added to his somber mood, as did the glow coming from Haern's bracelets, the ones Rsiran had made for all of his friends to prevent them from getting Read or Compelled. "The city has seen other changes over time. This will be just be one more."

"The city has stood for five hundred years," Rsiran said.

"How do we know what's changed and what hasn't in all those years? Think of your smithy. At some point, years ago, it was a well-maintained shop, surely a place its original owner was very proud of."

"I'm proud of it."

Haern grunted. "You've done plenty to get it to a condition you should be proud of it. But what is its history? Who owned it, and what happened to him? How long had the smithy stood empty?"

"Years."

Another grunt. "That might be an understatement, don't you think? There were holes in the walls if I remember correctly."

"Not the walls. The roof."

"Whatever. The smithy failed because something happened. Something changed and altered the course of whatever that owner had in mind for his future. Maybe he fell on hard times, like happened to most of those who live in these parts. So it was abandoned, until you came in and returned it to something that it once had been. The rest of the area where you have your smithy isn't any different. That's all part of Lower Town, and *old* Lower Town. You've been through there. You know the filth that's there."

"The people there aren't filth."

Haern shook his head. "Not the people. The trash, and the standing water from poorly repaired drains, and the theft. But it wasn't always that way, was it? Surely it was once like your smithy is now."

"I'd like the entire city to return to something like my smithy."

Haern stepped out of the shadows and continued through the streets of Upper Town. "Wouldn't we all, Lareth." When they reached the end of the street, Haern turned to him. "What do you intend? You going to Slide us into the palace or do we just walk in?"

"I Slid there once recently. That almost didn't end up so well for me."

"You heal fast." There was a question in there. Rsiran hadn't explained to many how he managed to heal from the crossbow bolt injury. Della knew, but not many others did.

"I heal fast," he agreed. "Della sees to that."

Haern grunted again. "More than only her, I think. Glad that you figured something out. If we're not walking up to the door, then you do intend to Slide in."

"I wanted to get a feel for the city before I did."

"And do you have a feel for it now?"

Rsiran sighed. All he knew now was that Elaeavn wasn't the city it had been when he'd been younger. Even that hadn't been the city that he thought it to be. The Elvraeth ruled, but he didn't think they had done so with the same autonomy they have now. The guilds had provided a certain influence, one he now knew the Elvraeth resented.

"I know what needs to get done."

"Why the two of us?"

"I don't want to risk too many others if this doesn't work."

"Not Jessa? Her Sight can help you navigate through the palace better than anything I can do."

"I don't need Sight to get through the palace, but I do need someone I can trust to watch over me and make certain I remain safe."

"You trust me now? What's it taken, a year?"

"I've trusted you."

"No, you haven't. Nor should you have. I didn't much trust you, either, so I guess we were even with that. Took me a while to discover what kind of man you were."

"And what kind did you find?"

"One that's too much like me for my liking."

"I'm not an assassin. Carth made it clear that she didn't think that I would ever be able to be much of one."

"And she still helped you. Seems that you've got something she respects."

"She respects Galen."

"Most who get to know him do."

"But he *is* an assassin."

"So was I. Not all men deserve to live, Rsiran. There are dangerous people in the world, some who want to do horrible things. Better to remove them and make the world a better place. Think of what your Jessa went through. Do you think I should have let those men live when I pulled her from them?"

Rsiran shook his head. Jessa had told him what the men had intended to do with her, but she hadn't gone into much more detail, thinking to spare him from it. What he'd heard troubled him enough. "No. I don't think those men should have lived."

"There are others like them. Evil men. They might not be with Venass, but they would just as soon hurt you than help you. It's what makes you a bit unique. You still manage to find reasons to help."

"I help those I care about."

Haern grunted softly. They stopped at the tall palace wall, and he leaned on it. "You didn't care so much about me, but you still helped. You didn't care so much for your sister and your pa, but you went and did everything you could to save them. You didn't care so much about that apprentice of yours, but you managed to make something out of him. That's not something that most would have been willing to do."

"I thought you said I was like you."

"Ah, maybe I was wrong. You're too kind for me. I would have let most suffer. The only person I look out for is Haern."

He flicked his gaze to the top of the wall. "You going to get us up there, or am I going to have to climb?"

Would Haern have let someone suffer? Rsiran had argued with Carth on behalf of Haern, claiming that he had changed, but what if he hadn't? What if men couldn't change?

Rsiran didn't believe that. *He* had changed. Haern might want to convey the gruff and occasionally angry exterior, but he had done much to ensure Jessa remained safe.

"You can climb if you think you can," Rsiran said.

"Not whether I think I can, but whether I'm wiped when I get up there."

Rsiran grabbed him, and *pulled* them to the top of the wall.

They emerged in a pool of shadows that reminded him of Carth and the way that she had used the shadows. Haern pressed himself flat against the stone, and with his dark shirt and pants, blended into the night. Rsiran copied him, lying flat so that he could hide from the eyes of Elvraeth or tchalit if they still roamed the grounds.

"What are you looking for up here?" Haern asked.

"Venass."

"They won't be patrolling the grounds."

"No, but I needed to be up here to act quickly. This is where you do your part."

"What part is that?"

"Protect me."

Haern grunted softly. "You're willing to place that much trust in me that I'll keep you safe?"

Rsiran shrugged. "You might not do it for me, but you'll for Jessa."

"Ah, damn, Lareth. I'd do it for you, too. Be safe."

Rsiran closed his eyes and focused on the inside of the palace.

He Traveled.

He still marveled at the strange sensation. It was something like a separation, a leaving of his body. Indescribable. Sliding was easy; you step into the Slide and emerge, or *pull* along the Slide. Traveling was both similar and quite different.

As he separated, he raced into the palace, emerging in a wide hall. Rsiran waited, hovering in an insubstantial form as he tried to find whether there were any Elvraeth around. At this time of night, the palace halls were quiet and mostly empty.

He needed to find Naelm for several reasons. Mostly to speak to him, but Rsiran needed to prove to Naelm that he could reach him, and that if he could reach him, he could do the same to those he might actually care about—like Cael. If he was right, maybe having Cael back would motivate him.

The other reason was to determine how strong a Venass presence there actually was in Elaeavn. He didn't know the numbers, but when Carth suggested that Venass didn't want power, it made Rsiran wonder if maybe there might be fewer than he believed. The threat of power—whether they truly had it or not—could be very effective, especially with the council on their side.

Rsiran moved into each room along the main hall. He found no one until he reached the end of the hall. There, in a small room no larger than a closet, he found a small, dark-haired man with a long, thin scar running down the side of his face. He sat in front of a lantern writing in a journal.

Hjan.

Rsiran returned to his body. "Wait for me," he said to Haern and Slid to the man.

The Hjan didn't have time to react. Rsiran grabbed him, *pulled* him to the place in between Slides, and used the power of the Elder Trees to incapacitate him. He bound the man and knocked him out and Slid him to the Forgotten Palace, where Valn had prepared a cell for him.

"Hjan?" Valn asked as he emerged from the shadows.

The walls here were lorcith and heartstone, woven together in a way that would prevent Sliding. "One. There might be others."

Valn grabbed the hilt of his sword and smiled. "We'll be ready."

Rsiran clapped him on the shoulder and Slid back to Hearn.

"One is secured."

"You sure about that?"

"As sure as I can be. He won't trouble us while we're here at least. Valn will keep him from getting free until I can reach him and remove his plate."

"Not sure how I feel about you going in and tearing the lorcith from the Hjan but leaving them alive."

"How many do you think there are?" Rsiran asked.

"Hundreds."

"And we're going to kill all of them? That doesn't make me feel any better than what they attempt."

"Some may have to die," Haern said. "That's the way it is with war. You think you can convince hundreds who sided with Venass that they were wrong? I doubt these are men who were

Compelled, Rsiran. They didn't need any reason other than a desire for power to have the implant, and they don't want anything more than a chance to continue gaining power. That the kind of man you think you can convince to integrate back into some sort of society? These men are extremists, Rsiran. I should know. I was there."

"But you changed."

"Maybe a little, but I'd still be tempted by power. Don't know if that ever goes away."

"We have to find something," Rsiran said.

Haern shook his head. "I'll do it your way, but only because you've proven that you can."

Rsiran watched him for a moment more. "Watch me again."

"That's why I'm here."

Rsiran Traveled. This time, he emerged first in the room where the Hjan had been making notes. He should have grabbed the man's book when he'd been here in person, but hadn't thought about it. He'd wanted to get free before the Hjan managed to attack him. At least in the place between Slides, he could use the power of the Elder Trees, and had an advantage that they didn't.

Moving through the halls, he made his way to an upper level in the palace. Rsiran had visited the palace several times, mostly sneaking in, but lately, he'd come as the guildlord on an invitation, and even then, he hadn't come to the upper floors. These were mostly the rooms of the Elvraeth.

He drifted in and out, occasionally finding Elvraeth sleeping, other times finding them sitting at tables, and other rooms that were empty. Some were as ornately decorated as the one he'd discovered Josun in. Many were simple, and reminded him more of Luthan than of Josun.

As he began to think that he might not find Naelm, he came across an empty room, one with an antechamber with the door closed to the back. Three voices drifted out from the door, and Rsiran paused to listen. One of them he recognized.

Rsiran floated through the door. In this form, there was a strange sense to it, something almost substantial, so that he could practically feel himself moving across the barrier of the doorway, and then it was gone.

On the other side of the door, Naelm sat at a small table.

Though he sat with his head down, and a deep bruise that had bloomed on his face, he wasn't what drew Rsiran's attention.

It was the other two facing him.

A Hjan he didn't recognize stood next to Naelm. His long sword unsheathed, catching the deep blue lantern light of the Elvraeth lanterns. Then there was Danis.

His grandfather looked up, as if looking *at* Rsiran, but he couldn't see him when he Traveled, could he?

Danis smiled with a flash of bright teeth. "Rsiran."

CHAPTER 13

Back to his body, Rsiran noted a faint sea breeze that gusted around him on the top of the wall, and nothing but moonlight lit his way. Haern watched him, knife in hand.

When Rsiran stood and prepared to Slide, Haern grabbed his wrist. "What did you see?"

"Danis is there. I can end this, Haern. All I need to do is—"

"Stopping Danis won't end this, Rsiran. If you go in there like you're planning, you'll just as likely end up dead as him. More, possibly, especially if there's more than one."

"We can't let him get away. He knows I was there, and we—"

Haern released his wrist, and pulled a pair of knives from hidden sheaths. "Good. *We.* You brought me to help watch over you, so let me watch over you."

Rsiran nodded. "We have to act quickly."

"Yes."

"It's a small room. Naelm is there. Beaten maybe. One Hjan is guarding him. Then there's Danis."

"I'm ready."

Rsiran took a deep breath, *pulled* on knives to establish the connection and Slid.

They emerged in the antechamber. He nodded to the door, and Haern nodded. Rsiran went to the door and kicked it open.

The Hjan leaped toward him.

Rsiran Slid to the side, emerging and *pushing* his knives at the Hjan. The man ducked, avoiding the knives. He swung his sword toward Rsiran, but Rsiran *pushed* another pair of knives at him, forcing him back.

"I can do this. You get Danis!" Haern shouted, moving to engage the Hjan.

Rsiran Slid into the back room.

Danis waited next to Naelm. The Elvraeth councilor could barely lift his head. His eyes were bloodshot, and the bruises on his face angrier in person than they had been when Rsiran had Traveled. Danis stood casually, his hands empty.

Rsiran tensed, prepared to Slide. For Danis to stand as he did meant he was unconcerned by their presence, which meant he was prepared in some way. He had to have something planned.

"Rsiran Lareth. It is good to see you in person this time."

"You're leaving Elaeavn," he spat.

"Ah, on that, we will have to disagree. I have yet to obtain what I came for, and Naelm is being most uncooperative. I'd expected more—being one of the family."

"He can't help you. I'm the reason you can't get to the crystals, Danis."

Danis frowned, something like a sad pout. "So formal. I had

always hoped my grandson would address me as Papa, but maybe your sister will find it easier to welcome me."

A flash of lorcith pressed behind him.

Rsiran Slid, emerging on the far side of the room, and sent a pair of knives streaking toward the Hjan who had appeared behind him. The man was thin, with pale green eyes and a scar that wrapped entirely around his face.

One of the knives connected, catching him in the stomach, and he fell.

"How many can you kill?" Danis asked softly. "You're too kind to do what you need, so how many will you come after?" He sneered at him. "And to think *you're* the one causing me all this trouble. Your mother was such a disappointment. She should have pulled you into line long ago, but now it must be me."

"My mother never cared about me." Rsiran *pulled* on the knives in the fallen Hjan and sent them toward Danis. His grandfather barely moved his hand, and the knives fell to the ground, held there in spite of how much Rsiran *pushed*.

Danis had grown stronger in his connection to lorcith. Rsiran briefly wondered how, but didn't take the time to search for answers.

What of heartstone?

Rsiran pressed on one of his pure heartstone knives, and sent that at his grandfather. Much like with the lorcith, it fell to the ground, and he couldn't move it.

"It is reassuring to know my enhancements worked," Danis said. "There are so few I can test them on." He waved his hand,

and all the lorcith and heartstone Rsiran carried pushed him into the wall.

Rsiran resisted, but Danis had grown powerful. He focused on lorcith, using the strength of Ilphaesn as he had so often before, and *pushed*.

In the past, that had been all that he needed to do. Connecting to the lorcith within the mountain had allowed him to push against someone who might be stronger than he was. This time, when he connected to Ilphaesn, it didn't give him enough strength.

Rsiran started to Slide, but Danis managed to tear him from it, and slammed him into the wall.

"I would like you to remain here, grandson."

Danis stopped behind Naelm and pulled his head back. "*I* was never exiled. Perhaps now it's time for me to re-establish my place in the city, and for new leadership to sit on the council," he said. He *pulled* on a knife and brought it toward Naelm. The blade skimmed across his neck, and blood bloomed to the surface. Naelm winced as blood started running down his neck. The blade pressed deeper, and blood poured out.

Danis looked to Rsiran. "You should have brought more than yourself to this," he said to him.

Haern appeared in the door and flipped a pair of knives at Danis. "He did."

Danis tried to *push* on the knives, but they were steel. Finely made—and crafted by Rsiran at Haern's request—but without lorcith or heartstone, Danis had no control over the metal within them.

One of the blades struck him in the shoulder. The other missed.

Danis flickered forward, and when he emerged, he caught Haern in the stomach with his sword.

Haern's eyes widened, and he sank to the ground.

"No!" Rsiran reaching for his sword, the only weapon that he had remaining. He wasn't as skilled with the sword as he was with his knives, but he had no other choice. He carried the blade he'd crafted in the heart of the Aisl, and as he unsheathed it, the metal practically blazed.

Danis tried *pushing* on it. It dipped slightly before the sword slipped past it, the blade itself managing to push back.

Rsiran swung his sword at Danis.

As he did, he felt a connection to the depths of the Aisl, to the Elder Trees themselves. Had he somehow forged that into the blade?

He *pulled* on that connection, sending it through the blade, and tried to wrap Danis in that power.

For a moment, Rsiran thought it might hold. Danis writhed in place, struggling against the power that bound him. Rsiran pulled on more power from the Elder Trees.

Haern gasped.

Rsiran's focus faltered. His friend was dying, and because of Rsiran, because of what he'd wanted, the fact that he had thought he could end the struggle in the city.

As he lost focus, Danis disappeared.

Rsiran wanted to chase him, and wanted to catch him, but didn't dare or he'd lose Haern.

RISE OF THE ELDER | 123

He sheathed his sword, Slid to Haern, and after a brief internal debate, grabbed Naelm as well. Then he Slid to the place between.

Rsiran left them long enough to Slide to Della. Her eyes widened as he appeared, and then he Slid with her to the place between as well.

"Can you help them?" he asked.

Della placed her hands on Haern, and closed her eyes. Rsiran used the power from the trees to help, funneling it into her. When her eyes opened, she shook her head. "He's too far gone, Rsiran. I'm so sorry."

Rsiran dropped to his knees. "Haern?"

Della left him as she went to Naelm. A connection between Rsiran and the Elder Trees remained, some of which he pushed into Della without knowing that he did. Most of the connection, he poured into Haern.

"There's nothing you can do," she whispered. "You can help the councilor, though."

"You help him. I'll see you've got the necessary strength."

"Rsiran—"

He ignored her, focusing on Haern.

The old assassin's breathing came in shallow gasps, each one labored and an obvious struggle. His brow was furrowed, and sweat poured from his face. Color had leached from him, bleeding out with the rest of his life. The long scar along his jaw became even starker.

"I'm so sorry, Haern," he whispered. Rsiran pressed all the power that he could draw from the Elder Trees into Haern, but he had none of Della's gifts. How had he managed to heal himself? Why couldn't he do the same for Haern? "This is my fault."

"Rsiran," Haern whispered. His eyes flickered open, and he grabbed Rsiran's hand. "Not... your fault. *Danis*. You did... what you could. Don't... let this change... you."

His breathing sped, and his eyes went wider.

Rsiran couldn't lose him. Not Haern. The man had done nothing but work with him, trying to train him, preparing him for a time like what he'd faced with Danis—a time where his abilities wouldn't matter. And Rsiran had failed him.

Closing his eyes, he focused on the connection to the Elder Trees, feeling the power all around him. There was strength here, immeasurable power, and he could *pull* on it. Why *couldn't* he use that power to save a friend? Why must Haern die because of Rsiran's weakness?

Drawing on that power, letting it fill him even more, he started pouring it into Haern. Rsiran might not know how to heal his friend, but the trees would, wouldn't they? They were ancient, older than the people who had once lived here, and tied into a greater power than anything Rsiran could imagine.

A hand touched his shoulder and he jerked.

"You didn't fail him," Della said.

Rsiran looked to Haern, hoping that he had somehow healed him. Haern's eyes were closed. He no longer breathed.

He was gone.

"No," he whispered. Rsiran drew on more power, *pulling* it to him, and sent that through Haern.

Della squeezed his shoulder, forcing him to look up at her. "You can't do anything more, Rsiran. He's gone. All that you do with this," she said, waving her hand around trees that appeared to Rsiran as bright glowing lights, "is consume the power of the Elder Trees. Even you cannot bring someone back from the dead."

Rsiran tore his eyes away from Della and looked at Haern. There was no more pain on his face. No more anger. Lying here, he almost seemed at peace, not gone. But he was gone, and he didn't know how he'd tell Jessa.

Della was right. There was nothing that he could do. The power of the Elder Trees couldn't even save him.

Rsiran released the connection to the trees and sat back on his heels. "It's my fault. He only tried to protect me, but I failed him. He'd been trying to get me to stop relying on my abilities to succeed. He had warned me that I might need to fight without them, but I never learned enough. I wasn't strong enough," he finished softly.

Tears flowed. They were tears he had not felt when his mother had died, but for Haern, they came easily.

"He chose to help, Rsiran." Della sank to the ground and slipped an arm around him. He rested his head on her shoulder, the closest family that he had. "You couldn't have forced him to help, just as you couldn't have stopped him when he decided to join. This was Haern's choice."

Rsiran sobbed. "I couldn't beat him."

"Danis is a dangerous man. He is intelligent, and the things Venass has discovered have only made him more powerful."

"I couldn't use lorcith or heartstone around him. I couldn't even Slide. If my abilities are gone, how are we going to beat him? How are we going to stop Venass?"

"Your abilities aren't gone. You have more than what Danis possesses. Can he Travel? Can he use the power of the Elder Trees?"

"That power is useless anywhere but here."

"Perhaps you cannot access it, but that doesn't mean it's useless."

Rsiran stared at Haern. Whatever else he did, he needed to stop Danis. No more of his friends could die because he failed. "The sword," he said. "I could use it through the sword. I almost had him…" Now Danis had escaped him twice. Rsiran feared he wouldn't get a third opportunity, and if he did, would anything end up any differently?

There was a cough behind him, and Rsiran turned.

Naelm sat up, running a hand along his neck. A shiny scar remained, but the councilor lived. "How… how is it that I still live? Where is this place?"

Rsiran glanced at Della. "I'll return," he said to her.

She nodded. "Take your time. There is much I can learn here."

He Slid to Naelm and grabbed him, then Slid to the Floating Palace. They emerged in the room where Rsiran had lost Danis, and he released Naelm. "You will welcome the guilds back to the city," he said.

Naelm somehow managed to quickly regain his composure. "Who are you to direct the council?"

Anger surged within him. Had the damned council not sided with Venass, he wouldn't have had to come here. He wouldn't have lost Haern. If this was about Naelm finding his daughter, what made her more important than all those who lived in the city?

"Who am I? Other than the reason that you still live?" Naelm touched his neck, his eyes widening slightly. "I am the smith guildlord, and I speak for all the guilds."

"The guildlords do not have a single voice."

"They do now. The council will no longer support Venass in the city."

"You cannot speak for the council."

"Then I will take a seat on the Elvraeth council."

Naelm's face contorted, and blotches of red rose in his cheeks. "The council consists of the Elvraeth. What you suggest is impossible."

Rsiran took a step toward him. "I'm descended from Elvraeth."

"You're no Elvraeth. You're Lareth, nothing more than a smith—"

Rsiran slammed his hand on the table next to Naelm. Knives floated up as he *pulled* on them without intending to. "I'll take that as a compliment. This smith is descended from Danis Ta'Elvraeth. As he left the palace voluntarily, I believe that grants me the right to remain in the palace. As I have held one of the great crystals—twice—I understand that grants me the right to sit on the council. You will see that it happens."

Naelm shook his head. "What you suggest can't happen."

"No? Then the guilds will return, and they will take residence in the palace." He didn't know if the threat would even work, but now that most of the guild halls were destroyed, they would have to have some place to come back to.

Rsiran wondered how many would even *want* to return to the city. Not all, he suspected. Some might be content to remain in the Aisl, but there were others—those like Brusus and Alyse—who longed to return to the city.

"The palace is home to the Elvraeth, not the guilds."

"The guilds preceded the rule of the Elvraeth. Perhaps it is time for the clans to return." Rsiran waited for Naelm's reaction. He took a deep breath and *pushed* the knives back into hiding. "I will sit on the council."

Naelm opened his mouth then closed it again. He sank into a chair, rubbing his hand on his neck. "All we wanted was the return of the crystal. Venass claimed they could see it returned to its proper home."

"Venass wanted to use the power of the crystals. They would never have returned it."

"I believe that now."

"You should have believed that before. And if this was about Cael, then you are even more of a fool, risking the city because you didn't understand, because the Elvraeth remain closed in the palace, thinking they can rule from above. The city—our people—deserve more."

Could he really do what he threatened? It wasn't anything that he planned, but how else would he join the guilds to the ruling Elvraeth without more violence? In many respects, it made sense.

"I will return the crystal," Rsiran said.

Naelm considered him a moment, continuing to rub his neck as he did. "If you do that, if you can return the missing crystal"—there was a hopeful tone in his voice, one that told Rsiran that Naelm wanted more than the return of the crystal —"I personally will see you sit on the council."

CHAPTER 14

Carrying Haern to the heart of the Aisl was one of the hardest things that Rsiran had ever done.

When he emerged with Della inside her forest hut, with the scents of mint and the smoke from her hearth rising around them, she left her small hut and went to find Jessa. When she raced in, she sank to her knees in front of Haern's body.

"Haern?" she whispered.

"I'm sorry," Rsiran said. He stood with his back to the hearth, wanting the warmth of the fire, but feeling no real warmth. He wasn't certain he would ever feel warm again. "He came with me to Elaeavn. We were going to find a way to…" He didn't finish. What did it matter now what they intended to do by returning to Elaeavn? What mattered was that Haern was gone, lost because of Rsiran. "I'm sorry."

"How?" Jessa said without looking up.

"Danis attacked. He's grown stronger. Haern tried to help. He even caught Danis using his steel knives, but Danis Slid to him and got him with his sword. I wasn't fast enough to help him. I wasn't strong enough."

Jessa wiped a tear from the corner of her eye. "He told me he wanted Venass toppled. After everything they had done to him, he hated what they were doing to you. He wanted to make sure no one else went through the same."

"I shouldn't have taken him with me."

Jessa stood and stormed over to him, jabbing him in the chest with her finger. "That's not the answer, either. You should have had more with you!"

"Then even more would have died."

"Rsiran—"

He sighed. There was something more that he needed to tell her, but he feared how she would react. He wasn't even sure how *he* felt about what he had decided. "I told Naelm I would return the crystal and that when I did, I would take a place on the Elvraeth council."

"You did *what*?"

He had worried how she would react to this. "It's a way we can bring the guilds and the council together without more violence. The council will no longer support Venass, but the guilds need to be in a stronger place than they've been. That means having a presence on the council."

"There are other ways, Rsiran. Besides, why would they even let you on the council?"

The door opened and Della entered, watching him with a puzzled expression. "Did I hear you say *you* were going to sit on the council?"

Rsiran blanched. "When I faced Danis, he made it clear to

Naelm that he was never exiled. He left the city of his own choosing. And since I'm descended from him, I'm Elvraeth."

Della chuckled, and Jessa shot her a look. "I would never have considered that, but I think you're right. I imagine Naelm did not take it well."

"I told him that I'd return the crystal."

"Which you were going to do anyway," Della said.

Rsiran nodded.

"An interesting plan."

They didn't get the chance to say anything more. Brusus entered, his eyes immediately going to Haern's body. His eyes flared a bright green. "You weren't supposed to go this way, friend," he said, crouching next to him and taking Haern's hand. "You were supposed to help me See our way through this. How am I going to do this without you?"

Rsiran took a step back, leaving the hut, and leaving Jessa and Brusus and Della to mourn. He didn't want to face their questions, and didn't want to face the continued reality that Haern was gone because of him.

As he made his way around the perimeter of the clearing, his eyes were drawn to the top of the trees, toward the massive branches overhead. Shortly, Jessa caught up with him. He wasn't surprised when she did, or when she slipped her hand into his.

"Haern liked sitting in the branches," he said.

"He said he could almost see back to Elaeavn from there," Jessa said.

Rsiran sighed. It was the sort of thing Haern would say.

"After this, I think I can remove Venass from Elaeavn. The

council no longer supports them, and Danis won't risk that confrontation. We could return to the city."

She squeezed his hand. "Do you want to?"

He kept his eyes focused on the treetops. "I want all of this over. I don't want to worry about my friends anymore. I want to get back to…"

He didn't know *what* he wanted to get back to. Did he want to return to when he couldn't Slide? Or when he feared capture by the Elvraeth, or the guilds, or the Forgotten? He didn't want to get *back* to anything, he realized, but to get to a point where he could be the person he'd become, and still not worry about his friends. To get there would take more fighting, and might make him do things he didn't want to do, but there was a chance he'd come out of it in a better place than he'd been.

There was hope.

"I'm sorry about Haern," he said.

"Haern knew what he did. Of all of us, he was the most prepared for what we faced. I know he never said it, but you impressed him. He enjoyed working with you, trying to find ways to test you and challenge you. That was something he valued."

"I wouldn't have learned nearly half of what I did were it not for Haern. Not how to fight, not the sword, maybe not even the extent of my connection over lorcith. Without him…"

He sighed, and shook his head.

Jessa patted his hand. "I know. What now?"

"Now we have to reach Galen and Cael. They had better have the crystal so I can force Naelm to let me participate on the council. And then we'll need to take the fight to Venass."

"It sounds..."

"Impossible. I know."

She smiled, her free hand reaching to grab the charm she wore. "I was going to say it sounded *easy* when you said it, but if you think it's impossible then you'll have to work a little harder, and I think we both know how much I like watching you work."

He held her hand and guided her toward the base of one of the trees. It was the Traveling tree, which suited him well, since that was what he intended now. "Good, then you can watch over me now."

"What are you going to do?"

"Travel."

"That's not much fun to do. Let's just Slide. Then you can at least take me with you."

"Not for what I need to do. Traveling is safer."

Jessa frowned. "What do you need to do? Where would you Travel?"

"I need to know if it's safe to return. And if it's not, I need to know where others of Venass might be in the city. I can seize them and take them to a cell I prepared—"

"You prepared a cell?"

"Valn watches over it."

"Why would you need to have someone watch over it? Wait... You've captured Hjan?"

"I can't keep bringing them here for Della to heal. I don't know how many I'll be able to remove the plate from, and this way, they can be held until I have a way to ensure they won't cause a problem."

"Do you intend to capture all of the Hjan?"

"I don't know what I intend, only that I can't kill them all. What would that make me?"

"Alive? You know what they will do to you if they get the chance."

"I'll fight, but I won't slaughter them." The more he thought about what he'd do with all the Hjan he would have to face, the more the idea disturbed him.

"Rsiran—"

"Haern would have been pleased to note your objections. He felt the same."

"Of course he did. Haern was always practical. He wouldn't have wanted you to risk anything unless you knew it was worth it. Do you think saving the Hjan is worth it? Will they suddenly stop wanting to hurt you, and wanting to gain power?"

"I don't know."

"Rsiran—"

"Watch over me, would you?"

Jessa clenched her jaw and tipped her head toward her empty charm as if she intended to smell the flowers that she normally kept there. "I'll watch you. Don't make me come after you."

He sat cross-legged near her and closed his eyes. As he did, the sense of the forest faded as he Traveled, returning to the city. He went to Naelm first, wanting to know if the man had done anything that Rsiran should worry about, but found him sitting in his room making a few notes in a small book. Rsiran glanced at the page, but couldn't make sense of what he wrote, as if he used some sort of code.

Moving on, he paused in the small closet where he'd found

the first Hjan he'd encountered that night. The one being held at the Forgotten Palace. Seeing Naelm writing in a notebook had reminded him of the one the Hjan had been writing in. It was still there, but he would have to come back for it when he finished.

Rsiran moved from room to room through the palace and found nothing to make him think the Hjan remained.

Would Danis have recalled them? How would he know?

Lorcith and heartstone. As usual, they would have to provide the answer.

Rsiran Traveled beyond the palace, taking himself above the city. For a moment, he hovered there, holding himself in place, but Traveling took energy Sliding no longer did. Holding himself here in this way fatigued him, and he would grow weak if he attempted to remain in this place for too long. If he went to Krali Rock, he could search more easily.

Atop the rock, he waited, holding himself in place.

The city spread out below him, glowing with orange and yellow lanterns that mixed with the white glow of lorcith and the blue of heartstone in numerous locations. First, Rsiran focused on the lorcith, drawing it toward him. With the connection, he could focus on the metal and watch for movement. Any movement he detected, he could track and determine if there were any Hjan still in the city.

Immediately, he detected two separate flashes.

Rsiran Traveled to them. One moved along the docks, an older man who Rsiran could tell carried one of his knives. Moving on, he Traveled to the other sense of lorcith that he'd detected. This was a woman carrying a stack of decorative bowls.

He paused near the woman. The bowls were not those he'd made, but given the cut of her dress, and the dirt on her hands, he doubted they were hers. With the guilds out of the city, that made it likely she'd stolen them.

The idea actually made him smile. Lorcith was not as rare as he'd once believed. Why shouldn't the people of the city have access to it, and own bowls or other finery the same as the Elvraeth? Now that the smiths had begun listening to lorcith again, even the creation of different items wasn't as difficult as it once had been. What would have taken planning and preparation in the past, now was a simple matter of listening to the lorcith, and a willingness to follow where it guided.

Rsiran returned to Krali. He focused on the sense of lorcith again, and found three other items that moved. Each time, it came from knives or decorative items carried by people who were clearly not of Venass.

Nothing else moved. He waited, holding onto his connection to the metals, and found nothing more.

What of heartstone?

Rsiran shifted his focus to it. Heartstone was less common than lorcith, and he didn't expect to find much moving. There were a few different collections in the city, but none that moved. He waited, holding that focus, and was about ready to abandon his search when he picked up the sense of heartstone flickering.

That meant Sliding.

Rsiran Traveled, following the heartstone that he detected,

and emerged in a quiet section of the city, one that he hadn't visited often. High above, the Floating Palace gleamed in the moonlight. There came a sound of cats, at least three separate yowls, and a distant cawing of gulls.

Where was the heartstone? He could still feel it even though he Traveled. It was nearby... Traveling again, he followed the trail of heartstone into a small house. The hearth and the cozy nature to the place made him think of Della's home, but hers was simpler. This had ornate decorations, and lorcith stacked along the wall, stone sculptures along another, and a few portraits leaning near the back. All of it was likely stolen.

The heartstone was probably stolen, as well, and most likely didn't really belong here, either. Whoever brought it here would be a thief, and not someone that he had to be concerned about.

Only, there was the fact the heartstone had seemed to flicker. It wouldn't do that unless whoever had it Slid.

Rsiran waited, holding onto the sense of heartstone. When it moved again, he Traveled, this time following it outside the city to a rocky shore near Ilphaesn.

Now he had no doubt that whoever had the heartstone could Slide.

The sense moved again, this time to the north. Rsiran Traveled again, drawn even farther away from Elaeavn. Each time he appeared, the sense shifted, and each time, it carried him north.

Toward Thyr, he realized.

One of the Hjan thought to draw him away. Danis had proven that they could detect him when he Traveled. He didn't know if they would be able to capture him, as well, but he wouldn't put it past them to have figured out some way, and if they could separate him from his body, he didn't know what might happen.

Rsiran Traveled back to the Aisl, and back to his body.

When he opened his eyes, Jessa was watching him. "Did you find anything?"

He considered sharing that he did, but it would only make her nervous. "The Hjan are gone from Elaeavn," he said.

Rsiran hoped that remained true.

CHAPTER 15

The coals burned in his smithy once more. It had been too long since Rsiran had felt comfortable in front of the forge. Jessa rested on the bed near the hearth, flipping through the pages of the notebook Rsiran had taken from the palace. He'd returned to the small room where he'd captured the first Hjan, and taken the journal with him, but couldn't decipher what was written. Without Haern, he wondered if they would be able to.

"You should probably have Luca help you," she said. "He *is* supposed to be your apprentice."

"Luca wanted to remain in the forest. He said the song was easier to hear in the forest."

Jessa looked up from the book and shook her head. "How many do you think returned?"

Rsiran rested on the anvil. "Maybe half the smiths. They wanted to get back to their smithies. Seval tried to get my father to return, but I don't think he did. Most of the miners returned to Ilphaesn. Ephram led the alchemists back to the Guild Hall, but there's not much left. The rest..."

"They're waiting for you to tell them it's safe to return."

Rsiran nodded. When word spread that he would join the council, the rest of the guild members were pleased, but they feared returning until Rsiran proved it was safe to do so. For now, they intended to remain in the Aisl, using the protections of the forest they had created over the last few months.

"Brusus plans to reopen the Barth tonight," Jessa said.

"I know. I still don't know if that's wise."

"You said there weren't any more Hjan in the city."

"Not that I can tell." Rsiran had Traveled through the city several more times since he tracked the heartstone from Elaeavn and hadn't found anything. After they returned to the city, he'd Slid to Krali Rock and attempted to track both lorcith and heartstone in person. So far, he'd not encountered anything. At least Haern's sacrifice had been worth something. "But we're still not wanting to draw the attention of Venass, not until I know how we're going to respond."

"You already know how you're going to respond. You just want to make sure that I don't have a problem with it."

"I'll need your help."

Jessa sat up and set the book down next to her, brushing her hair out of her face. "Will you? You've made a point of keeping me out of what you've been doing ever since you became this famous assassin in Eban."

"Only because I don't want you to get hurt." Rsiran Slid to

her and sat next to her on the mattress, taking her hand. "I can't let anything happen to you. What I've done is what I could to keep you safe."

"You have to stop thinking that you can keep those you care about safe. We get to make our own choices, the same as you."

"The same way Haern did?"

"Haern knew what he risked, Rsiran. He would have been angry had you tried doing to him what you're doing to me."

Rsiran squeezed her hand, not wanting to tell her that Haern knew how to protect himself, and even that hadn't been enough. Jessa didn't need him to remind her. Doing so would only upset her more.

"There are other ways you can help," Rsiran said.

"Like I did in Aisl? I don't think there was a whole lot I did there, other than spend time with your sister. I still don't think she likes me."

Rsiran laughed. "I once would have said I didn't think it likely that Alyse liked anyone before she met Brusus."

"I still think she'll hit him with a pot one of these days. You going to protect him from that?"

"Knowing him, he'll probably have deserved it," Rsiran said.

Jessa grinned. "Probably."

They sat in silence, enjoying the calm for a few moments. He picked up the notebook and tapped the plain leather cover. "Did you learn anything from the writings?"

"Other than that Venass uses some sort of code? Not a thing."

"It's something Haern would have been able to help us decipher," he said.

"Probably. Now we'll have to find some other way." She jabbed a finger at him. "And don't think you're going to your *cell* to see what you can find from the Hjan you have trapped there."

Rsiran stood. "Not the cell, but there might be another I could go to who won't be a danger to me."

He should have thought of Amin as soon as they recovered the journal, but the Hjan just hadn't come to mind. Rsiran didn't know if he would even help, but maybe Della could Compel him to. If she couldn't do that, at least she could Read him, and maybe find out some of what he knew so they could decipher it themselves.

"You're going back to the Aisl?" Jessa stood and took his hand.

"You don't have to return with me."

"And miss the excitement?" She shook her head and smelled the flower in her charm. Grabbing a new flower had been one of the first things she had done once she returned to Elaeavn.

Rsiran smiled again as he took her hand. They Slid, emerging in the Aisl.

As usual, the change came jarringly, jolting him with the difference between the hint of bitterness from lorcith in his smithy mixed with the sweetness of heartstone to the heady fragrance of the sjihn trees and the ripe scent of their leaves. They stood at the edge of the circle of the Elder Trees, the massive trunk of the miner tree rising near him. He took a few breaths, enjoying the change from the smithy to the forest and the heaviness in the air, the stillness that surrounded him, almost weighing on him.

"You're more at ease here," Jessa said.

Rsiran shook his head. "It's not that I'm uneasy in the city, but here... I can feel the power of the trees."

Jessa squeezed his hand. "It's fine if you admit that you're more comfortable here. Think of how many feel the same way."

She pointed toward the huts along the edge of the circle of trees. None were willing to build the small huts too close to the center of the clearing, as if they didn't want to risk angering the trees, or felt the need to leave that space for gathering. In the upper branches, there were different structures, built where branches were bent together, creating canopies that allowed coverage from the occasional storm or the winds that gusted through, more noticeable in those higher branches. Ropes and the earliest attempt at creating bridges stretched between branches, giving those without the ability to Slide the opportunity to move through the uppermost sections of the trees.

"I'm not more comfortable here."

"No? When you return, you have this air of relaxation. The lines around your eyes fade. And most of all, you smile more." She stood on her toes and kissed his cheek. "I feel it, too. There's something different about when we're here."

Rsiran took another deep breath, scanning the trees and everything that was around them. "Maybe it has to do with the fact that our people came from here long ago."

Jessa watched him. "Maybe."

Rsiran wondered if there might be something more to it, especially for him. The connection to the forest was a part of their people, and it was one that he felt as deeply as the rest of them, but for him it might be more. Since learning he could reach the power of the Elder Trees, he *had* felt more strongly about that connection. Not so much here, when he was physically in the forest, but when he stood in the place in between. That was when the feeling was strongest. He could use the power and didn't fear how Venass might find a way to overwhelm him. What he needed was some way to face Danis in that space, but doing that required that he catch him, otherwise Danis wouldn't know how to reach that place.

"What is it?" Jessa asked.

"Thinking about the future."

She leaned on his arm. "I'm always happy when you think about the future." When he didn't answer, she sighed. "But that's not the future that you're thinking about, is it?"

"We can't think about it yet. There's nothing in that future until we manage to stop Venass and my grandfather."

"You have to stop thinking about him as family. He's Danis Ta'Elvraeth, leader of Venass, and he wants to see you dead."

"He wants to see all of us enslaved."

Rsiran turned to see Della emerging from the depths of the forest. She held a small bundle of wood and some berries. A smudge of black dirt smeared across her dress, and the brightly colored shawl she wore over her shoulders stood out against the darkness.

"Danis would control us. All of us."

"What are you talking about?" Jessa asked.

Della met Rsiran's eyes. "Follow me."

She strode past them, across the clearing between the Elder

Trees, and reached her hut. Once there, she set the bundle of wood on the ground, but kept the berries. She opened the door and waited for Rsiran and Jessa to follow.

The heavy scent of the mint tea filled the air, mixing with the wood smoke. Della placed the berries in a bowl on a small table and began mashing them. Rsiran had seen her working before, and had even learned some of the herbs and leaves that she worked with, but there was something natural about seeing her in this place, using the berries she'd collected outside the Elder Trees, that felt right.

"What did you want us to see?" Jessa asked.

"Not what. Who."

Rsiran looked to the hearth and realized that someone sat in one of the chairs. All he could make out was the top of the person's head. An uneasy sense worked through him.

"Della?"

"Don't worry, Rsiran. You know I wouldn't do anything that placed you in danger."

He glanced to Jessa, who shrugged.

Making his way toward the hearth, he stopped next to the chair.

A man looked up at him, an anxious expression on his youthful face. He had moderate green eyes, and his hair was shorn close to his scalp, but it was the long scar along the side of his face that drew Rsiran's attention.

"Amin?" he asked. Had he not seen the scar, he wouldn't have been certain it was the same person.

Rsiran *pulled* on a pair of knives, already preparing for the possibility of an attack, but Amin sat in the chair, his hands clenched in his lap. Rsiran realized Amin was the one who was nervous.

"Della—you left him here *alone* while you went harvesting?" Jessa asked.

Della nodded. "Don't think I can't determine when it's safe to leave someone in my home. I think I've earned that right."

"How do you know he won't do anything?" Jessa unsheathed a long heartstone knife that Rsiran had made for her and held it ready. "Did you See something?"

Della touched Jessa's hand, pressing the knife down so she was forced to sheath it again. "I don't need to See anything to know he's not going to harm us. You seem to forget I have other talents."

"You've Read him," Rsiran said. "I thought he sealed himself off from you."

Della smiled at that. "I admit I thought the same. There aren't many who have that ability," she said, tapping Rsiran on the shoulder. "At least, not without assistance." Her gaze dropped to the bracelets he wore, but they didn't go cold. "In the time since we healed him, there has been another effect, and one I didn't expect."

"What was that?" Jessa asked. "What would make you think that you can trust him enough to leave him free in the camp while you go off in the woods? This man was an assassin!"

"I know what kind of man he is—or was," Della said. "Just as I know what kind of man my brother is. As I have said, he wants to enslave as many as he can, much as he attempted to enslave Amin's mind."

With the comment, Rsiran tore his gaze away from the Hjan and to Della. "What are you saying?"

Della sighed. "I'm saying that you were right, Rsiran. We can't destroy all of Venass, not without identifying those who could be saved. At least some of the Hjan were Compelled."

CHAPTER 16

R siran waited in the hall outside the heartstone room of
the Forgotten Palace. The guilds protected the palace
now, mostly those with the ability to Slide, but also miners and
a few alchemists. The protections here were not only to secure
the palace, but also to secure the prisoners Rsiran had started to
bring here.

"Decided to come back?" Valn asked. He wore a heavy jacket
that concealed a short sword, something that would have been
unthinkable only a few months ago.

"I wanted to see your pretty face," Rsiran said.

Jessa elbowed him.

"She's jealous," Rsiran said when Valn arched a brow.

"Can't say I can blame her. With looks like these, you'll be
fighting him for me."

Jessa rolled her eyes. "Between the two of you, I'm not sure
how we survived when Venass attacked. Both of you were
probably too busy looking at your swords."

Valn reached for his sword. "Well, Rsiran made mine, so he knows plenty about it." When Jessa shook her head, Valn turned serious. "I'm sorry to hear about Haern. He was a good fighter. He'll be missed."

Rsiran appreciated the fact that Valn directed the comment to Jessa. In many ways, Haern had acted as something of a father figure to her. He had certainly been as protective as most fathers.

"He's at peace now," Jessa said.

"Hope he's sitting next to the Great Watcher and guiding his hand," Valn said. "That way, we might have a chance. So damn many Venass, and all of them more powerful than us."

"That's why I'm here," Rsiran said.

Valn frowned. "You're going to start cutting them down? I don't really think that suits you, Rsiran, but if that's what you think is best."

"Not cutting them down, but Della thinks they've been Compelled."

"That's a lot of men to Compel. Do you think he could hold that control for all those years?"

Rsiran didn't know. Della hadn't been able to answer, either, other than to say that Danis was a more powerful Reader than anyone she'd met, which meant he could draw on that power when he Compelled.

"I don't know if he held them, or if he changed them," Rsiran said. The first sounded awful, but if Danis changed something about them permanently, that was worse.

"Why'd you come here?"

"To test whether it's true."

Valn cocked his head to the side and watched Rsiran for a moment before shrugging. "Whatever you want. You're the guildlord."

"He thinks he's more than that, too," Jessa said.

"Lareth? He's never even wanted to be guildlord."

"He thinks he can sit on the Elvraeth council."

"I don't want to sit on the council, but it might be the best way to ensure that the guilds and the council work together again."

Valn grinned. "Technically, he *is* Elvraeth, isn't he? Descended from Danis himself!"

"We're all *technically* Elvraeth," Jessa said.

Valn's smiled faded. "Not the guilds. We're descended from the ancient clans. That's where we get our abilities. Most of us, that is," he said, nodding to Rsiran.

Rsiran wondered whether it mattered that he didn't have any other abilities. Everything he possessed stemmed from the clans, and in that, he had aspects of *all* of the clans, while possessing none of those from the Elvraeth. If Naelm knew that, he might exclude him from the council for that reason alone, and Rsiran wouldn't have much of an argument.

They reached the heartstone chamber. Since the Forgotten had abandoned the palace, Rsiran had foraged and taken as much of the heartstone as he could, removing a piece at a time. The walls were now a patchwork of stone and the blue glowing light from the heartstone. The furniture Evaelyn once kept here had all been removed, carried into other rooms, mostly so that Rsiran could get to the heartstone more easily. The metal was rare enough he wanted to be able to use as much of what existed here as possible.

Passing through the heartstone room to get to the tunnels where the cells were located, Valn shivered. "Don't care for that room."

Jessa nodded. "Me neither. Evaelyn nearly forced me to attack Rsiran in this room."

"That's not why I don't care for it. Can't Slide."

"You can't Slide in here, either," Rsiran said, walking along halls lined with a strangely patterned lorcith. "That's why they created this place. It protected them from Thenar Guild."

"It didn't protect them from the Thenars," Valn said. "It was Venass and the way they intended to pull people with talent away from here that put them in danger. Building a place like this kept them safe from Venass."

"It's like they created a prison for themselves," Jessa said.

"When Evaelyn lived, I don't think they had to fear Venass," Rsiran said. "Danis was her brother."

"If that was true, why would she need a room coated in heartstone?" Jessa asked as they reached the line of cells.

Rsiran didn't have the answer. He had assumed Evaelyn didn't fear her brother, but maybe that wasn't true. Why else *would* she have built a room surrounded by heartstone, the one metal that Sliders struggle to get past? She had been surprised—alarmed—when he'd appeared, realizing he could get past heartstone. Only after that did she side with Venass. Rsiran thought it had been because she wanted to stop him and find the crystals, but maybe it was about more than that.

The row of cells had a strange quality to them. The forging

had been done so the lorcith pressed on him, making it hard for him to focus. Memories of his own imprisonment in one of these cells flashed into his mind. Without his ability to Slide by *pulling* himself, he wouldn't have managed to get free. Danis had nearly trapped them together as it was.

Two men armed with steel swords stood in front of the first cell. They nodded to Valn and glanced to Rsiran briefly. He knew one of the men's names, but not the other.

"Steel," Valn said. "Saw you eyeing the sword," he told Jessa. "They don't carry lorcith, even though Lareth's blades are the best, because they don't want to risk Venass using them against them."

"It probably wouldn't matter," Jessa said. "Venass has other weapons that they use."

"Not here," Valn said. He pulled a pair of orbs from his pocket and held them up.

Jessa jerked back, eyeing the spheres. "What do you think you're doing carrying those around here! One of those damned near killed Rsiran!"

"They killed plenty, not only almost Rsiran. We need to understand them if we're going to defeat them." He brought the spheres together in a quick motion.

Rsiran readied to Slide, hoping he could do it in a quick movement, and afraid he wouldn't be able to get Jessa away as quickly as he would need. In this place, his connection to the metal was different—faded—such that he would have to *push* with power energy more than he would otherwise.

Nothing happened.

"See? The orbs don't work here. The walls suppress it. I

think their ability is suppressed with lorcith, too, but we haven't risked testing it yet. Thought maybe you might be willing to try."

Rsiran *pulled* on his knives, sending a pair spinning in the air. "It's harder, but not impossible. And if I can do it, then Danis can."

"You're more powerful than Danis, especially when it comes to the metals."

Rsiran once would have thought the same, but seeing how easily Danis had stopped his knives before he'd killed Haern, he wasn't sure he was anymore. "They've come up with some way to overwhelm even my strength."

Valn's eyes widened. "If they can do that, how in the name of the Great Watcher do we think we'll stop him?"

Rsiran didn't have an answer. He wasn't willing to use the lorcith the same way Venass did, implanting it so it twisted the abilities they were given by the Great Watcher, but they would have to come up with something to stop Danis. Rsiran didn't even know if a cell like this would hold him anymore. The only thing that had even the hope of containing him recently had been using the power of the Elder Trees, and Rsiran wasn't sure he would have enough of a connection—even if he used it through the sword—for him to stop Danis.

"We have to find a way to neutralize Venass first," Rsiran said. "Then we'll go after Danis."

Valn watched him and shook his head. "Might as well figure out what he's done and copy it. That way, we might have a chance."

"We can't become like them or worse in order to stop them."

"We have to stop them if we want to survive. What's it matter how we do it?"

"It matters," Rsiran said.

The logic was the same as what Firell had used when justifying the way he'd betrayed Brusus. It was the same as what Shael had done when betraying all of them. If they abandoned what they believed in, and if they betrayed who they were, would it matter if they won?

"Lareth, you can't keep thinking that you'll—"

Rsiran ignored him as he *pulled* across the door into the cell.

On the other side, he found the small Hjan that he'd brought from the palace. The man glanced over from where he sat on a small stone pallet, almost as if expecting him. A dark sneer spread across his face.

"Lareth. You've finally come to taunt me?"

"Not taunt. Offer you a chance."

"What kind of chance? You chose not to kill me, so I don't think your threats will work as you might intend."

"No threats," Rsiran said.

The Hjan sniffed. "Then there's nothing you will do to convince me."

"Convince you of what?"

The Hjan tensed. "Isn't that why you've come? Don't you intend to convince me I need to share with you what Venass plans? Our scholars will find a way to release me, and even if they don't, it doesn't matter. He knows where I am."

Was there some connection shared between the Hjan? If there were, then it was possible Danis *did* know where he was, and maybe where Amin was, even after they had removed the implant from his head.

Did that matter?

It did, he knew. Danis might know where to find the Forgotten Palace, but he didn't know how to reach the heart of the Aisl Forest. The remaining Elder Trees protected it.

"Do you think I fear Danis?"

The Hjan looked over. "You should be careful saying his name."

"I don't fear him."

"Ah, that's not true, Lareth. I can see it in the way you frown when you look at me. You fear him, as you should."

"I can protect you from him. I can see to it that you're healed and the effect of his Compel is removed."

The Hjan touched the side of his face, running his finger along the scar. "Doing so would force me to give up the connection I fought so hard to gain. I think I would rather die, Lareth."

"You don't have to die for him."

The Hjan tipped his head. "For him? He promised me strength and power. Everything he said he would give, he has. What would you promise, Lareth? What do you think would convince me to abandon my lord?"

"Safety."

"There is no safety in this world. There is power, and the strength you can demonstrate. Anyone who tells you otherwise is a fool."

"I refuse to believe there can be no peace."

"Because you're strong, but not the strongest. He's learned your secrets, and now you will suffer." He pointed toward the door. "All of your friends will suffer as well. You would be better to support him than to fight. It would be less painful."

Rsiran wondered if this Hjan had even been Compelled. It was possible there were those with Danis who followed willingly.

He focused on the lorcith plate in the Hjan's head. It was fused there, but could he *pull* on it and remove it? Now that he'd done it once, he wondered if he could again, and this time without the incision.

It would take control, and it might require healing after he was done, regardless, but he needed to know.

Holding the connection to lorcith in his mind, he started to *push*. At first, it was slow, the resistance within the cell made it difficult, but the more that he did it, the softer the metal became, and the more attuned to it he became.

"What are you doing?" the man said.

He tried to stand, but Rsiran *pushed* slightly, enough to hold him in place.

He continued to work with the metal, *pushing* and *pulling* on it.

As he did, he realized he didn't need to remove it. All he had to do was modify it. Then the lorcith would be used differently.

The Hjan started to scream as Rsiran worked with the lorcith. The metal shifted, the soft hum from the song of it coming to his mind, and he knew what he needed to do.

With the implants, Venass forced the metal against the minds of the Hjan. This somehow connected them to it, and bound them to the potential of the metal. Teasing it away would require that he ease it back, away from the Hjan's mind.

Without Della's help, it risked harming him, but he had done the same with Amin, and if he didn't do this, there would be no way of determining if the Hjan could ever be released.

The Hjan tried to Slide.

Rsiran felt it as a flicker against his mind, but it faded.

He held onto the lorcith, and the Hjan lunged, trying to reach him.

Again, Rsiran *pushed*, holding him back.

The work was almost done. Another few moments, and the lorcith would be separated from him. There would remain a defect in the bone, a place where Venass had carved at his mind in order to place the implant, but he could shift the metal so it replaced the bone that had been lost, and so he wouldn't have to peel it completely away.

The Hjan screamed as Rsiran finished, drawing away the last of the metal from his mind.

The connection was deeper than he remembered with Amin, but then when he had removed the plate from Amin's head, he hadn't focused as much on how deeply he tore lorcith away. With Della along that time, he hadn't feared healing him. This time, any damage that occurred, he would have to repair, and Rsiran didn't think he could.

The last of the lorcith came away from deep within the Hjan's mind.

The Hjan slumped forward.

Rsiran watched him. Part of him wanted to check if he'd killed the man. If he had, it would be nothing more than cold-blooded murder. But he wouldn't risk the Hjan playing some sort of trick on him, and faking injury.

The Hjan breathed.

Rsiran waited. Moments passed before the Hjan opened his eyes and looked over to him.

"What did you do to me?"

"The implant remains."

The Hjan touched his face. What went through his head as he tried to use abilities that would no longer work?

"You shouldn't have been able to remove it!"

"As I said, I didn't remove it." If he could do the same with others of the Hjan, he might be able to end the battle much more easily. Somehow, the walls of this place created a buffer that allowed him to reach the lorcith, otherwise, he would not have been able to do so. Would he be able to find a way to do the same outside of the Forgotten Palace, or would he have to bring them all here?

"It's the same! When *he* discovers what you did—"

"As I said, I don't fear him."

The Hjan's eyes widened. "You *should*. We all should. He'll learn what you've done, and he'll find some way to counter it. You'll never be able to outsmart him."

CHAPTER 17

Rsiran couldn't stay in the cell with the Hjan anymore. The smell of lorcith clung to his nostrils, a strange heat to it that mixed with a bitter tang of blood. How much had he harmed the Hjan by trying to pull the lorcith from within his head? Without Della here, there wasn't anything that he could do to heal him, and Rsiran wasn't entirely certain that he would want to even if she were.

He *pulled* himself from the cell.

On the other side, Valn stood with his feet apart, his sword gripped tightly in hand. Jessa hunched over the door, her lock-pick set unrolled, and worked at the lock. When he appeared, she set the lock pick down and sighed.

"When we heard the scream," she said, a slight flush rising in her cheeks.

Rsiran glanced to Valn, who shrugged. "Don't look at me like that. I would have rushed in sooner, but she held me back. What took you so long?"

"I made it so he couldn't harm anyone again."

Valn studied the door, as if he could see through it, sheathing his sword. He started away from the cell, nodding toward the two guards. When he spoke, he lowered his voice. "What did you do—cripple him somehow?"

Rsiran shrugged. "Essentially. I reforged the implant so he can't use his Venass-given abilities."

"You reforged it?" Valn asked. "How did you heat... You used your connection to the metal to do that?"

Rsiran nodded. "I think I can do the same with others, but I'd need for whatever protects them to be removed."

"What protects them?" Valn asked. "We've searched him more than once—" It was Valn's turn for his cheeks to go a shade more red. "We had to know if he hid anything from us. We haven't found anything on him, though it's not for lack of trying."

With Amin, the connection had returned when they sliced open his flesh, revealing the plate, and with this other, the cell itself seemed to have released some of the protection that prevented Rsiran from accessing the plate and shifting the metal within it.

Could it be shadowsteel?

He had no connection to shadowsteel, but he knew Venass had used it to make the implants. That might even be how Danis gained extra abilities. If he could determine what they did, he might be able to counter it. He'd already seen how lorcith and heartstone could counter shadowsteel.

It was a question for Ephram. The alchemist guildlord owed him those answers.

"You don't know what it is," Jessa said.

Rsiran shook his head. "I don't know what it is. But it's neutralized in the cell."

"Well, maybe you can neutralize what they do as well. With your connection to metal, it seems we should be able to be stronger than the damn Venass."

"We're not going to use the metal the same way."

"You gave me these," Valn said, holding the bracelets up, and shaking them. In the darkness of the hall, the faint bluish white glowing from them visible only to Rsiran. "Don't you think there's something else you can do?" Valn shrugged. "Anyway, glad you came and fixed our friend. Maybe he'll be more cooperative."

"You should be ready. I might have others I'll bring to you."

"Neutered or will you leave us something to play with?"

Rsiran laughed. They reached the heartstone room and passed through. On the other side, Rsiran clasped Valn on the shoulder, then he Slid with Jessa to the smithy.

Once there, he faced his forge.

"What is it?" Jessa asked.

"Something that Valn said."

"He's pretty enough, but I don't think he's as pretty as you," Jessa told him. "He doesn't have the same strength as you have. Maybe if he spent a little more time hammering at metal, I might change my opinion..."

Rsiran shot her a look and shook his head. "Why can't I use lorcith to help augment my abilities?"

"I thought you didn't want to do anything that would mean you were no better than Venass?"

"Not quite like that, but haven't we already used lorcith and heartstone in something of the same way? We've used the bracelets, what would happen if I did something similar to try and augment my abilities?"

Jessa shrugged. "You could try. Didn't you say the lorcith had to agree to it?"

That was part of the problem for Rsiran that Venass didn't have. Rsiran wouldn't force lorcith to take on shapes that it didn't want to. Venass forced the metal, pushing it in ways the metal wouldn't naturally go. Doing so took some of the strength from the metal, but it allowed them to use it in ways Rsiran couldn't.

"Maybe if I find the right piece."

He could spend some time in the mines and find a piece of lorcith that would respond to him in the way that he needed. The problem for him was that he didn't know how he needed the lorcith to respond, but he could listen to the song and see if lorcith would react for him in a way that *could* be beneficial. Often, the metal knew what form it needed to take even more than he knew.

"The mine?"

Rsiran nodded. "You ready to return?"

"It's not my favorite—"

"I thought you liked the darkness."

She jabbed him. "The darkness is fine, but you make me follow you through those tunnels."

"I Slide us through the tunnels."

Jessa rested her hand on his chest. "That's the problem. You never pause and let us take advantage of the darkness."

Rsiran laughed softly. "I thought your time in the tunnels with Josun would have kept you from wanting to spend any more time there than needed."

"I always knew you'd come for me."

He took her hand and Slid to Ilphaesn.

As they emerged in the wide-open area of the mine, Rsiran saw a flash of orange light.

He Slid again, taking them deep into the mine, far below the usual places to mine.

"What was that?" Jessa asked as they emerged.

"A light. The mine is active again."

Some of the miners had returned, but that light was the same kind of light used when the Elvraeth controlled the mine. Could they have reopened Ilphaesn, once again using it to their own benefit, using prisoners as miners?

"You don't want to see what they're up to?"

Rsiran shook his head. As many times as he had returned to the mine, he hadn't wanted to visit with any of the miners sentenced here. He had been happy to escape. Many of the men sentenced had been sent here because they were criminals, but now, he no longer knew how to feel about those sentenced.

And lorcith wasn't as rare as so many had believed before. The Miners' Guild had controlled the flow to hold favor with the Elvraeth, and had prevented access to it in the past, but they could no longer deny the fact that lorcith overflowed Ilphaesn. It didn't take much time in the mine to know how much ore remained. There was enough to keep the smiths busy for as long as they wanted. Lifetimes. Generations. And this wasn't even the only place where lorcith could be found.

"Let's look here," he said, starting along one of the narrow tunnels. The shafts in this section reached deep beneath the earth. Rsiran suspected they would eventually connect to the palace, or at least to the Aisl if he were able to follow them that far, but the one time he had, he had nearly gotten stuck. The walls of the tunnel had closed in around him, as if made for a much smaller person.

Jessa took his hand as they walked along the tunnel. It wasn't wide here, only enough for them to go side by side, and not much wider than that. The walls glowed with the soft white of lorcith, but he knew Jessa saw only shades of gray. A soft breeze blew through here, Ilphaesn's breath, like that of the Great Watcher blowing past them.

Rsiran focused on the connection to the lorcith, letting that sense surround him. The song came with it, and he focused on it, listening for pieces of lorcith that called to him more than others.

Most of the lorcith here called to him in one way or another, but not all of the pieces called in quite the same way. Some were filled with a sense they didn't care what form they took. Others wanted to remain within Ilphaesn, bound to the rock, and others created images of decorative items—that of bowls or pots or even statues. None of that was what he needed to find.

What Rsiran wanted was lorcith that had something tied to him.

As he wandered, he let his mind go blank. Doing so allowed the metal to guide him, to draw him. He held Jessa's hand as he walked, pulling her along the tunnel with him. Neither of them spoke, and Rsiran appreciated her comfort in the silence. It allowed him to listen to the song, to hear the lorcith and search for what might work.

After a while, he stopped. "There's nothing here."

"Nothing? You've never struggled to find lorcith that would work for you before."

"This isn't just about finding any piece of lorcith, this is finding one with a willingness to work with me."

"You didn't have the same trouble with the bracelets."

He hadn't, but that had been tied to a request, and as he searched through the tunnels, he hadn't really sent a request to the lorcith.

Could he?

He focused on the song and the lorcith all around him, sending his need to it, feeding that into the song. What he needed was a way to get stronger working with lorcith. Not using it as an implant, but more like the bracelets. It would have to be attuned to him, and what he needed it for: to get stronger and to have a greater connection to the metal so that Danis couldn't hurt him—or anyone he cared about—again.

The song shifted.

Rsiran heard it distantly and felt drawn to it.

He Slid.

When he emerged in a distant part of the mine and much deeper underground, the song of the lorcith reverberated most strongly here. He could feel it racing through him, filling him, *energizing* him. He could barely stand, his head brushing the top of the tunnel, and Jessa squeezed against him, gripping his hand firmly.

This was the piece.

Rsiran *pulled* on the lorcith, expecting significant resistance, but the piece came from the wall with the barest of sound.

He caught it and was surprised to find it was nothing more than a tiny piece of lorcith, small enough for him to cup within his hand.

"What is it?" Jessa asked. "I can't see anything this deep, only gray."

He set the piece in her hand.

"This is what you came all the way down here for?" she asked.

He slipped it into his pocket. The piece sang more loudly to him than most, and there was the way that he felt when its particular contribution to the song flowed through him. "I think so."

"Can you find one for me?"

He hadn't considered it, but why couldn't he? Hadn't he made her and the others bracelets? It was possible he could use the connection to lorcith to do the same with other things, wasn't it? Could lorcith grant Jessa abilities the same way that it had granted them to Venass?

Shifting his attention to the call of the lorcith once more, he focused on what he wanted from it. This was not only a desire to find lorcith that could pair with Jessa, but lorcith that would help her, would strengthen her in some way. The steady call of lorcith changed again, and once more he Slid, emerging higher within Ilphaesn, almost to where the miners worked.

When he *pulled* the piece from the wall, it was larger than the other. He held it out, studying it, and when Jessa took it from him, the song surged.

"Can you feel it?" he asked.

The lump of lorcith was about the size of her fist, and heavy enough that she had to hold onto it carefully. "I don't feel anything. Am I supposed to?"

"I don't know. I don't even know if this will work, but we can find out."

"What do you expect?"

He shook his head. The piece that he'd found for himself, the one that was smaller, wouldn't be able to make anything of much size. When he got back to his smithy, he could heat it and see what shape it would take. With Jessa's, there were more options. The larger size could take on a knife or part of a sword, but he had the sense it didn't want to form either of those.

"I don't know what to expect. I've not gone looking for lorcith in quite this way before. Whatever I make out of these will only be attuned to you and me." But would it be enough to counter what Venass did with the metals?

CHAPTER 18

The pieces of lorcith were set off to the side, and the coals of Rsiran's forge glowed with a renewed warmth. Jessa leaned on the table rather than lying on the bed, watching him intently. A lantern glowed with a soft blue light, giving off enough light for Jessa's Sight. With all the lorcith in the smithy, Rsiran didn't need any additional light.

"You don't have to watch," he said.

"I want to see what you make."

The same curiosity she felt surged within him. What shape would the lorcith take when he heated it? This wouldn't be a forging where he'd tell the lorcith what he wanted. He'd already told the metal what he needed; now he had to learn what it would help him make.

"Then you can help—"

He looked up.

Had that been a flutter of heartstone?

He hadn't paid much attention to heartstone lately, especially since he'd convinced himself there weren't any Hjan or Venass remaining in the city, at least none with lorcith or heartstone. He still didn't know whether any with shadowsteel remained, but doubted many would risk themselves in the city. The Hjan using shadowsteel were too valuable to Danis for him to leave them isolated in Elaeavn and risk Rsiran attacking them.

The sense fluttered again.

It was nearby. Near enough that he couldn't wait to see what might have caused it.

"Stay here."

He *pulled* a dozen knives to himself and Slid.

When he emerged, he was near the row of warehouses. The darkness of night swirled around him, reminding him of Carth and the way that darkness seemed to love her. He stood in the middle of the street, waiting for another flash of heartstone, but detected nothing.

What had he sensed? Rsiran knew there had been something there, but now it was gone. If one of the Hjan had come to Elaeavn, he would either capture him, or chase him from the city.

There was a flicker, but nothing more than that, and not enough for him to act upon.

Rsiran drifted down the street, making his way between shadows. He saw nothing that told him what else might be here, nothing that alerted him to a greater threat.

As he walked, a shadow moved in the distance.

Rsiran Slid toward the shadow. At night in Elaeavn, many different kinds of people were out, so finding someone here didn't necessarily mean there was anything to worry about, but the streets had been quiet, and finding anyone tonight—especially after he'd detected Sliding—made him leery.

He watched as the figure continued to make his way along the street. He passed the Wretched Barth, the sound of music drifting out, and he paused and considered going inside to see how Brusus was handling the reopening, but his curiosity was piqued, and he wanted to follow this person. Beyond the Barth, the shadow turned, heading down a small alleyway.

Rsiran hesitated. He should get Jessa, and at least have her Sight, but if he did, he might lose track of this person. Something about the direction bothered him, though he couldn't quite place what it was.

Another turn. A cat meowed nearby.

Rsiran shivered, old superstitions returning.

Then the person paused at a house.

Rsiran's heart fluttered as the person entered.

He knew the place and had been there many times, but it should have been empty, abandoned since the attack on the city: Della's home.

Rsiran Slid inside the home, knowing it as well as he knew his smithy, and emerged to see the figure standing over the counter sorting through Della's collection of leaves and herbs, a collection that had once seemed incredibly complicated. The person standing there seemed comfortable, and quickly worked along the line of bottles as he took what he needed.

Galen.

Where was the woman?

If Galen had returned without Cael, then where was the crystal? And why would he have returned to Della's home?

Galen spun, readying something in his pocket.

Rsiran Slid slightly to the side, emerging with knives ready to *push*. Galen ducked behind a shelf, as if that would protect him from Rsiran if he sent knives at him. Maybe it would. But if Galen had his darts at the ready... He had nearly stopped Rsiran once, and it wouldn't surprise him if he managed a second time.

"I have not come to kill you, Galen."

"Lorst?"

Rsiran sniffed. The name was not one he could claim, but Galen didn't know, and didn't need to know. It had served the purpose so far, one that had allowed him to discover what happened to the crystal, even if he hadn't managed to return it quite yet.

Yet... Galen believed him to be Lorst, not Rsiran. Until he had the crystal, he had to ensure the deception remained. Later, he could explain the truth.

What would Lorst say?

Rsiran struggled with the answer, trying to think about the person Carth had created for him, the assassin who would hunt for money. That wasn't him, but Galen couldn't know that.

But Rsiran might need to share *some* of the truth, or Galen might be provoked to attack. Until Rsiran knew where the girl had gone—and the crystal—he needed to help him.

"You weren't to return to Elaeavn. I believe that you are one of the Forgotten?" Saying it that way disgusted him, but it was the kind of thing an assassin would say.

Galen shifted, and Rsiran Slid, careful to stay out of reach and avoid becoming an easy target for him. The one dart that had hit him had nearly killed him. Were it not for the connection to the place between and the Elder Trees, he might already be dead. He needed to be careful.

"Where did you take her?" Galen asked.

She was gone and Galen looked for her. That was unexpected.

"Your Elvraeth?" he asked. "You've lost her already?"

"Not lost. Taken by a Slider."

Galen knew about Sliding then. And someone else had grabbed his girl.

It must be Hjan and Venass, especially after what he'd detected. But if they had grabbed her and had already left the city, she might be impossible to track. There would be nothing he could do.

He Slid, emerging in front of Galen, *pulling* the knives back quickly and holding his palms out in front of him to demonstrate they were empty. As he did, he prepared for the possibility that he would need to Slide. He could reach the place between Slides and heal himself, but he could just as easily Slide away and reach the smithy if needed. That was where he should be anyway, staying there so that he could find out what the lorcith intended him to make, and whether there would be any way that he could use it to help him stop Venass.

But Cael was missing. What of the crystal?

Galen held a long, slender dart.

"Did you see them?" Rsiran asked, trying to placate him. He might need to disarm him, or even fully disable him.

"It was dark," Galen answered.

Rsiran grunted, studying Galen. The man had deep green eyes, and the way he watched as Rsiran shifted around the room told him his ability, even if the skill of using his darts did not. "Dark. And I thought you Sighted."

"And I thought you an assassin," Galen said.

What did he say to that? To Galen, Lorst *was* an assassin. "Only when I must."

His face contorted in confusion, and Rsiran nearly smiled. "Why are you here, Lorst?"

"I could ask the same of you."

He didn't know of Rsiran's connection to Della. If he shared —if he told him how he knew Della, and how she worked with him—would it make a difference to Galen?

Probably not.

What did Rsiran know of him? Della had shared some, and shared with him the sadness she felt about her former student's fate, and Haern had known more, and must have encountered him at other times. There might even have been some other sort of assassins' guild that had introduced him.

"Where's the girl?" Rsiran asked. He Slid over to a stool and sat, trying to appear less threatening. It was the answer that he needed the most. Would Galen share? If he didn't, would there be any way that Rsiran could force him?

Galen watched him and slipped the dart into a hidden pouch. "You never really wanted her, did you?"

"This has never been about her," Rsiran said.

Galen frowned. "Me? That's what this has been about? Damn, but Orly is a fool. He knew I would not simply take the job. That has never been how I operate."

Rsiran shrugged. What would Lorst say?

"I know," he said, thinking that might be the easiest answer.

Galen's hand reached into a pocket, and Rsiran prepared to Slide. If Galen attacked, the darts moved nearly as fast as crossbow bolts, and were nearly as hard to avoid. Worse, they were poisoned, leaving him more at risk.

"Why did you want her if not for the reward?" Galen asked.

His face twisted, and Rsiran couldn't decide if that meant he was angry or irritated. "I can see from your face that you already know why," Rsiran said.

"The crystal?"

Rsiran grunted. Did he have to play it this way?

Maybe Galen would react better to threats.

Rsiran *pulled* a knife to him, and flipped it in his hand much like Haern used to do. It had the added benefit that it cast a soft white glow on the room, giving him more light. Galen might be Sighted, but Rsiran didn't have that advantage.

What game was Galen playing? Did he have the information Rsiran wanted? He'd been gone from the city for a long time, and might not even *know* about what had happened. Exiled from the city, and not aligned with the Forgotten, it was possible he shared Rsiran's resentment toward the Elvraeth. Could he use that?

"You know that for so long I hated my ability? My father claimed it was a dark ability." He smiled, trying to foster a connection between them, but Galen ignored it. "Dark. I have seen those of the Elvraeth use their abilities for purposes far darker than anything I have ever done." He looked up, meeting

Galen's eyes. "The crystals have been kept from our people for too long, Galen."

"The Elvraeth protect the crystals for our people."

Had he made a mistake about Galen? Rsiran should have expected it, especially since Galen was with one of the Elvraeth, and had protected her, but he'd hoped that his anger over exile might override that. "Is that what you think? Is that what she told you?"

"She spoke little of the crystal. Only that she needed to return it." From the light off the knife, Rsiran could see that his hand tensed. Did he ready his dart? "Where is she, Lorst? Where have you taken her?"

Rsiran shook his head. Galen didn't know. He probably didn't even know about the damned Hjan and Venass. He had remained in Eban, killing for money.

Maybe Della was wrong about him. Carth too. This wasn't a man with a conscious.

"Not me this time, Galen. You think we're the only ones after the crystal?"

"I will get her back," Galen said.

"What do *you* want with the crystal?" Rsiran asked. "Do you think to use it?"

Rsiran watched Galen's face and noted the slight way that his eyes widened at the comment. Could he really want nothing more than to recover Cael and *not* have interest in the crystal?

"No. I see that you do not. Will you sell it?"

He shook my head. "I don't care about the crystal! I just want Cael back. And Cael wanted the crystal returned to the palace."

Rsiran sighed. If the same thing happened to Jessa, he knew what he would do, the lengths he would go to in order to bring her back. He'd already proven that, not only to himself, but to those who wanted to take her from him. It was what he feared the most.

"Then I will help."

CHAPTER 19

Rsiran sat in front of the Della's hearth, now with a fire blazing within, debating whether he should return to the smithy for Jessa or even to the Barth for Brusus. He'd agreed to help Galen, which meant finding Cael, but how would he begin to do so without any way of knowing where the Hjan would have taken her?

It was easy to understand *why* the Hjan would have taken her. As the daughter of Naelm, she would have value to Venass; maybe they would use her against the council. But if she had the crystal, as well, that was all the reason Venass needed to take her.

The problem was, Rsiran didn't even know where to begin. He had sensed the flickering of heartstone before Galen had appeared, which only told him that the Hjan took her, but nothing else. Not where they might have taken her. Other than possibly Thyr and the tower, Rsiran didn't know where Venass might have taken her.

"I found this," Galen said, breaking the silence as he reached into his pouch.

He held out a small bit of lorcith, barely more than a sliver. It pulled on Rsiran's senses, a throbbing that called to him. How had Galen gotten hold of unshaped lorcith, and how had he managed to find a piece so small?

Rsiran took the piece and held it out in front of him, studying it. Some of the firelight caught off the metal, and it glowed softly with the potential of the metal. "How did you find this?"

"I am Sighted, Lorst."

He turned and studied Galen. Did the man really think that he couldn't tell he was Sighted? "You found this where the Elvraeth woman was taken?"

He listened to the song from the sliver of lorcith, trying to determine where it had come from. As he listened, a familiar song came from it, one that he hadn't heard in quite some time.

This was from Ilphaesn.

Not only Ilphaesn, but a particular mine, one that he'd visited often enough to know it well, but one that few others should have been able to reach.

Galen's mouth twisted in distaste. Did he not care for lorcith? "Yes," he said.

If he'd found it there, that meant Josun.

The last place he'd found any evidence of Josun had been in Thyr, but Firell and Shael had known he lived, and had known he sided with Venass. If he'd returned to Elaeavn... they were all in more danger than he realized.

Was *that* who had come through his smithy when they were gone?

Rsiran hadn't discovered what had happened there, and seen no sign since their return to the city. If it had been Josun, that meant he could now Slide past the heartstone barriers he held in place. Which meant Jessa was in danger.

Galen seemed to wait for him to say something more. Rsiran clutched the piece of lorcith in his hand. "That is unfortunate."

Galen tensed, watching him with eyes that looked at him much the way that Jessa did—almost *too* knowingly. How powerful was his Sight?

"Why?" he asked.

Rsiran pulled himself up and opened his hand to show the piece of lorcith. "This comes from deep within Ilphaesn."

"Most of the ore does."

"No, it does not. Most comes from the mines the council has dug over the years through their forced labor. This," he said, holding it up, "comes from elsewhere in the mountain. They are similar but not the same."

"How do you know?"

"Just trust that I do."

"I have no reason to trust you, Lorst." He reached for something in his pocket—likely another dart.

Rsiran had thought they had moved past that. "As I have no reason to help you, Galen."

He blinked and pulled his hand back from his pocket with a sigh. "You know who might have her?"

Rsiran considered the best way to answer. What Galen

needed was an explanation for Sliding, and one that wouldn't confuse him. If he didn't know about the Hjan, and if he didn't know anything about Venass, how would he believe that lorcith and heartstone would grant them abilities?

"There are not many who Slide. At least not openly. I have already told you that it was considered a dark ability. A useful one, though, especially when you want to sneak around the city. Most with the ability never learn to use it."

"Why?"

"One of the Elvraeth once told me that the council has done all that they can to eradicate the ability, but still it appears." Did he share what he knew about the guilds—or even the Hjan—or would that confuse him more? Rsiran decided against it. When they had the crystal safely back, he would bring Galen to Della and let her decide what to share. "As I said, there were not many who openly Slide."

"You do."

"I do."

"Who else?"

"With the lorcith you found?" he asked. Galen nodded. Rsiran stared at the piece of lorcith, wishing that he would have ended Josun when he had the chance. He might not be an assassin, but Josun Elvraeth had caused him more trouble than anyone else ever had. If anyone deserved to die for his actions, it would be Josun. "It could only be one other. A dangerous man. One I once believed gone. If he wants the crystal for himself, then your friend truly is in danger."

"Where would he have taken her?" he asked.

Rsiran closed his fist around the tiny piece of lorcith,

listening to the sound of the metal as it hummed. If only the lorcith could explain where Josun had gone, and why he would have this piece with him. "I don't know for certain."

He *needed* to know the answer. Finding the crystal depended on it.

The song shifted and did something he hadn't known lorcith to do before: It created an image for him, one that he recognized.

Why would lorcith show him the warehouse?

How long had it been since he'd been there? It was the place where he'd first met Josun, and where he had nearly died more than once. Within the warehouse, there were countless treasures, items that the Elvraeth had been given but simply stored there, not willing to share with others. In hindsight, that might have saved them. Had they taken the cylinders into the palace, they might have damaged the Elder Trees sooner.

Rsiran stood and grabbed Galen and *pulled* them into a Slide.

They emerged within the musty warehouse. Motes of dust hung in the air, glowing from the light of his lorcith.

Rsiran *pushed* a pair of knives away from him, sending them sailing to create enough light to see. Stacks of boxes towered overhead, most he had examined at one time or another, but none recently. He released Galen and raised a finger to his lips.

Rsiran started forward when Galen grabbed his sleeve and nodded toward the top of the boxes. Rsiran shook his head, then tilted it toward another direction.

He started forward, not waiting for Galen to follow.

At the end of the column of boxes where it intersected with

another row, Rsiran paused and focused on heartstone, peering around the corner. There had to be something here, especially if this was what the lorcith had shown him, but why would Josun have brought her here?

It was the lorcith that Galen had found that led Rsiran here. But had Josun actually just intended for Galen to come?

Rsiran Slid, leaving Galen below, emerging on top of one of the boxes in a crouch. The dark shirt Carth had given him would protect him, and keep even Galen from seeing him easily.

As he crouched there, he noted another flickering, this time down in the clearing between boxes. Rsiran crept closer to see who was down there.

When someone spoke, he recognized the voice and tensed. Josun. "You should have left her, Galen, and returned to Eban. You will not find Elaeavn any more welcoming than when you last were here."

"You are mistaken," Galen said. "Elaeavn was never welcoming to me."

Rsiran saw Josun then. He had the same bright eyes and sharp jawline, but a long scar now ran along the side of his face with heartstone pulsing beneath the surface. His hair was longer now, and hung to his shoulders. His clothing, once so formal, was now a simple jacket and pants.

Josun smiled, and Rsiran readied a pair of knives. From where he hid, he suspected he could reach him quickly and be gone before Josun had a chance to react. Josun moved slightly, the briefest Slides as he did, emerging long enough to move again. Catching him with one of his knives would be difficult and would risk Galen and the woman chained down near him. "No. I suppose for one like you, it would not be," Josun went on.

Galen stepped closer to him, edging slightly in front to block the woman. "She is one of your family. Her father will be angered to learn what you have done to her."

Rsiran saw that Josun held a knife to the woman's neck. He'd seen Josun do the same with Jessa, and felt a surge of anger at Josun for repeating the same things that he'd done to those Rsiran cared about.

A small trickle of blood ran down the woman's neck. If something didn't happen now, she'd be killed, and with a knife across her throat, there wouldn't be anything that Rsiran could do that would bring her back.

Readying to Slide, he paused when Josun spoke again.

"You think I don't know who she is?" He laughed softly. In the warehouse, sounds were muted, heavy with the weight of all the stored riches that the Elvraeth held here. "Ironic that she would be the one to lose the crystal. Yet fitting. A shame you chose to kill her, Galen."

Damn it. He was going to kill her.

Rsiran started to Slide and realized that Galen attacked at the same time. A dart flew toward Josun, but missed as Josun Slid, taking Cael with him and emerging only a few paces away from where they had been.

Josun laughed, the knife pressing more firmly against Cael's neck.

Rsiran sent a pair of knives flickering across the distance, stationing them behind Josun so that he could *pull* them back toward Josun, to attack him unaware. All it would take was one knife, striking before Josun could Slide. One opportunity to end him so that Rsiran could move on to Danis. One strike, and he could return the crystal.

"How many darts do you have left, Galen? I know that you prepared only a few. I can keep this up far longer than you."

"Who are you?" Galen asked.

Josun laughed again, and Rsiran started *pulling* his knives toward him. "Someone who is ready to take the next step. Who is ready to do what others would not." He pressed the knife harder into Cael's neck. Rsiran could wait no longer, or Josun would do to her what he had intended to do to Jessa. "Who is willing to—"

Rsiran *pulled* himself in a Slide as quickly as he could, emerging long enough to grab Cael and move her to the other side of the small clearing. Then he returned, Sliding so that he stood across from Josun. The knives remained behind him, ready to attack.

"One who enjoys talking too much," Rsiran said, as if finishing his sentence for him. "Always too much, Josun."

Josun flickered his eyes to Galen then back to Rsiran. The bracelets on his wrist went cold for a moment. "Lorst." He said the name with amusement. How much did the Hjan know about the reason that he'd taken the name? Had it ever been useful, or had they been ready for him all along? "You have returned."

"I would say the same to you, only I think you *wish* you could really return. It's a shame that the council no longer thinks you should."

Rsiran Slid as he spoke, moving quickly, keeping himself

away from Josun. Taunting him in order to distract him, readying him for when Rsiran would send a pair of knives at him, but he needed to position him first.

Josun Slid with him. Each time he did, the heartstone now implanted beneath the skin of his face flickered, appearing briefly before Josun Slid. With the next Slide, Rsiran flung a pair of knives.

Both missed. Somehow Josun managed to Slide to the side, away from the knives.

Galen crept off. Rsiran hoped he was quick enough to rescue Cael. If he could, Rsiran could grab them both and Slide them to the safety of the Aisl so that he could get answers.

Josun was faster than he remembered, and he had been fast then. Now, with the skill he demonstrated, Rsiran wondered if he would be able to outmaneuver him.

"You should be dead, Lareth," Josun said. "Or would you prefer *Lorst?*"

"Call me whatever you want, but the only reason you had that implant placed is because you fear me."

Rsiran Slid again, *pulling* on a pair of knives. These nearly caught Josun, but missed, sinking into one of the boxes behind him.

"If you only knew how much *stronger* you could be if you were just willing to understand. You will never know what you've missed."

"I know that I don't need an implant to be able to do *this.*" He sent another pair of knives toward Josun, and again he managed to Slide fast enough to avoid it. Could Josun *pull* himself in the Slides? Had the implant given him the ability to Travel?

Rsiran was running low on his knives. He *pulled* on the ones that he'd used, and dragged them back to him, thankful that so far Josun hadn't managed to stop him. At least that was one ability Venass hadn't given him.

"And yet you continue to come here, Lareth. Look around you, at everything that *they* have kept from your kind. Don't you wonder about that?"

"My kind? You don't even know what I am. Or who."

"A smith. That is all you are."

Rsiran could almost laugh, but taunting Josun would come later. First he had to end this.

"Yet it's you who's here again, Josun. You have not given up on this delusion. Has not Brusus shown you that you were mistaken?"

Josun Slid, almost faster than Rsiran could track.

Rsiran chased Josun, emerging briefly before attacking again. Back and forth, neither of them leaving the clearing.

Only then did Rsiran realize that he'd been set up.

From the light of the lorcith, he saw movement near the corner of the boxes and the glint off a sword. Another Slide, and he saw a circle of sellswords, with Galen and Cael stuck in the middle. The crystal would be here, somewhere.

He Slid closer, and heard a soft cry as he emerged.

Rsiran glanced to Galen, thankful that the assassin had proven capable of stopping at least one sellsword with a dart. If he was right, they would be Neelish, and the poisons on swords —or crossbow bolts—deadly.

Now he understood why Josun delayed.

He knew he wouldn't be able to stop Rsiran, but if he could distract him, the sellswords might stop him.

Damn.

Rsiran debated Sliding away, but he *needed* Cael and the crystal. He wasn't about to let Josun escape with her, or with the crystal.

That meant fighting.

He Slid, emerging briefly.

As he did, pain surged through him.

He glanced down, clutching his stomach.

Josun laughed as Rsiran realized what had happened. From the burning pain of the crossbow bolt through his stomach, he suspected it was poisoned.

CHAPTER 20

Rsiran felt his vision begin to fade, clouding from a combination of pain and the likely poison that coursed through him. If he did nothing, he would fall here, dead because of Josun, and he'd lose the crystal as well. Somehow, he had to hold it together long enough to stop Josun.

"After all that, you let a simple crossbow kill you?" Josun asked.

Rsiran grunted and staggered forward a step before catching himself. He could still Slide himself to the place between, and to the Elder Trees. When he lost that ability, then he might be dead. "Not killed."

"You won't get the crystal. You might Slide off, but even then, you will not survive. Those were Neelish bolts." Josun turned to Galen, ignoring Rsiran. "I should thank you, Galen. Without your interference, none of this would have been possible. Young Cael there would have died in Eban, the crystal returned to the thief-master there. Eventually, the council would have come for it, and I would have lost my opportunity." A dark grin spread across his face as he Slid a few steps toward Galen. "But now? Because of you, now I have no use for the council. And Venass has promised quite the reward." He pulled the pulsing blue crystal out of a pocket and held it in front of him. "Have you ever wondered what it would be like to speak to the Great Watcher? What he might say?"

Rsiran tried *pulling* the crystal to him, but the poison prevented him from succeeding. "Are you certain that you're willing to risk that, Josun?"

Josun grinned at him, pocketing the crystal and Sliding toward Rsiran. This close, his deep green eyes shone in the light from the lorcith all around. Josun grabbed the crossbow bolt piercing Rsiran stomach, and twisted.

Rsiran fought not to scream and tried to Slide.

He failed.

Rsiran's heart hammered. He'd waited too long, and now Josun would succeed in killing him. After everything that he'd been through, he didn't want to die at Josun's hand, with Jessa not knowing what happened.

He tried to Slide again, and again he failed.

"You will die here," Josun taunted. "After everything you have been through, you failed here. And once I have used the crystal, the rest of your friends will fail, too. No longer will you be able to protect them."

Rsiran couldn't lift his head. He managed only to hold his gaze up, glaring at Josun. One last taunt, then. "I may die, but I will not do so alone."

He *pulled* on three knives behind Josun.

Josun managed to get away from one, but the other two hit.

One caught him on the shoulder, spinning him. The other streaked past his face, tearing a chunk of flesh free.

Josun screamed and grabbed at his face with his good arm. He tripped and fell to the ground, and pushed himself away from Rsiran.

Rsiran grunted with effort, and *pulled* on another knife. It streaked toward Josun, striking him in the back. He cried out again.

"You always underestimate me," Rsiran said, no longer able to stand, his knees gave way and he fell to the ground.

Rsiran felt the cool of the ground against his back. He might have failed, but he had stopped Josun. They had saved the crystal. That would be enough. It would have to be.

Galen reached toward him, but Rsiran pushed him away. "Don't," he said. "If you care for her, then save her. There will be other sellswords outside the warehouse. Move quickly." How many more Neelish sellswords would Josun have hired? He didn't know, just as he didn't know how many more might remain in the city. That was the warning he needed to get out.

"Let me stabilize the wound. I was apprenticed to Della for a time."

Rsiran looked up at him earnestly, trying to meet his eyes. "Why do you think I helped you?" He could no longer even move.

He tried to Slide again, but nothing happened. The poison somehow prevented him from Sliding.

Did Josun know that effect? Was that why he had used Neelish sellswords, or was it coincidence?

Galen knelt next to him and touched the bolt. Pain shot through Rsiran as he did, and warmth spilled over his dark shirt. No longer would it hide him from the Sighted. Galen reached into his pocket and started to smear something on the wound. The thick ointment stank, a bitter scent that was much like lorcith in a way. Rsiran knew it wouldn't matter.

"Can you Slide one more time?" Galen asked.

Rsiran swallowed hard and blinked at Galen.

"To Della's house. I might be able to help. Just get me back there and—"

Rsiran shook his head once. He tried to Slide, and realized that whatever Galen had done might actually have given him a chance. He felt a trickle of movement, and if he managed to *pull* hard enough, he thought he might be able to get away from here.

"Too hard. Too hard to take you with me." He swallowed. Blood dripped from his nose, running down his face. With every bit of effort he had left, he *pulled* on a Slide. "Just me, Galen. Get the crystal back to Naelm…"

With a scream, he Slid.

Rsiran emerged in the place between Slides, with the power of the Elder Trees all around him, and collapsed. The bright light of the trees pressed in on him, and he didn't feel the warmth from them that he normally did. Rsiran realized that it wasn't that the trees had lost their warmth, but his body growing cold, his life draining away. He tried *pulling* on the energy of the trees and failed. It had taken all of his remaining energy to simply reach this place.

Lying there, his blood oozing from his wound, he clutched

the ground, wishing that he would have managed to see Jessa one more time before he died.

He dreamt.

Rsiran didn't know where he was, but it was a place of darkness filled with spots of light. It felt as if he floated, but he was insubstantial, almost as if he Traveled. Perhaps that was what it felt like when you died. Maybe everyone Traveled in a sense, getting the chance to join with the Great Watcher.

He continued to float, noticing that the bright lights beneath him seemed to coalesce. They didn't remind him of lorcith as they had the last time he had experienced something like this. These were too scattered for them to be lorcith, and too bright to be heartstone. What then?

Strangely—or perhaps, not strangely—he felt no pain. There was no sensation at all, just an awareness, similar to when he had nearly died by the explosion in Seval's smithy. That time, he was certain that he was in a different place, and recognized that he moved without his body. This time was different, and he had a sense that he moved, similar to when he Traveled, but not the same. This time, it was almost as if he were substantial.

A sense of a great power flowed around him.

Rsiran tried to look around, searching for the Great Watcher. Each time he'd held the crystals, he'd had the same sense, that of the Great Watcher sitting off to the side, so close that he could practically reach him. This was no different, only, there was no crystal. Either Josun still had it and had escaped, or Galen had managed to rescue it, and would return it to the palace. If Naelm took possession of the crystal, he could get word to the guilds so they could return it to the chamber.

But they wouldn't be able to.

Rsiran had bound the crystals in the protections granted by the Elder Trees. He'd used their power, and had sealed the crystals off. No one could access the chamber except for Rsiran. Even were Galen to get the crystal back in their hands, there wouldn't be anything anyone could do to return it to the chamber, all because Rsiran had thought he knew best and had blocked the council from accessing the crystals. Now, none would ever have the opportunity to hold one of the great crystals. He had wanted to give others the chance, and now with his death, he will have taken it from everyone.

He continued to move, carried by some invisible wind in the darkness. As he floated, he noted additional flashes of color, but none came any closer. All seemed extremely distant, nothing more than a vague shifting in the darkness.

The sense of power didn't change.

It didn't come any nearer, but the power still flowed all around. Rsiran almost believed there was something familiar about it, a sense from it he had known before but not from when he had last held the crystal. This was a personal connection.

Realizing that sent a chill through him.

Could it be that he wasn't near the Great Watcher? Could this be something else—something darker? He had seen power in the world that seemed to come from something other than the Great Watcher. Having worked with Carth, he knew that there were others with abilities that were different from his. In some ways, her abilities might exceed his. What else might exist in the world that he didn't know and understand?

What else might Venass have attempted to discover?

If not in this form, he might have shivered.

Rsiran had long assumed that Venass only sought power similar to the gifts given by the Great Watcher, but what if there were other abilities they had discovered, and other ways of augmenting that power? Haern had warned him to be careful, alerting him that there *were* other people in the world with power, but Rsiran hadn't given it the thought he should have.

As he continued to move, he wondered why he floated like this. If this was death, was this all there was to it? Would he float endlessly above the world, staring at flashes of color he didn't understand, or would there be something more? Was this what happened to Haern, or had he suffered a different fate?

A particularly bright surge of light appeared beneath him.

Rsiran focused on it, and tried *pulling* himself to it.

With the attempt, there came movement, a kind of motion that was more a rustling against the steady wind blowing him along.

He tried again, *pulling* harder.

The light zoomed closer.

Rsiran studied it, wondering what it might be. Not lorcith this time. The size wasn't large enough to be lorcith. And he thought he'd seen heartstone in the past, but this didn't seem to be heartstone, either.

What then?

Rsiran continued to *pull* himself toward the light. It grew brighter and brighter. There was no sense of warmth, not as he wished for, and he hesitated.

Maybe this was a mistake.

He stopped *pulling* and *pushed*.

With that, he flew away from the light, moving more quickly than he had. It was effortless, and he soared, reaching a height above the flash of light once more, and remained there. Whatever lights he had seen below unsettled him for reasons that he couldn't explain.

If he was dead, if this was the end, would there be any way for the barrier he'd placed around the crystals to be lifted? If it remained, if the barrier persisted, his friends would suffer even more because of him.

But he was gone... wasn't he?

He'd collapsed in the midst of the Elder Trees, at the place of their power. Were he alive, he could use that power, and undo the protections that he'd placed there.

Could he unravel them in this state?

If this was some sort of place before his passing, some way of moving him beyond and to the Great Watcher, would there be any way for him to connect to that power?

Rsiran turned his attention to trying to reach the power of the Elder Trees. Normally, reaching that power was difficult, something that he could only do when he was in the place between Slides. The sword he'd forged might have acted as a kind of intermediary, but it still hadn't given him the same connection that he had while in that place. Lying there, with his body there, shouldn't he be able to reach it?

He *pulled*, thinking of the power.

At first, nothing happened.

Rsiran floated, the scattered lights below him still unsettling.

He *pulled* again. This time, he felt a stirring, the faintest of fluttering.

Rsiran fixed a desire in his mind. The crystals couldn't remain apart from their people forever. Doing so was a mistake.

When he *pulled* again, power surged. Rsiran felt it within him, something that occurred to him as more of an unraveling. The lights below brightened, now mixing with faint blue hues and greens. Other colors flashed.

Power raced through him.

For a moment, he worried he'd made some sort of mistake, that he'd accidentally unleashed something, but then he felt the steady hum of energy, a familiar sense of the Elder Trees. They glowed brightly near him.

Rsiran *pulled*, this time returning to his body.

CHAPTER 21

W hen Rsiran awoke, his body was restored. There was no evidence of the crossbow bolt that had nearly ended him, and the poison that coursed through his veins no longer burned as it once had. He took a deep breath, and noted the strange bitter lorcith odor he associated with the place between Slides.

Sitting up, he saw that he sat at the edge of the clearing. The four remaining sjihn trees glowed a bright light as they did in this place, and the fifth remained darkened near him. Each time he saw it, he knew he would have to find a way to restore that tree.

At least he still lived.

Rsiran didn't know how it was possible. The Elder Trees had healed him before, but that hadn't been nearly the injury he'd sustained this time. Facing Josun had nearly killed him, and he was lucky to have survived.

The crystals.

Had he released the protections upon them?

Rsiran *pulled* strength from the Elder Trees and Slid.

When he emerged, he stood amidst the crystals. Four crystals rested atop wooden pedestals, glowing with the bright bluish light. None pulsed more brightly than any of the others, not the way that they had when he had held the crystal the first time—or even the second time while Traveling. Though he might want to, Rsiran doubted that he would be able to claim any of the crystals a third time.

The fifth was still missing.

He hadn't *really* expected it to have returned yet. He had barely released the protection around the crystals. The council —even if the crystal had been returned—would not have been aware that they could now access the chamber, much less had the time to replace it.

Had he made a mistake in releasing the protection around the crystals?

Without that, there would be no way to prevent Venass from reaching them. Already, they had damaged one of the Elder Trees, harming it enough that one of the crystals had been vulnerable. He didn't doubt they would come searching for it again, trying to take another—possibly all of them.

He'd never considered the question of who would release the barrier if not for him. Pride had made him think that he would survive. In spite of everything that had happened to the others, including losing Haern, there was a part of him that still believed he would live when others failed. If Josun Elvraeth had nearly killed him—and not even Josun, but a sellsword using a poisoned crossbow bolt—others could harm him as well.

They would have to find a different way to protect the crystals.

The crystals had been safe for generations before Rsiran appeared, protected by the Elder Trees and the guilds. Somehow, he would need to restore that protection.

After making a steady circle around the crystals, he Slid, emerging in his smithy.

The smithy was empty. The coals had long since burned out. The lantern was missing, and a new layer of dust coated the floor. Where was Jessa?

He Slid to the door, and checked the locks, finding them intact.

She must have sneaked off, leaving the smithy, but would she have done so knowing that he'd disappeared after something he'd detected?

Doubtful.

Something had happened.

Rsiran Slid to Krali, his favorite place for detecting lorcith and heartstone, and focused on the charm he'd made her. It was small, but he'd used it so often to search for her, and was so attuned to it now, that finding it was easy. In the distance, he detected it.

Why would she have returned to the Aisl?

He Slid to her.

When he emerged, he appeared in the clearing of the Aisl. Not only did he find Jessa, but also Della and Brusus and Luthan and Seval.

Jessa gasped when he appeared, and rushed over to him,

throwing her arms around him and squeezing him tightly. "Where have you been?"

Rsiran noted the relieved expression in Seval's eyes. Della appeared more concerned than anything. Brusus had a neutral face.

Only then did he realize that there was another in the clearing, someone he hadn't expected to find. "Cael?" he asked. "How did you get here so fast? And what happened to Galen?"

Had someone Slid her to the forest?

No... Considering the way Jessa clung to him, that wasn't the answer.

How long had he been gone?

"You rescued me a week ago," Cael answered.

A week. He'd lain in the place between for a week? It explained why his stomach rumbled as it did. "I've been gone a week?"

Della stepped forward and touched his cheeks. A surge of cold washed over him. Rsiran didn't fight her healing attempt. "You were gravely injured," she said softly. "That you live..."

"The Elder Trees healed me," he said.

Della frowned. "What happened with you seems different from that. I cannot tell what saved you."

"Cael told us what happened to you," Jessa said. "She told us you took a crossbow bolt to the stomach and that it was poisoned. We couldn't find you... Valn returned, and we searched, but we couldn't find you..." She leaned on him, sobbing. "I thought... I thought that you didn't make it wherever you wanted to go and were dying."

"I was dying. I didn't."

She pressed her hand on his chest. "I see that you *didn't*."

"I'll explain what happened to me later, if I can. What happened with the crystal? Where is Galen," he asked Cael again.

Cael's mouth pinched together, darkening her otherwise lovely face. His bracelets went cold and she blinked, shaking her head. "Josun survived," she said. "The crystal is gone. Galen is—"

She cut off abruptly as Della shook her head.

Rsiran glanced at her. What had happened to Galen?

It didn't matter. What mattered was that Josun lived. In spite of nearly dying, Rsiran still hadn't managed to kill him.

"It's not your fault," Jessa said.

Rsiran clenched his jaw. "It *is* my fault. Had I only finished him when I had the chance, none of this would have happened. Venass wouldn't now have the crystal."

"We don't know that Venass has the crystal," Jessa said.

"What else would he have done with it?" Rsiran asked. "If he managed to get the crystal—"

"Venass does not yet have it," Luthan said. His voice was thin, and he rubbed a knuckle into his eyes. "What I can See tells me that there remains hope we can reclaim the crystal. Something else changed," he said, watching Rsiran intently.

"I removed the barrier preventing access to the crystals," Rsiran said.

"You did *what?*" Brusus asked. "Wasn't that barrier the only thing keeping Venass from reaching the other crystals?"

"Maybe," Rsiran said, "but what happens if I die and the barrier remains intact? None of our people would be able to access the crystals then. After what happened to me, I couldn't leave the barrier in place. I couldn't risk it, not when the crystals are about more than me."

Luthan's eyes flared a brighter green, the intensity lasting only a moment. "I can't See what will happen now that you've released the barrier around them, but you were right to do so. Too much would be lost if you fell."

"What happened to you?" Brusus asked. "Cael told us about your injury, and how you Slid away, but you should have been back by now."

Rsiran glanced to Della. The others didn't know about the space between Slides, or about the power of the Elder Trees. To them, the trees were a symbol, not real power, but Rsiran knew them differently. He'd held their power, had used it to defeat Venass.

"There's a place between Slides where the trees healed me."

That was the only answer that he could come up with. Nothing else made any sort of sense. Even *that* answer didn't make much sense to him. He should have died. Given what Josun's hired forces had managed, Rsiran should have fallen the same as Haern. Why should he live when Haern died?

The trees had seen it differently. Rsiran didn't understand why, and maybe he wouldn't ever know.

"There is power here," Della said. "And I can see why they would wish to have you healed. You have been chosen to protect them."

"I haven't done such a good job so far," Rsiran said. "I already lost one of the Elder Trees—"

"Before you knew they existed," Jessa said.

Rsiran smiled, appreciating the fierce way that she defended him.

"The girl is right," Luthan said. "Too much has been held from you—from all of our people—and for too long. That must change moving forward."

The crystals. All of this was about the crystals. Wasn't that the reason he was here? The reason for Venass and the Forgotten and for everything.

The people needed to reach the crystals.

Where did he start? When would they start?

In a flash of inspiration, he knew the answer. Rsiran took Jessa's hand and Slid to Brusus. "It will start now," he said to himself.

He Slid them into the crystal room.

Brusus gasped.

"How is it that you can *Slide* us here? I've never thought that I would be able to see this place, and you easily reach it."

"I don't know how I can."

"Rsiran—" Jessa released his hand and stared at the crystals. "I shouldn't be here. I'm not Elvraeth born."

"I didn't think I should be here, either, but I don't think that matters to the crystals, only that the right people are chosen."

"What did you see when you held one?" Brusus asked.

"I don't know that you can hold one unless it calls to you," Rsiran said. The steady glow of the crystal Josun held made it unlikely he'd been called. Yet.

Rsiran reached toward the crystals, choosing one at random. For all he knew, the crystal might have been the same one he had held before.

As he did, it *pushed* against him.

"See? It won't allow me to hold it."

"If that's true, then Venass might not be able to reach them, either."

"Maybe not," Rsiran said, "but I wouldn't put it past them to figure out some way of overwhelming the crystals' defenses." That was what he feared the most. And if they managed to reach the crystals, they would probably find some way to drain the energy that they stored.

Jessa started making a circuit around the room. "What do you mean 'call' to you?" She paused as she made her way around, stopping in front of a crystal on the far side of the chamber. "This one"—she reached toward one of the crystals —"is a little different from the others, isn't it?"

Rsiran didn't know what would happen as she reached for it. Would the crystal *push* against her, the same as it had done with him? Or would Jessa manage to reach it?

Her hand closed on the crystal.

Light flashed.

And then she stepped back, blinking. "Did you see that?" she asked, her voice excited.

"See what?" Brusus said. He had stopped in front of another crystal and studied it. The light radiating off of the crystals was bright enough for Rsiran to see the way his eyes blazed a bright green. "How did you reach that?"

He hovered his hands just off the crystal, almost touching it, but the crystal *pushed* back.

Rsiran felt it as it did.

The effect was strange. Why should he be aware of how the crystal resisted Brusus?

Brusus looked over to Rsiran. "Guess I'm not worthy."

"You didn't see that?" Jessa asked again. She blinked slowly as she looked around her, as if coming out of a daze.

"I don't know what you're talking about," Brusus said. "The only thing I see are these damned crystals that I can't even reach. Guess they don't think I'm worthy," he muttered. He reached the next one. "And this one... it flickers differently than the others. I think there's something wrong here." Brusus reached the crystal and held it. As it had with the one Jessa touched, light flashed.

Brusus was gone.

Jessa sucked in a breath.

The crystal was still there, but Brusus was not.

"Is that what happened when I touched the crystal?" she asked.

Rsiran shook his head. "You touched it and then released it. It was sort of the same motion."

"The same motion? I saw clouds and sky and stars all around me! It had to have been hours that passed!"

Rsiran smiled. "I had something similar when I reached the crystal. It felt like I was sitting next to the Great Watcher. When I looked down, I knew the connections between lorcith and heartstone. I was able to see it everywhere. That was what I was meant to see."

He stopped in front of one of the other crystals. For some reason, it seemed to have moved.

Before he knew what he was doing, he reached for it.

When his hand touched it, there came a flash of light.

Heat and energy throbbed through him. Everything glowed, a mixture of colors unlike anything that he'd seen before, but reminding him of the potential that he saw from heartstone and lorcith. It was everywhere. As it faded, Rsiran had a sense that he moved, falling toward the ground.

Then everything returned to the way that it had been. The light faded and there were only the crystals. Had he held another of the great crystals?

"Rsiran?" Jessa asked.

Rsiran looked at the crystal, trying to understand what had happened. How should he be able to hold another of them? They were meant to be held once, the gift that came from them meant for the receiver once. And now Rsiran had seemingly managed to hold them three times.

Why did the crystals choose to allow this?

"Rsiran?" Jessa said again.

"What is it?"

She pointed.

Rsiran followed the direction of where she pointed. Brusus lay in a heap on the ground, convulsing violently.

CHAPTER 22

Rsiran Slid them back to the clearing within the Aisl with Brusus still convulsing.

When they emerged, Della rushed to them, sending a Healing over Brusus. "What happened?" she demanded.

"He held one of the crystals."

Della's eyes widened slightly. "I will see what I can do, but I cannot find anything wrong with him."

Luthan crouched next to Brusus. "If he has truly held one of the crystals…" He looked up at Rsiran with a question in his eyes. "This happens to some who hold them. Not all come away intact. That is why we screen those who attempt it."

"You should have warned me," Rsiran said.

"I didn't think that you'd be foolish enough to try and have them hold one of the crystals."

"What happens to those like this?" Jessa asked. Her face was ashen, and Rsiran suspected she thought about what could have happened to her. The crystal hadn't affected her the same way as it had Brusus.

"It either passes or it does not. For most, it will pass, and they will be given the gifts that holding the crystal will bring, but others will not be so lucky. They continue to convulse until it burns out, but they are never the same, as if the convulsions have burned out what was once them.

Della pressed another Healing through Brusus, and the convulsions eased.

"Bring him to my place. I will keep him safe until we learn what effect this will have." She glanced at Rsiran askance. "You are often so impulsive," she scolded. She glanced over to Jessa. "What of her? Did she attempt to hold one of the crystals?"

Jessa smiled. "I did."

"What did you see?" Luthan asked. She described what she saw, and Luthan smiled. "Ah, you have been given the gift of Sight."

"Sight? I'm already Sighted," she said as Rsiran lifted Brusus and carried him toward Della's hut.

"This would be an extension of Sight, something more than what you already possess. It is a great gift, but one that can be difficult as well."

"You mean that I'll be able to See? Like you?"

Luthan shrugged. "I do not know. What you describe is much like the vision I had when I held the crystal. We have taken to comparing experiences, so we can learn what others have seen. Through this, we have taken to naming the crystals, though they all look the same when we are standing in the room." He nodded to

Rsiran. "You have held the crystal of wisdom." He grinned. "That is what we call it at least. There is something where you sit above the world, almost as if watching with the Great Watcher, and looking down on the world. Few are given the chance to hold that crystal."

"He held another," Jessa said.

Luthan frowned. "Another? That you have held a crystal more than once... and now a third? That is unprecedented."

Della nodded. "As I have said. The trees have chosen him to be their protector. Now they're giving him all the knowledge and strength that he needs in order to succeed."

They stopped at the hut, and Della threw the door open. Once inside, Rsiran set Brusus down near the makeshift hearth while Della started brewing mint tea like she usually did. She mixed something together and then crouched next to Brusus, rubbing a thick paste on his neck and face.

As she did, his breathing continued to ease, getting more regular with every passing breath. Another wave of Healing washed over Brusus, enough that he sighed with it.

"I think that he will be fine," Della said.

"Do you know which crystal he held?" Luthan asked.

Rsiran shook his head. "Not the same one as Jessa or I did."

"That doesn't matter. They have been known to shift."

"Even while we're in there?"

Luthan shrugged. "It is difficult to say what happens with the crystals. They appear to be connected to the pedestal, but they are not. Their positions change, often quickly, so there is no way to predictively know which one you'll be called to hold. As few are lucky enough to be called to hold them at all, it usually doesn't matter. It is strange that all three of you would be given the chance to hold one."

"Not strange," Della said, looking up from Brusus as she continued to smear another layer of the medicine across his face. "These are the two closest to him. The crystals would have chosen them to work with him, especially if the Elder Trees needed him to be able to do so."

Brusus took a deep breath and his eyes fluttered open. He smiled. "Damn, Rsiran. That was something..." He looked around, realizing that he was in Della's hut and that he wasn't with only Rsiran and Jessa anymore. "Didn't go so well for me, then?"

Luthan tipped his head to the side, and his eyes flashed. "I think it went as it needed to go for you, Brusus. It is fortunate that your friends were with you to bring you out of the chamber. When others have convulsed, they have needed more help."

"Others? How many have gone through this?" Brusus asked.

Luthan inhaled deeply. "The Elvraeth have monitored the crystals for generations. There have been hundreds who have suffered the same way."

"Hundreds?" Della paused as she poured a mug of steaming tea. "Why are none warned of this possibility?"

"Would it change anything?" Luthan asked. "Would you have done anything differently if you had known that there was more of a risk to hold one of the great crystals?"

Della handed the mug to Brusus, who took it and sipped carefully. "What else doesn't the council reveal to others? What more haven't you shared with us?"

"You of all people should understand there are things the council cannot share. Doing so puts others in danger."

"Like hiding the truth about the crystals?" Rsiran said. Luthan's glance seemed to beg him to silence. "Jessa was able to hold one of the crystals, Luthan. When I first held one, the explanation was that I am descended from the Elvraeth, so it made sense that I should be able to hold one. What is the answer regarding Jessa? Why was she able to? Her parents weren't Elvraeth."

Luthan glanced from Jessa to Rsiran without answering.

"How many have the potential to hold one of the crystals?" Rsiran asked.

"Anyone can," Luthan answered.

Della pressed her lips together in a tight frown.

"Everyone in the city? Not only the Elvraeth, but all of the people?"

"Anyone who possesses one of the Great Watcher's abilities," Luthan said. "They would be able to hold one of the crystals, though few are given the opportunity."

"None," Rsiran corrected. "None are given the opportunity. Only the Elvraeth. Holding the crystals unlocks potential, doesn't it?"

Luthan nodded. "It unlocks something in the person who manages to reach it. There is permanence in what is unlocked, and that person can pass their ability on to their heirs."

"That's why you keep the crystal to the Elvraeth?" Brusus rubbed his neck as he sat up, and a frown crossed his mouth. "You're afraid of who else might get the same powers as you?"

"You are the result of such a pattern," Luthan said to him.

"The council has long tried to breed for increased abilities, to find strength where there has not been strength before."

"What does the council search for?" Brusus asked. He had set the cup of mint tea down and started to stand. He propped himself up on the wall and stood there, somehow managing to making himself look threatening. "Why try to interbreed in the first place?"

Rsiran thought he understood. "The guilds. That's the reason, isn't it? The council knows the guilds possess a different kind of power than the Elvraeth. They have gifts of the Great Watcher, but they are never as strong as their guild gifts."

Luthan sighed and nodded. "We—they—have wanted to discover if the clan gifts could be replicated. There were some who thought that time and drawing out the power from the crystals would allow us to eventually replicate the abilities of the guilds."

"They're different abilities!" Rsiran said.

Luthan nodded. "I See that. Others do not."

Rsiran turned to the door, frustration surging through him. Luthan Saw that. What else might he have Seen? What else might there be to the abilities that he didn't understand?

He needed to get Jessa and Brusus away from the rest so they could discover what abilities might have changed for them. Given what Luthan said, Jessa might now be a Seer, but if the change was anything like what Rsiran had experienced, it would be gradual.

There was something more about what he'd heard that troubled him. It wasn't just that the council had held back information that would have helped the others. There was the fact that *he* didn't have any of the Great Watcher's abilities, but he was able to reach the crystals. Why should he be able to hold one of the crystals—and why should it have affected him the way that it had—without the abilities of the Great Watcher? He might be descended from the Elvraeth, but he was more guild born than anything else.

Would others like him have the same potential?

Better yet, were there any others like him?

Rsiran didn't think he was alone, but what if he was? What if there were no others like him? In some ways, he was more like the Elvraeth and their collection of abilities.

"I think it's time for Brusus to rest," Della said, shooing Luthan, Jessa, and Rsiran toward the door.

"I'm fine," Brusus said. She shot him a hard look and he took a deep breath, laying himself back. "I don't know why she's concerned about me. I think that I'd know if there was anything wrong." He muttered the comments to the air, as if speaking to himself.

As they reached the door, Della grabbed Rsiran's arm and held him back as the others departed. Jessa glanced at him before motioning to the center of the clearing.

"What is it?" Della asked.

"It's nothing, Della," Jessa assured her.

Della shut the door after the others left and lowered her voice. "I can see from your face that something's bothering you. I may not be Jessa, but I think I know you well enough to know when there's something troubling you."

"It's the crystals," he admitted, glancing over to Brusus. His friend rested now, his eyes closed and his breathing heavy.

Every so often, he would take a deep, sonorous breath. "I've been thinking about the crystals and how I don't have any of the Great Watcher's abilities. Why should I have been able to hold one of the crystals?"

"I believe you have held more than one of the crystals," Della said.

"Fine. More than one of the crystals, but that doesn't change the fact that I don't have any of the Great Watcher's abilities."

"Are you so certain of that?"

"I don't have Sight. I'm not a Reader. I'm not a Seer. I'm not a Listener," he said, tapping on each of his fingers as he went. "I can Slide and I can use metals. Those are the abilities of the guilds."

Della released his arm and touched Brusus's face, wiping a bead of sweat off of his forehead. "There are many abilities beyond those. Think of Brusus and his ability to Push you. Or the ability to Compel. Even mine—the ability to Heal. To say that what you possess is any different, or lessened, takes away from what the Great Watcher has given us."

"But what I can do is tied to the ancient clans," Rsiran said. "It's not the same as the others."

"No, but then, the others are newer abilities. What you possess is more closely aligned with the clans, and what they would have known when the crystals were first discovered. I think in some ways, you have a purer connection than others. Or maybe it's something else."

"Like what?"

She shook her head. "I am not certain. The longer I am here

beneath these trees, the farther back I can See. I think... No. It doesn't matter."

Rsiran squeezed his hands together, debating what to say. "I know that you're disappointed I took Jessa and Brusus to the crystals."

"Are you so certain?" she asked.

"You looked as if—"

Della lifted the mug resting next to Brusus and poured the contents into the fire. "I might be many things, Rsiran, but I don't think I am so easy to know as that. I recognize you have been given a unique ability, one that allows you to reach the crystals when no one else can. With that ability, you are given the right to decide who to reveal them to. There is a reason for that, I think. I am only surprised that it took you as long as it did to bring those you care about to them."

Rsiran looked at Brusus and noted the easy way he breathed, thankful nothing more had happened to him. He hadn't imagined the crystals might be dangerous. He had thought there could only be two outcomes—either you could hold the crystals or you could not.

"What will happen to them?"

"Now that they have held the great crystals?" Della asked. When Rsiran nodded, she shrugged. "It is hard to say. You have seen how your abilities change. You have always been sensitive to lorcith, but since holding the crystal, you can see its potential. The Great Watcher knows I can't even tell you what will happen to you now that you've held one of the crystals a third time. Maybe nothing, or maybe there will be some other great change." She shook her head. "Although, you seem to have as much ability as anyone these days. It is hard to imagine what more you would be able to do."

"And Jessa? Do you think that she'll become a Seer now?"

Della studied Brusus. "I don't know what will become of them. Luthan might be right. The Elvraeth have followed the abilities of those who have held one of the crystals for years, trying to determine what would happen to others who managed to hold the crystals. There is value in knowing what to expect, even when the outcome is uncertain. But I don't think that even he knows quite what to expect from those who emerge from the crystal chamber."

"Is that the only reason you wanted me to stay behind? You wanted to know what bothered me?"

Della smiled at him. "I worry about you, but that is not the reason that I asked you to remain."

"Why then?"

"There are two things that you still must do, Rsiran, and they are linked. The first is finding the crystal. Cael reported she had the crystal, and that she attempted to return it to the city, especially after learning that Orly was after it."

"I saw it. Josun had it."

"That man," she whispered, shaking her head. "Unfortunate that he would be the one to recover it. He was a handful before holding one of the great crystals. Now that he has…"

"He has an implant as well," Rsiran said. "Heartstone. It makes him a more skilled Slider."

Skilled enough that Rsiran almost hadn't been able to stop him. And he hadn't, not really. He'd nearly died, and Josun had still escaped with the crystal. How did Rsiran expect to defeat

Danis—especially now that he would have the crystal—when he wasn't even able to stop Josun?

He needed to return to his smithy to see if he could figure out how to use the lorcith to augment his abilities. That was what he'd been doing when he'd detected Josun, and now he was a week behind.

"You said there were two things I needed to do. The first was to find the crystal, which I was going to try and do, regardless. What was the other thing?"

Della nodded. "The other will require that you return to Ilphaesn."

Rsiran frowned, and as Della explained what she needed of him, he began to nod.

CHAPTER 23

Heat filled the inside of his smithy. After all the time that he'd been away from the forge, standing this close to the blast of the coals left a sheen of sweat coating him. It was a good sweat, and one he needed. He watched the nugget of lorcith, barely larger than his thumb, as it took on heat, worried that he might leave a piece this small in for too long.

He needn't have been concerned. The song from the lorcith called to him, and he could listen to that song, and use that to guide him as he heated the metal, but the smith part of him—that part that had been instructed by his father and remembered—made him watch the ore as it took on the heat from the coals.

The door to the smithy opened with a gust of cool air, and Jessa entered, quickly closing the door behind her and slipping the massive heartstone locks into place. Rsiran didn't know if they would even keep Josun out anymore, especially now that he had the implant, but he felt more comfortable with them than without.

She joined him near the forge. A pale yellow flower curled around the heartstone charm, and it carried a heavy fragrance with it. "Did you find Galen?" she asked.

Rsiran took a deep breath and nodded toward the dark gray clothes folded on the bench. He hadn't worn the miner's garb in months, and putting them on once more had taken him back to a difficult time, back before he Slid openly, back before he had grown comfortable with his abilities.

When Della had told him how the council—really, Naelm—had sentenced Galen to Ilphaesn, Rsiran knew what he had to do. At least he hadn't been executed. That was the usual punishment for those who returned from exile. Sneaking into the mine had been easy, but he'd worn his old clothing in case he couldn't easily find him.

"I found him."

"I can't believe they still exile people to the mines," she said. She rested her head on his shoulder and took a deep breath.

"At least he could have earned his way out," Rsiran said. "My father didn't give me that opportunity."

She looked up at him, biting her lip as she did. A frown crept across her face. "You don't sound so... bitter when you talk about it. Not like you once did."

Rsiran shrugged. "What would bitterness get me? Besides, I can't complain about what happened. Everything that did brought me closer to the life I was meant to lead."

"You really mean that."

"I do."

She smiled and brushed the strands of hair out of her face. "Was it hard to find him?"

"Not once I got in there. I Traveled first so that I knew where to find him."

"And now he's with Della?"

"With Cael, at least. That was what she wanted."

"I still think it's surprising that Della had an apprentice."

"What's surprising is that her former apprentice is an assassin."

"Do you really think he was an assassin?"

Rsiran shrugged. "More assassin than me, but that's what he did in Eban. The stories about him…" He hadn't shared with her that he'd gone back to Eban. Before rescuing Galen from Ilphaesn, he wanted to know more about him. It was helpful knowing what kind of man he would be helping, regardless of Della's feelings on the matter. Everything that he heard told Rsiran that Galen was a skilled—and dangerous—man.

"Sort of like the stories about you."

"What stories?"

Jessa smiled. "You should hear the way the guilds talk about you. It's like you're more than a man. I keep telling them that they're wrong, but they keep wanting to believe there's more to you than even I know."

Rsiran grinned. "Maybe I *am* more than a man."

Jessa grunted. "You keep telling yourself that."

Rsiran laughed.

"Are you finally going to try it?" she asked, nodding toward the forge.

"I'm going to see what the lorcith wants of me. And it's just about ready."

"Then I'll watch and see if you do something amazing." She patted his arm, lingering on his shoulder for a moment before going to sit on their bed.

He pulled the piece of lorcith off the coals and set it on the anvil. He studied it, thinking about what he needed while listening to the song of the lorcith. Heated as it was, the song came like a steady hum, a loud sound that filled his mind as he focused on it.

Rsiran had thought to *push* on the metal to get its shape, but the song wasn't clear about what shape it would take if he did that. What he needed was a clear head, and there was only one way for him to do that.

He lifted a hammer, choosing from the tools he had lined next to his bench, and not surprised that he should grab the hammer that he'd used in the mines all that time ago. First he'd donned the gray uniform once again, and now he chose to use the hammer from that time.

With a first tap, he struck the heated metal, letting the lorcith sing to him.

Rsiran pounded steadily. Each blow was sharp, and with less force than he usually needed, mostly because of the small size of the nugget of lorcith. He continued, one strike after another, falling into a rhythm. He turned the piece as he went, forming a ball of lorcith, focusing not on a shape that he wanted, but on need.

Rsiran breathed out.

With each tap of the hammer to the ore, his mind became clearer. All he heard was the song.

To this, he added the sense of urgency, a desire for strength, one that would help add to his abilities, but only in a way that honored the Great Watcher.

The lorcith hummed louder.

Rsiran continued to hammer, turning the piece over and over.

Now he no longer needed the hammer. He *pushed*, forming a ring of metal, the shape coming to him now, though not the reason behind it. The process repeated. Each time he turned the metal, he *pushed* again, the shape coming forth.

The band complete, now Rsiran pressed into the sides. The lorcith guided him in this, as well, creating an intricate pattern, one he would not have managed with tools. The pattern came from his mind and was one he *pushed* onto the metal, creating the outline. With one more *push*, the forging was complete.

Rsiran carried it to the quenching bucket where it released a hiss of steam.

Jessa looked up, setting down the journal that he'd taken off the Hjan. "Are you done?"

Reaching into the bucket, he pulled the ring free and held it in his palm. Surprisingly, the song from the lorcith hadn't changed. Usually with forging, the song changed as he worked with the metal, but this time, it had not, remaining the same strong sound that hummed within his mind. It reverberated in him, calling to him. None of the other things that he had created did the same. Why should this be different?

But then, he had chosen this piece of lorcith for the song,

and because it sang to him more loudly than any others. Why *wouldn't* he still hear it?

"It's done."

She stood and took the ring from his hand, holding it up to study it, pursing her lips as she did. She tilted the ring from side to side, making a funny face as she studied it. "Do you even see what it is that you do when you work with the metal?"

He shook his head. "You know I can't see as well as you. Had I more Sight—"

"You'd probably mess it up if you had any Sight," she commented. "You go by feel."

"This one I went with what I saw in my mind."

She set the ring back on his palm, and he left it there, afraid to slip it on. What if it didn't work? What if there was no difference when he wore the piece of lorcith that was attuned to him after forging it? What would he do then? He had placed all of his hope into the possibility he would be able to use the connection to lorcith to create something that would augment his abilities, but if he couldn't, he would have no way to counter even Josun, let alone what his grandfather might do.

Jessa shook her head. "Now you're creating what you *see*? You have an amazing gift, Rsiran." She glanced at the piece of lorcith sitting on the bench, the one that he had found for her. "Are you going to try it?"

"I... I worry it won't work."

"Like the bracelets?"

Rsiran glanced to his wrist. The bracelets were now a constant presence for him, but they were different. They didn't augment anything for him.

Maybe the ring would do the same.

Rsiran slipped the ring onto his finger.

Jessa watched, waiting for a reaction. "Anything?"

He listened for lorcith, but that hadn't changed. Heartstone was the same. "I don't think it did anything. At least not with metal. Maybe it will help me Slide?"

"Do you really need help Sliding? You're already stronger than anyone else as a Slider, and there aren't any others who can Travel."

"Josun is faster than I am and was able to Slide with as much control as me when I faced him. If I were only a little faster..."

"I don't think speed has anything to do with it with Josun. Your problem with him is deeper than that."

"Deeper?"

"I think you're still afraid of him. Which is strange, because you haven't been afraid of much else these days."

"I'm not afraid of him," he said. "He's stronger than me when it comes to Sliding."

Jessa laughed. "If you believe that, then he is. But you've discovered not one but *two* different aspects to your ability. I doubt he has done the same."

"You don't understand. He has the crystal and he's taken an implant—"

"And you're able to do all of those things without needing to rely on either. I think they fear you, Rsiran. You need to remember you're as strong as you are."

He sighed, staring at the ring. It felt strange to wear a ring, but not surprisingly, it was a perfect fit for his middle finger. The metal still had some warmth from the forging and was heavier than he would have expected given its size. The song within the lorcith still hummed, and maybe that was the only thing that would be different for him, but why would he hear the song so loudly if there was nothing else that the ring helped him do?

"Why don't you try mine and see what it does?" Jessa suggested.

Rsiran didn't have anything else he could offer, so he took the lump of lorcith—this one much larger than the one he'd pulled from Ilphaesn for himself—and set it on the coals. As it took on the heat, he readied a hammer, wanting to clear his head.

"Has anything changed for you?" Jessa asked as it heated.

He frowned. "Changed?"

"Since holding the crystal a third time. Has anything changed?"

"I haven't noticed anything. Maybe there's only so much that can change after holding the crystal. I've held one of them twice now."

"The second one wasn't the same, was it? You Traveled to it."

"I still held it. I don't know how to explain it, but when I reached it the second time, I felt more attuned to the metals. This time... this time there wasn't anything like that. Maybe nothing will change for me." He noted the orange glow of the ore and lifted it to the anvil. "Has it for you? Have you noticed anything?"

"No visions, if that's what you're asking. Luthan said that I might become a Seer, but so far, I've had nothing more than vivid dreams, and those were of holding the crystal."

"I'm sorry."

She shrugged. "I didn't expect anything. From what you'd said, I didn't think that I'd even be able to reach the crystals, so to hold one and to see what I did... I think that was the reward." Jessa closed her eyes and took a deep breath. "When I sleep, I can still see it, like I'm there. I wonder if it's the same for Brusus."

"Brusus hasn't said much about what he experienced. Mostly he's afraid that we'll tell Alyse what happened."

Jessa grinned. "I might, especially if he's giving us too much trouble."

"That... that wouldn't be kind."

She shook her head. "No. I suppose it wouldn't. Your sister can be hard at times."

Rsiran lifted a hammer—this one the striker he usually used—and rested it on his shoulder. "I'm just glad I'm not the target for her frustration anymore."

Jessa eyed the hammer and stepped back, giving him space.

Rsiran started, swinging the hammer with a quick stroke, trying to clear his mind. As he worked, he couldn't help but think of the way that Josun had trapped Cael, and what Rsiran would have done were he to take Jessa again. What she needed was a way to protect herself, one that was stouter than bracelets or knives, one that might give her a chance to stay safe, but would the lorcith allow him to create something like that, or was something like that not even possible?

CHAPTER 24

The link necklace fit snuggly around her neck. Rsiran thought it might be too tight, but she claimed it was fairly comfortable. The lorcith necklace connected to the charm that he'd made before, almost as if they had been crafted to go together. She ran her fingers over it as they walked through the streets, and every so often, she'd smile.

"There's something here."

"You said that yesterday," Rsiran noted.

"I don't know how to explain it, but I can feel that this is more than a chain."

When the lorcith guided him into making this chain, one that reminded him far too much of the Elvraeth chain that had trapped him, he had almost stopped, but something compelled him to continue. Now she wore it proudly.

They stopped in the Barth, looking around for signs of danger before settling onto stools that brought back the feeling of the comfort they'd offered long ago. Those days were now gone. Jessa sat across from him and pulled a set of dice from her pocket, shaking them to spill onto the table.

"You need to relax," she said.

Brusus emerged from the kitchen, carrying a tray laden with plates and a few steaming mugs. He smiled when he saw them sitting in the corner, and dropped off his drinks before weaving toward them.

Rsiran grunted. "I don't know if I can relax. Not after what happened last night…"

"It was a mistake, Rsiran. A misunderstanding."

Galen had come to the tavern the night before, sent by Della Rsiran later found out, because she intended for them to work together. Cael was with him, and almost as soon as they arrived, she had tried to Read Jessa and Rsiran, as if she had reason to distrust them after all the help they had provided.

Galen assumed they had attacked Cael when he saw her suffering—the effect caused by her attempting to Read them while they wore the protections of the bracelets. At least now, Rsiran doubted she would attempt doing so again. Considering she had held one of the crystals, her ability to Read would have been powerful, making him thankful for his protections.

When Galen had used one of his poisoned darts on Brusus, thinking him part of the attack, Rsiran had used his lorcith knives to counter him. There had been a fleeting moment when he thought Galen might have killed his friend.

"Use him," Della had suggested afterward. "Galen has skills that we need."

"You want me to use an assassin?"

Rsiran had Slid to Della's, needing to find out if what the

man had claimed about the dart was true and that Brusus wouldn't die from it. Had Haern lived, he would likely have been with them in the Barth, he would have provided the answers they needed, but then, had Haern lived, he likely would have known how to handle Galen better. Della confirmed what Galen claimed about the coxberry poison, and Brusus had recovered quickly.

"You need to use his skills, and the assassin is a part of them."

"Why should I trust him?" Rsiran had asked.

"Because I do."

"I don't even know where he should start."

Della had closed her eyes. "Asador. There is something there I cannot fully See. I don't understand what has changed."

"Why Asador?"

"Because Josun Elvraeth is there."

Since Della suggested he use Galen, he'd "hired" the assassin to go after Josun. It freed Rsiran to focus on the rest of Venass, and on finding the crystal, but more than that, it got Galen out of the city. His presence in Elaeavn risked the peace he intended to form between the council and the guilds.

"Della says we can trust him," Brusus said.

"I know what Della says," Rsiran told him. "That doesn't make it easier."

"If you go after Josun, it draws you away from the city. That's dangerous, Rsiran, especially as we know that he'd probably only try to drag you to Danis. And this way, someone else can do the digging, see if he can come up with answers."

Rsiran had to admit that it was easier for Galen to search

than for him. He'd started him in Asador, but only because he didn't know where else to go. What he needed was more information.

"You look like you just heard three cats fighting," Brusus said.

"He wants to go searching for information," Jessa said. "He doesn't like the idea that we're trusting Galen to search while he remains here."

"Galen isn't the only one who searches," Brusus reminded her.

"I know," Jessa said. "And he doesn't like that, either. He thinks he should be the one bouncing all over the countryside trying to find where Josun might have disappeared."

"I know where he's gone," Rsiran said.

As soon as he'd learned that Josun had disappeared with the crystal, he had suspected that he'd taken it to Thyr. Even though the one time that he'd Traveled to Thyr, he'd had no sense of the crystal, nothing that suggested that Josun might be there. But until he could confine Josun—and recover the crystal—he couldn't abandon Elaeavn and go after Danis. Each step had to follow the one before. The delay was maddening.

"You don't know that he's in Thyr. Luthan can't See Thyr, but he can't See Asador, either," Jessa reminded.

Rsiran lifted the dice and shook them. They landed a pair of ones; most considered that unlucky. "I can still get in and out faster than most."

"And we can't risk you, not with the unpredictability of Venass," Brusus said.

He leaned on the table, holding the tray to the side. It was good for Brusus to feel a part of the coming fight, even if his greatest battles these days were waged with Alyse about what ale to serve. But Brusus didn't really understand the stakes, not as he once had. Rsiran wondered if he ever *really* understood the stakes. Though his intentions were always the best, and he always sought to protect them all, he had risked them interacting with Josun without knowing that Josun sought to serve the Forgotten, and before they had any idea about Venass.

Jessa rested her hand on his arm. "How else do you want to search for Josun?"

Rsiran shook his head. How else *could* he search for him? He'd Traveled, but hadn't found any sign of him. If Rsiran could figure out how to track the heartstone implanted in Josun, he might be able to detect him, but he hadn't managed to hold that focus long enough while fighting him, not enough for him to be able to use it to detect him once more.

He'd done it with Amin, and he'd removed the implant from the other Hjan they'd captured, but they had both used lorcith, not heartstone. But was there something about the heartstone they used that he could track?

"What is it?" Jessa asked.

"A thought. Nothing more at this point."

"That sounds dangerous," Brusus said, smiling. "You get something in your head, and usually it means that you put yourself in danger."

"If we can stop Venass, isn't that worth it?"

"Didn't say that it wasn't worth it, only that I've been through this with you, Rsiran. I wish I had Haern's ability to

See what might come. I miss that—not as much as I miss the man, but still miss it."

"Haern could never See me easily," Rsiran said.

"No, but he could See around you. There was value in that was well." Brusus took a deep breath and clasped Rsiran on the shoulder. "Just… just be careful, will you?"

"I'll try."

Rsiran stood and reached for Jessa's hand. She pocketed the dice and stood, studying the tavern a moment, as if seeing it for the last time. When she clasped his hand, he Slid.

He emerged in the depths of the Forgotten Palace, the strange walls of lorcith pressing around him. Jessa stayed near him, gripping his hand tightly.

"Why here?" she asked.

"I need to know if there's something with the metal they use that I can follow."

"I thought that you said you lose the connection when it's placed beneath the skin."

He nodded, starting toward the cell. "It conceals it. The sense of lorcith—or heartstone—is still there, but I can't connect to it the same way. It's like implanting it prevents me from connecting to it the way I would if it weren't inside someone."

Jessa held her wrist up, nodding to the bracelet. Bluish white light glowed softly, giving more than enough light for him. "Can you connect to this?"

"It's not under the skin."

"Maybe not, but the effect is the same. You told me that. Can you connect to it?"

Rsiran listened for the metal and felt it pulling on him softly. He'd rarely used the bracelets to follow since forging them for Jessa, but wasn't surprised when he focused on them and found that he *could* track them. "I forged those, Jessa. That creates more connection than anything else."

"What about this?" She touched her new lorcith-chain necklace around her neck.

Studying the necklace, he noted that it didn't glow the same way that the bracelets did. There was the soft white light from lorcith, and the charm glowed, as well, but it seemed muted. He focused on the necklace, trying to pull on the connection... but failed.

He'd forged it, he should be able to use it, but he couldn't even *pull* on it. It was similar to what he noted with those from Venass and their implants, only Rsiran hadn't expected that something he had created would refuse him like this.

"What is it?" Jessa asked.

"Not what I expected. It's there... I can see the glow, and I'm aware of the lorcith, but I can't use the potential."

"Like with Venass."

"Like with Venass," he agreed. He looked around at the walls of the strange undulating lorcith that Venass or the Forgotten had placed here. "Maybe it has more to do with where we are than anything about the necklace." Hadn't he been able to *pull* on it before they came here? He couldn't remember, but thought that he had.

"See if you can overcome it."

"This isn't the best place to try to overcome something in the metal, especially if it's on your neck."

She pressed on a clasp around the back, releasing it from her neck. "What about now?"

The sense of lorcith surged with it off her. He *pulled*, able to use the connection once more. Why should it matter if it was around her neck? The bracelets weren't like that... but then, the bracelets hadn't been designed with the same intent. He'd asked the lorcith to help him create something that would augment Jessa's abilities to keep her safe. That meant that *she* would be attuned to the potential within it, not him.

"Why should I be able to detect it now?" he asked.

Jessa took the necklace and secured it around her neck once more. "You can practice with me. See if you can figure out a way to overcome what resists you."

They stopped at the cell. Only one guard stood outside, a Slider name Mara. She wore a pair of short swords strapped to her waist, and nodded as he approached. "Guildlord," Mara said. "Valn thought you might return for him."

"How is he?" Rsiran asked.

"Valn or your prisoner?"

Rsiran chuckled. "Valn probably isn't any different from when I saw him last, so I guess I should say the prisoner."

"Quiet. Since you were here last, he's been quiet."

Rsiran Slid through the door, leaving Jessa behind as he appeared on the other side. The Hjan sat in a corner and barely looked up as he entered. His hair had a greasy appearance, and a thick shadow of a beard formed on his face. The cell stank.

"Have you returned to torment me again?" the Hjan asked.

"I didn't torment you the last time."

"No? You tear from me the gifts—"

"I tore nothing from you. It remains in your head."

The Hjan grunted. "Remains but is nothing. Everything that I gained is gone."

This man was no threat. Not the way he had been before Rsiran had twisted his implant. He was broken, no longer the danger he once had been. Should Rsiran even keep him confined like this anymore or would it be kinder to release him?

"Why have you come then, if not to taunt me?" the man asked.

"To learn about the implants the Hjan use."

The man looked up with squinted eyes. For a moment, Rsiran thought he might try to attack, but then he sank back to the wall, resting his head against the lorcith. "Talk to the forgers."

"Forgers?"

The Hjan's mouth curled into a slight smile and then tapped the side of his head. "I didn't place this here myself, Lareth."

"Where are your forgers?"

"You might be skilled, Lareth, but I doubt that even you can face our forgers. There is a reason they are exalted among Venass. When they free me, I will see to it they repair what you've done. Then I will come after you—"

Rsiran didn't wait for him to finish and Slid to the other side of the wall.

"What is it?" Jessa asked. "Did you discover anything you can use?"

He sighed. "I found answers, but none I wanted."

"What answers then?"

"Only that Josun and Danis might not be the only people I need to worry about."

How would he find these forgers if he couldn't even find Josun? How would he ever defeat Danis if he couldn't reach them?

CHAPTER 25

Wind gusted through the Aisl more briskly than usual. Rsiran Slid into Della's hut and found it empty. The hearth glowed with a soft heat, and the two chairs sitting near it reminded him of her home in Elaeavn. Unlike others who had come to the Aisl, Della had made her small home something more permanent. More and more followed, but she had been the first.

The door opened and she entered. Wind stirred up the coals, and she shut it quickly before the fire could flare.

Rsiran turned to see her adjusting her striped shawl. A few gray hairs hung wildly around her head, and she smoothed them down as she tottered to the table that held her collection of herbs.

"You don't intend to return," he said. He hadn't asked why she remained in the Aisl, thinking that it had something to do with the project she had been researching while here, but what if that wasn't the case at all? What if Della intended to remain in Aisl?

"I think my time in the city has come to a close," she said. "There is more for me to learn here."

"What do you think you can learn?"

She closed her eyes and took a deep breath. "There is history in this place, Rsiran. I can feel it. And when I look, I can See it."

Rsiran stood across the table from her and watched as she mixed a few spices together, stirring them with a long fingernail. She tipped the mixture into a cup of water and brought it to the hearth where she set it, leaving the cup on the coals to heat.

"There is something like a memory here. I don't know how to explain it any other way, but here... here there is our story, that of our people before we went to Elaeavn, leaving the trees for the shore."

"Can Luthan See it?"

She shook her head. "Luthan's gift works a different way. Following his Saenr, he was granted greater vision, allowing him to See what others could not. Mine has never been my strength."

"You're a skilled Seer."

She nodded. "Skill is not the same as strength. Luthan has both. I have skill, but not the strength. Here... at the heart of our ancient home, my skill changes, allowing me to See in ways I could not in Elaeavn." She took her cup off the coals and turned to him, sipping it carefully. "When I look back, I can see the first clans, watch as they founded their home here. If I stare long enough, I think I can even See the time they left the Aisl, when they went to the shores and founded Elaeavn."

"Is it difficult to look back like that?" Rsiran thought about what it was like when he Traveled. Sliding didn't weaken him the same way anymore, but Traveling still did. Would it be the same for Della with these visions?

"There is always difficulty in spending too much time looking back and not enough looking forward. It becomes easy to lose yourself in the past. That is the risk, and I force myself to pull away from that, though it is not always possible."

"But if you stay here—"

"Remaining in the Aisl gives me the chance to continue to learn. There are others with the strength and skill to look forward and to See what might come, but there aren't many willing to look back. Once I leave here, I'm not certain I will have the same capability."

"You'll be missed in Elaeavn."

"You can always find me here, Rsiran. Besides, this is the true home of our people. Before there ever was an Elaeavn, and before there ever were the Elvraeth, we had the Aisl. Perhaps it is only right that at least some of us return." She took a seat and motioned for him to join her on one of the other chairs. "That is not why you came here, though."

Rsiran shook his head. "I went to the Forgotten Palace."

"Where you keep your prison."

"There are cells there, but I don't know that I'd call it a prison."

Della took a drink of her tea and breathed out through the steam. "What else would you call it, Rsiran? They were built to hold you—or one like you—and now you use them to hold the Hjan."

"I wanted to know if there was anything that I could learn about the metal they used. The man I have detained told me to talk to the *forgers*."

Della nodded. "How else did you think that Venass managed to create not only the implants, but the shadowsteel devices?"

"I thought my father was involved, or the other smiths they abducted, but the way he spoke made it seem like these forgers are valued, like they wanted to be a part of Venass."

"It is unfortunate that we lost Josun Elvraeth. He would have answers. Perhaps not all that you wanted, but answers, nonetheless."

"Do you think Galen can find him?"

"Galen is skilled, but I'm not certain he will be able to capture him." She glanced at him. "That's what you asked him to do, isn't it?"

Rsiran sighed. "Galen is an assassin, Della. I asked him to do what he trained to do."

"You haven't learned anything about Galen. He might serve as assassin, but the man is much more than that. He could be an ally, but you choose to use him like a tool."

Rsiran clasped his hands together in his lap. "What would you have me do? By taking him from Ilphaesn, I've already put the peace between the council and the guilds at risk." It was already a tenuous peace. Until Rsiran returned the crystal, it would not hold.

"Work with him. There is much he can do to help. We may have lost Haern, but Galen might have answers even Haern

242 | D.K. HOLMBERG

would not have been able to obtain." Rsiran leaned back in the chair, and Della smiled. "Don't pretend you don't have some way of tracking him. I believe that you've taken to slipping your lorcith coins into other's possession?" She pulled a small piece of lorcith from her pocket and held it out to the light. The coin glowed softly, not as much as a larger piece of metal might, and one Rsiran hadn't realized she knew he'd given her.

"You knew?"

Della chuckled. "Of course I knew."

"After you disappeared when Danis attacked the city..."

"I don't disagree with placing a way for you to find me. Any of us you might care about, really. I presume you did the same with Galen?"

Rsiran nodded. The coin he'd used with Galen had a hint of heartstone worked into it, enough that Rsiran could detect it from a distance. He didn't want to risk not finding him again, especially if Galen somehow managed to find Josun.

"That is good. I can See that you need to find him," she said.

"When?"

"Soon."

"Do you See Josun?"

"He is a Slider, much like you. I See nothing when it comes to him. Luthan doesn't, either, so there would be no point asking him."

"Luthan can See something when it comes to me."

"When he focuses on those around you. It is the same for me, Rsiran, but that doesn't paint a very clear picture and requires that I know who might be with you. With Josun

Elvraeth, I don't know who else might be with him. I don't know who else to attempt to See."

"What do you See with Galen?"

Della leaned her head against the back of the chair. "With Galen, I See that he risks himself once more and that he is in danger. Besides, I believe you have overlooked a potential ally."

"You already told me that I needed to find a way to work with Galen." Rsiran wasn't sure how he felt about working with him, especially without Haern. Would it be too hard and make him think of his friend too often? But Galen had skills they could use, especially as they faced others of Venass. He had nearly defeated Rsiran once, so it was possible Galen would be able to stop Josun… or maybe he could even help incapacitate Danis.

"This is not about Galen. This is about others who might be interested in working with Elaeavn."

He frowned. "Who?"

Della leaned forward, fixing him with a heated stare. "The same allies you took Galen to see." When he frowned, she went on. "From what I can See, it's time for you to return to him."

CHAPTER 26

Rsiran emerged from his Slide in Asador, making a point of appearing near the docks, not wanting to draw attention to himself. This was the same place he'd brought Galen when he'd Slid him to Asador, at least near enough he should be able to detect him.

Standing in the street, with the dark night overhead and the steady lapping of waves against the shore, it was enough to almost make him think he was back in Elaeavn. He checked the knives he'd brought with him, wanting to have an adequate supply in case he did find Josun, and checked the heartstone alloy chain he'd brought as well. This was one of his own creations, slightly different from the Elvraeth chains Josun had used on him, but ones that might be strong enough to hold Josun. Testing them himself, they didn't prevent him from Sliding, but as Jessa had reminded him, he *was* a more skilled Slider than Josun. At least, he hoped that was still true.

The city was alive in ways that Elaeavn was no longer.

There was the hum of activity along the docks that mixed with the waves, a crowd of people wandering the streets, music that drifted from open doors of taverns, loud enough he could hear it easily from where he stood on the street. Tall buildings loomed above the streets, creating shadows he suspected Carth would have appreciated. The occasional cry of gulls swooping overhead pierced the night.

Rsiran focused on lorcith and heartstone. Within Asador, there were hundreds of items made out of lorcith, but fewer of heartstone. That was the reason he'd chosen to plant a coin with a hint of that metal on Galen. Along with his connection to the metal, he thought that he should be able to detect the heartstone, or possibly even the lorcith knives that he'd given Josun.

There came a flicker of lorcith somewhere nearby.

Rsiran readied a pair of knives and Slid.

When he emerged, he noted shadowed figures outside what appeared to be a tavern. One of them turned toward him, lorcith sword blazing from beneath a cloak. The shadow flickered.

Sliding.

Rsiran *pushed* on his knives, catching one of them in the leg and continuing to *push* until he fell. If they *weren't* Hjan, he would see them healed and apologize later. If they *were* Hjan, then he'd be thankful that they were incapacitated and unable to chase him.

Once the man was down, he Slid to him. Even in the light from the thin crescent moon, Rsiran could tell that the man had deep green eyes and a jagged scar along his cheek.

He *pulled* on the lorcith sword, sending it sailing across the street and out of reach. He didn't know how much the other would be able to *pull* on it, but he wasn't willing to risk one of them having control over the metal the same way he did. He struck the man on the top of his head, knocking him out.

Another shadow appeared, separating from the darkness. The moonlight cast a faint glow upon a woman's skin. She approached cautiously, appearing only as he knelt over the unconscious man.

Rsiran had never known Venass to use women, but it didn't surprise him that they would shift their tactics, especially now that he had started coming after them.

"You won't succeed," she said. She had a hint of an accent, and eyes that weren't green at all, possibly a faint blue, though it was difficult to tell in the night.

"I disagree," Rsiran said.

He grabbed her and the man and Slid them to the cell within the Forgotten Palace, separating them. Rsiran paused long enough to focus on the man's implant, and *pushed*, deforming it as he had the Hjan who was still in the nearby cell. When finished, he Slid to the woman but didn't find an implant on her.

He hadn't been able to find an implant on Danis, but that didn't mean he didn't have one. He *had* to have some way to augment his ability.

"Who are you?" he demanded.

She watched him with anger flaring in her eyes. "This will not hold me," she said.

"I will take away your power, one by one if I have to."

"Better to kill us all rather than risking us coming after you." She stood with her arms crossed and glared at him.

Rsiran waited for her to lunge and attack, but she made no effort to do so. "You're not even of Elaeavn. Why do you support them?" he asked. He kept knives ready in case he needed to attack, but she simply stood.

"Support? I came only for death."

"Then you'll stay here, wishing for death."

Her eyes flashed with anger. "I think you're mistaken."

"I understand enough."

She smiled darkly. As she did, Rsiran realized the temperature in the cell began to climb. The wall behind her took on a soft glow, the song within the lorcith shifted.

"What are you doing?" Rsiran demanded.

"Demonstrating how little you know, Elvraeth."

Rsiran laughed bitterly. "If you think that I'm Elvraeth, then you're the one who knows little."

Heat continued to rise. The wall began to bulge. If Rsiran did nothing, the cell would fail.

He *pushed* on one of his knives. As he did, it began to glow, and slowed before reaching her, falling harmlessly to the ground.

"You will fail—"

Rsiran *pushed* on three knives with more effort than he normally would, and sent them streaking toward her, no longer interested in trying to keep her alive. Why did it have to come to killing?

Two began to glow as they streaked toward her. The third struck her in the chest.

As it did, the heat dropped quickly. The wall began to cool. A smile formed on her face.

Blood pulsed from her chest and congealed quickly. He considered whether he should check on the other captive, but that man had been Elaeavn born. Sliding back to Asador, he paused on the street outside the building he'd nearly entered.

What were they protecting and were there others?

Rsiran Slid around the street, searching for the possibility that he might find more of the Hjan. When he didn't encounter any others, he paused, and looked up and down the street.

There came another flicker of lorcith, this time from within the building.

He readied his remaining knives and Slid across the doorway.

Rsiran almost froze.

Josun was bound to a wall, his head hanging low. A few others lay unmoving on the ground near him. Galen turned toward him, a dart held lightly in his hand. His eyes widened at Rsiran's sudden appearance.

How had Galen succeeded when Rsiran could not?

Rsiran quickly cut Josun free from the wall and slapped the cuffs and chain he'd forged onto his wrists. Josun didn't move. "What did you use to catch him?" Rsiran asked.

"Slithca."

His mouth twisted in an expression of disgust, thinking of how slithca had once been used on him. He remembered all too well the way that it had poisoned him, preventing him from Sliding, all so the Forgotten could Read him.

But used on Josun... that might have been the only way that Galen could stop him.

He scanned the room, noting the dark-haired woman near the back. Not Cael, and not of Elaeavn from the color of her eyes, or the low cut to her dress.

Maybe he didn't know Galen at all.

A dark smile pulled on the corners of Rsiran's mouth. "A foul thing, but probably necessary for him."

Galen nodded toward the cuffs that Rsiran had forged, still clutching the dart in his hand. "Those will hold him?"

"They'll hold most Sliders."

"Most?"

"They won't hold me."

Rsiran started to Slide, ready to carry Josun to the cells, when Galen called after him, "What are you going to do with him?"

He paused and glanced over his shoulder at Galen. He *should* kill him and be done, but he already knew he wouldn't. "I haven't decided. But he'll answer for what he did."

Rsiran Slid.

He emerged within the Forgotten Palace. Lorcith flared against him, pulsing with a steady rhythm that had changed since he'd been there only moments before.

Rsiran looked down the hall. A body lay unmoving outside the cells. He dragged Josun with him, and checked.

Mara.

Her neck was slit.

The door to the cells was open, and Rsiran glanced into each, finding them empty. Even the woman was gone.

What had happened here?

Josun started to stir, and he dragged him into one of the cells. The palace might not be safe for holding him, but he could use the lorcith in the walls to reduce the suppression that prevented him from reaching the implant. Rsiran focused on the heartstone implanted in Josun's head. With the lorcith in the walls, he reached it and began to *push* and *pull*, slowly deforming it. Now that he had done it several times, changing it was easier.

The metal began to pry free, slowly moving away from Josun's mind, separating from him. Rsiran debated cutting through his skin and prying the metal free, but that wouldn't do anything more than what he did changing the implant.

Then a thought occurred to him. Was there a way to change it so that it could help them?

Rsiran focused on the metal, listening to the soft song of the lorcith.

He began to push, folding it in a way that resonated with him, not with Josun. Rsiran wished that he knew *what* this did, but he trusted the heartstone to work with him, much as he trusted lorcith to work with him. Listening to the song of the metal allowed him to coax it into a shape that would do what he needed.

Josun screamed suddenly, and his body thrashed.

Rsiran continued *pushing*, not sure what effect this had on Josun—and not wanting him killed—not yet, not while there was still so much for them to learn from him.

The song shifted, the indication that he was done.

Rsiran stopped *pushing*.

Heat started building.

He'd felt it before, and didn't hesitate, Sliding free from the cell, dragging Josun with him.

Outside the cell, three people faced the door. They looked different from others he'd seen. Could these be the forgers he'd heard about? Somehow, the woman he thought he'd killed stood in the lead.

Rsiran *pushed* on his knives.

Two struck, and the Hjan fell.

The woman turned. Her face seemed to glow, her dark eyes flashing in anger. "You were mistaken not finishing this, Elvraeth."

"You won't take him back alive."

"Do you think that I want him alive?"

Rsiran hesitated. "You don't?"

"That bastard attacked me, and thought to do other things to me," she said, touching the side of her face. "Why would I want to let him live?"

"You're not with Venass?"

Her face soured. "Venass," she spat, saying the word with a strange accent to it. "The Hjan seek only darkness and death. That is what they brought to my country when they attacked."

"What country is that?"

"Nyaesh."

Rsiran hadn't heard of Nyaesh, but if there were others like this woman, others who could control the temperature around them... they would be a powerful resource fighting Venass.

Unless even they hadn't managed to stop Venass.

Why else would this woman be here, if not for the fact that Venass had destroyed her home, and her people?

"Release him, Elvraeth, and I might let you live."

Rsiran glanced to Josun. "I can't do that. He's hurt too many I care about too often. And he's stolen something I must recover."

"I'm sorry, Elvraeth, I must see him dead. Only then can I return home."

With that, she attacked.

Considering that he'd thought her dead only a short time before, she moved with more speed that he would have believed possible for someone without obvious enhancements. How had he managed to stop her the first time?

Rsiran Slid, dragging Josun with him so she couldn't get to him and kill him before he got answers about Danis and the crystal. Ironic that he wanted nothing more than to kill Josun, but here he was trying to save him.

The hall grew hotter, the lorcith in the walls starting to glow with a bright orange light.

The woman had found a pair of swords, and swung them toward him with as much control as any Neelish sellsword.

He emerged briefly from one of his Slides. "We could work together against Venass," he said.

The woman struck, piercing his shoulder. Rsiran winced and paused in between Slides long enough to draw on the power from the Elder Trees before returning.

"You're a fool, Elvraeth, if you think I'll work with you." She almost cut him again, this time coming dangerously close to his neck.

Rsiran jerked back just in time. He doubted that even the Elder Trees would be able to heal him if he were harmed like that.

What he needed was some way to confine her, but she'd already shown that she could escape one of the cells. But those were designed to hold *him*, would he be able to do anything that could hold *her*?

The glowing lorcith along the walls gave him an idea.

Pulling on the metal, he began to curve it around her. As he did, he pressed into the lorcith, changing it enough that it raised the temperature required to soften the metal. Doing this required adding grindl and iron to the composition, and he discovered that pulling the lorcith over the stone, he picked up enough of both to add to the alloy he created. The metal continued to fold around her, creating a cage of sorts. If she could Slide, she'd be able to escape. If not, then he hoped the magical heat she generated would be trapped within.

Rsiran took a step back, letting out a tired breath.

Pulling on as much metal as he did here required more effort than he'd used in a while. Next to him, Josun started writhing. Rsiran wished he had asked Galen to dose him again before he'd slid to the Forgotten Palace.

Josun's eyes flashed open. He glanced toward the metal barricade Rsiran had created, and down to his wrists. "What did you do?"

"Quiet!" Rsiran said. "Or I'll let her have you."

Josun tried Sliding.

Rsiran *saw* it.

How would he be aware when someone else Slid?

There were colors that started to swirl before stopping, thwarted by the cuffs Rsiran had placed on him.

Heat pressed against him, rising from behind the metal cage. Even with the addition of grindl and iron, the barricade began to glow. Rsiran doubted that it would hold for much longer.

"Time for me to leave," Rsiran said. "She's after you, anyway."

Josun looked to the glowing lorcith, his eyes wide. "You wouldn't leave me to her, Lareth."

At least he admitted that he knew the woman. "Give me a reason to take you to safety."

Josun shook his head. "I'll tell you what you want to know about your grandfather. Not that it will do you any good."

"Not only him. The crystal. I need to know what happened with the crystal."

Josun's face clouded. "I don't have it."

"Not good enough."

"It will have to be. I brought it from Elaeavn to Asador, and *they* took it from me."

"Who? Galen?"

Josun's face contorted. "Galen didn't take anything. That fool is too stupid to know what he got himself into."

"That fool managed to capture you." Rsiran glanced to the lorcith spiraling around the woman. Much longer and the heat would cause the metal to buckle and fold, and then he'd have to deal with her. He didn't fear her—he could Slide from here if needed—but he didn't want to kill her again, not until he understood why she wanted Josun. "Time is running out, Josun. Who has the crystal?"

He stared at the wall of glowing lorcith before finally shaking his head. "The Forgotten. That's who has it."

"The Forgotten are no more. When I killed Evaelyn, the rest scattered."

"Scattered. The rest of *that* group joined Venass. But that's not who I mean. There were others who had chosen not to organize, who had wanted nothing more than to live out their lives in peace. They have the crystal."

"Why would they get involved if they wanted only to live out their lives in peace?"

"They were given a choice."

The lorcith barricade began to sag. "What kind of choice?"

"Work with Venass or…" He shrugged.

Rsiran's temper flared. "That's not much of a choice."

"Most were going to side with Venass, but then they learned about the crystal. Now they have it." Josun turned his attention back to the lorcith that now started to flow toward the ground. The energy and heat required to melt that much lorcith was enormous, and this woman managed to generate it by herself?

"What do they intend to do with it?" Rsiran asked.

Josun shrugged. "It doesn't matter. Venass won't let them keep it."

"Where is it?" Rsiran asked.

Josun shook his head.

"Fine. Good luck with that," Rsiran said, nodding toward where the top of the woman's head was becoming visible over the sagging metal from the barricade.

Josun's eyes widened again. "You'll never learn what happened to the crystal if you leave."

"I'm not the only one looking. I think you've already discov-ered how talented Galen can be. And there are others as well."

Josun closed his eyes, shaking his head. "Asador," Josun said. "They are in Asador. But you won't be fast enough, not now that Venass knows where it is as well."

Rsiran considered leaving Josun to the flame woman, but grabbed the cuffs and angrily Slid him away. As he did, he had the briefest image of her face fully appearing from behind the lorcith before it sank completely to the ground.

CHAPTER 27

As Rsiran emerged in the heart of the Aisl Forest, Josun kicked a moment before settling, his eyes taking in the massive sjihn trees, and tension fading from his arms. Rsiran watched as Josun noted the row of huts along the edge of the clearing, and the structures in the trees overhead, those that housed dozens of people choosing exile from the city.

"You're a fool, Lareth."

"Maybe," Rsiran said. "But I have you, don't I?"

"Do you really think that you can hold me here? Once I'm free—"

Rsiran tapped him on his forehead. "Feel your implant, Josun. What does it tell you?"

Josun's eyes narrowed. "What did you do? You couldn't have removed it, or I would have died."

"You can believe that if you want, but know that I have more control over heartstone than even the Venass forgers can understand." He hoped that was true. The way the muscles in Josun's face twitched, Rsiran knew he'd hit on the right concern for Josun. He'd thought the fire woman one of the forgers, and with the control she had over heat, it would make sense, but he believed that she wanted to oppose Venass.

"You—"

Jessa didn't let Josun finish. She ran over to Rsiran, saw Josun, and punched him in the face, leaving him with a bloody lip. "That's for nearly killing Rsiran."

Josun licked the blood off his top lip. "You have a harder punch than your man."

"He caught you again," Jessa said. "Rsiran will always catch you."

Josun grinned at Rsiran. "You mean *Lorst*, don't you? Wasn't that the name you chose when you played at assassin?"

"I found you, didn't I?" Rsiran asked.

"Luck, Lareth. That is all it is."

"Why do you feel so certain it was luck? Haven't I proven I have different skills than you do? Different from any that Venass understands?"

Josun smiled at him, a dark expression that made Rsiran want to throw him back in the cave within Ilphaesn where he would be trapped. Maybe this time, he would leave him without food or water.

"You've proven that you don't have the stomach to do what's needed, Lareth. You've shown time and again that you're not willing to do what's needed."

"I've done what was needed to protect those I care about."

"Like with Haern?" Josun's smile spread more widely across

his face. "Ah, see? You still mourn him, when you should be seeking revenge."

"Revenge won't change what happened."

"It might change what's to come," Josun said. "Or do you believe you can do what is necessary when your grandfather attacks next?"

"I'll do what I have to do," he said, but even as he did, a part of him wondered if he could. How many times had he been given the chance to confront Danis, and how many times had he failed? His grandfather had proven not only more capable than Rsiran, but cleverer, and able to find new ways to overcome Rsiran's natural ability.

"You will fail. I can see that now. A shame, really. You've proven yourself more interesting than I would have expected."

Jessa took a knife and slammed it into the back of Josun's head. He crumpled without another word. She sheathed her knife with a quick flourish. "What are you doing bringing him here?"

"The Forgotten Palace is compromised."

"Compromised?"

"Can you get Della? I'll stay here with him, but I need to ask her a few questions."

Jessa glanced at Josun before nodding and hurrying off toward Della's hut.

Rsiran stared at Josun. The heartstone implant under the skin of his face thrummed in Rsiran's mind, but with something like a steady song, not painfully as before he had managed to change it. He didn't know *what* he had done to Josun's implant, only that it no longer augmented him the same way.

A shadow appeared from between two of the massive sjihn trees. Luthan wore a long robe, and his slippered feet barely made a sound as he approached. "You caught him," he noted, studying Josun.

"I wasn't the one who managed to capture him, but he's caught."

"Galen?"

Rsiran nodded.

"A skilled man. A valuable ally, don't you think?"

"What do you See from him?"

Luthan shrugged. "From him?" he motioned toward Josun. "I See about as much as I can manage when I try to See you. I believe that the two of you share an ability that obscures you."

"Not Josun." He hesitated. "Did you know him? When he lived in Elaeavn, did you know Josun?"

Luthan shook his head. "There are many Elvraeth who live in the palace, Rsiran. It is difficult to know them all. The council interacts with many but not all of them."

"You didn't think it strange you weren't able to See some of the Elvraeth who live in the palace?"

"The Elvraeth are descended from the ancient clans, no differently than you. But they have been given access to the crystals for years, where as the rest of the population has not."

"What does that mean?"

"The Elvraeth are concealed for the most part. It is not all that surprising or strange for me to not See anything when it comes to the Elvraeth within the palace."

Rsiran had thought it came from the ability to Slide, but then, Josun had been wrong about that ability, and was probably wrong about the Elvraeth trying to remove it. One of the first clans possessed the ability, an Elder ability, not Elvraeth, and it would have been protected by them.

"What of Galen? Can you see anything about him?"

"If I knew Galen, it's possible I would be able to See something. You'll have to ask Della, especially as she knows him much better than I."

"Josun claims the Forgotten now have the crystal."

Luthan frowned. "I thought you said the Forgotten were eliminated when you removed Evaelyn Elvraeth."

"I thought so as well. These are Forgotten who had chosen to remain neutral, but Venass pulled them back, forcing them to choose a side."

Luthan's brow furrowed, and his eyes flickered to the side, flaring a brighter green for a moment. He stood unmoving, not changing his posture even as Della and Jessa joined them.

"What happened?" Jessa asked.

"He Sees," Della said.

She waited, hands clasped behind her back, ignoring the fact that Josun lay motionless on the ground and bound in heartstone chains.

Finally, Luthan opened his eyes.

"They have it," he whispered.

"Who?" Della asked.

Luthan blinked, shaking his head. "Lareth told me that the Forgotten have claimed the crystal."

Della nodded knowingly. "You were able to find it?"

Luthan nodded. "I do not know where it is, but I know who has claimed it."

"It's in Asador," Rsiran said. He kicked at Josun. "At least, that's what he claims, and I have no reason to doubt that is true."

"Then you must return to Asador, Rsiran. You must go for the crystal."

"Who has it?" Jessa asked.

A troubled look passed over Luthan's face. "Someone I have not seen for many years, but someone I cared very much for."

"No…" Della shook her head, closing her eyes. They opened in a flash, and she met his gaze. "We can't tell him that we've found her. After everything that he's been through, this will only pull him back in. I have been pleased he removed himself from everything."

"Who?" Jessa pressed.

"It's Brusus," Rsiran said, making the connection. That would be the only person that Della would be concerned about discovering one of the Forgotten. He turned to Luthan. "But who is his mother to you?"

The Barth was relatively quiet today. A lutist played in the background, the soft sound doing nothing to fill the gloom of the tavern. In the few times that Rsiran had been to the Barth since returning from the Aisl, he had found it similarly somber.

The fire burning in the hearth gave the tavern a sense of warmth, but not the same way it normally did. The lorcith sculpture of the sjihn tree that Luca had forged rested on the mantle. Rsiran still didn't understand the power the sculpture possessed, but there was *something* to it.

Jessa sat next to him on the stool, her hands resting on the table, and her eyes staring straight ahead. "Can't believe we're this concerned about telling Brusus."

"Della is right," Rsiran said. "When we tell him about his mother, how is that going to affect him? Does it draw him back into a fight that he's essentially abandoned?"

Jessa bit her lip and didn't say anything.

Alyse appeared from the kitchen carrying a plate for a man sitting in the corner near the hearth and set it down in front of him. She noted Rsiran and Jessa and nodded before making her way toward them.

When she reached their table, she glanced from Jessa to Rsiran. "What's wrong?" she asked.

Rsiran shook his head. "It's nothing."

Alyse crossed her arms over her chest. "I can tell when something is bothering you, Rsiran! Is this about the tavern? Something about grandfather? Tell me!"

"Neither," he said. "It's about Brusus."

Her brow furrowed and she placed her hands on her hips. "What is it about Brusus?"

"We think we know where to find his mother."

Her hands slipped off her hips. "Oh."

The door to the kitchen opened again and Brusus strode out, a wide smile splayed on his face. He greeted the few people in the tavern, and even paused to nod to the lutist, whispering something that only he could hear before heading toward

Rsiran and Jessa. "About time you got back here. Rumor has it that you caught Josun."

"I didn't catch him. Galen did."

"Ah, don't sell yourself short, Rsiran. Galen may have slowed him, but you caught him." He leaned on the table. "Did Galen tell you *how* he stopped Josun?"

"Slithca."

Brusus sucked in a breath and then whistled softly. "Do you think he learned that from Della, or did he pick it up from Isander?"

"I don't know. Either way, it doesn't matter. He stopped Josun."

Brusus nodded. "And a good thing. We have the crystal then?"

Rsiran shook his head. "That's actually why I'm here."

Brusus grinned. "You want a few mugs of ale to forget about it for a while?" Seeing Rsiran's face, his smile faded. "Not here to forget about it then. Something you learned affects me, doesn't it?"

Rsiran took a deep breath. "It does. Brusus, I—"

"You found her didn't you?" When Rsiran didn't answer, he shook his head. "Where is she?"

Rsiran swallowed, looking to Jessa for support. Both of them knew how much Brusus had wanted to find his mother, and that it had been the reason he had spent so much time trying to find the Forgotten in the first place. Now, they finally had word of her, and Brusus wanted to know.

"Rsiran, if you know anything about her, please... don't keep it from me. You don't understand how long I've searched for answers. I still don't even know what she did to warrant exile."

"Asador," Rsiran said. "That's where she is. Josun told us that the Forgotten who hadn't chosen a side before were forced by Venass to choose. That's why she's there."

"And the crystal?"

Rsiran nodded. "She has it. Luthan saw it and realized that." Rsiran hesitated. "There's more, Brusus."

"More than my mother? What more can there be?"

"It's about Luthan. He knew your mother before her exile."

Brusus shrugged. "Many would have. She was Elvraeth, and fairly highborn from what I've managed to learn. I haven't learned anything about my father... unless you're telling me that it's Luthan." He said the last with a grin. "Though I can't imagine Luthan ever young enough to take a wife."

"He's not your father."

"I know that, Rsiran. Had it been one of the council, I would have learned."

"Luthan... he's not your father. He's your grandfather."

CHAPTER 28

The Slide carried Brusus to the Aisl, and Rsiran left him. He didn't want to be a part of the meeting. That was something private, something that should be between only Brusus and Luthan. Rsiran could easily imagine the questions Brusus had, questions like how Luthan had abandoned his daughter, or how long he had known that Brusus lived in the city, or whether he had any role in his mother's exile in the first place.

Rsiran had other things he needed to do, anyway. In addition to preparing for a return to Asador—and he wanted to forge knives of both lorcith and heartstone before he did—there was someone he needed to see.

Jessa refused to leave him, and Rsiran wasn't about to return to the Floating Palace alone. Now that Haern was gone, and with Brusus trying to understand his heritage, who else *could* he bring? The obvious answer would be someone from the guild—maybe Valn or even Sarah, someone he'd grown to trust enough to watch him while in the palace, but would either of them want to keep him as safe as Jessa would? And if he left her behind, he knew he'd suffer her anger.

The Slide back to Elaeavn took them into the palace. They emerged in a long hall with the lanterns glowing softly around him. He squeezed Jessa's hand reassuringly. "This leads to the council chamber," he whispered.

"It's strange, you know?" she said. "Coming here like this, when I'm *not* afraid of getting caught."

Rsiran sniffed. "I'm still a little afraid of that."

"But you're the guildlord."

"It doesn't mean anything to the Elvraeth, and certainly not to the council. They fear the threat to their authority more than anything. They see the guilds as competing for the rule of the city."

Rsiran pushed open the door to the council hall, and found it empty. He hadn't really expected to find Naelm there, but had hoped he'd have chanced upon a council meeting. Rsiran needed them to understand he didn't intend to drop the issue of joining the council. As much as the idea of sitting on the council didn't appeal to him, there was a need for him, one that came from the same place that needed him to settle the strife in the city once the battle with Venass was over.

He Slid with Jessa, this time emerging on one of the upper levels where he'd found Naelm the last time. The outer chamber was empty, but Rsiran noted the movement of lorcith behind the door. Was that Naelm, or was that something else?

He Slid, pulling Jessa with him, and emerged on the other side.

Naelm stood from where he sat behind a narrow table as Rsiran emerged, and the bracelets on his wrists surged with a hint of cold before it faded. "Lareth."

Rsiran tilted his head. "I apologize for the intrusion. I doubted you'd see me otherwise."

"Do you think I'll agree to meet with you now, after you forced yourself into my room?"

"I seem to recall I could have let you die when last here."

Naelm frowned. He reached for his pocket, and Rsiran prepared for the possibility he would need to Slide, but he only detected steel knives on him.

"You promised that you'd return the crystal," Naelm said. "You haven't lived up to that side of the bargain."

"Recovering the crystal is taking longer than anticipated," Rsiran agreed, "but I'm close to getting it back." He stepped to the side, searching for the lorcith he'd detected, but there was none. What had he detected before coming into the room? "Your daughter Cael returned to Elaeavn."

"You will not speak her name, Lareth."

Rsiran frowned. "Why? Did you exile her as well?"

Naelm shook his head. "She returned with a man the council had exiled and thought she would force us to reconsider."

"He saved her life."

"What do you know about it?"

Rsiran smiled. "More than you, I suspect." He didn't want to tell Naelm that Lorst had been hired to kill Cael, along with Galen. That would only give the Elvraeth councilor more ammunition against him, and he had enough as it was. "And then you sentenced Galen to serve in the mines."

"He's lucky to live," Naelm said.

Rsiran shook his head. "You still think in such absolutes, don't you? The man who brought your daughter back to Elaeavn—"

Naelm pounded his fist on the table. "A man who had been punished by this council before!"

"For what?" He leaned toward Naelm, anger rising in him. Jessa pulled on his arm and he resisted. "What was the crime that earned Galen his exile? Do you even remember?"

Naelm glared at him. "Is this why you have come to me, Lareth? Do you wish to argue? I have already agreed to your terms. Find the damn crystal, and I will see you sit on the council."

"I have found the crystal. And I have found Josun Elvraeth." He watched Naelm as he said it. The slight twitch at the corner of his eyes made it clear that he recognized the name. "Did you know he went to serve the Forgotten, and then when they fell, he went to Venass?"

"He chose his path."

"Because his sister was exiled. Because the council ripped apart his family. When will the council realize they are responsible for many of the horrors that have befallen the city? When will the council realize it is partly their fault so much has been lost?"

"Nothing has been lost because of the council. We protect—"

"Your power," Rsiran said. "That is all that you protect."

"The Elvraeth protect the people, Lareth. We are the only ones able to reach the ancient crystals. Without the Elvraeth, there would be no connection to the Great Watcher."

Rsiran glanced to Jessa, wondering if she would ever begin manifesting any additional abilities. She had now held the crystal, but so had Brusus, and Rsiran wasn't sure that he had begun showing any signs of them, either.

"Tell me, Naelm, what would you say if I suggested that any within Elaeavn could hold one of the crystals?"

Naelm's face reddened. "I would say you know nothing about them. You might have managed to hold one, Lareth, but that doesn't mean that you understand them, not the way the council does. We have protected them, and seen they are attended, for generations."

Rsiran sighed. "Too long, I think."

"Even if you join the council," he began, and the tone of his voice made it clear he didn't think Rsiran should be allowed onto the council, even if he recovered the missing crystal, "you are one voice."

"Luthan would get a vote."

"And you know how the old one will vote? What about when he passes, are you so certain that you know how the next will vote?"

Rsiran watched Naelm. Arguing would get him nowhere. He wondered if Naelm already had a plan to prevent him from reaching the council when he did bring the crystal back. Could he have something in mind for preventing what he'd agreed to?

Probably. As one of the Elvraeth, he would want to maintain his power, and wouldn't want to risk losing it, especially not to someone like Rsiran, a man he saw as less than the Elvraeth.

What had Rsiran hoped to achieve by coming here?

He had wanted to know whether Naelm would undermine him. Did he have the answer?

"I'll tell Cael you send your regards when I see her next."

Naelm clenched his fist and seemed as if he might hit the table again. "You have seen her?"

"I've seen her."

"Where? She must be in the city. She cannot remain away from the palace for much longer. She has responsibilities here."

Rsiran snorted. "That's not up to me. And I don't think it's up to you, either. Cael is old enough to make her own choices."

"She has sided with the exiles!"

"And that's a problem for you?" Rsiran asked. "Those outcasts might be the only reason we manage to recover the crystal. They might be the only thing between us and what Venass intends to use it for."

"And what is that?" Naelm asked.

Rsiran shook his head. "I don't know, but whatever it is, they intend to draw away the power within the crystal. I suspect they will drain it completely. Then the crystal will be lost forever."

"You're the guildlord. You know that cannot happen!"

"Why do you think I continue to fight?" Rsiran asked.

Naelm watched him intently for a few moments. "What is it that you want, Lareth?"

He didn't know if Naelm would care about the real reason he'd come to the palace, but he had to ask. For any plan to work, they would need the council to help. "If it comes to fighting, will you help?"

Naelm's eyes narrowed. "Do your duty as guildlord. Find the crystal. Then let the Elvraeth worry about the rest."

Rsiran opened his mouth to object, but decided against it. He watched Naelm for a moment before reaching for Jessa and Sliding away.

Emerging in his smithy, Rsiran sighed deeply, staring at the lorcith piled along one of the walls. "The council is part of the problem," he said. "Even if we stop Venass, that doesn't change anything with the council."

"We do what we can," Jessa said.

Rsiran didn't know if that was all they would need to do. There had to be more to it. Somehow, when all of this was over, it had to be about more than simply stopping Venass, about more than opening the crystals to the people, and even about more than the people getting sent to the mines or fearing exile from the city. With the rule of the Elvraeth, how were the people any different from those inside places like Thyr or Eban, places where they were forced to serve?

They had to provide freedom, but would anyone even want that kind of freedom?

Rsiran hadn't known he needed it until meeting Brusus. Before then, he thought the Elvraeth ruled because they should. Others would have thought the same. But they didn't rule because they should, they ruled because no one had ever thought to challenge them. No one had ever questioned whether they *should* rule.

"First the crystal," Jessa said.

"Then the Elder Tree."

"The tree?"

"The crystals will never be safe with the tree damaged," he said. "So when we find the crystal, then we have to restore the tree. Only then can I face the rest of Venass."

"Do you know what you'll do yet?"

"By that, you mean whether I think we'll have to slaughter all of Venass?"

"Slaughter is a loaded term, Rsiran. They've attacked us, and those we have cared about."

"How many have been Compelled like Amin?"

Jessa shook her head. "And how many are like the man you kept in the cell?"

Rsiran turned away. Jessa knew he didn't have an answer to that, just as he didn't have an answer about what had happened to those men. Had the woman attacked them? Rsiran had forged the lorcith implants, preventing them from using them, so he wasn't sure how he felt about the possibility that they had been killed. "They weren't a threat there."

"Not then, but they weren't Compelled, either."

"I don't know that. I didn't have a chance to bring them to Della."

"I can't say I feel bad for them or for what happened to them. They would have done the same to you, or worse, if given the chance."

Rsiran glanced at the lorcith and came to a quick decision.

He Slid, carrying them to the Forgotten Palace.

The tunnel smelled of burned lorcith. Amazingly, the wall of rolled lorcith still carried some of the heat from what the woman had done, though now, it was nothing more than a pool of slowly hardening lorcith.

"Why here?" Jessa asked.

"If we're going to take Brusus to Asador," he started, thinking of what they had promised to Brusus and wondering if that was the right decision, "I need to know more about why *she* was there."

"You said she wanted to attack Venass."

"She did, but I don't know anything about her. She would have killed me if she could in order to get to Josun."

"I know the feeling."

"Look at this, Jessa," he said. "Look at what this one woman could do. What if I encounter her again?"

"You can Slide away."

"What if I can't?"

"Why wouldn't you be able to get away? What prison has worked to hold you?" She squeezed his hand. "I know you fear the way that first Josun, and then Venass trapped you, but you've always managed to escape. I don't think there's anything that can hold you."

"That's not what worries me," he said. And it was true. There had been a time when he had been more concerned about whether Josun or Venass would come up with some new way to hold him, but his ability with Sliding was different from what others managed. Even the cell designed for him hadn't managed to hold him in place. Shadowsteel might have been effective, but Rsiran had destroyed their source for that, leaving them without even that secret.

"What is it, then?"

"If I need to reach Danis and she's there." He shook his head.

"Whatever else happens, I need to see this ended. We can't keep at this anymore."

"Then send her at him. If she wants to see Venass destroyed, as well, then use her."

He stopped in front of the pool of melted lorcith that had peeled free of the walls, leaving bare rock. The pressure upon him from the lorcith that had once been here was no longer. Now there was only the strange, almost sorrowful sense from the lorcith. It hummed to him, the song disappointed. Heat radiated up from it, and Rsiran *pushed*, smoothing it out. It was the only thing he could really do for the lorcith.

Could he use the woman? Were there others like her?

If he managed to find the crystal, that would be one of the next things he'd have to determine. Somehow, they needed to find allies, even if they were as dangerous as this woman had been. Maybe *especially* if they were as dangerous as she was.

Rsiran took Jessa's hand and Slid her back to Elaeavn.

CHAPTER 29

W hen Alyse came to see him, Rsiran wondered what was wrong.

She found him in the Aisl as he made preparations to leave for Asador. Luthan claimed the crystal remained safe, but for how much longer? If they didn't act, they ran the risk of Venass managing to secure the crystal before they could. So far, Luthan's visions told them that the Forgotten—and Brusus's mother in particular—still had the crystal.

"Rsiran," she said, catching his attention.

He looked up from where he stood near the open-air forge, choosing this place rather than his smithy in the city with the hope that his forgings might connect him to the Elder Trees. The other smiths working nearby had given him space, leaving him to work alone. Rsiran had tried to ignore their watching eyes as he worked, feeling slightly awkward at the way they studied him as he hammered at the lorcith, but the longer he hammered, forming the dozen knives now splayed out along the table, the more he fell into a rhythm and was able to ignore them.

"Alyse," he said. She wore a long dress, more formal than he would have expected for the forest, and held her hands in front of her, fidgeting. "You left the tavern?" The walk would have taken several hours, unless one of the Sliders had brought her here, but the sheen of sweat on her face made that less likely.

"I need you to do something for me."

He set the hammer down, resting it along the wide stump that served as an anvil. "If I can."

She thrust her jaw forward, but her hands remained clenched together. "I... I want to help Brusus."

"We all do. That's why we're planning this trip to Asador. Once I get these knives ready—"

"That's not what I mean," she said, glancing to the row of knives. "I want to go with you."

Rsiran shook his head. "That's not the best idea, Alyse. You don't know what you'll be facing. These people—especially Danis if he appears—they're dangerous. You saw the way he used our mother and the way he had her use Father."

"That's why I need to go. I *know* how dangerous they are. Brusus... he thinks he'll be fine, that he can go with you as you Slide in"—Rsiran noted the slight edge to the way she said "slide," letting him know that she still wasn't *quite* comfortable with that ability—"and then disappear. But I know how much he's wanted to find his mother, how much he's wanted to learn what happened to his father. I know what he'll do to get that chance. I need to go with him."

Rsiran wiped his hands on the leather apron that he wore.

Since working in the Aisl smithy—that was what the masters had come to call it—he had begun wearing the leather apron, something he did not when working in his smithy in Elaeavn. The weight felt right, especially here, and the pockets had been useful now that he didn't have a place for the usual tools he liked.

"I don't think that's a good idea," Rsiran said. "And I'm sure Brusus wouldn't, either." She started to open her mouth, and Rsiran stepped forward, touching her on the shoulder. "Brusus wasn't always a tavern owner," he said. "The skills he had when I first met him made him more dangerous. And you know his background. He has abilities I don't even fully understand. That at least gives him a way to defend himself."

"I can defend myself."

"Alyse—this isn't like Elaeavn. You haven't been outside of the city before. You don't know what it's like." He lowered his voice, glancing toward the massive sjihn tree near the edge of the clearing where Jessa sat. She looked up, almost as if she knew what he was thinking. "There are men outside the city who take women from Elaeavn. They use them. They're forced into—"

"I know all about what they're forced into." Alyse took a deep breath, and a flush rose in her cheeks.

Rsiran realized that he might be *too* protective of his sister, especially given what he'd seen her go through, and what he had rescued her from. She probably *did* know what women from Elaeavn were often forced into.

"Brusus isn't a fighter anymore. He's changed. You know

that he has, or you would have used him more in your plans before now."

Rsiran swallowed. "I know he's changed. That's why I hated even telling him what we discovered. I know Brusus. Maybe not as well as you do now"—her cheeks flushed even redder —"but I know him. I knew what his reaction would be when we discovered where his mother might be. Like you, I don't want him to go, but I can't keep him from this."

"You can't keep me from this, either."

"Yes, I can. You're my sister, Alyse. I can just choose not to Slide you with me."

"And I'm his betrothed!"

Rsiran blinked. "You're his *what?*"

Alyse fingered the fabric of her dress and looked at the ground. "We didn't get a chance to tell you together. We wanted to. When you came to the tavern that night… that was when we were going to, but you came with word of his mother, and… and it changed everything."

"How? When?"

Alyse looked up. "You don't think he should marry me?"

Rsiran smiled and hugged his sister, trying not to think of how long it had been since she'd let him get close. She stiffened with the hug, but relaxed the longer he held her. "I think it's wonderful," he whispered. "Brusus is… well, he's Brusus. He will treat you well, and I can see the way he looks at you, so I know how much he cares. Does Father know?" he asked, releasing the hug.

"That was the other reason I came today."

Rsiran nodded and reached for her hand. "I'm sure he'll be proud of you."

"Are you? Even knowing Brusus's past? It doesn't matter to me, but—"

"Any more, I don't think it will matter to him. I think he's only wanted you happy, too. And if he can't see that you *are* happy, then you'll just have to ignore him." He released her hand and stepped away. Alyse smiled and looked around the clearing, searching the smiths for signs of their father. He was one of the smiths who had remained here in the Aisl when others had returned to the city. Rsiran didn't know why, but it was a question he hadn't yet asked. "You haven't told me how he asked you."

She smiled. "He took me to the top of the Barth. There's a balcony there where we stood, looking out at the city, and he asked me. It was... lovely." She finished in a whisper.

Rsiran smiled, thinking of Brusus asking his sister. Once, it would have seemed impossible to believe that his sister would marry a former thief like Brusus, or even that she would be such a part of Rsiran's life, but he was thankful she had come back to him.

"I'm sure it was."

She met his eyes. "You see why I have to go with him? I need to be there. I've seen too much already... more than enough to know something could happen to him. I can't say my being there would protect him, but you have to let me come."

Rsiran glanced at the knives lined up along the ground. If Alyse came with them, it would be another person he'd have to worry about, one more person's safety he'd have to worry about, but wouldn't one more person help? If they encountered Venass, wouldn't it be useful to have others with him who he trusted?

And maybe there was another way for her to help. "If I do this, if I let you come, there's something that I will have to do first."

Alyse nodded quickly. "Whatever it takes."

"And there is something you will have to do."

She frowned as he told her what he needed, but the frown faded, and a resolute expression crossed her face. "Whatever it takes," she repeated.

———

After Alyse shared her news with their father—Rsiran had left Alyse alone with their father to share the news privately—she rejoined him near the Aisl smithy. He couldn't tell from her expression how their father had received the news of her engagement. The determined lines around her eyes could just as well be due to what they planned to do now, rather than anything that their father might have said to her.

"Are you ready?" he asked.

Alyse nodded. "Do you think this will work?"

"You're my sister, which means you share the blood of the smiths and that of the Elvraeth. There's a reason that Danis thought you were the one that he could use." It was why Rsiran had to see if taking her to the crystals would work as well. The more people who held them, the more likely it was that they would succeed.

"I'll never let him use me," she said with intensity.

"I know that." There had been a time when he thought that Alyse would side with their mother, a time when he had feared that she worked with her willingly. But Rsiran had learned that their father had attempted to protect her by giving her the gift of a lorcith charm that would provide protection. "You'll want these," he said, handing her a pair of bracelets that he'd forged while she spoke with their father.

The forging of the bracelets came more easily for him now that he'd made several of them. As he had with Jessa, Brusus, and Haern, he had focused on the connection to the metal, and tried to keep the desire at the forefront of his mind as he worked. Rsiran wasn't surprised that Alyse's bracelets were much like his, the band of heartstone running through them almost matching the ones that he wore. Even when he held them—they were too tight for his wrists to wear—they gave an echoing sort of sense.

Her eyes glanced toward his wrists as she pulled them on. "I thought you said the necklace Father made would protect me." She pulled that necklace from beneath the collar of her dress. It caught the light, but had a soft glow to it as well.

"It will protect you to a certain extent, but these will keep powerful Readers and Compellers from reaching you."

Alyse nodded.

"Are you ready?"

"I think I have to be."

"You don't have to do this, Alyse. You could choose to stay here. The forest will protect you, and Brusus wouldn't be upset." He'd probably be happier if Alyse stayed behind. Rsiran didn't look forward to telling Brusus what he'd done, but then, Alyse was her own woman—she had always been strong—and if Brusus didn't understand that, then they had other issues to work through.

"I don't have to. I want to."

Rsiran Slid with her, emerging in a place somewhere beneath them.

The four crystals glowed with a soft bluish light, slightly dimmer than it had been before.

That realization worried him. Did it mean that the crystals were tied to the trees, and with the loss of one of the Elder Trees, the others failed... or did the crystals need to remain together in order to maintain their strength?

That was a question for another time. For now, he needed to learn if Alyse could hold one of the crystals.

"They're beautiful," she said.

"They are. The first time I came here, I didn't know what I would find. I knew that Venass and the Forgotten were after something, but I couldn't learn what it was. The second time I came, I nearly died." He walked with her as she made a steady circuit around the crystals. The fifth location, where the missing crystal *should* be, had only a twisted platform of dark wood. Rsiran didn't know if it was the root of one of the Elder Trees, or if a long ago craftsman had created the platforms. "You might not be able to hold any of them," he reminded her. "The Elvraeth, during their ceremony, don't all get the chance to hold one of the crystals. Most will never reach them."

"I understand. But even to be given this chance..."

"I've said I think everyone should be given the chance," Rsiran said.

"You're not afraid of what will happen if the wrong person reaches them?"

Rsiran shrugged. "The Elvraeth have had control over the crystals for generations. Centuries. Have all of those they sent here been the right people?"

"The Elvraeth were given the crystals by the Great Watcher," Alyse said.

"You're falling into the trap they want you to believe. They need for the rest of Elaeavn to believe they were destined to rule, but that wasn't the case at all. The ancient clans found the crystals, even if they couldn't use them at the time. That's why the guilds have protected them all these years."

"Maybe I shouldn't be here, then," Alyse said. "If this is supposed to be a place of the Elvraeth—"

Rsiran touched her arm. "You're descended from the Elvraeth, Alyse. You cannot forget that. And I'm the guildlord. So I guess even in bringing you here, we're still satisfying the conventions set all those years ago."

Alyse smiled. She continued to make a steady circuit around the crystals. "How will I know if there will be one that I can hold?"

"It calls to you," he said. "When I first held one, it was like... it was like the crystal *wanted* me to hold it."

"What happened then?"

"I sat by the Great Watcher."

Alyse shot him a frown. "Don't play games with me, Rsiran. Not here, and not when I'm risking myself like this."

"No games. When I held the crystal, it felt like I was sitting next to the Great Watcher."

"And then you became more powerful?"

"Has Brusus?"

Alyse tipped her head to the side as she frowned. "Well... no."

"I don't know when the change takes place. Mine was gradual. I didn't realize at the time, but I was able to see the potential in lorcith and then heartstone. I'm not Sighted, but that ability has provided me with more protection than Sight ever could, and it suited me better than Sight. With it, I can go to the mines, and I can *see* where the lorcith is, where before I could hear it, and feel it. That potential is the same as what the alchemists possess, but in some ways, what I'm able to do is even more powerful than that."

"I thought you said the crystals unlocked the gifts of the Great Watcher? Elvraeth gifts?"

Rsiran shook his head. "I don't have any abilities like that. I never have. Mine are all descended from the earliest clans. Smith, sliding, alchemist, miner, and even thenar."

"I don't understand any of this," Alyse said. "I thought you said the ancient clans couldn't hold the crystals?"

"From what Della told me, they couldn't."

"But you're basically like one of the ancient clans, aren't you? If you have no abilities of the Great Watcher, that means you're like... like the Elders. How is it that you've been able to hold the crystals?"

Rsiran had given it some thought but still didn't have an answer. Alyse was right—he *shouldn't* be able to hold the crystals. Mostly because he was more like one of the ancient clan leaders than like the Elvraeth. "I think that it has to do with Danis. We're descended not only from the smiths, but from the Elvraeth. That bloodline gave me the ability, I think. Without it, I don't know if I would be able to hold the crystals."

"Have you tried it with others of the guilds?"

"Not yet. Jessa and Brusus were the first. And now you."

Alyse stopped in front of one of the crystals. "I don't feel called to any of them. This isn't working for me." She didn't keep the disappointment from her voice, and Rsiran couldn't blame her. He felt the same disappointment. He had *wanted* her to be able to reach one of the crystals, if only to see whether it would unlock something inside her, the same way that it unlocked something for him. "There's nothing like what you describe, only the way this one seems to pulse a little brighter."

Rsiran Slid next to her. When he emerged, he saw it pulsing as well.

Why should he see it again?

"Reach for it," he said.

"Rsiran?"

"That's the call from the crystal. You need to reach for it."

Alyse started to, but then pulled her hand back. As she did, the pulsing started to fade.

Rsiran grabbed her hand, and stretched with her. "You need to do this, Alyse. Let me help."

Then together, they touched the crystal.

CHAPTER 30

D arkness surged around them. Rsiran was aware of his sister, but in more of a spiritual sense, not physical. In some ways, it was like he Traveled, carried along with her.

They seemed to float, hovering above everything. Rsiran felt power all around him, but it was weakened in some way, incomplete. It took him a moment to realize he detected the missing Elder Tree, and that was the reason the power was not what it should be.

Rsiran turned to his sister and found her as nothing more than an insubstantial form, like a wisp of light, similar to what he detected from the Elder Trees. He glanced at his hands, and noted that he appeared in the same way, nothing more than his spirit, his body left with the crystals.

Had it been like this the last time he'd held one of the crystals?

Rsiran hadn't been aware of his body any of the other times, but didn't think that it had.

"What happened?" Alyse's question came without sound, but somehow he heard it. "What is this?"

"This is like Traveling. This is the crystal."

"What happened to us? How are you here?"

"I don't know. I shouldn't be able to touch the crystal a fourth time." Which one had he yet to touch? The missing one? Had he touched each of the four crystals that remain? What might it mean if he had?

"This doesn't feel like we're sitting next to the Great Watcher," she said.

"This is different from the other times that I've reached the crystal."

"How?"

"The other times, I was alone."

They continued to move, drawn away from the sense of the Elder Trees, leaving the brightness of the light glowing from them behind as they stretched higher into the darkness. Rsiran felt the pull of power from the Elder Trees, and wished that he could restore the damaged tree, but even Della didn't know if that were possible.

The farther that he drifted, the more everything seemed like a distant glow far below. After a while, even the sense of his sister began to fade into nothingness.

He was alone. Blackness surrounded him, a darkness so absolute that it terrified him.

Rsiran tried *pulling* on the sense of the Elder Trees, wanting to draw himself back toward his body, but he had never been in control while holding the crystals.

Where was the sense of the Great Watcher?

There was no answer.

Had something happened?

Rsiran could imagine Venass coming up with a way to destroy the Great Watcher, finding some way to sap that ancient power, but how could you capture and destroy a god?

Then, slowly, there came a presence.

At first, it was faint, but the presence came nearer. As it approached, Rsiran felt it as an overwhelming power. Had he a body, he would have shivered, though had he a body, he would have cowered in fear from it.

A vision flashed in his mind.

Rsiran saw the crystal returned, and the Elder Tree restored. In that vision, the people of Elaeavn lived in the city or the forest, a part of the same, connected in ways that the ancients had not been. Then there had been the clans, and later the Elvraeth. In this vision, there were both.

The vision faded, leaving him in darkness again.

The presence remained, heavy and overwhelming.

Another vision followed. This was different, a surge of darkness, even blacker than before. In this vision, Rsiran knew the Elder Trees were gone and the crystals had flickered out. There was no power that he knew remaining, everything had disappeared in this vision. Other powers appeared, almost as if battling to overwhelm each other.

In many ways, it was more terrifying than the presence that he detected.

The vision faded.

"Is that what will happen if Venass succeeds?"

He asked the question in the same way he had spoken to his

sister, using the connection that felt as if it shouldn't exist, almost a question within his mind.

There was no answer.

Had he expected the Great Watcher to answer him?

"What of the others?" Rsiran asked. He formed an image in his mind, that of the woman he'd thought he'd killed who had used the power of fire to escape. "How do she and her kind fit in with what you have created?"

There came no answer.

"Help me to understand!"

The presence *pulled* on him.

Rsiran had no other way to describe it. The darkness parted, and flashes of light flickered into existence below him. He saw white—that of lorcith, he suspected—and blue—heartstone—mixed with green and silver and gold and orange. Countless splashes of light below him. He still felt the presence near him, but it didn't frighten him in the same way. This was a reassuring sense, one that left him feeling as if he and his people were looked after.

As he stood above everything, an even greater presence throbbed against him, this time distantly.

Rsiran tried to turn, but he was restrained, as if the Great Watcher didn't want him to move.

He tried to focus on the greater presence that he detected, and another vision appeared, nothing more than a flash.

This one was difficult to put words to. A man—or perhaps, something more than a man—watching over the land, guiding it when needed, but mostly observing. Five other beings—some greater than the others—were arrayed behind the nearest. The

Great Watcher, Rsiran suspected. Somehow, the Great Watcher oversaw the others.

The vision faded.

As it did, Rsiran thought that he understood.

There were others like the Great Watcher.

He wanted to return, to get away from the sense of power, the presence he felt behind him, but the Great Watcher held him in place.

"Why show this to me?" Rsiran asked.

He didn't expect any answer.

Rsiran remained, and the colors below shifted, growing brighter, slowly melding together, like metals in an alloy. He felt that he neared the ground, the presence—the Great Watcher— slowly pushing him back until the bright light of the Elder Trees surrounded him.

Now as he stood among them, he felt the discord, the disconnect, that came from the missing Elder Tree. He felt an urgency to restore it, and realized that he *had* to restore it.

"How?"

Rsiran was pushed deeper, back toward the crystals, but still not into his body. He floated, almost as if Traveling, and saw the crystals beneath him. They flashed, each of them pulsing, and the steady pulsing of light gradually grew stronger until he felt almost as if he were pulsing with it. As he did, he realized he had, indeed, touched each of the crystals here. The only one that he hadn't held was the crystal that wasn't here.

What would happen if he managed to reach that crystal?

He wished that he had looked around when floating from above to see if he could find the missing crystal. If he could see it, he could Slide to it. Instead, he had to rely on what Luthan Saw, and hope that they were able to find it.

The sense of the presence near him pressed even harder against him, this time forcing him down toward the crystals. Toward the center of the ring. Each time before when he'd come to the crystals, he had stood outside of them.

Did the Great Watcher *want* him to stand in the middle of the crystals?

What would happen if he did?

Slowly, Rsiran settled, surrounded by the crystals.

With another flash, a vision so brief he couldn't track what he was seeing, he was back in his body.

Rsiran jerked his hand back.

Alyse still stood next to him, her hand gripping the crystal where he'd forced her to touch. She trembled slightly, and her eyes were open, but rolled back in her head.

He waited, knowing that he couldn't do anything to disturb her while she was holding the crystal. What did she see while holding it? Had she been made aware of the Great Watcher? Would she return changed, able to use abilities that she had not before?

She started to tremble harder.

Rsiran reached for her then, not wanting the same thing to happen to her as happened to Brusus, fearing that she would start convulsing as he had.

When he touched her hand, she settled.

Light streaked from him and arced between the remaining crystals before fading.

Alyse staggered back with a gasp. "Rsiran?" she asked. "What happened?"

The light from the crystals began to fade. When they had first arrived, he thought that they had seemed dimmer than before, but now it was clear that they were.

"I don't know," he answered. Alyse didn't need to know about the visions he'd experienced while touching the crystal, or about the presence that he'd felt behind him, the presence that made him think of the Great Watcher, but also something else that was there, that seemed to be tied to the crystals.

Regardless of what happened, he knew what he needed to do now more than ever. After the visions that he'd had, he recognized the need to recover the crystal. If he didn't, more was at stake than he had previously believed; all of the crystals could be lost.

If that happened... he feared the darkness he saw in his vision.

CHAPTER 31

The landscape outside of Asador had an undulating quality, rolling from a gentle hillside as it swept toward the sea. The air here carried with it a hint of filth, the stink of the city that reached far beyond its walls. Clouds obscuring the nearly full moon spoke of rain, as did the distant rolling of thunder and the occasional flicker of lightning in the sky.

Rsiran stood with Brusus. Jessa and Alyse remained behind for now. This was only to be a chance to scope out where they would go, not to see his mother or recover the crystal or attack Venass were they to appear.

"I wish you hadn't let her reach the crystals," Brusus said.

Since returning, Brusus had been silent about the fact that Rsiran had taken his sister to the crystal chamber. Rsiran hadn't told Della or Luthan that *he* had touched another one, worrying about what that might mean. If he managed to reach the missing crystal, and if he managed to hold it, what would happen—other than the fact that he would become the first person in Elvraeth memory to have touched each of the crystals?

"She needed to. We share the same bloodline, only she has abilities of the Great Watcher, unlike me," Rsiran said. A ribbon of smoke rose in the distance, but Rsiran couldn't tell if it came from within the city or outside. The city was too far away for him to easily tell. "And... well, it's Alyse."

Brusus breathed out and shook his head with a laugh. "I know how your sister can be. The stubbornness. The way that she gets something in her head and thinks she has the right of it, but this?" He pointed to Asador. "She's never left the city, Rsiran."

"Neither had I before all of this started."

"You had ways to protect yourself."

"Because I can Slide? She has Sight, and she's a Reader, and the Great Watcher knows what else she'll be able to do now that she's touched that crystal."

"Maybe nothing," Brusus said.

"Has anything changed for you?"

"Not that I can tell. I've always had strength with my abilities, but..." He shrugged, but Rsiran could tell that it bothered him that he wasn't able to do *more* now that he'd held one of the crystals.

"Like I told Alyse, it took time for me to realize that my connections changed."

There was another concern that Rsiran had, one that he feared *might* be tied to it. What if all the crystals had to be together for something to change?

If that was how they worked, what would happen to Rsiran

when they were brought back together? Yet, he didn't understand why that would matter. Why would it matter if all the crystals remained together for their influence?

Did Venass understand they might need to be together to be effective?

He'd given up hoping that Venass might have overlooked something. With Danis—and the other "scholars" of Venass—he suspected they had thought through all the angles. If so, then what else would they do?

Rsiran suspected they would somehow drain the crystal of its power, and if it *was* connected to the others, then they ran the risk of Venass managing to drain *all* the crystals having only acquired one.

That gave even more urgency to finding the crystal.

"You don't really think she should come with us to Asador," Brusus said.

Rsiran shook his head. "I don't, but since she told me about your other piece of news..."

Brusus sighed. "Look, I'm sorry I wasn't the one to tell you."

Rsiran smiled. "You don't have to apologize for anything. I'm happy for you and Alyse."

His friend flushed slightly, noticeable even in the rising darkness. "I'll tell you, after what happened with Lianna, I didn't think that I'd let myself get close again, but Alyse... she's so *strong*. I think that's what I like best about her." He looked at Rsiran, meeting his eyes. "Which is what worries me with her, too. Sometimes, she doesn't recognize when it doesn't make sense to get involved. I worry that with this, she's stepping into something bigger than she knows."

"I feel the same when it comes to Jessa."

Brusus grinned. "With Jessa, you know that she's strong enough to handle whatever comes. And you know that with her Sight and training as a sneak, she's a lot less likely to get into trouble than most."

"It doesn't make it any easier," Rsiran said.

Brusus let out a sigh. "No. I suppose it doesn't." He surveyed the city lit up in the distance. "What now? We came to scout because you said it would be too hard for you to Slide us all at the same time." He shot Rsiran a sideways glance. "You think we can figure out where the crystal might be?"

"Figure it out, claim it, and return it."

"All of that?"

"That's my intent."

"What of the others."

"If it comes to more than sneaking in and claiming the crystal, we'll involve the others."

"Your sister isn't going to like that you left her behind."

Rsiran shook his head. "Neither will Jessa, but going with a larger group is more likely to get us caught. Better that just you and I move in, swiftly and quietly. Better chance that we get back out."

Brusus nodded. "What do you need from me?"

"For now, just watch me."

Rsiran sat on the hillside overlooking Asador. From here, he could Travel, and it wouldn't require as much strength, not nearly what it would take if he were to Travel all the way from the Aisl, or from Elaeavn. He didn't know if what he planned would even work, but he had to try. Would he be able to somehow *feel* the connection to the crystal from here? Now that he had held the others, he thought that he should be able to find it, but if he was wrong, it meant that he would have to search a different way. It might mean involving Jessa and his sister as they wanted, bringing Luthan with him so that they could use his visions to find it.

It would be simpler if his connection to the crystals would allow him to find it.

His hand fell to the hilt of the sword he'd forged at the Aisl smithy that connected him to the Elder Trees. As he did, he separated from his body and Traveled.

The connection took him above his body. He stayed there for a moment, looking at Brusus and himself. Brusus looked so much wearier than he had when Rsiran had first met him. Though he had willingly chosen to come, this was not a fight that he relished. His posture revealed his anxiety, and the darting glances as he studied the night told Rsiran that he was much less comfortable with these missions than he once had been.

It was a mistake to have brought Brusus, just as it would be a mistake to bring his sister. Jessa would be better equipped—she hadn't stopped fighting alongside him—but even she didn't need to be out here.

This was a fight he should take on alone.

If he could recover the crystal, the connection would return. He would then restore the Elder Tree—if he could find the way. And then he would defeat Danis. He was the real threat. Once he was gone, the rest of Venass wouldn't be easy to hunt down, but it would be *easier*.

In this insubstantial form, it was all so clear to him in a way that it wasn't when he remained in his body.

He could Slide Brusus back to the Aisl, and return in this form, but he still needed someone to watch over him while he Traveled. Without that, he feared any of Venass finding him, stabbing a knife through him or slitting his throat, injuries that he doubted he'd easily recover from, even with the Elder Trees helping.

Focusing on Asador, he Traveled.

Rsiran hovered above the city. In this way, he felt more like he had when he held one of the crystals, looking down at the city splayed out below. Even Traveling, he could feel the connection of lorcith and heartstone, and wondered if he could use it while Traveling. Doubtful, at least not without a body to *pull* or *push* from. There came a sense of lorcith and heartstone flickering, and he focused on that, realizing it meant Sliding and Venass.

How many could he detect?

As he focused, he realized it was dozens.

They flickered, moving quickly through the city, but why would Venass Slide so aggressively?

The same reason that he Slid.

Venass had discovered the crystal in Asador.

Rsiran had known they would. They were too well connected, too smart, not to learn where it was. Did they know that he'd captured Josun as well?

He couldn't worry about what Venass might do. If he found the crystal first, he could remove it and return it to the Aisl, but doing so required that he force himself away from the sense of the flickering lorcith.

Was there another way he might find it?

Without Luthan, and someone Sighted as he was, he needed another connection to find the crystal... one that already existed within the city.

Rsiran focused on the coin that he'd placed on Galen.

Finding it was easier than reaching for connections with Venass. The coin didn't move and flicker like the sense from Venass did.

Once he discovered it, he Traveled there.

Rsiran appeared inside a tight passageway. Galen was there, tall and lean and wearing a heavy leather overcoat that hung to the floor. Cael was there, as well, wearing a dirty brown dress that brushed the floor. Her dark hair was tied behind her neck, and as he appeared, she looked up.

"There's someone here," she said.

Galen stood and swept his gaze around the passageway, a pair of darts clutched in his hands. Rsiran noted that he had a gash on his forehead that had been stitched closed. "I don't see anyone."

"Not see," Cael said. "This is... this isn't anything like I've felt before."

She could tell that he was here, the same way that Danis could tell. What was it about Traveling that revealed him to them? With Sliding, he'd learned to *pull* himself along to avoid detection and influence from those with the ability, but Traveling didn't have a similar technique, or if it did, he wasn't skilled enough yet to know how to do it.

"Where?" Galen said.

Cael walked toward Rsiran and practically stood in front of him, as if he were there in physical form. "I can almost Read whoever it is," she noted. "But it's like there's not enough for me to Read." She tipped her head to the side, focusing on where he was. Rsiran remained, curious whether she would be able to detect him or not. A hint of a smile curved her lips. "Rsiran?" she whispered.

Galen turned quickly. "He's here?" He reached into his pouch and pulled out other darts, preparing to throw them.

"He's here, but he's not. I don't understand."

"He already claimed Josun, what else does he want?"

"He wants… the crystal," Cael said.

Galen grunted. "Everyone wants the crystal."

Cael turned to Galen. "Yes, but I think Rsiran is the only one who should have it."

Rsiran returned to his body, grabbed Brusus and Slid, emerging in the passageway.

When they appeared, Galen stood and held his darts out in front of him. "How did you find us?"

"The same way I did before," Rsiran said. He turned to Cael. "Do you have the crystal?"

"I know that it needs to be returned to the council," Galen said.

Rsiran shifted his focus to him. "If you really think that, then you wouldn't be here. *She* wouldn't be here. As I think I have told you, the crystal belongs to the people. *All* the people. We have to return it or we'll lose the others."

"What?" Brusus asked.

Rsiran nodded. "I haven't told anyone that because there's nothing that can be done other than what we are already doing."

"Are you certain?" Cael asked.

Rsiran looked at her. She had eyes that reminded him of her father, with the same depths and intensity to the gaze, but rather than radiating a cold cunning, she exuded warmth. He understood Galen's attraction to her. "I've held the other four crystals," Rsiran said.

Galen stepped in between Rsiran and Cael. "That's not possible. The crystals can only be held once."

"It's possible, and I have."

Galen turned to Cael. "We can't listen to him. You know what the others have said."

"We don't know whether we can trust the others."

"We can trust them more than *him*," Galen said, nodding to Rsiran.

Rsiran didn't know whether to be annoyed or amused that Galen turned his back on him, almost as if it didn't matter that Rsiran could Slide and use his knives on him. But then, Galen had seen him nearly die. Without Galen's help, it was possible he would have died. They didn't have to agree, but they *could* work together.

It only required trust.

Not only on their part, but on his.

Rsiran took a deep breath and peeled the bracelets off his wrists.

"What are you doing?" Brusus whispered.

"We have to trust them, and they have to trust us," Rsiran

said. He nodded to Galen. "They know where the crystal is. Maybe they even have it."

"I can't tell," Brusus said.

Rsiran studied Galen and Cael. "No. I don't think you'll be able to Read her, and I suspect she protects him as well."

Cael watched him and nodded.

Rsiran set the bracelets at his feet. "Read me."

He lowered the barriers he kept in his mind at the same time, willingly letting someone Read him for the first time in a very long time.

Cael nodded again.

There was a presence in his mind. It was soft, quick, and with a sense of urgency to it.

Then it was gone.

"He *has* held the crystals," she whispered. "And he must return the last, or more than the crystals will fail." She watched Rsiran as he placed the bracelets back onto his wrists. Having them on provided him a reassurance that he wouldn't be controlled and Read, even if he believed that his smith blood protected him from others Compelling him. "The trees. When the crystals fail, so will the trees, and that which powers them."

Brusus frowned, but Rsiran was taken back to the vision that he had while holding the last crystal, when he'd felt a presence behind him. He hadn't been able to see anything, but there had been no doubt that *something* had been there.

"They power the trees?" Galen asked.

Cael walked toward him, and met his eyes. "What did you feel?"

"I thought... I thought it was the Great Watcher."

304 | D.K. HOLMBERG

She nodded. "When I held the crystal, I thought the same. And maybe it is. There are powers beyond the Great Watcher, and I think those are the powers the crystals—and the Elder Trees—tap into."

Rsiran had a sudden sense of those powers, almost as if they were sitting behind him, urging him to act. "Do you know where we can find the crystal?" he asked.

She closed her eyes and nodded.

"Where?"

"It will be dangerous to reclaim," she said. "They have protected it against Venass."

"The Forgotten?" Rsiran asked.

"It's more than the Forgotten," Cael said. "It's always been more than the Forgotten."

Rsiran frowned, wondering who else would have an interest in keeping the crystals from Venass. "The Forgotten won't be able to protect the crystal. I've seen how Venass attacks."

"But it's not only them. They sought help, those with other abilities."

A fluttering anxiety stirred within him at the memory of the woman who used fire. "What others?"

Cael sighed. "Many others."

CHAPTER 32

Rsiran released Brusus's arm as they emerged from a
Slide on the edge of the city. From here, Asador
reminded him more of Elaeavn with the massive boulders that
dropped off toward the water. Waves crashed below, the sound
filling the night.

"We should return to the Aisl for others," Brusus said.

Rsiran had considered that, but dismissed the idea. "You
heard what Cael said."

"I don't know if we can trust what she says. She's the
daughter of a man on the Elvraeth council who wants to see
that you fail. Doesn't that strike you as a bit risky to trust her?"

Rsiran shrugged. "No riskier than her trusting me. She
knows what I can do."

"What if they won't meet with us?"

That had been the biggest fear. If they wouldn't meet with
him, he would have to force his way in. If the "others" that Cael

306 | D.K. HOLMBERG

mentioned were the type that he suspected, there were no guar-
antees that he would succeed.

"Then we have to find another way."

Brusus nodded. "What of this business with the trees? Will
they really die if we don't recover the crystal?"

"Why don't you ask about your mother?"

Brusus squeezed his eyes shut. "That will come, Rsiran. But
the crystals…"

"I've been so focused on the crystal, I haven't paid as much
attention to the Elder Trees." And he'd used the power stored
within the trees, not even giving thought to whether doing that
damaged them. After losing the one tree, how could he have
ignored the risk to the others?

"You think it's possible?"

"From what I can tell, the crystals are connected to the
trees," Rsiran said. "I think that's why the one crystal was lost in
the first place. It's possible they work together." He shook his
head. "Even after holding each of the others, I don't know the
answer. Are they separate powers, or are they connected?"
Similarly, were the ancient clans separate from those who eventually were able to reach the crystals, or were they connected?
The answer might be somewhere in between.

A shadowy figure appeared, making its way toward them.

"You see this?" Brusus asked.

Rsiran nodded. "Well enough." The shadows seemed to
swirl, and he stepped toward them. "Why are you here, Carth?
Where's Galen?"

"Galen's friend claims you must return the crystal to
your home."

"That's why I'm here."

"The others won't allow it."

"Others?"

Carth nodded. "I believe you met one of them? Sayanne tells of a powerful man who nearly killed her, one who can use metal like Venass, but who speaks as if he despises Venass. I can only imagine that was you?"

"Sayanne was the one who wanted to kill Josun Elvraeth?"

Carth tipped her head slightly. "There are many who wish to see him dead, Rsiran Lareth. He made the mistake of offending far too many, including those with powers he doesn't fully understand. It is the same mistake your grandfather made."

"Josun remains in my custody."

Carth smiled. "For now."

"What of the crystal?" Rsiran asked.

Carth took a step around them, glancing at Brusus as she did. "You won't be able to use your mind abilities on me, Elvraeth," she said to him.

Brusus flushed slightly and shrugged when Rsiran shot him a look. "Worth a try."

"You believe you can protect the crystal," Carth said.

"I think I'm the only way the remaining crystals survive."

Carth paused in front of him. "I have secured the crystal, and I doubt you will be successful in persuading the A'ras to allow you to reclaim it."

A'ras. Had he heard that before? "That's what Sayanne is?" Rsiran asked.

Carth nodded. "Leave the crystal, Rsiran Lareth. It is protected now."

"It's not protected. Once Danis reaches it—"

"What do you think you can do, Rsiran Lareth? He has proven he will outmaneuver you, outsmart you. I cannot risk him gaining any more influence than he has."

She started to turn away from him, the shadows again swirling around her.

"And I can't leave the crystal here," Rsiran said. "Too much is at risk."

"Even you won't be able to reach it," Carth said.

She stepped to the edge of the rock and disappeared.

Rsiran turned to Brusus. The hope that they could recover the crystal without a battle was gone. If it was only about keeping the crystal protected, he thought that Carth might actually be the right person to do it, but there was more to it than protection. The crystal needed to be recovered and returned to the chamber with the others.

"What will you do now?" Brusus asked.

"I can't leave it to Carth to protect," he said. "I don't know much about the A'ras"—had Haern still lived, he suspected he would have known something—"but I can't leave it here."

"What then?"

"We'll need help," he said.

"Who?"

"Someone who knows Carth better than I do. Someone she respects."

After searching for the heartstone-infused coin, Rsiran Slid into Asador long enough to grab Galen and Cael. He didn't give them an opportunity to resist and Slid them to the Aisl, emerging in Della's hut.

Smoke drifted from the fire, and the air smelled of mint tea, but Della wasn't here.

Galen spun toward him as Rsiran released him, a pair of darts already prepared to throw. Cael touched his arm and he relaxed.

"Can't you see where we are?"

Galen quickly scanned the room. "No. It's like he tried to create a place that would remind me of Della's but this is not her home."

The door opened and Della strode in, glancing from Rsiran to Galen. "This *is* my home, Galen, and if you could only see clearly you would recognize that."

Galen flushed slightly and placed his darts back into his pouch. "Della. I didn't know you were here. Your student grabbed us and brought us here."

"After you proved you couldn't help him recover the crystal, it seems," Della said. Rsiran suspected she Read Galen.

Galen nodded. "I ensured the crystal was protected. If anyone could, it would be her."

Della looked to Rsiran. "This is the same woman who wanted Haern?"

"She is. The same who helped establish me as Lorst."

"Carth set you up as Lorst?"

Rsiran nodded.

A slight smile twisted on Galen's mouth, and he glanced at Cael. "Damn that woman."

"Which one, Galen?" Della asked. "The one you're with, or the one who has been working with Rsiran as well?"

Galen started pacing, his eyes taking on a distant look. Rsiran couldn't help but feel annoyed at him. "Is that all this is?" He said it mostly to himself, stopping at the hearth to stare.

"What?" Rsiran asked.

He turned and looked at each person in the room. "It's a game to her. That's all this is. When it comes to Carth, everything is a game."

"Losing the crystal isn't a game to me," Rsiran said. "It won't be to the people of Elaeavn if the crystals fail and the Elder Trees die."

"Carth won't lose," Galen said. "I've never known her to lose."

"All it takes is one time," Brusus said. "One bad hand, one poor roll of the dice. That's all it takes. Then we lose everything. Do you really trust this Carth to be able to survive even when the odds are against her?"

Galen turned to Brusus, matching the intensity on his face. "I trust Carth more than I trust you," he said softly. "More than I trust the council that exiled me. More than I trust damn near anyone." He met each of their eyes, his burning a deep green. Had they been that green the last time that Rsiran had seen him? "You talk of odds, like that matters to someone like Carth. She won't play the game if the odds aren't in her favor. Even then, she has a way of forcing them into her favor."

"No one can do that," Brusus said. "Luck always plays a role."

"Not when you're prepared. You ever hear of Tsatsun?" he asked.

Della nodded thoughtfully. "That... is an old game," she said slowly. "When I was a younger woman, I used to play, but I was never any good."

"What is it?" Brusus asked.

Della looked at Galen. "Not a game that I would expect anyone to still play. It's an ancient game, one of skill and fore-sight. One that requires the player to think dozens of moves ahead. True masters can plan a hundred moves in advance."

Galen grunted. "Dozens. I'm lucky if I can plan even ten in advance. Stupid game, with stupid rules." He shook his head. "Carth tried to teach me, but I never had the mind for it, but the only other person I've ever feared was also a master of it. They played one time. I thought I followed, and thought Carth was getting outsmarted, but she played Orly in such a way he didn't even *know* that he was getting played. Even when it was over, he thought he'd played her close."

"The thief-master?" Rsiran asked. "That's who you compare Carth to? Do you really expect us to trust your comparison of her abilities when you use the thief-master?"

"How long have you known Orly?" Galen asked.

"I don't."

"I do. I was in Eban when he started taking control of the city. I was there as he consolidated his power. I was there as he maneuvered himself so that he could be protected from the city council. This is a man who is smarter and more ruthless than you can understand. And Carth toyed with him."

Della rested her hand on his arm, silencing him.

"If Carth is the master that you say, then we need to deter-mine what game she's playing. What does she have in mind?"

Galen shrugged. "Maybe she's reached the end point."

Della considered him a moment. "You don't think so."

He shook his head. "I don't think so."

"Why?" Rsiran asked.

"When I was in Asador—when you dropped me in Asador—I learned from someone close to her that she was dead."

Dead. Carth had mentioned her willingness to die to capture Danis. *Had* it all been a game—even the time she spent with him? "Yet she lives."

"She faked her death. There would be a reason for Carth to do so."

"And now that she revealed herself to us?" Rsiran asked.

"I think that's all part of the game she's playing. She's after something. It has to do with the Hjan, but more than that, I don't know."

Rsiran had thought he would find a way to force Josun to help, maybe trade Josun for the crystal if the A'ras really wanted him that badly, but he worried even that wouldn't be successful, not if Carth protected it. After facing her, he didn't think he would be able to defeat her if it came down to it. Somehow, her abilities countered what he was capable of doing.

How would he get the crystal back?

Rsiran didn't know how much time they had remaining, but he suspected time was growing short. Why else would the Great Watcher reveal the visions that he had to him? Why else would it seem like the power in the crystals seemed to wane?

They had to do something now.

"If she won't return the crystal, then she intends to use it for something else," Brusus said, jarring Rsiran from his thoughts.

Galen frowned. "That is possible. I hadn't considered she would use the crystal in such a way, but then, as I said, she's the master. I can barely last with her more than a few moves."

"I think you underestimate yourself," Cael said.

"Perhaps he's playing a game with *us*," Della said.

Brusus looked from Galen to Della, his deep green eyes no longer hidden. How long had it been since he'd Pushed on the faintness of his eyes? "We need to find out what she wants. Then we can figure out how to trade that for the crystal."

But Rsiran thought he knew what she wanted. Hadn't she told him?

It was the same reason that she had wanted Haern. The same reason that she had probably faked her death, playing a long game that he didn't fully understand. But he could see the end of that game clearly.... It was the same ending that he wanted.

They needed to work together, and for all that he knew, Carth *wanted* them to work together, even if she'd denied it when he'd asked.

Could she be playing him?

He looked at the others, trying to read from their faces whether they had come to the same conclusion he had He couldn't tell.

"What is it, Rsiran?" Brusus asked.

"Danis," Rsiran said. "She wants Danis."

And somehow, they had to use him to coax Carth into returning the crystal.

CHAPTER 33

"This is about as stupid as anything we've done," Valn said to Rsiran.

Rsiran clasped him on the shoulder as he grinned at him. Crouching on the ridgeline overlooking Thyr, with the sun setting in the distance, reminded him of the times he'd spent with Valn searching for Venass. Since they'd moved to the trees, their times together had grown less frequent, and he missed his new friend. Rsiran had no idea if what he planned would even work, but this was the only thing they had managed to come up with.

"You don't have to stay if you're scared," he said to him. Jessa jabbed him with the blunt end of a knife, and he turned his grin to her. Since deciding what they would try, he'd felt a little... punchy. He couldn't think of any other way to describe it. The plan would either work, and they would be rid of Venass and recover the crystal, or it would not.

Valn glared at him, and turned to stare at the distant tower as it rose up into the sky. "I think I've proven I don't scare easily."

"It sounded to me like you wanted to return to the cozy Forgotten Palace."

"At least I have privacy there. Sarah likes that."

He glanced at Sarah standing next to him, the wind catching her blonde hair, and she flushed. "Stop it. We need to focus on what we're doing."

"Which is what, exactly?" Valn said. "Sitting here isn't what I thought you intended for us. I thought you wanted us to get into the city and get noticed."

"I do. But I wanted to determine how many Venass I can detect."

"Fine, and then what?"

Rsiran shrugged. "Then we make our run."

Valn sighed softly. "You say so."

"Can you do this, Lorst?" Galen asked.

Rsiran shook his head. Galen hadn't taken to referring to him by his real name, preferring to use the one that Carth had given him. It stopped mattering to him. When they had decided to draw Venass out this way, Galen had offered to come. Rsiran hadn't known whether that was a good idea or not, but Della pushed, so Rsiran relented. And maybe Lorst was who was needed here. Facing Venass required the assassin, especially if they were to end this.

He focused on the sense of lorcith within the city of Thyr. There were nearly a dozen different moving pieces of lorcith, all of which he suspected to be implants for Venass. He tried to search for heartstone, but didn't detect anything clearly. That didn't mean that there was no heartstone there; Rsiran had seen Venass mask their implants before. He also couldn't tell if there were any with shadowsteel implants. That might be the most worrisome to him.

"Ready?" he asked.

The others grabbed onto his arms.

Rsiran Slid.

They emerged in a small room. The man sitting at the desk glanced up as they appeared, and tried Sliding, but Rsiran caught him with a knife in his arm. Sarah used her ability and held him in place, preventing him from Sliding away.

"How many do you think you can kill?" the man asked.

Rsiran shook his head. "Not kill."

Squeezing his focus through the lorcith ring on his finger, he could *feel* the lorcith within the implant more solidly. As he did, he *pulled* on it, *pushing* at the same time. The man screamed, but Jessa clamped her hand over his mouth, silencing him.

Rsiran worked quickly and shifted the intent of the lorcith implant. Once done, they released the man.

"What did you do?" the scholar asked.

Valn shook his head. "Why is it they always say the same thing?"

"There are other ways to silence them," Galen suggested.

"No. Not silence. We need them to talk," Rsiran said.

The man tried Sliding again, but the implant failed him.

"I'm coming for each of you," Rsiran said. "You can let Danis know that I know how to stop him."

With that, they Slid, emerging where he'd detected the next person of Venass. The man wasn't alone, and the other with him—a younger girl with a fresh scar along her face—tried attacking, but Valn held her back.

Focusing on the lorcith implanted in the man first, he reforged it, neutralizing the effect of the lorcith. He did the same with the girl. As with the first, they left them alive.

Four more times, they did the same, and each time, the question was the same.

"How many more times do you intend to do this?" Jessa asked after he had modified the implant in an older man.

They were inside a wide, empty room, deep beneath the ground. The stone walls rising around them reminded Rsiran of the time when he'd come to Thyr with Brusus and Jessa, when they had tracked Venass beneath the ground. There was a single candle resting on a table at the center of the room, and the man they had found here had almost seemed like he expected them to come, looking up at them with a resigned expression. Rsiran would take his time with this man. For his plan to work, he needed to.

"As many as it takes to get his attention."

"You've already got his attention," the man said. "Why else do you think I am here?"

Rsiran felt it before he saw it: a surge of lorcith mixed with heartstone. There was a sickly sense of something else—likely shadowsteel, he decided—and seven Hjan appeared.

Knives streaked toward them.

Rsiran *pushed* on lorcith knives, attempting to block them all. Even as he did, he knew he wouldn't be fast enough.

Grabbing Jessa, he Slid to the side, dragging her with him as he got out of the way of the knives. Valn had done the same, and now fought with his sword, trying to face three Venass. Sarah attacked from his side, the two of them battling with as much skill as the guilds possessed. Still, they weren't enough.

Rsiran had another four Hjan focused on him. Somehow, they had ignored Galen.

The assassin spun, flicking a handful of darts all at the same time. The speed and the accuracy he possessed were alarming, but at least they weren't coming for Rsiran. All of the darts hit, catching the Hjan with their poisoned tips, and they fell, leaving two standing.

Valn with Sarah's help finished them quickly, then turned to Galen. "Damn glad we have you with us," he said. "Where did you say you found him?" he asked Rsiran.

"Eban. He was exiled and turned to assassinations for his livelihood."

"You say that as if you haven't killed, Lorst."

Rsiran turned to him and shook his head. "Not the way you do it."

"There are times when you have to attack. Other times, you have to sit back and try to understand. The key is knowing the difference."

Rsiran sniffed. "Did Della teach you that?"

"Not Della. My other instructor."

"Isander. That doesn't seem like something he would have said."

"You wouldn't know him."

"I've met him."

Galen reached into his pouch, pulling out a few more darts

and rolling them between his fingers. "You wouldn't. Isander is dead."

Rsiran debated telling him that Isander lived, but hadn't wanted to antagonize Galen any more than necessary.

Jessa looked up at him. "Now that the two of you have that done, how about we keep moving?"

"What about him?" Valn asked, pointing with his sword toward the Venass scholar sitting behind the table. His face had paled watching them, and Rsiran wondered if he had expected them to fail.

"I think he's seen what he needed."

The man's eyes widened. "You *knew*?"

Rsiran shrugged. "Eventually, Venass learns. I've found it doesn't take long, especially this close to the tower."

"You still risked coming here?"

Rsiran looked at the Hjan lying on the ground. "I'm not sure I'm the one who risked anything coming here. Make certain Danis knows I'm ready for him. Tell him his grandson controls the crystals. He'll know where to find me."

"You're a fool if you think to challenge him!" the man said. "He's more powerful than you know."

"I have friends," Rsiran said. "And you've seen how powerful *I* am. Make sure he knows."

The Venass man rubbed his eyes. "And he has the Hjan. How many do you think you can stop? A hundred? Five hundred? What of a thousand?"

"If you had a thousand Hjan, you would have come after me already."

"Maybe we didn't, but the forgers have been busy. They place new implants each day."

"Like yours?" Rsiran asked. "You won't be able to receive another." That was one of the side effects of what he had done. He wasn't certain about much when it came to the implant that he'd left within those of Venass, but he knew that they wouldn't be able to receive another. Removing it would kill them, and placing another wouldn't work with the lorcith that he'd left. Doing what he did reduced the numbers of Venass. Maybe not as quickly as he'd like, but he didn't have to slaughter them, either.

"I won't. Others will. They have discovered you don't need to have abilities of the Great Watcher to receive the implant for it to work. There are ways to grant power without that. Now our numbers will—"

He slumped forward, and Rsiran noted the dart sticking out from the back of his neck.

Galen shrugged. "Coxberry. He'll sleep. This way he stops talking."

Sarah grinned. "I like this one."

Valn shot her a look.

"He's taken," Jessa reassured him.

Rsiran wondered what else the Venass scholar might have been able to tell him. Probably not much, but he'd learned enough to worry. If Venass really had discovered a way of using the implants on those without natural abilities, how many would they have to face? How many could the forgers place in a day?

He had thought to use Danis to draw Carth out, thinking to

join in her game, but maybe she was such a skilled player that would be foolish. And from what he'd seen of Danis, he would be equally skilled.

Was it possible that they were trapped between two masters, each positioning for power?

The idea worried him. If that was the case, what could *he* do but try to get out of the way and stay alive? What could he do to help those he cared about?

Somehow, he had to find a way to keep everyone safe. He thought that meant he would face Danis, and force Carth to act, but he began to wonder if that might have been a mistake.

As he looked at the Venass lying on the ground, most dead, he realized it was too late to second-guess the decision. They had to move forward and hope they would be able to find a way to pull out victory from those playing a game around them.

"Rsiran?" Jessa asked. She watched his face with that way she had, almost as if Reading him.

He nodded. "It's time we return. We've made our point. Now we have to hope Danis takes the bait."

CHAPTER 34

The guilds collected in the heart of the Aisl Forest. As Rsiran waited for the rest of the guilds to arrive from Elaeavn, he searched for Luthan. He found him with Della near the edge of the clearing, leaning against one of the sjihn trees. Della stared into the depths of the forest, and the worried crease in her brow left Rsiran unsettled.

"What is it?" he asked.

Luthan turned away from the forest. "There is something I have Seen. I cannot explain well. A darkness, similar to what I See when I try to turn my attention to you, but this comes from within the forest."

Rsiran used his connection to lorcith and heartstone, fearing Venass might have been approaching from a different direction, but came up with nothing. "Danis would have gotten the message by now," he said.

"The message, but will he come after you here?" Luthan scanned the guilds within the forest and shook his head. "I can't believe he would bring his people here, especially knowing that you taunt him."

"That's my concern, as well, but at least here, we can prepare."

"I wonder if maybe we were mistaken drawing him here," Della said, practically tearing her eyes away from the forest. Rsiran recognized the worried expression she wore. He'd seen it before when Brusus had nearly died. It was the same expression she wore when she'd learned of the connection to the Forgotten with Evaelyn and to Venass with Danis.

"They can't do anything to the Elder Trees," Luthan said. "Rsiran destroyed the forge, so they shouldn't have the supply of shadowsteel they had before."

"With Danis, I've learned that might not matter. He will likely find other ways to attack the Elder Trees if that's his goal," Della said, "yet I'm not certain that's his move."

"What do you think he intends?" Rsiran asked.

"I wish I could See that more clearly," Luthan said. "Unfortunately, what I can See is limited. Perhaps if there was a way of determining what I could See around them, much like I do when I try Seeing with you, Lareth, but I haven't been able to find anything."

"Maybe there's something *I* can do," Rsiran said.

"You will Travel?" Luthan asked, looking to Della.

He nodded and sat next to the tree, resting his back against the smooth bark, and closed his eyes. Taking a deep breath, he Traveled.

He didn't have a destination in mind and hovered over the forest, similar to what he'd done when he went with Brusus to

Asador. He rose above the forest, and in this form, Traveling as he did, he had a hint of the power of the Elder Trees, and could reach them from here.

Della and Luthan watched over him, keeping him safe.

Rsiran drifted toward the forest, wanting to see if there was anything within the forest that he had to worry about. He swept through the trees, finding nothing. The forest once had intimidated him, but there was nothing to fear from the forest. This was a place of his people, a place that should be their home.

As he drifted, he heard an occasional howl. In all the time that he'd spent in the forest, he hadn't discovered the source of the cry. Most suspected it came from wolves, but Rsiran had never seen wolves in the Aisl Forest.

Moving in a steadily widening arc, he reached out from the forest, searching for anything that would explain the darkness that Luthan saw. There was nothing.

Making another pass, and now starting to feel the strain of the effort required to continue, he paused back near the heart of the Aisl, gaining strength from the Elder Trees. What would Luthan have Seen?

He shifted toward the city, moving into Elaeavn.

Lorcith, and it moved.

Rsiran focused on the lorcith, trying to determine how many of Venass might be here.

Dozens of dozens. This was the attack.

What would Danis want from Elaeavn—other than revenge?

Rsiran returned to his body and jumped to his feet.

"What is it?" Della said.

"They're in Elaeavn. Hundreds of them. It's like they waited…"

"For us to leave the city open and then they would attack," Luthan said.

"Why would Danis attack Elaeavn?" Della said. "There is nothing about the city that gives them an advantage."

"Other than trying to draw Rsiran and us into protecting those within the city. They can attack with impunity while we must be cautious," Luthan said. "It is a particularly brutal plan. And will be effective, I fear. This city will be lost."

There was only one answer. "I need to get everyone back into the city," Rsiran said.

"If they've already attacked, it will be too late," Luthan told him.

"Not for me."

"You can't Slide that many people into the city!"

Couldn't he? Rsiran had never tested the limits of his ability, and there seemed no better time than now to try. They *needed* to reach Elaeavn, and needed to stop the attack, and with as many of Venass and the Hjan as there were within the city, he didn't think he could take multiple trips.

"I have to try. I can *pull* us, and that should give us enough advantage to reach the city."

He hurried to the center of the Aisl where the others were waiting. Jessa ran over to him and noted his expression. When he explained what he wanted to do, she shook her head at him. "Too many, Rsiran. Even you have limits."

"What limits?" He looked around at the people arranged

around them. "We don't have much time, not if we intend to save *any* of the city."

He noted Cael watching him from where she stood near Galen. When they reached the city, Rsiran wanted Galen with him. Whatever else he might be, having the assassin's skills would be valuable.

Rsiran guided Jessa toward them. "Do you have everything that you need?" he asked Galen, glancing to the pouch that contained the poisons the assassin used.

Galen almost smiled. "Do you, Lorst? I presume you think we can retake the city?"

"We never lost it. But Venass has focused their attack on the city. It's time to finish this."

Galen swept his gaze over the people standing near them. "With these? Are they ready for where you'll take them?"

Rsiran hoped that everything they had been through would be enough. There were several hundred with him, more than he should even consider attempting to Slide, and he doubted they would all escape unscathed. Rsiran needed to attack Venass, and knew that not all who were with him now would survive. That pained him.

Jessa touched his arm, almost Reading him in the way that she did.

Rsiran sighed. "They're as ready as we can make them. This is what we wanted."

Galen did smile then. "We? This is what you wanted, Lorst. You brought the Hjan to Elaeavn."

Rsiran shook his head. "I didn't bring them to Elaeavn, but I will see that they never return." He started to turn away. "Be ready."

As they left, Jessa leaned into him. "How many do you think you'll be able to Slide?"

Rsiran glanced around the clearing. "I don't know."

"This many?"

"I—"

"I ask because if you attempt this and it fails, what happens to all of us?"

"It won't fail."

"How can you be so certain?"

Rsiran pointed to the Elder Trees. "For this, I'll have to use the power of the trees."

"Why do I get the sense that's not a good thing?"

"Because I don't know how much strength they can continue to offer."

Would he be the reason the other vision that he'd had while holding the last crystal came true? Would it be his fault that they darkened?

If he tapped away the rest of the power simply to Slide people to Elaeavn, it was possible.

But they needed to go now.

"It's time," he said.

Valn hurried over to him with several others of the Sliding guild. All told, there were seven. The guild was a small one, without enough people to make this easier on Rsiran.

"How can we help?" Valn asked.

"We're returning to Elaeavn to face Venass."

"Good, because if you said we were returning to fish, I'd be upset. Don't much care for fishing," Valn said.

Rsiran considered those around them. "Take the best fighters. As many as you can carry. Arrange yourselves throughout the city."

Valn nodded and reached out his hand. Rsiran took it, clasping wrists with Valn.

"Whatever happens, Lareth, I've enjoyed fighting with you."

Rsiran nodded. "Me, too. May the Great Watcher keep his gaze on you."

Valn grinned. "Someone has to."

They departed, grabbing a few from those waiting in the clearing. Rsiran knew most who the Sliders chose—all skilled fighters—but not all. Valn took two, and most of the others took one. It helped, but not as much as what he needed.

And they couldn't wait any longer.

Rsiran stood in the center of the clearing and raised his hands. Those standing around started to quiet, and quickly turned their attention to him. It shouldn't have surprised him how quickly the focus shifted to him, and the open willingness for him to assume command, but it still did.

What did he say? From the faces that he saw and recognized—Luthan and Sarah and Seval and dozens of others—they expected him to say something.

He cleared his throat and touched the hilt of his sword as he searched for reassurance. "Venass has reached Elaeavn. If we fight—and if we win—we can end this. We can return to the lives we want to lead, and we can stop fearing another attack." He swallowed. "More than that, we need to capture Danis so that we can reclaim the crystal. If we don't, the other crystals will fade."

Jessa squeezed his hand.

Rsiran took a deep breath. "We've faced Venass before. We know the powers they are capable of using, and the destruction they can cause. Whatever we have experienced before, this will likely be worse. They will have discovered some new trick, and come up with some new threat." Rsiran looked at those standing around him, meeting as many in the eye as he could. "Not all of us will survive. I will do everything I can to save those who choose to fight, but not all of us will live. I understand if you don't want to come with me."

He fell silent, expecting some to depart. Jessa held his hand tightly, and the rest of the forest around him seemed to hold its breath, waiting for the others to respond.

No one left.

"Grab onto each other," Rsiran said.

As everyone started to squeeze closer together, Jessa leaned into him. "Where are you going to Slide this many people that it will be safe?"

There was only one place that he could think of in the city, but he feared that it would be the hardest to reach.

"The palace."

Jessa sucked in a breath and nodded.

Rsiran closed his eyes. He wasn't entirely certain what he planned would succeed. Could he *pull* all of these people with him? He'd done the same with massive amounts of lorcith in the past, but never had he attempted it with such a large group of people. If he failed, so did the hope of Elaeavn surviving the Venass attack.

Yet he knew he couldn't Slide people separately. Even as quickly as he could Slide, it would take too long—and would ruin any chance that they might have at surprise. They needed to act now, and quickly.

He *pulled*.

As he did, he remembered vividly the first time that he tried Sliding with another, and how hard that had been. Then there had been the time when he had Slid Brusus and Lianna to the heart of the Aisl after she'd died. That had been so difficult that he couldn't Slide again afterward. Why did he think he could Slide this many now?

The effort was enormous, and almost too much.

He anchored to the place he intended to Slide, knowing it as well as he could. That familiarity helped, but there were so many with him.

Rsiran screamed.

Pain shot through him. Moving this many people—even with the need that they had—was more than he should have attempted.

Maybe it would have been better to have Slid smaller groups, after all.

But that would risk Venass knowing they were coming.

Rsiran *pulled* harder, forcing them along the Slide.

Then he paused the Slide in the place between.

Power flowed around him, and Rsiran bathed in it, taking as much of that power as he could, knowing that he would need it to succeed. He *pulled* on the power of the Elder Trees. There was no question that the power faded, weakened in some real way. Whatever had happened with the crystal had weakened the Elder Trees as well.

Rsiran felt his strength return, and he *pulled* more, drawing as much as he could within him. When they reached the palace, he couldn't be so weakened that he couldn't fight.

The power of the trees energized him.

Jessa squeezed his hand.

Rsiran Slid again, *pulling* everyone with him toward the palace, continuing to draw on the power of the Elder Trees, feeling it coursing through him.

CHAPTER 35

The fading sun reflected off the bars of heartstone and lorcith as they emerged. Rsiran looked around, worried that he hadn't managed to bring everyone he intended along with him, but they were all accounted for. How weakened had the Slide left him?

Not as much as it should have. Without the help of the Elder Trees, he wouldn't have been able to manage it. Had he drained the trees of their power so much that they wouldn't be able to help him with what else he needed?

He didn't have a chance to think about it.

Lorcith and heartstone flickered in the city. Some of it was nearby.

Rsiran recognized the sense from when he'd detected Venass before. There were hundreds. Too many to take on, even with his small force.

But what choice did they have?

"We have to go," Rsiran said.

He searched for Galen. That was who he wanted with him as they tried to capture Danis. With the slithca Galen could use, they could neutralize him as a threat, then they could trade Danis for the crystal. Galen knew Carth well enough that she would have to work with them, wouldn't she?

He found Galen and Cael arguing softly.

"I need your help," he said to Galen.

"You're the great assassin, Lorst. You don't need me."

"I think we both know that I'm no assassin. And I need to capture someone, which seems to be your specialty, not killing."

"I can't leave Cael. She thinks she's going to convince her father to fight."

"I *will* convince him to fight," she said.

Rsiran doubted that Naelm would get involved, not if he didn't have to, but let Cael try. There was no harm in the attempt, even if it wouldn't lead to anything. Rsiran had already tried and failed.

"Luthan can go with you," Rsiran suggested. "Take another councilor to convince him."

"Even if the council agrees," Galen began, "what do you expect them to be able to do?"

Cael frowned. "Most of the Elvraeth are skilled with swords."

"Swords?" Rsiran asked. Even Luthan hadn't shared that.

"Why do you think the Elvraeth value swords as much as they do?"

Galen's eyes widened. "I suppose they have nothing else to do."

Rsiran laughed.

"Let her go, and please," he said, "come with me."

Cael and Galen hugged quickly, whispering something softly to each other before he released her to search for Luthan.

"Do you think you can do this?" he asked.

"There are several hundred of Venass within the city," Rsiran said. "We have about as many as they do, but they use their implants to give them even more power than we possess."

"Difficult odds," Galen said. "Good thing we have the great assassin Lorst with us."

"You and I. We will move quickly to reach Danis."

"What of your girl?" he asked, glancing to Jessa as she approached.

"Jessa will stay here to help coordinate." He turned to her. "I need your help, but I need to be able to move quickly."

"I know."

"You can keep things organized here. If Cael manages to rouse the council, then we will need to organize them into our attacks."

"I know."

"I can't risk losing you."

She smiled and squeezed his hand. "I know."

Rsiran had expected more of an objection from her, but this was better than he could have hoped for.

She kissed him, the warmth of her lips lingering on his cheeks. "Come back to me."

He nodded. "Coordinate with the others. The Sliders will be sweeping in from the perimeter of the city. Work with them."

"We'll take care of this. You take care of yourself."

Rsiran turned to Galen, and the assassin nodded.

Together, they Slid.

They emerged where Rsiran detected nearly a dozen of Venass—all lorcith.

When they appeared, they were attacked.

Rsiran *pushed* on the lorcith within them, deforming it as quickly as he could. Working as he did, he almost missed another attacking him.

Galen did not, catching the knife with one of his own, and throwing a dart at the man.

"Where's the assassin Lorst?" Galen demanded, turning to him.

Rsiran realized he couldn't continue with the soft approach. As much as he might want to disable them and avoid killing, doing so risked his life—and Galen's.

There was no other choice.

Rsiran flicked knives, *pushing* them at Venass fighters. Galen spun, moving quickly in a dance of death. Each of his darts struck. Between the two of them, they subdued all of the fighters within a few moments. Rsiran *pulled* the knives back to him, and wiped each of them off, pocketing them for the next attack.

"That might not be so—"

Galen cut off as heartstone flickered to them. Someone Sliding.

This came in a wave larger than before. Nearly two dozen, all enhanced with metal implants.

Rsiran *pushed* on his knives, but he didn't have enough.

Galen threw darts, flicking handfuls at a time, leaving

Rsiran wondering how many the man possessed. Would there come a time when he ran out of darts?

One of the Hjan grinned wolfishly at Rsiran.

What did he know?

They formed a ring around him, and he felt pressure against him.

They were trying to hold him.

His connection to lorcith and heartstone faded.

The Hjan had attacked him similarly in the past, but this was a new technique. This time, they used their own people, risking sacrifice.

"Galen! I need a little help."

Galen rolled, sending a spray of darts. Some missed, the first time that Rsiran had seen the man miss. Thankfully, most hit, and the circle of Hjan that had formed around him sagged, leaving him freedom to move.

Rsiran *pushed,* sending knives streaking toward the Hjan, curving the trajectory in the air so that they would hit. Most of the Hjan Slid, disappearing, and Rsiran only managed to catch a few of them.

Galen leaned forward, panting. "I'm not going to be able to keep up with this." He made his way around the fallen, claiming his darts. He slipped most of them into his pouch, and then stood. "This isn't an attack."

"What do you mean?"

Galen surveyed the Hjan. "They knew they couldn't win. You could see it in the set of their jaw. They came expecting to die, but they wanted to hold you."

Not hold, Rsiran realized. Venass had enough experience with him that they wouldn't expect to be able to hold him.

But they could *delay* him.

Why? What did they hope to accomplish delaying him?

Danis had another plan.

Rsiran knew it as certainly as he knew that Carth played him in her own way. Both of them would be masters of the game, and Rsiran had become a mere pawn, seemingly unable to make his own moves.

But that had to end. He had to find a way to stay in the game, to control the next move. Because he knew if he failed, if he couldn't reclaim the crystal, more than Elaeavn would be lost. Power would fade. He had seen that in his visions, and though he might not know what they meant, he believed that he was shown those visions for a reason.

Where was Danis?

He had to find his grandfather. That was how he would stop this. Find Danis, then trade him to Carth. But the attack proved that it would be difficult to stop Venass. If he was having this much difficulty, how would the others have any easier a time?

"What would they be after?" Rsiran asked aloud.

Galen started filling his darts. Rsiran watched, noting the steady way that he worked, the quick tip of a vile of liquid as he poured it into the darts. "You have to think like Carth. What would the next step be? Then the one after? What would be there? And after that... You can keep going, but that's the point. Carth will be looking a dozen of steps out."

So would Danis. And with that being the case, he might have attacked the city, but what if that wasn't his end game? What if he knew what Rsiran wanted, and tried to make it appear that he'd attacked?

Rsiran couldn't help but think that Danis would have a different goal in mind.

Before he could think about the answer, an explosion rocked the city. Then another. Then another. The ground rumbled, as if the city itself were separating from the rocks to slide into Aylianne Bay.

Smoke rose throughout the city. There were fires near the shore and in Lower Town, but it appeared there were ones in the higher in the city as well. The palace remained untouched, for now.

Another explosion, this time behind him.

Rsiran turned and noted debris falling from the palace.

"Why would they want to destroy the palace?" he asked.

"Cael." Galen started up the street, but Rsiran grabbed him. "Don't, Lorst—Rsiran, whatever your name is. I'm going for Cael, and you're not going to stop me."

"I'm not trying to stop you. Let me take you there."

Galen glanced toward the palace and nodded.

Another explosion came.

Rsiran Slid.

They emerged on the palace grounds. Rsiran was surprised to see dozens of people hurrying across the grounds, most of them people he hadn't brought with him from the Aisl. Jessa was there, speaking with Cael and waving her hands. When he appeared, she ran to him, a relieved expression on her face.

Galen hurried over to Cael, leaving Rsiran with Jessa.

"They're trying to destroy the city!"

"I don't think that's all that they want," Rsiran said. "It's part of something else."

"You don't think that they're angry at what you did, and the way that you went after Venass?"

"That might be part of it, but he's going after something else. I just don't know what it is." Rsiran motioned to the people that had joined them in the yard. "This is—"

Jessa nodded curtly. "The Elvraeth. Yes. They think they're going to take over."

"And do what?"

Jessa shrugged. "The council intends to direct the attack. Now that they've finally been pushed out of the palace—and they only came when the attacks struck the palace—they want to take over."

"I think that's a great idea," Rsiran said.

"You *what?*"

"Let the council direct things in the city. They might not have the experience fighting Venass, but the council has several powerful Seers."

"Seers? None of them can detect lorcith the way that you do."

He shrugged. "Detecting lorcith and heartstone doesn't matter when they can Slide away. What they can See will be as much help as anything I can do."

"What of you?"

Another explosion sounded down in the city. Rsiran saw Luthan speaking to someone, and as they turned toward him, he saw that it was Naelm. His face was grim, and he only nodded to Rsiran before turning his attention back to Luthan.

340 | D.K. HOLMBERG

Naelm raised his hand and two men hurried forward. Naelm said something to them and they hurried off, gathering a dozen men as they did.

They were already coordinating, and doing a better job than he would manage.

Why had it taken getting to this point for them to get help from the Elvraeth? When Venass attacked the first time, the Elvraeth had done nothing to intervene. Now that their palace was under attack... Rsiran would be angry if he weren't so thankful for their help. Even with the Elvraeth, it still might not be enough to stop Venass.

But their presence let him turn his focus away from the city. With the Elvraeth involved, he could focus on finding Danis and determining what his grandfather might be up to.

Why would he destroy the palace and the city?

There had to be something he would gain by it.

Not drawing Rsiran out. They didn't need to attack the palace itself for that, but what else?

He turned slowly, trying to understand what he might be missing, and wishing that Haern were with him. He always saw things differently, his experience granting him a unique perspective. What would Danis want that he hadn't yet seen?

"Rsiran?"

He shook himself, trying to clear his mind.

"Venass is here," he said. "But what if Danis is not?"

"Where would he be?" she asked.

As another series of explosions rocked the city, Rsiran stared at the palace, wishing that he had answers.

CHAPTER 36

Rsiran Slid back to the Aisl, emerging at the heart of the forest. There were few who'd remained behind, and those who did were either older, or had no interest in fighting. Luca was there, hammering away at the forge, the rhythmic sound of his hammering the only sound in the otherwise quiet and somber air.

He hurried to Della's hut. The inside was quiet, and he looked for Josun where he should be bound and held on a cot near the fire. It was empty.

Della groaned near the corner and Rsiran hurried to her. She sat up, her eyes glazed, holding a massive gash on her forehead that still oozed.

Rsiran grabbed her and Slid to the place between, *pulling* on the power of the trees as he attempted to heal Della, fearing that he might be too late.

He pressed the power of the Elder Trees through her.

She took a deep breath, letting it out with a sigh. Her eyes

342 | D.K. HOLMBERG

opened, and the gash on her head slowly sealed closed. Her breathing eased, and the hint of confusion in her eyes faded.

"What happened?" he asked.

"Danis."

"He was in the Aisl? He shouldn't have been able to even reach it!"

"Not in the forest, but he sent some of his Hjan for Josun Elvraeth. I don't know how they would have found him."

Rsiran thought that he did. They would have placed something on him to track, much like Rsiran had done with Galen, or had once used on Brusus.

"It's my fault," he said.

Della shook her head. "This isn't your fault. This is Danis."

"Why would they want Josun? He doesn't have the crystal."

"I don't know," Della said. "It's possible that they don't know he no longer has it."

"Or maybe he thinks to make a different bargain," Rsiran said. "What kind of bargain do you think he'll make that will keep him safe? Either Venass has him or the A'ras."

Della wiped the dried blood off her hand onto her dress and started to stand. "With Danis, I'm not sure you can know. Why are you here? What happened in Elaeavn?"

"Venass attacked, but they're not doing anything."

"Nothing?" Della said with a frown.

"Destroying the city. The palace. Nothing else. It doesn't make sense. I know Venass wants power, but they're sacrificing all of the Hjan and those of Venass for nothing."

"Unless they're not," Della said.

Now that Della seemed to be doing better, he Slid her back

to her hut. "What would they hope to achieve?" he asked. "What does destroying the city gain them?"

Della started mixing powders, starting a brew of mint tea, as if they weren't in a middle of a battle. Rsiran knew that he needed to get back to the city, but with Josun missing, he needed to understand what else he might be missing before he did.

"Access, Rsiran. That would be what Danis wants. That's all he's ever wanted since leaving the city."

"What kind of access?"

"The kind that the guilds have protected."

Rsiran knew instantly what she meant. "Will you be okay?"

"Go, Rsiran. See if you're already too late."

He Slid.

When he emerged, he appeared in the crystal chamber.

The soft blue light from the crystals seemed faint, much weaker than it had been when he'd been here last, and that had only been a few days before. How much longer did the crystals have? For that matter, how much longer did the trees have? If he didn't recover the crystal soon, they would lose the trees as well.

A flicker of movement caught his attention.

Rsiran Slid to the center of the crystals.

From here, he made a slow spin, looking at the four remaining crystals as he did, and searching for the source of the movement. Where was it?

Nothing else moved.

Rsiran reached for lorcith, then heartstone, fearing that Venass had infiltrated this room, but found nothing. This room

344 | D.K. HOLMBERG

was what the guilds protected. This was what Venass had tried to reach one time before, and if the explosions *were* meant as some kind of diversion, they risked giving access to the crystals.

There was nothing.

Rsiran stood for a moment longer, then Slid.

He emerged in his father's smithy, fearing that it might be destroyed, but the building stood. There was dust over everything, and the smithy itself remained empty. The massive forge where he'd learned the trade remained cold. The air still had the smell of lorcith mixed with that of copper and steel, though the odor of dust hung over everything.

Beneath him was the chamber leading to the Hall of Guilds. He Slid, emerging in the tunnels, but they remained intact. Another Slide, and this time he emerged closer to the now-destroyed Alchemist Guild house. He found nothing.

Where else might they have attacked?

It couldn't have only been the palace, could it?

What else would Danis want to destroy? What else would draw Rsiran's focus?

With a sickening sensation growing in his stomach, he thought he knew.

Rsiran Slid, emerging in his smithy.

Or, where his smithy should be.

Rock and debris littered the ground. The walls that had stood for centuries had crumbled. In the middle of all of it was the remains of his forge, the anvil still somehow surviving.

They had attacked the one place he considered home.

Emotions welled inside of him as he stared at what had been his smithy, the only place he'd ever felt that he belonged. Anger at what Danis and his Venass fighters had done. Sadness at what he'd lost. And an overwhelming desire to see that he didn't lose his smithy for nothing.

Another explosion sounded, and this time, it seemed farther away.

Had he not been near his smithy, he doubted that he would have heard it. This came from deep beneath the ground, like thunder that rolled from beneath him and to the north.

Why north?

The only thing that he could think of that was there was Ilphaesn.

He Slid, appearing inside Ilphaesn.

The walls trembled around him, the lorcith in them shaking.

Not shaking. Charged. Something had changed with the lorcith here.

Rsiran raced through the tunnel and used his connection to lorcith to attempt to calm it. If he didn't, he didn't know what would happen, but the tunnels felt like they would collapse. The entirety of Ilphaesn might collapse. That by itself wouldn't be a problem, but they were close enough to Elaeavn that the mountain might crumble and roll toward the city, destroying it.

Even as he went through Ilphaesn, he wouldn't be strong enough to stabilize it, or fast enough.

The entire mountain started to tremble around him.

Rsiran Slid, emerging on the top of the mountain. From the peak, he could feel all of the mountain below him shaking. He *pushed* on the lorcith, trying to hold it steady, but there were limits to his strength, even when it came to lorcith.

How had Venass done this?

The only thing that he could think of was that they had used some sort of connection to shadowsteel, but when?

Unless they had been planning this for longer than he had realized.

Rsiran didn't dare move, fearing that the moment he did, the entire mountain would begin to collapse.

As he stood there, a vision flashed through his mind.

He'd had this vision before. It was the one where the crystals went dark, the Elder Trees went dark, and the powers sitting behind the Great Watcher suddenly failed.

His heart fluttered. Why should he have that vision?

Why now? What did the Great Watcher want him to see?

Unless the crystals were in danger.

What he needed was some way to stabilize Ilphaesn while he searched. If he could connect to the Elder Trees, it might be possible, but he couldn't do that, not without Traveling, and he didn't dare risk losing that much of a connection to make Traveling work.

Was there another way?

Could he reach for the energy of the Elder Trees through his sword? It had worked once before, so it was possible that it would work for him again.

Grabbing the hilt of the sword, he *pulled* on lorcith, this time, attempting to do so *through* the sword, through its connection to the Aisl. There came a sense of a deep groaning, and something of a shift. Whatever happened was subtle, nothing more than the barest of movements, but it was enough for him to know that the mountain would not collapse. Stable, but not sturdy.

It would have to be enough.

How much of the Elder Tree power had he drained doing what he had just done? Rsiran couldn't even argue the necessity. If he hadn't, they would have lost the mountain—the lorcith—along with the city.

The flash of the vision worried him. Had the flicker of shadow in the crystal chamber been real? If it had, then he might already be too late... and perhaps he should have remained there.

If he had, then he would have missed whatever was happening to Ilphaesn.

They needed help, but he didn't dare spend time trying to find others. If he did—and if the vision was close to coming true—then he needed to act. Would he be strong enough to stop Danis? Would he at least be able to keep him from reaching the other crystals?

But stopping wasn't enough. He needed to *capture* Danis, not kill him.

As skilled as he believed himself, he wasn't certain that he could do that by himself. For that, he needed help, but he'd have to find it quickly.

Rsiran listened for the familiar pull of lorcith, readying to Slide.

As he did, he wondered—in all of this, where was Carth?

CHAPTER 37

Finding Galen proved easier than he expected. The assassin had still been in the palace yard, so when Rsiran emerged, he grabbed him and Slid again. Galen had barely had a chance to react.

They emerged in the crystal room. The crystals glowed with a faint blue light.

"What is this?" Galen demanded, jerking free as they emerged.

"I need your help. I think Venass intends to attack here."

Galen quickly glanced at the crystals and shook his head. "And you only bring me?"

"Look at them," Rsiran said. "They're dying."

"The crystals can't die," Galen said.

"I think they can. Whatever Venass is doing is killing them." He looked around the room, but saw nothing. There was no sign of movement, nothing that would make him think that the crystals were in danger.

"The crystals cannot die. They are or they are not."

Rsiran watched Galen a moment. "You've held one."

The assassin flushed a moment. "I traveled with the missing crystal for a time. I think I would know if they were changing."

"This isn't just about changing, though. This is about power fading." Rsiran motioned overhead. "Venass has already proven they can damage the Elder Trees. The crystals are tied to the Elder Trees somehow, so if a tree fails—"

"That's how the crystal disappeared," Galen said.

"I think so."

"Why would the crystals fade with the dying of a tree?" Galen asked.

"They're connected. That's all that I can tell." Now wasn't the time to explain to Galen about the vision of powers stronger than even the Greater Watcher who he suspected powered the crystals—and maybe even the trees. That could come if they succeeded. For now, he needed to protect the crystals. "Do you see anyone here?"

Galen studied the crystals, and then looked beyond them. "There's nothing but darkness here. I don't see…"

With a fluid motion, he pulled a dart from his pouch and flicked it.

There was a grunt, and someone dropped to the ground.

"Damn," Galen breathed. "Barely saw him. Shadowed. I've never seen anything like that before."

Rsiran tensed, trying to peer into the darkness and failing. "I have."

Galen glanced at him, but Rsiran shook his head. "There will be others. If Danis has sent others here, they will already be here."

"Why wouldn't they have come any closer?"

"Because the crystals create their protection," Danis said. His voice sounded as if it came from everywhere, a heavy, booming quality that filled the crystal chamber.

As he spoke, the light from the crystals seemed to dim even more.

How much time did they have?

Rsiran began to suspect that capturing Danis wasn't enough. Then he'd still somehow have to figure out a way to coerce Carth into a trade. And if they were running out of time, what would happen when the crystals finally went dark?

Rsiran jerked his head around, searching for Danis.

"Isn't that right, grandson?"

Rsiran readied the knives on him, nodding to Galen. The assassin had already grabbed a handful of darts, and prepared to throw them, but the rapid way that he looked around told Rsiran that he didn't know where to target.

"Danis. Why don't you show yourself?"

"I think I have time to wait. Not much longer, grandson. Then I'll be able to claim these crystals."

"Much longer, and the crystals won't be of any use to you."

"Is that what you think?" Danis said. "A good thing that you won't be responsible for watching over them for much longer. It doesn't seem as if you're the right fit, though you haven't been the right fit for many things, have you? First you lose one of the Elder Trees, then you lost the crystal, and now... now you'll lose the rest."

Danis appeared at the edge of the light coming off the crystals for a moment before disappearing. Galen threw a pair of darts, but Danis Slid and the darts missed.

His laughter echoed in the small chamber. "Decided that you can't do this on your own? I thought you were stronger than this, grandson."

"I thought you were smarter than to risk yourself against me," Rsiran said.

"I am smarter than that," Danis said. "Why do you think you're in there?"

Rsiran started to Slide, intending to chase Danis, but Galen grabbed his arm. "Don't let him taunt you like this. I don't know what he wants, but he keeps dancing around the outside of these crystals."

"That's why I'm going after him."

"Think, Lorst! That's what he wants you to do. Play the game!"

Rsiran studied the crystals, trying to think of what Danis might be attempting.

As he did, he realized that Galen was right. Danis wasn't attacking, not because he waited for the crystals to fade, but because he *couldn't*. The crystals prevented him from accessing this part of the chamber. Galen could because he'd held one of the crystals before—the same as Rsiran. But if Rsiran went after Danis—if he left the protection of the ring of crystals—then Danis could attack.

What did Danis *really* want?

All along, Rsiran had thought that he wanted the crystals. Rsiran had attempted to seal them off, but that had only risked preventing everyone else from reaching them. Were something to happen to Rsiran, he couldn't leave the crystals blocked like that. He'd be doing as much damage as the others if he did.

But could he move them?

The crystals no longer blocked him, and from what he could tell, he'd held each of the crystals once before. Shouldn't he be able to move them?

Where would he take them if he did?

The answer came to him quickly. There was only one place he *could* take them.

"Can you watch me?" Rsiran asked.

Galen glanced over to him. "What are you going to do?"

"Something either really smart or really dumb."

Galen offered a half-smile. He grabbed a handful of darts and readied them. "Sounds like me."

Rsiran approached the first crystal and held his hands up to it. Would it even work?

"If this goes right, you'll need to stay close so I can Slide you to safety."

Galen took a few steps back.

Rsiran reached for the crystal.

There was no resistance. It was almost as if the crystal knew what he intended. He lifted it, and rather than having a vision, or anything like he'd experienced before, the crystal simply felt warm in his hands. He chose not to think about it and slipped it into his pocket.

Moving to the next, he hurried, grabbing it and placing it next to the other.

"Lorst!"

Rsiran glanced over as he reached the third crystal. Shadows had started to separate from the walls. What had Danis discovered? Was Carth somehow involved?

He grabbed the third crystal and slipped it into his pocket.

When he reached the fourth, they were attacked.

It felt like the night closed around him. Pain shot through him, burning up through his legs and through his arms, feeling much like when he'd been poisoned. He tried taking a step forward, but couldn't. He tried Sliding, but couldn't.

His arm worked.

Reaching for the hilt of his sword, he *pulled*, trying to draw the power from the Elder Trees. It came slowly, oozing through him. With this power, he *pushed* against the darkness, forcing it back.

The darkness moved slowly, but it moved.

The remaining crystal started to flicker, as if it would go out.

Rsiran reached for it, but was too late. Someone else touched it first.

"Galen!" he shouted.

Galen grabbed onto him, and flicked darts into the darkness. Rsiran *pushed* on lorcith, using the power from the Elder Trees as he did, drawing more and more strength. It almost wasn't enough.

Light surged from him, and the darkness evaporated.

A man with a gray face and shaggy dark hair lay on the ground outside the circle, the crystal gripped in his hand.

Rsiran felt a flicker of metal.

Danis.

He Slid, emerging and grabbing the crystal before Danis could and Sliding again.

When he emerged, he stood inside the base of one of the Elder Trees. He hadn't come here since their people had first returned to the forest, but this was the source of the Elder Trees power, and he would use that power to protect the crystals in a way that not only he could remove.

But which crystal should go where?

He didn't think they were paired, but didn't know. Taking the crystals from his pockets, he noted that one seemed to pulse in his hands. He set it in a small shelf that seemed as if it were made for the crystal.

"Lorst?" Galen whispered. "Where are we?"

"Inside an Elder Tree."

"*Inside?*"

"Hold on." Rsiran Slid to the next tree, and again there was a steady pulsing to one of the crystals. The light within it hadn't changed, and when he set it on the shelf much like he had the other one, nothing really changed.

He did the same with the other two.

Would restoring the last crystal matter at this point? Returning them to the chamber wouldn't be possible, not unless he stopped Danis, and he didn't think he was strong enough. He might not even be strong enough to keep him from the trees, especially if the power that the trees stored faded.

"What now?" Galen asked.

"Now we need to—"

Rsiran hesitated. The vision of the crystals and the trees fading flashed through his mind again. Why would it do that?

The last time that it had, the crystals had been in danger, but the crystals were in the trees... unless it was the missing crystal.

He Slid, dragging Galen with him, and emerged in the crystal chamber once again.

Rsiran stood in the middle of the chamber, a battle taking place around him.

Lorcith and heartstone flickered as the Hjan Slid, but that didn't surprise him. What surprised him was the change in temperature within the chamber. Heat intensified, reminding him of when he'd faced that woman with the strange power.

Galen gasped softly. "She's here."

"Who?" Rsiran asked, looking around.

Galen moved out of the center of the circle, pulling two fistfuls of darts and scanning the chamber.

"Galen?" Rsiran asked.

He nodded toward the back of the chamber. "Carth. She's here."

CHAPTER 38

As Rsiran readied to move within the crystal chamber, heartstone flickered.

He recognized it as a knife he'd forged, but when the person with the heartstone appeared, he was shocked to realize that it was Josun.

Josun glared at Rsiran and aimed a crossbow at him.

"You will suffer for what you did," Josun said.

"I stopped you once," Rsiran said.

"You may have stopped me, but you will not stop *him*. He's too powerful for even you now. I have seen it."

"You support him after the way he used you?"

"Used? I would gladly be used if it helped him find this place, if it meant I would learn what he knows! I would gladly—"

He fell over, a pair of darts sticking out from his neck.

Galen shrugged. "Coxberry. You can decide if you kill him later."

Rsiran stared at Josun a moment and then Slid toward the far wall. If Carth had come, then there was some part of her plan he needed to know. But rather than Carth, he found a younger woman with bright red hair swinging a sword with amazing precision. Heat radiated from her, and flames practically licked along the blade as she fought with Venass. Three fallen Hjan lay scattered around her, and there was another lying unmoving—a man with a similar sword and long robe— who she stood over.

One of the Hjan appeared behind the woman. Rsiran *pushed* on his knives, catching the Hjan as he did.

The woman glanced toward the fallen Hjan before turning to Rsiran.

He readied his knives, not certain if she would attack. Could they work together, at least for now? If she fought the Hjan and Venass, couldn't they find a way to work together so that they could stop them? She started to raise her sword, and Rsiran prepared to fight.

"Easy, Isha." Carth appeared as if from the darkness and laid a hand on the woman's sword, pushing it away.

Isha turned away with a nod, hurrying toward another clash. All around, fighters of Venass attacked. Most faced people like Isha, but there were a few of Elaeavn. Rsiran saw Valn and Sarah, as well as Galen throwing his darts, and Cael was there with Naelm of all people.

"Was this all your plan, Carth?"

"Do you think that I could have planned this?"

Rsiran surveyed the chaos around him. Had she planned this—as part of her game strategy that Galen spoke of—or had she simply reacted, the same as he had? He no longer knew.

"Galen seems to think you played all of this like some game of Tsatsun."

She briefly glanced over her shoulder. "Ah, well he has seen the game from a different direction, so I suppose it's not surprising for him to feel that way. What do you think?"

"I think you want to stop Venass."

She nodded. "Venass. Danis Elvraeth. All of them."

"You waited for them to attack." She nodded again. "You intended for me to draw him out."

She shrugged. "When I learned you were his grandson, I found the move I'd been missing. Danis is far too clever to be easily pulled into action, but you unsettled him. I had never seen him react so… predictably."

"And the crystal?"

Carth grinned. "We could never keep it safe."

She started to reach for her pocket when a blast of energy hit her, sending her sliding back toward the wall. Danis appeared briefly and dismissed Rsiran as he tried to *push* knives at him, waving them away as if they were nothing.

He sent another surge of energy, this time striking the A'ras fighting against Venass, almost all at the same time.

They fell.

Within the blink of an eye, he attacked Valn, and Sarah, and Naelm. All fell.

Rsiran didn't have a chance to check on his friends.

"Do you think you can win, grandson?" Danis asked. He started to turn toward Rsiran as he reached for his sword.

Danis *pushed*, and Rsiran was unable to unsheathe his sword. "You may take the crystal from here, but I have learned how to control more power than you will ever understand. I will destroy this city and all that you care about. I will destroy—"

"You talk too much," Rsiran said.

He *pulled* himself to Carth and then Slid, praying that he reacted faster than Danis.

Emerging in the dying Elder Tree, he grabbed for the crystal in Carth's pocket.

As he did, Danis appeared.

He glanced at Rsiran, and then around him, as if recognizing where he was, and grinned. "You are such a fool." Looking to Carth, his smile widened. "All this time, facing the great Carth of C'than, and she'll fall like this? She has evaded me for years, but no more. I'll have the crystal *and* I'll have succeeded in removing the only threat I had."

Carth moved. It was nothing more than the flicker of shadows.

Something pressed into Rsiran's hands.

The crystal.

"He *does* talk too much," Carth said.

Danis's eyes widened.

Then everything went black.

Rsiran felt like he was floating, bodiless and without pain. It was like he Traveled, but different from when he'd held the other crystals. This time, there was the sense of the movement, and the sense of wind, and the sense of a vastness all around him, an enormity that he could never understand even were he to stare at it for centuries. There was everything.

And nothing.

Rsiran was aware of both, just as he knew that he wasn't strong enough to fully comprehend what he saw around him. There was life, and there was nothing.

Elder.

It seemed as if a voice spoke in the vastness. Rsiran shivered —or would have, if he had a body—and tried to withdraw.

Elder. You must rise.

Rsiran tried turning to see if he could find the person or being that spoke, but he saw nothing.

Only, that wasn't true. There was the vastness that he sensed. Within that, there was the sense of power and creation, that of the Great Watcher, much as he had seen him before.

Rsiran looked toward that sense, trying to peer into it, but there was nothing for him to see.

Elder.

Visions flashed through his mind in a dizzying succession.

With them came knowledge and understanding. Rsiran saw the beginning of the world. He saw the first of his kind appear in the forest. He saw them leave the forest, and some went farther, wandering beyond these lands and beyond the sea. The visions flashed faster than he could comprehend, faster than his mind worked, until all that remained was one: that of the crystals.

They pulsed, each of them, throbbing much like they had when he'd attempted to place them within the trees. The pulsing crystals strengthened, drawing power from the Elder Trees, and somehow feeding them as well. They were incomplete, the missing crystal leaving the defect in the strength of the crystals. All he had to do was return the missing crystal and...

The visions stopped.

Rsiran floated.

Rise, Elder.

Was the Great Watcher talking to one of the Elders?

Rsiran thought they were in the vision he'd had, but with those visions, none had spoken. This was unlike any of the other visions.

Did the Great Watcher want the dying tree to rise?

Those answers didn't come.

Darkness faded.

Rise.

The voice was like a distant memory, lingering at the back of his mind.

Then Rsiran was back within the tree, holding the crystal that now throbbed in his hands much like the others had done. Rsiran knew what he needed to do, but didn't know if he could be fast enough.

Danis stood, his attack building. Rsiran could *feel* it, and wondered what that meant.

Before Danis could act, he Slid, pressing the crystal into the cove within the tree.

Danis grinned. "Do you think that will stop me now?"

Rsiran took a deep breath and unsheathed his sword. Power surged through him as he did. It was the power of the Elder Trees, and stronger than he'd felt since he had first discovered them. It washed over him, filling him, demanding that he use it. Light filled the inside of the tree.

Rsiran *saw* it as Danis tried to Slide. Using the power from the Elder Trees, Rsiran held him, *pulling* him back and wrapping him in bands of power. For the first time, he detected hidden implants in Danis. He *pulled*, tearing them free. Lorcith, heartstone, and even shadowsteel all peeled through his flesh.

Danis screamed.

Wrapped in light as he was, Rsiran healed him, but the screaming didn't stop.

Danis tried Sliding again, but couldn't. Cold burned against Rsiran's wrists as Danis tried to Read or Compel him, and his grandfather grabbed his head, dropping to his knees.

"What have you done?" he demanded.

"Less than you deserve," Rsiran said.

He should kill him. After all he had done, Danis deserved to die.

Danis reached for the metal from the implants, but Rsiran *pulled* it from him. How was he able to *pull* even shadowsteel?

That would be a question for later.

Wrapping the metals together, he formed a ball and then turned that into a liquid that he vaporized. Danis screamed again.

Carth slumped forward, and Rsiran pushed the light and power over her, letting a healing wash over her, not certain that it would work. She looked up and took a deep breath. When she breathed out, some of the light dimmed. It was faint, but it was how he knew that she would be fine.

She stood and watched him, waiting.

What would he do?

"He's yours," Rsiran decided, nodding to Danis.

Carth unsheathed a knife. For a moment, Rsiran thought she might kill Danis, and he wondered if that would be acceptable within the tree, but she used it to jab into each of his shoulders and then his hips. Whatever she did, it looked like darkness sliding into him, and Danis screamed again.

Then she sheathed her knife.

"What did you do?" Rsiran asked.

Carth watched Danis, as if gauging how he would react. "Danis Elvraeth is now powerless."

"Carth," he started, not certain she would answer. "What are you?"

"I am shadow born, Rsiran Lareth. And I will take Danis Elvraeth where he can no longer harm anyone."

"What can I do?"

"I need to get to Asador. From there, I will take care of the rest."

Rsiran nodded. "I can do that."

Carth lifted Danis as if he were nothing more than a child. Rsiran Slid them from inside the Elder Tree and emerged outside of Asador. Carth narrowed her eyes and nodded. "You will tell Galen of Elaeavn that he has my thanks?"

"I will tell him whatever you would like."

She studied Danis before looking to Rsiran. "You might share the same bloodline, but you are nothing like him, Rsiran Lareth." She lifted Danis. He didn't fight, and in the fading light, Rsiran realized that streaks of black ran up his arms. He wondered if the same worked along his legs.

"I'm not," Rsiran agreed. "He's Elvraeth born and I'm—"

"Elder born," Carth said.

She winked at him and started away.

As she did, shadows swirled around her until she disappeared, leaving nothing but black night.

Rsiran closed his eyes, holding tightly to his sword and feeling the power of the Elder Trees flowing through him. It was time to return to Elaeavn and end the war.

EPILOGUE

B right sunlight gleamed overhead. Rsiran stood in the middle of the lawn within the Floating Palace, looking up at the masons as they worked to repair the damage. Much of the city had been destroyed, and many buildings—like the palace—had been damaged enough that they would spend a long time trying to repair them, if they ever could fully.

He had returned to Elaeavn carrying with him the power of the Elder Trees. Even here, he could *pull* on it. His first act had been removing the power of the implants placed within the Venass fighters. After that, the battle had changed, quickly ending.

Cael stood next to Galen, holding his hand. Luthan, with his gray hair and eyes that could seem both clear and incredibly clouded at the same time, watched over everything. Rsiran wondered what he now Saw, if anything.

"What will you do with the council?" Rsiran asked Luthan. He couldn't meet Cael's eyes, unable to mourn the same as she would at her father's loss, and he had returned hoping that he could avoid serving on the council. With what had happened here, he would if Luthan pushed, but the old councilor knew about Rsiran's resistance.

"The council seeks to add another member," Luthan said.

"Do you have someone in mind?" he asked carefully.

A wry smile parted Luthan's mouth. "There is someone I would choose," he started. When he shifted his gaze to Cael, she looked away. "You have wisdom your father occasionally lacked, and compassion that most of us lack. You would be a great addition to the council," Luthan said to her.

Rsiran smiled.

Cael looked up, shaking her head. "I don't deserve—"

"Why? Because your father couldn't see beyond the past to accept the present?" Luthan asked.

"I'm not experienced enough—"

Luthan waved his hand, cutting her off once more. "Not experienced? How many from Elaeavn do you think have ever ventured beyond the borders of the city? After the attack, how many do you think will ever attempt it? We would ask Lareth, but he has no interest in ruling."

"My responsibility is to the guild." To all of them now, and perhaps in ways he still didn't fully understand. There was a part of him that wondered if the comment about the Elder in the vision while holding the last crystal had not been about the fallen tree, but about him. It was a question for Della, but later. Now, he had much he still had to do.

Cael turned to Galen. "What do you think?"

The assassin looked up at the palace, then over to Cael. "I

was banished for my impulsivity and anger, trained to use that anger for profit, and now find I want nothing more to do with it." He took her hands and met her eyes. Rsiran noted that Galen's hard features seemed to soften. "That's my way of saying that I'll go wherever you go, Cael."

Luthan looked at Rsiran. "What of you, Lareth? Where will you go?"

"I have a few other things I need to do."

"Will you remain in the city? You can claim your Elvraeth heritage if you want."

Rsiran smiled. "I can Slide, Luthan. I am never far from the city. And I'm a Lareth, not Elvraeth. I might be descended from the Elvraeth, but it's the blood of the Elders that drives me, not the blood of the Watcher."

The old councilor clapped him on the shoulder and nodded. "Be that as it may, I pray for the Great Watcher to look upon you favorably, Rsiran Lareth."

"The council—and the Elvraeth—have to change, Luthan," Rsiran cautioned. "You know what I think."

Luthan nodded. "We are bound to the forest in ways we had forgotten." He glanced to Galen, a deep frown across his face. "The council and the Elvraeth will lead, but all will be offered the chance to hold one of the crystals. Besides, now it will require the guilds even more. We won't be able to reach them otherwise."

The crystals remained within the trees. With the return of the missing crystal, he had considered moving them, but for now, he thought they *needed* to stay. The alchemist tree, the one that had been dying, already began to heal. Eventually, Rsiran wondered if he would need to place them back beneath the forest in the crystal chamber, but they seemed as if they belonged within the Elder Trees for now.

"There's the other thing I mentioned," Rsiran said.

Luthan's brow furrowed, and his jaw clenched slightly. "That will be more difficult, Rsiran. You know what happened."

"I know that many were exiled for reasons no better than Galen's, and many for much worse reasons. Not all will want to return, but they should be offered the chance. Don't you want your daughter to return?"

Luthan lowered his eyes. "We've all made mistakes that weigh upon us. Mine are as heavy as any."

"Then change what you can."

Luthan forced a smile. "You should be careful, Rsiran, you're getting close to ruling with statements like that."

"Not ruling, but even you can't deny the consequences of the way it had been done. We have to find a way for fairness. Letting all have the chance to see—and hold—the crystals is one step. Not exiling those who should be a part of the city is another."

Luthan nodded slowly. "The council has much work to do."

Cael looked to Galen before she spoke. "I know what I would do. My father made a mistake once. The entire council did. We will find a better way, Rsiran, and we will work with the guilds."

Rsiran glanced at the palace and the dozen men working along the wall trying to repair the stone. Some were of the Miners' Guild. Already, they began to work together in ways that they had not for many years. "That's all I can ask."

He Slid.

Rsiran emerged in the Aisl. The forest was busy with activity. The small, temporary huts would become more permanent, and countless new faces moved through the forest. Word had gotten out about the Aisl as a refuge for those displaced during the attack, and many had quickly sought the protection here.

Jessa worked with Della, coordinating the activity here. She saw him emerge and hurried over to him. "Well?"

"Luthan suggested Cael serve on the council."

Jessa bit her lower lip and leaned toward a small white flower that she'd found somewhere and stuffed into the charm. "Cael? She would be a good fit. Elvraeth born, so that would satisfy many. What of the other part?"

"We'll see. The crystals will remain here for now, and I've made it clear that I think they should be available for any to *try* to reach. Not all will be able to. And I've suggested they call the Forgotten back. There should be no exiles."

From what he'd learned from Galen, there was a large pocket of Forgotten who wanted only to return. Most had no greater crime than Galen's. Others were even less.

"When will you leave again?" Jessa asked.

"Soon."

"You'll be safe?"

"As safe as I can be."

"You'll return before the services?"

Rsiran swallowed and glanced toward the forest. They had lost so many in the attack. Friends and those he had cared about. Valn was gone, and with him Sarah. Master Kevan and two other master smiths. Nearly a dozen miners. Almost thirty of the Elvraeth had fallen. And thousands had fallen in the explosions. People Rsiran had never met, but mourned nonetheless. Those responsible were gone now, either powerless like Danis and Josun, or destroyed, but it didn't change the sense of loss they all had. Neither did holding Josun imprisoned, but they had yet to decide what to do with him.

"I'll return before then."

"Do what you have to."

Rsiran nodded and left her to work with Della organizing the growing population of the Aisl.

He found his father near the Aisl forge, working without a shirt, a sheen of sweat covering his body. Rsiran watched him work for a while, noting the way his father paused, likely listening to lorcith now—something that he hadn't done when Rsiran was his apprentice before hammering once more.

His father glanced up, and he smiled at him. "Rsiran. I thought that you'd be too busy…"

"There's something that I need your help with, Father."

His father set the hammer down and left the pot he'd been working on atop the stump to cool. "You're the guildlord."

"It can wait until you finish."

His father nodded to a younger man working the coals. "Let Therin finish. He's been doing good work these days. Helps that he can hear the lorcith as well as he does."

Rsiran smiled, still shocked by the change in his father. "And you? What do you hear these days?"

"I hear how Ilphaesn nearly collapsed. The lorcith sings of something…" He tipped his head, frowning.

Rsiran had heard it as well. He'd returned to Ilphaesn and

used the power of the Elder Trees to save the mines and stabilize the mountain. With that much power, he'd been able to *pull* on so much more than he ever had. After he did, the lorcith seemed to change, almost speak to him instead of only singing. He wondered what that meant.

"Come then," Rsiran said.

He Slid his father into Elaeavn, and into his family smithy.

It still stood. In spite of all the destruction, most of the smithies still stood.

"What is this?" his father asked.

Rsiran grinned. "I thought you'd recognize this. It's the Lareth smithy."

"I see that, but why bring me here?"

"Because you need to return. This is a Lareth smithy."

His father shook his head. "This is yours. *You're* the Lareth master smith now."

Rsiran swallowed back the lump in his throat at the comment. How long had he wanted to hear something like that from his father? How long had he wanted that kind of acknowledgment? And now to get it, but have to refuse?

"This isn't for me," Rsiran said.

His father clasped Rsiran's shoulder. "I heard about what happened with your smithy, son. This should be yours. I was too blind to see that when you were my apprentice, but I see it now. A guildlord needs a smithy."

"But I have one."

"It wasn't destroyed in the blasts?"

"Oh, that smithy was destroyed, but that isn't what I mean. The forge in the Aisl will be my home. I intend to continue serving as guildlord, and with that, I can connect to our clans better. Besides, I think I need to be there."

Rsiran wasn't sure that he could remain in the city after what he'd lost here. He could always visit, but would he ever feel safe?

"I... I can't believe it," his father said.

"Treat her well. Work hard." Rsiran smiled. "You have a demanding guildlord, you know."

His father nodded, "I know. But a great one as well."

Rsiran Slid, leaving his father in the smithy.

He emerged in the Barth. It had also somehow survived. The old buildings nearest the shore might be among the oldest in the city, but they were among the stoutest as well. Brusus and Alyse sat talking quietly, the tavern otherwise slow. Both looked over as he emerged.

"Rsiran," Alyse said warmly. "You look well."

Rsiran smiled, glancing from Brusus to Alyse. "And you?"

"Besides Brusus playing with his new abilities?" she asked.

"They've come?" he asked.

Brusus laughed. "I don't understand it, but after the attack... I've always been a decent Reader, but this is something else. I feel a connection in ways I can't understand. Sort of like I know when I need to find those I care for." He shrugged. "And I haven't tested it nearly as much as your sister would have you believe. What of Jessa?"

"She... Sees... now. Not well, but it's coming. Each day is stronger. That's part of why I'm here."

"And the other?" Alyse asked.

"Father is in his smithy," he told her. "I'm sure he'd love to see you."

"You… you gave it back to him?"

"It wasn't really mine to give." That wasn't entirely true. As guildlord, he could make assignments, but it felt right. He turned to Brusus. There's something more I need to do, and I'd like you to come with me."

"What is it?"

Rsiran let out a deep breath. "Something for Haern."

Brusus nodded. "When?"

"How about now?"

He glanced to Alyse, and she patted him on the hand. Brusus kissed her on the cheek and then stood, grabbing Rsiran's arm.

They Slid, emerging on the rocks outside of Thyr. The Tower of Venass rose like a dark finger against the sky, a painful reminder of what they had been through. Shadows parted around the tower, reminding him of Carth. A part of him wondered what had become of her, and what she had done with his grandfather, but for the most part, he didn't care. The man was gone.

"Why here?"

Rsiran stared at the tower. "Haern tried escaping the tower and failed. I think it's time that we honor his memory."

"In what way?"

Rsiran had thought about what needed to be done to fully recover from what Venass had done to those he cared about. He still hadn't found the forgers, likely smiths with abilities no different from his. He suspected they were in the tower, but even if they weren't, he intended to search until he found them.

374 | D.K. HOLMBERG

"By destroying the tower."

Brusus started to laugh, until he realized that Rsiran was serious. "How do you expect to destroy the tower? And why do you need me?"

"You're here to watch, and celebrate. I'll do the destroying." He hesitated. There was another reason he wanted time with Brusus. "The council will allow the Forgotten to return, Brusus. It won't happen quickly, but it will happen."

Brusus swallowed and nodded. "Thank you."

"Now. For the reason we're here." Rsiran unsheathed the sword that connected him to the Elder Trees. Now he understood that *anything* he forged in the Aisl smithy did the same, which was more reason for him to remain in the forest, not only for the crystals and the safety.

Drawing on the power of the Elder Trees, he *pulled*.

Venass had too much lorcith, and too much heartstone, to resist.

The tower began to buckle, and with a loud explosion, it fell, crumbling into ruins and leaving a cloud of dust that rose into the otherwise clear sky.

Rsiran sheathed his sword. Neither of them spoke.

After a while, Brusus chuckled. "You're right. Haern would have loved that."

"Venass is gone, Brusus."

"For the most part."

"There's a part of me that doesn't know what to do. I went from hiding my abilities, to battling the Forgotten and then Venass, and now to a place where I'm expected to have responsibilities."

Brusus smiled. "You've come a long way, Rsiran. None of us would be where we are without you."

"What do I do now?"

Brusus clapped him on the shoulder, and his eyes blazed a bright green, no longer hidden as they once had been. "Now? Now we are finally free to live as the Great Watcher intends."

Rsiran stared at the ruins of Venass a moment longer, and then he took Brusus's arm and they Slid.

I'm excited to share with you book 1 of a new series, The Lost Prophecy: The Threat of Madness, available now!

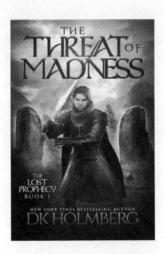

The arrival of the mysterious Magi, along with their near invincible guardians, signals a change. For Jakob, apprentice historian and son of a priest longing for adventure, it begins an opportunity.

When his home is attacked, Jakob ventures out with the his

master, traveling alongside the Magi, beginning a journey that will take him far from home and everything he has ever known. As he travels, he gains surprising skill with the sword but begins to develop strange abilities, along with a growing fear that the madness which has claimed so many has come for him.

With a strange darkness rising in the north, and powers long thought lost beginning to return, the key to survival is discovering the answer to a lost prophecy. Only a few remain with the ability to find it, and they begin to suspect that Jakob has a pivotal role to play.

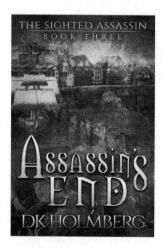

Want to learn about Galen during the events of Rise of the Elder? Check out Assassin's End, book 3 of The Sighted Assassin:

After returning to Elaeavn from his exile, Galen is caught up in a fight he wants nothing to do with. When Lorst offers him a job that requires he leave the city, he gladly accepts as there's no role for an assassin in his homeland.

The assignment brings him back into danger, and forces him to reconnect with a woman he'd left behind long ago, leaving him with mixed emotions and Cael with jealousy. Completing the job is only the beginning, and forces a discovery that even those who hired him hadn't expected.

If he fails, the dangerous Hjan will gain the power of the crystal, but succeeding means that he's brought deeper into something even his skills haven't equipped him to face. Galen must use friends old and new to survive, but even that might not be enough to stop the Hjan.

Want to read more about Carth? Check out her beginning in Book 1 of The Shadow Accords trilogy: Shadow Blessed

The A'ras of Nyaesh have a terrifying reputation: skilled

swordsmen, owners of powerful magic, and ruthless killers. When they kill her parents, Carth discovers her father has trained her for shadow magic she never knew she possessed.

She must use those skills to stay alive, discover a way to find answers, and avenge her parents if she can. Only the discovery of a greater threat than the A'ras forces her to risk herself for new friends and a home she never wanted but now can't imagine losing.

AUTHOR'S NOTE

Thanks for sticking with me for Rsiran's journey. In my mind, he began as the assassin in a novella I wrote for a writing workshop, now included in The Forgotten. In that initial draft, he was a cold and competent assassin named Rsiran, hired to kill Cael and Galen. I found myself thinking about how he would have reached the point in his life that he did in the novella. I renamed him Lorst to hide his identity, started on the Dark Ability, and if you're reading this, you know the rest! He was a troubled character, wanting nothing more than a family, and I enjoyed helping him find the relationships he desired—and deserved. Through it all, I knew that in the end of the series, I would have to get him back together with Galen, and have enjoyed the twists it took getting there.

I've been asked whether there will be more stories in this world, and though I think Rsiran's story is complete, there are others I'd eventually like to discover. I love hearing from fans, so let me know if you have any favorites you'd like to explore more. For now, you can read about Rsiran (The Dark Ability series), Galen (The Sighted Assassin), and Carth (The Shadow Accords).

Galen's story will finish soon with Assassin's End, a book with overlap of the events in Rise of the Elder. Everything with Galen has been building up to the point where he needs to decide what he wants for himself, and he needs to decide whether to be the assassin or the hero.

When I first wrote about Carth, I knew I'd have to visit her backstory. Shadow Blessed is the first of what will probably be 5 or 6 books, detailing her early years and the development of her network. After reading this book, you know how incredible Carth is, but it takes time, training, and experience to get her there. She's proven to be one of my favorite characters to write.

Thanks again and keep reading!

DK Holmberg
dkh@dkholmberg.com

ABOUT THE AUTHOR

DK Holmberg currently lives in rural Minnesota where the winter cold and the summer mosquitoes keep him inside and writing.

Word-of-mouth is crucial for any author to succeed and how books are discovered. If you enjoyed the book, please consider leaving a review at Amazon, even if it's only a line or two; it would make all the difference and would be very much appreciated.

Subscribe to my newsletter to be the first to hear about give-aways and new releases.

For more information:
www.dkholmberg.com

ALSO BY D.K. HOLMBERG

The Dark Ability

The Dark Ability

The Heartstone Blade

The Tower of Venass

Blood of the Watcher

The Shadowsteel Forge

The Guild Secret

Rise of the Elder

The Sighted Assassin

The Painted Girl (novella)

The Binders Game

The Forgotten

Assassin's End

The Shadow Accords

Shadow Blessed

Shadow Cursed

Shadow Born

Shadow Lost

Shadow Cross

The Lost Prophecy

The Threat of Madness

The Warrior Mage

Tower of the Gods

Twist of the Fibers

The Teralin Sword

Soldier Son

Soldier Sword

The Endless War

Journey of Fire and Night

Darkness Rising

Endless Night

Summoner's Bond

Seal of Light

The Cloud Warrior Saga

Chased by Fire

Bound by Fire

Changed by Fire

Fortress of Fire

Forged in Fire

Serpent of Fire

Servant of Fire

Born of Fire

Light of Fire

Cycle of Fire

The Lost Garden

Keeper of the Forest

The Desolate Bond

Keeper of Light

The Painter Mage

Shifted Agony

Arcane Mark

Painter For Hire

Stolen Compass

Stone Dragon